blueeyedboy

JOANNE HARRIS

Doubleday

LONDON · TORONTO · SYDNEY · AUCKLAND · JOHANNESBURG

TRANSWORLD PUBLISHERS
61–63 Uxbridge Road, London W5 5SA
A Random House Group Company
www.rbooks.co.uk

First published in Great Britain
in 2010 by Doubleday
an imprint of Transworld Publishers

A CIP catalogue record for this book
is available from the British Library.

ISBNs 9780385609500 (hb)
9780857520081 (tpb)

Addresses for Random House Group Ltd companies outside the UK
can be found at: www.randomhouse.co.uk
The Random House Group Ltd Reg. No. 954009

The Random House Group Limited supports The Forest Stewardship
Council (FSC), the leading international forest-certification organization. All our
titles that are printed on Greenpeace-approved FSC-certified paper carry the FSC logo.
Our paper procurement policy can be found at www.rbooks.co.uk/environment

Typeset in 11/14pt Goudy by
Falcon Oast Graphic Art Ltd.
Printed and bound in Great Britain by
Clays Limited, Bungay, Suffolk

4 6 8 10 9 7 5 3

Mixed Sources
Product group from well-managed
forests and other controlled sources
FSC   www.fsc.org   Cert no. TT-COC-2139
© 1996 Forest Stewardship Council

To Kevin,
who also has blue eyes.

ACKNOWLEDGEMENTS

Some books are easy to write. Some are rather more difficult. And some books are just like Rubik's cubes, with no apparent solution in sight. This particular Rubik's cube would never have been solved without the help of my editor, Marianne Velmans, and my agent, Peter Robinson, who encouraged me to persevere. Thanks, too, to my PA, Anne Riley; to publicist Louise Page-Lund; to Mr Fry for the loan of Patch; to copy-editor Lucy Pinney; to Claire Ward and Jeff Cottenden for the cover art; to Francesca Liversidge; Manpreet Grewal; Sam Copeland; Kate Tolley; Jane Villiers; Michael Carlisle; Mark Richards; Voltaire; Jennifer and Penny Luithlen. Thanks, too, to the unsung heroes: the proofreaders; sales executives; book reps and booksellers who are so often forgotten when it comes to handing out the laurels. Special thanks to my friends in fic and fandom, especially to: gl-12; ashlibrooke; spicedogs; mr_henry_gale; marzella; jade_melody; henry_holland; divka; benobsessed. And, of course, to the man in Apartment 7, whose voice was in my mind from the start.

> and what i want to know is
> how do you like your blueeyed boy
> Mister Death
>
> e e cummings, 'Buffalo Bill'

PART ONE

blue

Once there was a widow with three sons, and their names were Black, Brown and Blue. Black was the eldest, moody and aggressive. Brown was the middle child, timid and dull. But Blue was his mother's favourite. And he was a murderer.

1

You are viewing the webjournal of **blueeyedboy** *posting on:*
badguysrock@webjournal.com
Posted at: *02.56 on Monday, January 28*
Status: *public*
Mood: *nostalgic*
Listening to: *Captain Beefheart:* 'Ice Cream For Crow'

The colour of murder is blue, he thinks. Ice-blue, smokescreen blue, frostbite, post-mortem, body-bag blue. It is also *his* colour in so many ways, running through his circuitry like an electrical charge, screaming blue murder all the way.

Blue colours everything. He sees it, senses it everywhere, from the blue of his computer screen to the blue of the veins on the backs of her hands, raised now and twisted like the tracks of sandworms on Blackpool beach – where they used to go, the four of them, every year on his birthday, and he would have an ice-cream cone, and paddle in the sea, and search out the little scuttling crabs from under the piles of seaweed, and drop them into his bucket to die in the heat of the simmering birthday sun.

Today he is only four years old, and there is a peculiar innocence in the way he carries out these small and guiltless slayings. There is no malice in the act, merely a keen curiosity for the scuttling thing that tries to escape, sidling round and round the base of the blue plastic bucket; then, hours later, giving up the fight, claws splayed, and turning its vivid underbelly upwards in a futile show of surrender, by which time he has long since lost interest and is eating a coffee ice cream (a sophisticated choice for such a little boy, but vanilla has never been his taste), so that when he rediscovers it at the end of the day, when the time comes to empty his bucket and to go home, he is vaguely surprised to find the creature dead, and wonders, indeed, how such a thing could ever have been alive at all.

His mother finds him wide-eyed on the sand, poking the dead thing with a fingertip. Her main concern is not for the fact that her son is a killer, but for the fact that he is suggestible, and that many things upset him in a way that she does not understand.

'Don't play with that,' she tells him. 'It's nasty. Come away from there.'

'Why?' he says.

Good question. The creatures in the bucket have been standing undisturbed all day. He gives it some thought. 'They're dead,' he concludes. 'I collected them all, and now they're dead.'

His mother scoops him into her arms. This is precisely what she dreads. Some kind of outburst: tears, perhaps; something that will make the other mothers look down their noses at her and sneer.

She comforts him. 'It's not your fault. It was just an accident. Not your fault.'

An *accident*, he thinks to himself. Already, he knows that this is a lie. There was no accident, it *was* his fault, and the fact that his mother denies this confuses him more than her shrill voice and the feverish way she clasps him in her arms, smearing his T-shirt with sun-tan oil. He pulls away – he hates mess – and she fixes him with a fretful gaze, wondering if he is going to cry.

He wonders whether perhaps he should. Maybe she expects it of him. But he can sense how very anxious she is, how hard she tries to protect him from pain. And the scent of his ma's distress is like the coconut of her suntan oil mixed with the taste of tropical fruit, and suddenly it hits him – *Dead! Dead!* – and he really does begin to cry.

And so she kicks sand over the rest of his catch – a snail, a shrimp, a baby flatfish all landed and gasping, with its little mouth pulled down in a tragic crescent – smiling and singing; *Whoops! All gone!* – trying to make a game of it, holding him tightly as she does, so that no possible taint of guilt may darken the gaze of her blue-eyed boy.

He is so sensitive, she thinks. So startlingly imaginative. His brothers are another race, with their scabbed knees and their uncombed hair and their wrestling matches on the beds. His brothers do not need her protection. They have each other. They have their friends. They like vanilla ice cream, and when they play at cowboys (two fingers cocked to make a gun) they always wear the white hats, and make the bad guys pay.

But he has always been different. Curious. Impressionable. *You think too much*, she tells him sometimes, with the look of a woman too much in love to admit to any real fault in the object of her devotion. He can already see how she worships him, wants to protect him from everything, from every shadow that may pass across the blue skies of his life, from every possible injury, even the ones he inflicts on himself.

For a mother's love is uncritical, selfless and self-sacrificing; a mother's love can forgive anything: tantrums, tears, indifference, ingratitude or cruelty. A mother's love is a black hole that swallows every criticism, absolves all blame, excuses blasphemy, theft and lies, transmuting even the vilest deed into something that is not his fault –

Whoops! All gone!

Even murder.

Post comment:

Captainbunnykiller: *LOL, dude. You rock!*

ClairDeLune: *This is wonderful,* **blueeyedboy**. *I think you ought to write more fully about your relationship with your mother and the way it has affected you. I don't believe that anyone is born bad. We simply make bad choices, that's all. I look forward to reading the next chapter!*

JennyTricks: *(post deleted).*

JennyTricks: *(post deleted).*

JennyTricks: *(post deleted).*

blueeyedboy: *Why, thank you . . .*

2

You are viewing the webjournal of **blueeyedboy**.
Posted at: *17.39 on Monday, January 28*
Status: *restricted*
Mood: *virtuous*
Listening to: *Dire Straits*: 'Brothers In Arms'

My brother had been dead for less than a minute by the time the news reached my WeJay. That's about how long it takes: six or seven seconds to film the scene on a mobile phone camera; forty-five to upload the footage on to YouTube; ten to Twitter to all your friends – *13:06 OMG! Just saw a terrible car crash* – and after that the caravan of messages to my WebJournal; the texts; the e-mails, the oh-my-Gods.

Well, you can skip the condolences. Nigel and I hated each other from the day we were born, he and I, and nothing he has ever done – including giving up the ghost – has caused any change to my feelings. But he *was* my brother, after all. Give me credit for some delicacy. And Ma must be feeling upset, of course, even though he wasn't her favourite. Once a mother of three, today only one of her children remains. Yours truly, *blueeyedboy*, now so nearly alone in the world –

The police took their time, as usual. Forty minutes, door-to-door. Ma was downstairs, making lunch: lamb chops and mash, with pie for dessert. For months I'd hardly eaten; suddenly now I was ravenous. Perhaps it takes the death of a sibling to really give me an appetite.

From my room, I followed the scene: the police car; the doorbell; the voices; the scream. The sound of something in the hallway recess

14

– the telephone table, at a guess – slamming against the wall as she fell, cradled between two officers, clutching the air with her out-stretched hands, and then the smell of burning fat, probably the chops she left under the grill when she went to answer the door –

That was my cue. Time to log off. Time to face the music. I wondered whether I could get away with leaving in one of my iPod plugs. Ma's so used to seeing me wearing them that she might not even have noticed; but the two officers were a different matter, of course, and the last thing I wanted at such a time was for someone to find me insensitive –

'Oh, B.B., the most *terrible* thing—'

My mother's a bit of a drama queen. Contorted face, eyes wide, mouth wider, she looked like a mask of Medusa. Holding out her arms to me as if to pull me under, fingers clawing at my back, wailing into my right ear – defenceless now without my iPod – and shedding tears of blue mascara down the collar of my shirt.

'Ma, please.' I hate mess.

The female officer (there's always one) took over the business of comforting her. Her partner, an older man, looked at me with weary patience, and said:

'Mr Winter, there's been an accident.'

'Nigel?' I said.

'I'm afraid so.'

I counted the seconds in my head, whilst mentally replaying Mark Knopfler's guitar intro to 'Brothers In Arms'. I knew I was under scrutiny; I couldn't afford to get this wrong. But music makes things easier, reducing inappropriate emotional responses and allowing me to function, if not entirely normally, then at least as others expect of me.

'I knew it, somehow,' I said at last. 'I had the weirdest feeling.'

He nodded, as if he knew what I meant. Ma continued to rant and rail. *Overdoing it, Ma*, I thought; it wasn't as if they were especially close. Nigel was a ticking bomb; it had to happen sooner or later. And car accidents are so common these days, so tragically unavoidable. A patch of ice, a busy road; almost the perfect crime, you might say, almost above suspicion. I wondered if I ought to cry, but decided to keep it simple. So I sat down – rather shakily – and put my head in my hands. It hurt. I've always been prone to headaches, especially in moments of stress. *Pretend it's just fiction, blueeyedboy. An entry in your WeJay.*

Once more I sought the comfort of my imaginary playlist, where the drums had just come in, ticking gentle counterpoint to a guitar riff that sounds almost lazily effortless. It isn't effortless, of course. Nothing so precise ever is. But Knopfler has curiously spatulate, elongated fingers. Born for the instrument, you might almost say, destined from birth for that fretboard, those strings. If he had been born with different hands, would he have ever picked up a guitar? Or would he have tried it anyway, knowing he'd always be second-rate?

'Was my son alone in the car?'

'Ma'am?' said the older officer.

'Wasn't there – a girl – with him?' said Ma, with the special contempt she always reserves for any discussion of Nigel's girl.

The officer shook his head. 'No, ma'am.'

Ma dug her fingers into my arm. 'He never used to be careless,' she said. 'My son was an excellent driver.'

Well, that just shows how little she knows. Nigel brought to his driving the same temperance and subtlety that he did to his relationships. I should know; I still have the marks. But now he's dead, he's a paragon. That hardly seems fair, does it now, after all I've done for her?

'I'll make you a cup of tea, Ma.' Anything to get out of here. I made for the kitchen, only to find the officer obstructing my way.

'I'm afraid we're going to need you to come with us to the station, sir.'

My mouth was suddenly very dry. 'The station?' I said.

'Formalities, sir.'

For a moment I saw myself under arrest, leaving the house in handcuffs. Ma in tears; the neighbours in shock; myself in an orange jumpsuit (really, *not* my colour); locked up in a room without windows. In fic I'd make a run for it: knock out the officer, steal his car and be over the border before the police could circulate my description. In life –

'What kind of formalities?'

'We'll need you to ID the body, sir.'

'Oh. That.'
'I'm sorry, sir.'

Ma made me do it, of course. Waited outside while I put a name to what was left of Nigel. I tried to make it fictional, to see it all as a film set; but even so, I passed out. They took me home in an ambulance. Still, it was worth it. To have him dead; to be free of the bastard for ever –

All this is fic, you understand. I never murdered anyone. I know they tell you to *write what you know*, as if you could ever write what you know, as if *knowing* were the essential thing, when the most essential thing is desire. But wishing that my brother were dead is not the same as committing a crime. It's not my fault if the universe follows my WebJournal. And so life goes on – for most of us – much the same as it ever did, and *blueeyedboy* sleeps the sleep of the just – if not *quite* that of the innocent.

3

That was just two days ago. Already we're back to normal, apart from planning the funeral. Back to our comfort rituals, our little everyday routines. With Ma, it's dusting the china dogs. With me, of course, it's the Internet: my WeJay, my playlists, my murders.

Internet. An interesting word. Like something brought up from the deep. A net for something that has been interred, or something as yet to be interred; a holding-place for all the things we'd rather keep secret in our real lives. And yet, we like to watch, don't we? Through a glass, darkly, we watch the world turn: a world peopled with shades and reflections, never more than a mouse-click away. A man kills himself – live, on cam. It's disgusting, but strangely compulsive. We wonder if it was a fake. It could be a fake; anything could. But everything looks so much more real when you're watching it on a computer screen. Thus even the things we see every day – perhaps *especially* those things – gain an extra significance when glimpsed through the eye of a camera.

That girl, for instance. The girl in the bright-red duffel coat who walks past my house nearly every day, windswept and oblivious to the camera's eye that watches her. She has her habits, as do I. She knows the power of desire. She knows that the world turns not on love, or even money, but on *obsession*.

Obsession? Of course. We are all obsessed. Obsessed with TV; with the size of our dicks; with money and fame and the love-lives of others. This virtual – though far from virtuous – world is a reeking midden of mind-trash, mish-mash, slash; car dealerships and Viagra sales, and music and games and gossip and lies and tiny personal tragedies lost in transit down the line, waiting for someone to care, just once, waiting for someone to connect –

That's where WeJay comes in. WebJournal, the site for all seasonings. Restricted entries for private enjoyment; public – well, for everyone else. On WeJay I can vent as I please, confess without fear of censure; be myself – or indeed, someone else – in a world where no one is quite what they seem, and where every member of every tribe is free to do what they most desire.

Tribe? Yes, everyone here has a tribe; each with its divisions and subdivisions, binary veins and capillaries branching out into a near-infinity of permutations as they distance themselves from the mainstream. The rich man in his castle, the poor man at his gate, the pervert with his webcam. No one has to hunt alone, however far from the pack they have strayed. Everyone has a home here, a place where someone will take them in, where all their tastes are catered for –

Most people go with the popular choice. They choose vanilla every time. Vanillas are the good guys, common as Coca-Cola. Their conscience is as white as their perfect teeth; they are tall and bronzed and presentable; they eat at McDonald's; they take out the trash; they come with a PG certificate and they'd never shoot a man in the back.

But bad guys come in a million flavours. Bad guys lie; bad guys cheat; bad guys make the heart beat faster – or sometimes come to a sudden stop. Which is why I created *badguysrock*: originally a WeJay community devoted to villains throughout the fictional universe; now a forum for bad guys to celebrate beyond the reach of the ethics police; to glory in their crimes; to strut; to wear their villainy with pride.

Membership is open right now; the price of admission a single post – be it a fic, an essay or just a drabble. Though if there's something you'd like to confess, this is just the place for it: no names, no rules, no colours – but one.

No, *not* black, as you might expect. Black is far too limiting. Black presupposes a lack of depth. But blue is creative, melancholy. Blue is the music of the soul. And blue is the colour of our clan, embracing all shades of villainy, all flavours of unholy desire.

So far, it's a small clan, with less than a dozen regulars.

First comes *Captainbunnykiller*: Andy Scott of New York. Cap's blog is a mixture of jackass humour, pornographic fantasy and furious invective – against niggers, queers, fucktards, the fat, Christians and, most recently, the French – but I doubt he's ever killed anything.

Next comes *chrysalisbaby*. Aka Chryssie Bateman, of California. This one's a typical Body Freak – has been on a diet since she was twelve, and now weighs over three hundred pounds. Has a history of falling for vicious men. Never learns. Never will.

After that there's *ClairDeLune*; Clair Mitchell, to her friends. This one's a local; she teaches a course on creative self-expression at Malbry College (which explains her slightly superior tone and her addiction to literary psychobabble) and runs an online writers' group as well as a sizeable fansite devoted to a certain middle-aged character actor – let us call him Angel Blue – with whom she is infatuated. Angel is an irregular choice, an actor specializing in louche individuals, damaged types, serial killers, and other assorted bad-guy roles. Not A-list, but you'd know his face. She often posts pictures of him on here. Curiously enough, he looks something like me.

Then there's *Toxic69*, aka Stuart Dawson, of Leeds. Left crippled in a motorbike crash, he spends his angry life online, where no one needs to pity him; and *Purepwnage9*, of Fife, who lives for Warcraft and Second Life, oblivious of the fact that his own life is surely but swiftly slipping away; plus any number of lurkers and irregulars – *JennyTricks*; *BombNumber20*, *Jesusismycopilot*, and so on, who exhibit a diverting range of responses to our various entries, from admiration to outrage; from cheeriness to profanity.

And then, of course, there's *Albertine*. Definitely not like the rest, there's a confessional tone to her entries that I find more than a little promising, a hint of danger, a dark undertone, a style perhaps more akin to my own. And she lives right here in the Village, no more than a dozen streets away –

Coincidence?

Not quite. Of course, I have been watching her. Especially so since my brother's death. Not with malice, but with curiosity, even a measure of envy. She seems so self-possessed. So calm. So safely cocooned in her little world, so unaware of what's happening. Her online posts are so intimate, so naked and so oddly naïve that you'd never believe she was one of us, a bad guy among bad guys. Her fingers on the piano keys danced like little dervishes. I remember that, and her gentle voice, and her name, which smelt of roses.

The poet Rilke was killed by a rose. How very *Sturm und Drang* of him. A scratch with a thorn that got infected; a poison gift that keeps on giving. Personally, I don't see the appeal. I feel more kinship with the orchid tribe: subversives of the plant world, clinging to life wherever they can, subtle and insidious. Roses are so commonplace, with their whorls of sickening bubblegum pink; their scheming scent; their unwholesome leaves, their sly little thorns that poke at the heart –

O rose, thou art sick –

Still, aren't we all?

4

You are viewing the webjournal of **blueeyedboy**.
Posted at: *23.30 on Monday, January 28*
Status: *restricted*
Mood: *contemplative*
Listening to: *Radiohead:* 'Creep'

Call me B.B. Everyone does. No one but the police and the bank ever use my real name. I'm forty-two and five foot eight; I have mousy hair, blue eyes and I've lived here in Malbry all my life.

Malbry – pronounced *Maw-bry*. Even the word smells of shit. But I am unusually sensitive to words, to their sounds and resonances. That's why I don't have an accent now, and have lost my childhood stammer. The predominant trend here in Malbry is for exaggerated vowels and clumsy glottals, coating every word in a grimy sheen. You can hear them on the estate all the time: teenage girls with scraped-back hair, shouting *hiyaaa* in shades of synthetic strawberry. The boys are less articulate, mouthing *freak* and *loser* at me as I pass, in half-broken voices that yodel and boom in notes of lager and locker-room sweat. Most of the time I don't hear them. My life has a permanent soundtrack, provided by my iPod, into which I have downloaded more than twenty thousand tracks and forty-two playlists, one for every year of my life, each with a specific theme –

Freak. They say it because they think it hurts. In their world, to be labelled a freak is obviously the worst kind of fate. To me, it's just the opposite. The worst thing is surely to be like them: to have married

22

too young; to have gone on the dole; to have learnt to drink beer and smoke cheap cigarettes; to have had kids doomed to be just like themselves, because if these people are good at anything, it's reproduction – they don't live long, but, by God, they populate – and if not wanting any of that has made me into a freak in their eyes –

In truth, I'm very ordinary. My eyes are my best feature, I'm told, though not everyone appreciates their chilly shade. For the rest, you'd hardly notice me. I'm nicely inconspicuous. I don't talk much, and when I do, it's only when strictly necessary. That's the way to survive in this place; to keep my privacy intact. Because Malbry is one of those places where secrets and gossips and rumours abound, and I have to take exceptional care to avoid the wrong kind of exposure.

It's not that the place is so terrible. The old Village is actually very nice, with its crooked York stone cottages and its church and its single row of little shops. There's rarely any trouble here; except perhaps on Saturday nights, when the kids hang around outside the church while their parents go to the pub down the road, and buy chips from the Chinese takeaway and push the wrappers into the hedge.

To the west, there's what Ma calls Millionaires' Row: an avenue of big stone houses shielded from the road by trees. Tall chimneys; four-by-fours; gates that work by remote control. Beyond that there's St Oswald's, the grammar school, with its twelve-foot wall and heraldic gate. To the east, the brick terraces of Red City, where my mother was born, then to the west, White City, all privet and pebble-dash. It's not as genteel as the Village, though I've learnt to avoid the danger zones. This is where you'll find our house, at the edge of the big estate. A square of grass; a flowerbed; a hedge to keep out the neighbours. This is the house where I was born; hardly anything has changed.

I do have a few extra privileges. I drive a blue Peugeot 307, registered in my mother's name. I have a study lined with books, an iPod dock, a computer and a wall of CDs. I have a collection of orchids, most of them just hybrids, but with one or two rare *Zygopetala*, whose names bear the scent of the South American rainforests from which they were sourced, and whose colours are astonishing: violent shades of priapic green, and mottled, acidic butterfly-blue that no chart could possibly duplicate. I have a darkroom in the basement, where I develop my photographs. I don't display them here, of course. But I like to think I have a gift.

At 5 a.m. on weekdays I clock in at Malbry Infirmary – or I did, until very recently – wearing a suit and a blue striped shirt and carrying a briefcase. My mother is very proud of this, of the fact that her son wears a suit to work. What I actually *do* at work is a matter of far less importance to her. I am single, straight, well-spoken, and, if this were a TV drama of the type favoured by *ClairDeLune*, my blameless lifestyle and unsullied reputation would probably make me a prime suspect.

In the real world, however, only the kids notice me. To them, any man who still lives with his mother is either a paedo or a queer. But even this assumption comes more from habit than real belief. If they thought I was dangerous, they would behave very differently. Even when that schoolboy was killed, a St Oswald's boy, so close to home, no one thought me remotely worthy of investigation.

Predictably, I was curious. A murder is always intriguing. Besides, I was already learning my craft, and I knew I could use any information, any hints that came my way. I've always appreciated a nice, neat murder. Not that many qualify. Most murderers are predictable, most murders messy and banal. It's almost a crime in itself, don't you think, that the splendid act of *taking a life* should have become so commonplace, so wholly devoid of artistry?

In fiction, there is no such thing as the perfect crime. In movies, the bad guy – who is invariably brilliant and charismatic – always makes a fatal mistake. He overlooks the minutiae. He succumbs to vainglory; loses his nerve; falls victim to some ironic flaw. However dark the frosting, in film, the vanilla centre always shows through; with a happy ending for all who deserve it, and imprisonment, a shot through the heart, or better still, a dramatically pleasing – though statistically improbable – drop from a high building for the bad guy, thereby removing the burden to the State, and leaving the hero free of the guilt of having to shoot the bastard himself.

Well, I happen to know that isn't true, just as I know that most murderers are neither brilliant nor charismatic, but often subnormal and rather dull, and that the police force is so buried under its paperwork that the simplest murders can slip through the net – the stabbings, the shootings, the fist-fights gone wrong, crimes in which the perpetrator, if he has left the scene at all, can often be found in the nearest pub.

Call me romantic, if you like. But I do believe in the perfect crime. Like true love, it's just a matter of timing and patience; of keeping the faith; of not losing hope; of carping the *diem*, of seizing the day –

That's how my interests led me here, to my lonesome refuge on *badguysrock*. Harmless interests, to begin with at least, though soon I grew to appreciate the other possibilities. And at the beginning it was just curiosity: a means of observing others unseen; of exploring a world beyond my own, that narrow triangle between Malbry town, the Village and Nether Edge moors, beyond which I have never dared to aspire. The Internet, with its million maps, was as alien to me as Jupiter – and yet, one day, I was simply *there*, almost by chance, a cast-away, watching the changing scenery with the slowly dawning awareness that *this* was where I truly belonged; that *this* would be my great escape, from Malbry, my life, and my mother.

My mother. How it resonates. *Mother* is a difficult word; so dense with complex associations that I can barely see it at all. Sometimes its colour is Virgin-blue, like the statues of Mary; or grey like the dust-bunnies under the bed where I used to hide away as a child; or green like the baize of the market stalls; and it smells of uncertainty and loss, and of black bananas gone to mush, and of salt, and of blood, and of memory –

My mother. Gloria Winter. She's the reason I'm still here: stuck in Malbry all these years, like a plant too pot-bound ever to thrive. I have stayed with her. Like everything else. Apart from the neighbours, nothing has changed. The three-bedroomed house; the Axminster; the queasy flowered wallpaper; the gilt-edged mirror in the kitchen that hides a hole in the plaster; the faded print of the *Chinese Girl*; the lacquer vase on the mantel; the dogs.

Those dogs. Those hideous china dogs.

An affectation to start with, that since has got totally out of hand. There are dogs on every surface now: spaniels, Alsatians, chihuahuas, basset hounds, Yorkshire terriers (her favourites). There are musical dogs, portraits of dogs, dogs dressed up as people; dogs eager-tongued and lolloping, sitting to attention, paws lifted in silent appeal, heads topped with little pink bows.

I broke one once, when I was a boy, and she beat me – though I denied the crime – with a piece of electrical cord. Even now, I still hate those dogs. She knows it, too – but they are her babies, she explains (with a terrible, girlish coyness), and besides, she tells me, she never complains about all *my* nasty stuff upstairs.

Not that she even knows what I do. I have my privacy: rooms of my own, all of them with locks on the doors, from which she is excluded. The converted loft and study room, the bathroom, the bedroom; and the darkroom in the cellar. I've made a home for myself here, with my books, my playlists, my online friends, while she spends her days in the parlour, smoking, doing crosswords, dusting and watching daytime TV –

Parlour. I always hated that word, with all its fake middle-class resonances, and its stink of citrus potpourri. Now I hate it even more, with her faded chintz and her china dogs and her reek of desperation. Of course, I couldn't leave her. She knew that from the very first; knew that her decision to stay kept me here, chained to her, a prisoner, a slave. And I am a dutiful son to her. I make sure her garden is always neat. I see to her medication. I drive her to her salsa class (Ma drives, but prefers to be driven). And sometimes, when she's not there, I dream . . .

My mother is a peculiar blend of conflicts and contradictions. Marlboros have ruined her sense of smell, but she always wears Guerlain's L'Heure Bleue. She despises novels, but loves to read dictionaries and encyclopaedias. She buys ready meals from Marks & Spencer, but fruit and veg from the market in town – and always the cheapest fruit and veg, bruised and damaged and past their prime.

Twice a week, without fail (even the week of Nigel's death), she puts on a dress and her high-heeled shoes and I drive her to her salsa class at Malbry College, after which she meets up with her friends in town, and has a cup of fancy tea, or maybe a bottle of Sauvignon Blanc, and speaks to them in her half-bred voice about me and my job at the hospital, where I am indispensable (according to her) and save lives on a daily basis. Then at eight I pick her up, although it's only a five-minute walk from the bus stop. *Those hoodies from the estates*, she says. *They'd stab you soon as look at you.*

Maybe she's right to be cautious. The members of our family seem unusually prone to accidents. Still, I pity the hoodie who tries to mess with my mother. She knows how to look after herself. Even now, at sixty-nine, she's sharp enough to draw blood. What's more, she knows how to strike back at anyone who threatens us. She is a little more subtle, perhaps, than in the days of the electrical cord, but even so, it isn't wise to antagonize Gloria Winter. I learnt that lesson very young. In that, if nothing else, I was a precocious pupil. Not as smart as Emily White, the little blind girl whose story has coloured so much of my life, but smart enough to have survived when neither of my brothers did.

Still, isn't that all over now? Emily White is long dead; her plaintive voice silenced, her letters burnt, the blurry flashgun photographs curled away in secret drawers and on bookshelves in the Mansion. And even if she were not, somehow, the Press have almost forgotten her. There are other things to squawk about; newer scandals over which to obsess. The disappearance of one little girl, over twenty years ago, is no longer cause for public concern. Folk have moved on. Forgotten her. Time for me to do the same.

The problem is this. Nothing ends. If ever Ma taught me anything, it is that nothing is ever truly over. It just works its way slyly into the centre, like yarn in a ball. Round and round and round it goes, crossing and re-crossing, until eventually it is almost hidden beneath the tangle of years. But just to be hidden is not enough. Someone will always find you out. Someone is always lying in wait. Drop your guard for even a second and – *wham!* That's when it all blows up in your face.

Take that girl in the duffel coat. The one who looks like Red Riding Hood, with her rosy cheeks and her blameless air. Would you believe that she is not what she seems? That beneath that cloak of innocence beats the heart of a predator? Looking at her, would you ever think that she could take a person's life?

You wouldn't, would you? Well, think again.

But nothing's going to happen to me. I've thought this out too carefully. And when it *does* go up – as we know it must – *blueeyedboy* will be half a world away, sitting in the shade by a beach, listening to the sound of the surf and watching the seagulls overhead –

Still, that's for tomorrow, isn't it? Right now I have other things on my mind. Time for another fic, I think. I like myself better as a fictional character. The third-person voice adds distance, says Clair; gives me the power to say what I like. And it's nice to have an audience. Even a murderer loves praise. Maybe that's why I write these things. It certainly isn't a need to confess. But I do admit to a leap of the heart every time someone posts a comment, even someone like Chryssie or Cap, who wouldn't know genius if it poked them in the eye.

I sometimes feel like a king of cats, presiding over an army of mice – half-predatory, half in need of those worshipful voices. It's all about approval, you see, and when I log on in the morning and see the list of messages waiting for me I feel absurdly comforted –

Losers, victims, parasites – and yet I can't stop myself from collecting them, as I do my orchids; as I once collected scuttling things in my blue bucket on the beach; as I was once collected.

Yes, it's time for another murder. A public post on my WeJay, to balance these private reflections of mine. Better still, a *murderer*. Because, although I say *he* –

You and I know this is all about *me*.

5

You are viewing the webjournal of **blueeyedboy** *posting on:*
badguysrock@webjournal.com
Posted at: *03:56 on Tuesday, January 29*
Status: *public*
Mood: *sick*
Listening to: *Nick Lowe*: 'The Beast In Me'

Most accidents occur in the home. He knows this only too well; has spent much of his childhood avoiding those things that might potentially do him harm. The playground with its swings and round-abouts, and the litter of needles along the edge. The fishpond with its muddy banks on which a small boy might so easily slip, to be dragged to his death in the weedy depths. Bikes that might spill him on to the tarmac to skin his knees and hands – or worse, under the wheels of a bus, to be skinned all over like an orange and left in segments on the road. Other children, who might not understand how special he is, how susceptible – nasty boys who might bloody his nose, nasty girls who might break his heart –

Accidents happen so easily.

That's why, if there's anything he should know by now, it's how to create an accident. Maybe a car accident, he thinks, or a fall down a flight of stairs, or a simple, homely electrical fire. But how do you cause an accident – a *fatal* accident, of course – to happen to someone who doesn't drive, who doesn't indulge in dangerous sports, and whose idea of a wild night out is popping into town with her friends (they always *pop*, they never just *go*), for gossip and a glass of wine?

It isn't that he fears the act. What he fears are the consequences. He knows the police will call him in. He knows he will be a suspect, however accidental the deed, and he will have to answer to them, to plead his innocence, to convince them that it isn't his fault –

That's why he has to choose his time. There can be no margin of error. He knows that murder is a lot like sex: some people know how to take their time; to enjoy the rituals of seduction, rejection, reconciliation; the joy of suspense; the thrill of the chase. But most of them just need to *see it done*; to get the need of it out of themselves as quickly as they possibly can; to distance themselves from the horrors of that intimacy; to know release above all things.

Great lovers know it's not about that.

Great murderers know it, too.

Not that he *is* a great murderer. Just an aspiring amateur. With no established modus operandi, he feels like an unknown artist who yet has to find a style of his own. That's one of the hardest things to do – for an artist or for a murderer. Murder, like all acts of self-affirmation, requires a tremendous self-confidence. And he still feels like a novice: shy; uncertain; protective of his talents and hesitant to make himself known. In spite of it all, he is vulnerable; fearing not just the act itself, but also the reception it may have to endure; those people who will, inevitably, judge, condemn and misunderstand –

And of course, he hates her. He would never have planned it otherwise; he is no Dostoyevskian killer, acting at random and thoughtlessly. He hates her with a passion that he has never felt for anything else; a passion that blooms within him like blood; that sweeps him away on a bitter blue wave –

He wonders what it would be like. To be free of her for once and for all; free of the presence that envelops him. To be free of her voice, of her face, of her ways. But he is afraid, and untested; and so he plans the act with care, selecting his subject (he refuses to use the word *victim*) according to the rules, preparing it all with the neatness and precision that he extends to all things –

An accident. That's all it was.

A most unfortunate accident.

To challenge the boundaries, he understands, you first have to learn to follow the rules. To approach such an act, one has to train, to hone one's art on some baser element, just as a sculptor works in clay – discarding anything that is not perfect, repeating the experiment until the desired result is achieved – before creating the masterpiece. It would be naïve, he tells himself, to expect great things of his first attempt. Like sex, like art, the first time is often inelegant, clumsy and embarrassing. He has prepared himself for this. His aim is merely not to be caught. It has to be an accident – and his relationship with the subject must, though real, be distant enough to defy those who will come looking for him.

You see, he thinks like a murderer. He feels its glamour in his heart. He would never harm someone who does not already deserve to die. He may be bad, but he is not unfair. Nor is he degenerate. He will not be a commonplace, bludgeoning, thoughtless, messy, remorse-sodden killer. So many people die futile deaths – but in her case, at least, there will be reason, order and – yes, a kind of justice. One less parasite on the world, making it a better place.

A strident call from downstairs intrudes upon the fantasy. He feels an annoying tremor of guilt. She hardly ever comes into his room. Besides, why should she climb the stairs when she knows that a call will bring him down?

'Who's there?' she says.

'No one, Ma.'

'I heard a noise.'

'I'm working online.'

'Talking to your imaginary friends?'

Imaginary friends. That's good, Ma.

Ma. The sound a baby makes, the sound of sickness, of lying in bed; a feeble, milky, helpless sound that makes him feel like screaming.

'Well, come on down. It's time for your drink.'

'Hang on. I'll be right there.'

Murder. Mother. Such similar words. *Matriarch. Matricide. Parasite. Parricide,* something used to get rid of parasites. All of them coloured in shades of blue, like the blue of the blanket she tucked around his bed every night when he was a boy, and smelling of ether and hot milk –

Night night. Sleep tight.

Every boy loves his mother, he thinks. And his mother loves him so much. *So much I could swallow you up, B.B.* And maybe she has, because that's how it feels, as if something has swallowed him, something slow but relentless, something inescapable, sucking him down into the belly of the beast –

Swallow. There's a blue word. Flying south, into the blue. And it smells of the sea and tastes like tears, and it makes him think of that bucket again, and the poor, trapped, scuttling things dying slowly in the sun –

She's so proud of him, she says; of his job; of his intellect; of his gift. *Gift* means poison in German, you know. Beware of Germans bearing gifts. Beware of swallows flying south. South to the islands of his dreams: to the blue Azores, the Galapagos, Tahiti and Hawaii –

Hawaii. Awayyy. The southernmost edge of his mental map, scented with distant spices. Not that he's ever been there, of course. But he likes the lullaby lilt of the word, a name that sounds like laughter. White sands and palm beaches and blue skies fat with fair-weather clouds. The scent of plumeria. Pretty girls in coloured sarongs with flowers in their long hair –

But really, he knows he'll never fly south. His mother, for all her ambitions, has never been a traveller. She likes her small world, her fantasy, the life she has carved for them piece by piece into the rock of suburbia. She will never leave, he knows; clinging to him, the last of her sons, like a barnacle, a parasite –

'Hey!' She calls to him from downstairs: 'Are you coming down, or what? I thought you said you were coming down.'

'Yes, I'm coming down, Ma.'

Of course I am. I always do. Would I ever lie to you?

And the plunge of despair as he goes downstairs into the parlour that smells of some kind of cheap fruit-flavoured air-freshener – grapefruit, maybe, or tangerine – is like going down into the belly of some huge, fetid, dying animal: a dinosaur or a beached blue whale. And the smell of synthetic citrus makes him almost want to gag –

'Come in here. I've got your drink.'

She's sitting in the kitchenette, arms folded across her chest, feet camel-backed in her high heels. For a moment he is surprised, as always, at how very small she is. He always imagines her larger, somehow; but she is smaller than he is by far, except for her hands, which are surprisingly large compared to the bird-bony rest of her, the knuckles misshapen, not just with arthritis, but with the rings she has collected over the years – a sovereign, a diamond cluster, a Campari-coloured tourmaline, a piece of polished malachite and a flat blue sapphire gated with gold.

Her voice is at the same time both brittle and oddly penetrating. 'You look terrible, B.B.,' she says. 'You're not coming down with something, are you?' She says *coming down* with a certain suspicion, as if he has brought it on himself.

'I didn't sleep too well,' he says.

'You need to take your vitamin drink.'

'Ma, I'm fine.'

'It'll do you good. Go on – take it,' she says. 'You know what happens when you don't.'

And take it he does, as he always does, and its taste is a murky, rotten mess, like fruit and shit in equal parts. And she looks at him with that terrible look of tenderness in her dark eyes, and kisses him gently on the cheek. The scent of her perfume – L'Heure Bleue – envelops him like a blanket.

'Why don't you go back to bed for a while? Get some sleep before tonight? They work you so *hard* at that hospital, it's a crime they get away with it—'

And now he's *really* feeling sick, and he thinks that maybe he will lie down, go back to bed and lie down with the blanket pulled around his head, because nothing could be worse than this; this feeling of drowning in tenderness –

'See?' she says. 'Ma knows best.'

Ma-ternal. Ma-stiff. Ma-stodon. The words swim around inside his head like piranhas scenting blood. It hurts, but he already knows that it will hurt much more later; already the edges of things are garlanded with rainbows that in the next minutes will blossom and swell, driving a spike into his skull just behind his left eye –

'Are you sure you're all right?' his mother says. 'Shall I sit beside you?'

'No.' The pain is bad enough, he thinks, but her presence would be so much worse. He forces a smile. 'I just need to sleep. I'll be fine in an hour or two.'

And then he turns and goes upstairs, holding on to the banisters, the filthy taste of the vitamin drink lost in a sudden surge of pain, and he almost falls, but does not, knowing that if he falls, she will come, and she will stay at his bedside for hours or days, for as long as the terrible headache lasts –

He collapses on to his unmade bed. There is no escape, he tells himself. This is the verdict. Guilty as charged. And now he must take his medicine, as he has done every day of his life; medicine to purge him of bad thoughts, a cure for what's hidden inside him –

Night night. Sleep tight.

Sweet dreams, *blueeyedboy.*

Post comment:

chrysalisbaby: *wow this is awesome*

JennyTricks: (*post deleted*).

ClairDeLune: *This is quite intriguing,* **blueeyedboy.** *Would you say it represents your true inner dialogue, or is it a character portrait you're planning to develop at some later stage? In any case, I'd love to read more!*

JennyTricks: (*post deleted*).

6

You are viewing the webjournal of **blueeyedboy**.
Posted at: 22.40 on Tuesday, January 29
Status: restricted
Mood: vitriolic
Listening to: Voltaire: 'When You're Evil'

The perfect crime comes in four separate stages. Stage One: identification of the subject. Stage Two: observation of the subject's daily routine. Stage Three: infiltration. Stage Four: action.

So far there's no hurry, of course. She is barely a Stage Two. Walking past the house each day, the collar of her bright red coat turned up against the cold.

Red isn't her colour, of course – but I don't expect her to know that. She doesn't know how I like to watch: noting the details of her dress; the way the wind catches her hair; the way she walks with such precision, marking her passage with almost imperceptible touches. A hand against this wall, here; brushing against this yew hedge; pausing to lift her face to the sound of schoolchildren playing in the yard. Winter has stripped the leaves from the trees, and on dry days their percussion underfoot still smells dimly of fireworks. I know she thinks that too; I know how she likes to walk in the park with its alleys and walled gardens and listen to the sound of the naked trees shushing to themselves in the wind. I know how she turns her face to the sky, mouth open to catch the droplets of rain. I know the unguarded look of her; the way her mouth twists when she is upset; the turn of her head when she listens; the way her face tilts towards a scent.

She notices scents especially: lingers in front of the bakery. Eyes closed, she likes to stand by the door and catch the aroma of warm bread. I wish I could talk to her openly, but Ma's spies are everywhere; watching; reporting; examining . . .

One of these is Eleanor Vine, who called round early this evening. Ostensibly to check on Ma, but really to enquire after me, to search for signs of grief or guilt in the wake of my brother's death; to sniff out what was happening at home, and to collect any news that was going.

Every village has one. The local do-gooder. The busybody. The one to whom everyone applies when in need of information. Eleanor Vine is Malbry's: a poisonous toady who currently forms part of the toxic triumvirate that makes up my mother's retinue. I suppose I ought to feel privileged. Mrs Vine rarely leaves her house, viewing the world through net curtains, occasionally condescending to welcome others into her immaculate sanctum for biscuits, tea and vitriol. She has a niece called Terri, who goes to my writing-as-therapy class. Mrs Vine thinks that Terri and I would make a charming couple. I think that Mrs Vine would make an even more charming corpse.

Today she was all sweetness. 'You look exhausted, B.B.,' she said, greeting me in the hushed voice of one addressing an invalid. 'I hope you're taking care of yourself.'

It is common knowledge in the Village that Eleanor Vine is something of a hypochondriac, taking twenty kinds of pills and disinfecting incessantly. Over twenty years ago, Ma used to clean her house, though now Eleanor reserves that privilege for herself, and can often be seen through her kitchen window, Marigolds on standby, polishing the fruit in the cut-glass dish that stands on the kitchen table, a mixture of joy and anxiety on her thin, discoloured face.

My iPod was playing a song from one of my current playlists. Through the earpiece, Voltaire's darkly satirical voice expounded the various virtues of vice to the melancholy counterpoint of a gypsy violin.

> And it's so easy when you're evil.
> This is the life, you see,
> The Devil tips his hat to me –

'I'm quite all right, Mrs Vine,' I said.

'Not sickening for anything?'

I shook my head. 'Not even a cold.'

'Because bereavement can do that, you know,' she said. 'Old Mr Marshall got pneumonia four weeks after his poor wife passed on. Dead before the headstone went up. The *Examiner* called it a double tragedy.'

I had to smile at the thought of myself pining away for Nigel.

'I hear they're missing you at your class.'

That killed the smile. 'Oh yes? Who says?'

'People talk,' said Eleanor.

I'll bet they do. Toxic old cow. Spying on me for Ma, I don't doubt. And now, thanks to Terri, a spy for my writing-as-therapy class, that little circle of parasites and headcases with whom I share – in supposed confidence – the details of my troubled life.

'I've been preoccupied,' I said.

She gave me a look of sympathy. 'I know,' she said. 'It must be hard. And what about Gloria? Is she all right?' She glanced around the parlour, alert for any telltale sign – a smear of dust on the mantelpiece, a speck on any one of Ma's collection of china dogs – to suggest that Ma might be cracking up.

'Oh, you know. She manages.'

'I brought her a little something,' she said, handing me a paper bag. 'It's a supplement I sometimes use when I'm feeling under the weather.' She gave her vinegary smile. 'Looks like you could do with some yourself. Have you been in a fight, or something?'

'Who, me?' I shook my head.

'No. Of course,' said Eleanor.

No, of course. As if I would. As if Gloria Winter's boy could ever be involved in a fight. Everyone thinks they know me. Everyone's an authority. And it always irks me a little to think that she, like Ma, would never believe the tenth of what I am capable –

'Oh, Eleanor, love, you should have come through!' That was Ma, emerging from the kitchen with a tea-towel in one hand and a vegetable peeler in the other. 'I was just making him his vitamin drink. D'you want some tea while you're here?'

Eleanor shook her head. 'I just popped in to see how you were.'

'Holding up all right,' said Ma. 'B.B.'s looking after me.'

Ouch. That was below the belt. But Ma *is* very proud of me. A taste like that of rotten fruit slowly crept into my mouth. Rotten fruit mixed with salt, like a cocktail of juice and sea water. From my iPod, Voltaire declaimed with murderous exuberance:

> *I do it all because I'm evil.*
> *And I do it all for free –*

Eleanor gave me a sidelong glance. 'He must be such a comfort, love.' She turned once more to look at me. 'I don't know how you can hear a word we're saying with that thing in your ear. Don't you ever take it out?'

If I could have killed her then, right then, without risk, I would have snapped her neck like a stick of Blackpool rock without so much as a tremor of guilt – but as it was I had to smile so hard it made my fillings ache, and to take out one of my iPod plugs, and to promise to go back to my class next week, where everyone is missing me –

'What did she mean, go back to your class? Have you been skipping sessions again?'

'No, Ma. Just the one.' I did not quite dare meet her eyes.

'Those classes are for your own good. I don't want to hear you're skipping them.'

Of course, I should have known that sooner or later she would find out. With friends like Eleanor Vine, her net covers all of Malbry. Besides, I quite enjoy my class, which gives me the chance to disseminate all kinds of misinformation –

'Besides, it helps you cope with stress.'

If only you knew, Ma.

'OK, I'll go.'

7

You are viewing the WebJournal of **blueeyedboy**.
Posted at: *01.44 on Wednesday, January 30*
Status: *restricted*
Mood: *creative*
Listening to: *Breaking Benjamin:* 'Breath'

Most accidents occur in the home. I'm guessing that's how I came about; one of three boys, all born within five years. Nigel, then Brendan, then Benjamin, though by then she'd stopped using our real names, and I was always B.B.

Benjamin. It's a Hebrew name. It means *Son Of My Right Hand*. Not so very flattering, really, when you consider what guys actually *do* with their right hand. But then, the man we knew as Dad was hardly a dutiful father. Only Nigel remembered him, and then only as a series of vague impressions: a big voice; a rough face; a scent of beer and cigarettes. Or maybe that's memory doing what it does sometimes, filling in the gaps with plausible detail while the rest turns over in darkness, like a spindle laden with black sheep's wool.

Not that Nigel *was* the black sheep – all of that came later. But he *was* destined to always wear black, and with time, it affected his character. Ma worked as a cleaner in those days: dusting and vacuuming rich people's homes, doing their laundry, ironing their clothes, washing their dishes and polishing their floors. Time spent on our own house was unpaid work, and so of course it took second place. Not that she was slovenly. But time was always an issue with her, and had to be saved at every turn.

And so, with three sons so close to each other in age and so much laundry to do every week, she hit upon an ingenious system. To ensure that items could be easily identified, she allocated to each of her sons a colour, and bought our clothes accordingly from the local Oxfam shop. Thus Nigel wore shades of charcoal, even down to his underwear; Brendan always wore brown and Benjamin –

Well, I'm sure you can guess.

Of course, it never crossed her mind what such a decision might do to us. Colours make a difference; any hospital worker can tell you that. That's why the cancer unit in the hospital where I work is painted in cheery shades of pink; the waiting rooms in soothing green; the maternity wards in Easter-chick yellow –

But Ma never really understood the secret power of colours. To Ma, it was just a practical means of sorting laundry. Ma never asked herself what it might be like to have to wear the same colour day in, day out: boring brown or gloomy black or beautiful, wide-eyed, fairy-tale blue –

But then, Ma always was different. Some boy's mothers are sugar and spice. Mine was – well – she was something else.

Born Gloria Beverley Green, the third child of a factory girl and a steelworker, Ma spent her childhood in Malbry town, in the maze of little brick terraces known locally as Red City. Washing strung across the streets; soot on every surface; cobbled alleyways leading to nothing but blind and litter-lined spray-painted walls.

Ambitious even then, she dreamed of far pavilions, distant shores and working girls rescued by millionaires. Even now, Ma believes in true love, in the lottery, in self-help books, in boosting your word power, in magazine columns and agony aunts and TV advertisements in which the floors are always clean and women always *worth it* –

Of course, she was neither imaginative nor particularly bright – she left school with only five CSEs – but Gloria Green was determined enough to compensate for her failings, and instead turned all of her considerable willpower and energy towards finding a means of escape from the grime and small-mindedness of Red City into that TV world of clean babies and shiny floors and numbers that can change your life.

It wasn't easy, keeping the faith. Red City was all she had ever known. A rat trap, that lures you in, but seldom lets you out again. Her friends all married in their teens; found jobs, had kids. Gloria stayed with her parents, helping her mother keep house and waiting day after tedious day for a prince who never came.

Finally she gave in. Chris Moxon was a friend of her dad's; he ran a fish-and-chip shop and lived on the edge of White City. He wasn't exactly Catch of the Day – being older and balder than she'd planned – but he was kind and attentive, and by then she was getting desperate. She married him at All Saints' Church in white tulle and carnations, and for a while she almost believed that she had somehow escaped the rat trap –

But she found that the smell of frying fat crept into everything she owned – her dresses, her stockings, even her shoes. And however many Marlboros she smoked, however much scent she dabbed on to her skin, there was always that stink – *his* stink – underlying everything; and she realized that she *hadn't* escaped the rat trap, she had simply fallen deeper inside.

Then she met Peter Winter at a Christmas party later that year. He worked at a local car dealership and drove a BMW. Heady stuff for Gloria Green, embarking on her first affair with the coolness of a professional poker player. Certainly, the stakes were high. Gloria's Pa thought the world of Chris. But Peter Winter looked promising: he was solvent, ambitious, untroubled, unwed. He spoke of moving out of White City; of finding a house in the Village, perhaps –

It was good enough for Gloria. She made him her personal project. Within twelve months she was divorced, and pregnant with her first child. She swore that the boy was Peter's, of course, and when she was able, she married him, in spite of her family's protests.

This time, there was no fanfare. Gloria had shamed them all. No one attended the ceremony, which was held on a dismal November day at the local Register Office. And when things started to fall apart – when Peter started drinking, when the dealership went broke – Gloria's parents refused to back down, or even to see the little boy that she'd named after her father –

But Gloria was undaunted. She took an evening job in town, as well as her daily cleaning shift; and when she became pregnant again she hid it, wearing a girdle right up until the eighth month, so that she could keep earning money. When her second son was born she took in mending work and ironing too, so that the house was always filled with the steam and the smell of other people's washing. The dream of a house in the Village had become increasingly remote; but at least in White City there were schools, and a park for the kids, and a job at the local laundrette. Things looked good for Gloria, and she faced her new life with optimism.

But two years of unemployment had wrought a change in Peter Winter. Once a charmer, now he'd grown fat, spending his days in front of the TV, smoking Camels and drinking beer. Gloria was carrying him, much to her resentment; and unbeknownst to her, by then she was pregnant once again.

I never knew my real father. Ma seldom spoke of him. He was handsome, though. I have his eyes. I think Gloria secretly thought that he might turn out to be her ticket out of White City. But Mr Blue Eyes had other ideas, and by the time Ma learnt the truth, her ship had sailed for sunnier shores, leaving her to weather the storm.

No one knows how Peter found out. Perhaps he saw them together somewhere. Perhaps someone talked. Perhaps he just guessed. But Nigel remembered the night he left – or at least, he said he did, though he can't have been five years old at the time. A night of broken crockery, of shouted oaths, of insults – and then the sound of the car starting, the slammed door, the squeal of rubber on the road – a sound that to me always conjures up the smell of fresh popcorn and cinema seats. Then, later, the crash, the broken glass, the howl of sirens in the air –

Of course Nigel never heard all that. That was the way she told it, though; that was Ma's version of the tale. Peter Winter took three weeks to die, leaving his widow pregnant and alone. But Gloria Green was tough. She found a childminder in White City and simply worked harder, pushed herself more, and when she left her job at last, two weeks before the baby was due, her employers took a collection that raised a total of forty-two pounds. Gloria spent some of it on a washing machine and banked the rest, to make it last. She was still only twenty-seven.

At this point I think I might have gone home to my parents. She had no job, hardly any savings, no friends. Her looks, too, had begun to fade, and little remained of the Gloria Green who had left Red City with such high hopes. But to crawl back to her family – defeated, with two children, a baby and no husband – was unthinkable. And so she stayed in White City. She worked from home; looked after her sons; washed and ironed and mended and cleaned, while all the time she was searching for another escape, even as her youth left her and White City closed around her like a drowning man's arms.

And then Ma had a stroke of luck. Peter's insurance paid out. Turns out he was worth more dead than he'd ever been worth alive; and finally, Ma had some money. Not enough – there was *never* enough – but now she could see a light ahead. And that piece of good fortune had come along just as her youngest entered the world, making him her lucky charm; her chance at the winning ticket.

In certain parts of the world, you know, blue eyes are thought to be bad luck, the sign of a demon in disguise. But to carry a blue-eye talisman – a glass bead on a piece of string – is to divert the path of malchance, to send back evil to its source; to banish demons to their lair and to bring good fortune in their place –

Ma, with her love of TV drama, believed in easy solutions. Fiction works to formula. The victim is always a pretty girl. And the answers are always right under your nose, to be revealed in the penultimate scene: by accident, or perhaps by a child – tying up all the loose ends in a pretty birthday-party bow.

Life, of course, is different. Life is nothing but loose ends. And sometimes the thread that seemed to lead so clearly into the heart of the labyrinth turns out to be nothing but tangled string, leaving us alone in the dark, afraid and consumed with the growing belief that the *real* action is still going on somewhere without us, just around the corner –

So much for luck. I came very close. Almost close enough to touch before it was taken away from me. It wasn't my fault. But still she blames me. And ever since, I have tried to be everything she expects of me; and still it's never quite enough, never enough for Gloria Green –

Is that what you feel? says Clair, from Group. *Don't you think you're good enough?*

Bitch. Don't even go there.

You're not the first to try it, you know. You women, with your questions. You think it's so easy to judge cause and effect, to analyse and to excuse. Do you think you can fit me into one of your little boxes, a neatly labelled specimen? That, armed with a few choice details, you can pencil in the rest of my soul?

Not much chance of that here, *ClairDeLune*. You people really have nothing on me. You think I'm new to this game? I've been in and out of groups like yours for the greater part of twenty years. As a matter of fact, it's kind of fun: recalling childhood incidents; inventing dreams, spinning straw into fantasy –

In this way, Clair has come to believe that she knows the man behind the avatar. Fat Chryssie – aka *chrysalisbaby* – also thinks she understands. In actual fact, I know more about them than they could ever know about me; knowledge that may come in useful some day if ever I choose to exploit it.

Clair thinks she is trying to help me. I think she is in denial. Clair's therapeutic writing class is really nothing but a disguised attempt at amateur psychoanalysis. And Clair's online fascination for all things damned and dangerous suggests that she, too, feels damaged. I'm guessing an early experience of abuse, perhaps by a family member. Her fixation with the actor Angel Blue – a man so much older than herself – suggests that she may have daddy issues. Well, of course, I can sympathize. But it's hardly reassuring in a lecturer. Plus it makes her so vulnerable. I hope it doesn't end in tears.

As for Fat Chryssie's interest in me – it seems to be purely romantic. Well, it makes a change from her usual posts, which normally consist of a series of lists detailing her calorie consumption – *Diet Coke: 1.5 cals; Skinny Cow: 90 cals; nacho chips, lo-fat cheese: prolly about 300 cals* – punctuated by agonizing monologues on how ugly she feels, or interminable pictures of skinny, fragile Goth girls that she refers to as *thinspiration*.

Sometimes she posts pictures of herself – always body shots, never the face – taken on a mobile phone in front of the bathroom mirror, and encourages people to rant at her. Very few indulge her in this (with the exception of Cap, who hates fatties), but some of the other girls leave *ana – love,* or saccharine messages of support – *Babe, you're doing great. Stay strong!* – or half-baked advice about dieting.

Thus Chryssie has acquired an almost evangelical faith in the properties of green tea as a metabolism booster, and in 'negative calorie foods' (which to her mind include carrots, broccoli, blueberries, asparagus and many other things that she rarely eats). Her avatar is a manga drawing of a little girl dressed in black with butterfly wings growing out of her shoulders, and her signature line – at the same time hopeful and unutterably sad – reads: *One day I'll be lighter than air . . .*

Well, maybe she will. There's always hope. But not all Body Freaks die thin. Maybe she'll end up as some of them do, dead of a stroke or a heart attack on the porcelain phone to God.

One of her online friends – *Azurechild* – has been urging her to try something called syrup of ipecac. It's a well-known purgative, with potentially fatal side effects, but which causes rapid weight loss. Of course it's irresponsible, one might say downright criminal, to encourage someone with Chryssie's weight problem, and with her already weakened heart, to take such a dangerous substance.

Still, it's her choice, isn't it? No one is forcing her to take the advice. We do not create these situations. All we do is hit the keys. *Control. Alt. Delete.* Gone. A fatal error. An accident –

So – *How Well Do You Think You Know Me Now?*

That's this week's *meme,* posted by Clair, snagged by Chryssie, who always tags me, like a child in a crowded playground trying to summon a circle of friends.

Clair and Chryssie, like so many of our online clan, are addicted to *memes:* Internet chain-letters, whose purpose is to simulate interest and conversation, often in the form of a questionnaire. Sweeping the Net like a schoolyard craze – *Post three facts about yourself! What did you dream about last night?* – passing from one person to another, disseminating information both useful and otherwise; these things behave like viruses, some going global, some dying out, some ending up on *badguysrock*, where talking about oneself – *Me! Me!* – is always a popular pastime.

When tagged, I tend to reciprocate. Not because I enjoy self-promotion, but I find these exercises intriguing for what they reveal – or not – about the recipient. The questions – to be answered at speed – are designed to create the illusion of intimacy, and to answer them correctly sometimes requires a level of detail that might challenge even the closest friend.

Thanks to this medium I know that Chryssie has a cat called Chloë and likes to wear pink socks in bed; that Cap's favourite film is *Kill Bill*, but that he despises *Kill Bill 2*; that Toxic likes black girls with big breasts; and that *ClairDeLune* likes modern jazz and has a collection of ceramic frogs.

Of course, you don't have to tell the truth. And yet, so many people do. The details are designed to be trivial enough to make the lie seem unnecessary – and yet, from those details a picture emerges, the little things that make up a life –

For instance, I know that Clair's computer password is *clairlovesangel*. It's her hotmail password too, which means that now I can open her mailbox. It's so easy to do these things online; and fragments of gleaned information – names of pets, children's birth dates, mothers' maiden names – all make it so much easier. Armed with such seemingly innocuous data, I can access more intimate things. Bank details. Credit cards. It's like nitrogen and glycerine. Each fairly harmless on its own, but pair the two together, and – *Wham!*

Tagged by **chrysalisbaby** *posting on* **badguysrock@webjournal.com**
Posted at: *12:54 on Tuesday, January 29*
If you were an animal, what would you be? *A rat.*
Favourite smell? *Petrol.*
Tea or coffee? *Coffee. Black.*
Favourite flavour of ice cream? *Bitter chocolate.*
What are you wearing right now? *A dark-blue hooded top, jeans, blue Converses.*
What are you afraid of? *Heights.*
What's the last thing you bought? *Music for my iPod.*
What's the last thing you ate? *A toasted sandwich.*
Favourite sound? *Surf on the beach.*

Siblings? *None.*
What do you wear in bed? *Pyjamas.*
What's your pet hate? *The slogan 'Because I'm worth it.' Because you're not, and you know it –*
Your worst trait? *I'm devious, manipulative, and a liar.*
Any scars or tattoos? *A scar across my upper lip. Another on my eyebrow.*
Any recurring dreams? *No.*
Where would you most like to be right now? *Hawaii.*
There's a fire in your house. What would you save? *Nothing. I'd let it all burn.*
When did you last cry? *Last night – and no, I won't tell you why . . .*

See how you think you know me?

As if you could possibly form a judgement on the basis of how I drink my coffee, or whether I wear pyjamas in bed. In fact, I drink tea, and I sleep naked. Has that changed your impression of me? Would it have made a difference if I'd told you that I never cry? That my childhood was bad? That I've never been outside of a hundred-mile radius of the place where I was born? That I'm afraid of physical violence, that I suffer from migraines, that I hate myself?

Some – or all – of those things might be true. All or none of the above. *Albertine* knows some of the truth, although she rarely comments here, and her WeJay is password-protected so that no one can read her private posts –

But Chryssie will study my answers with care. She will establish a profile from my replies. There's more than enough to intrigue her there, plus there's a hint of vulnerability, which will counterbalance the veiled aggression to which she responds so readily.

And I *do* come across as a bad guy – but I may be redeemable, through love. Who knows? It happens in movies all the time. And Chryssie lives in a rose-tinted world in which a fat girl may find true love with a killer in need of tenderness –

Of course it isn't the real world. I save all that for my writing group. But I like myself so much better as a fictional character. Besides, who is to say that what she sees isn't some fragmentary part of the truth –

truth, like an onion, layer upon layer of tissue and skin, wrapped tightly round something that brings tears to your eyes?

Tell me about yourself, she says.

That's how it always starts, you know, with some woman – some girl – assuming she knows the best way to mine the motherlode at the centre of me.

Motherlode. Mother. Load. Sounds like something you'd carry about – a heavy burden, a punishment –

So let's begin with your mother, she says.

My mother? Are you really sure?

See how quickly she takes the bait. Because every boy loves his mother, right? And every woman secretly knows that the only way to win a man's heart is, first of all, to dispose of Ma –

8

You are viewing the webjournal of **blueeyedboy** *posting on:*
badguysrock@webjournal.com
Posted at: *18:20 on Wednesday, January 30*
Status: *public*
Mood: *vibrant*
Listening to: *Electric Light Orchestra:* 'Mr Blue Sky'

He calls her Mrs Electric Blue. Appliances are her thing: novelty door-chimes, CD players, juicers, steamers and microwaves. You have to wonder what she does with so many; her guest bedroom alone contains nine boxes of obsolete hairdryers, curling tongs, foot spas, kitchen blenders, electric blankets, video recorders, shower radios and telephones.

She never throws anything away, keeping them 'for parts', she says, although she belongs to that generation of women for whom technical ineptitude counts as a charming sign of feminine fragility rather than just laziness, and he knows for a fact that she hasn't a clue. She is a parasite, he thinks, useless and manipulative, and no one will grieve very much for her, least of all her family.

He recognizes her voice at once. He has been working part-time in an electrical repair shop a couple of miles from where she lives. An old-fashioned place, rather obsolete now, its small front window packed with ailing TVs and vacuum cleaners, and dusty with the grey confetti of moths who have flown in there to die. She calls him out on his mobile number – at four on a Friday afternoon, no less – to look over her menagerie of dead appliances.

She is pushing fifty-five by now, but can look older or younger according to necessity. Ash-blonde hair, green eyes, good legs, a fluttering, almost girlish manner that can change to contempt at a moment's notice – and she likes the company of nice young men.

A nice young man. Well, that's what he is. Slim in his denim overalls, angular face, slightly over-long brown hair and eyes of that luminous, striking grey-blue. Not the stuff of magazines, but nice enough for Mrs Electric Blue – and besides, at her age, he thinks, she can't afford to be particular.

She tells him at once that she is divorced. She makes him a cup of Earl Grey tea, complains about the cost of living, sighs deeply at her solitude – and at the gross neglect of her son, who works down in the City somewhere, and eventually, with the air of one about to confer an enormous privilege, offers him her collection for cash.

The stuff is totally worthless, of course. He says so as gently as he can, explaining that old electrical goods are fit for nothing but land-fill now, that most of her collection doesn't conform to present safety standards, and how his boss will kill him if he pays as much as a tenner for it.

'Really, Mrs B.,' he says. 'The best I can do is dump it for you. I'll take it down to the rubbish tip. The council would charge you, but I've got the van—'

She stares at him with suspicion. 'No, thanks.'

'Only trying to help,' he says.

'Well, if that's the case, young man,' she says in a voice that is crystalline with frost, 'you can *help* by taking a look at my washing machine. I think it's blocked – it hasn't drained for nearly a week—'

He protests. 'I'm due at another job—'

'I think it's the least you can do,' she says.

Of course, he gives in. She knows he will. Her voice still has that blend of disdain and vulnerability, of helplessness and authority, that he finds irresistible . . .

The drive-belt has slipped, that's all. He unbolts the drum, replaces the belt, wipes his hands on his overalls, and in the reflection from the glass door he sees her watching him.

She may have been attractive once. Now you'd call it *well-preserved*; a phrase his mother sometimes uses, and which to him conjures up images of formaldehyde jars and Egyptian mummies. And now he knows she is watching him with a strangely proprietary look; he can feel her eyes like soldering irons pressing into the small of his back – an appraising glance as careless as it is predatory.

'You don't remember me, do you?' he says, turning his head to meet her gaze.

She gives him that imperious look.

'My mother used to clean your house.'

'Did she really?' The tone of her voice is meant to suggest that she couldn't possibly remember all the people who have worked for her. But for a moment she seems to recall *something*, at least – her eyes narrow and her eyebrows – plucked into insignificance, then redrawn in brown pencil half an inch above where they should be – twitch in something like distress.

'She used to bring me with her, sometimes.'

'My God.' She stares at him. '*Blueeyedboy?*'

He's killed it now with that, of course. She'll never look at him again. Not in *that* way, anyhow – her languid gaze moving down his back, gauging the distance between the nape of his neck and the base of his spine, checking out the taut curve of his ass in those faded blue overalls. Now she can *see* him – four years old, hair undarkened by the passage of time – and suddenly the weight of years drops back on her like a wet winter coat and she's old, so terribly *old* –

He grins. 'I think that's fixed it,' he says.

'I'll pay you something, of course,' she says – too quickly, to hide her embarrassment – as if she believes he works for free, as if this might be some kind gesture of hers that will put him for ever in her debt.

But they both know what she's paying him for. Guilt – maybe simple, but never pure, ageless and tireless and bittersweet.

Poor old Mrs B., he thinks.

And so he thanks her nicely, accepts another cup of lukewarm and vaguely fishy tea, and finally leaves with the certainty that he will be seeing a lot more of Mrs Electric Blue in the days and weeks to come.

*

51

Everyone's guilty of something, of course. Not all of them deserve to die. But sometimes karma comes home to roost, and an act of God may sometimes require the touch of a helping human hand. And anyway, it's not his fault. She calls him back a dozen times – to wire a plug, to change a fuse, to replace the batteries in her camera, and most recently, to set up her new PC (God only knows why she needs one, she's going to die in a week or two), which prompts a flurry of urgent calls, which in their turn precipitate his current decision to remove her from the face of the earth.

It isn't really personal. Some people just deserve to die – whether through evil, malice, guilt or, as in the present case, because she called him *blueeyedboy* –

Most accidents occur in the home. Easy enough to set one up – and yet, somehow he hesitates. Not because he is afraid – although he is, most terribly – but simply because he wants to watch. He toys with the idea of hiding a camera close to the scene of the crime, but it's a vanity he can ill afford, and he discards the scheme (not without regret), and instead contemplates the method to use. Understand: he is very young. He believes in poetic justice. He would like her death to be somehow symbolic – electrocution, perhaps, from a malfunctioning vacuum cleaner, or from one of the vibrators that she keeps in her bathroom cabinet (two of them modestly flesh-toned, the third a disquieting purple), amongst the bottles of lotions and pills.

For a moment he is almost seduced. But he knows that elaborate plans rarely work, and firmly dismissing the beguiling image of Mrs Electric Blue pleasuring herself into the grave with the aid of one of her own appliances, on his next visit he sets up the makings of a dull but efficient little electrical fire, and gets back home in time for a snack in front of the TV. While meanwhile, in another street, Mrs Electric gets ready for bed (with or without her purple pal), and dies there sometime during the night, probably of smoke inhalation, he thinks, although, of course, one can only hope –

The police call by the following day. He tells them how he tried to help, how every appliance in the house was some kind of accident waiting to happen, how she was always overloading the sockets with her junk, how all it might take was a little surge –

In fact, he finds them ludicrous. His guilt, he thinks, should be plain for them to see, and yet they do not; but sit on the couch and drink his mother's tea and talk to him quite nicely, as if trying not to cause him distress, while his mother watches suspiciously, alert for any hint of blame.

'I hope you're not saying that was his fault. He works hard. He's a good boy.'

He hides a smile behind his hand. He is trembling with fear, but now laughter overwhelms him, and he has to fake a panic attack before someone realizes that the pale young man with the blue eyes is actually laughing fit to split –

Later, he can pinpoint the moment. It is a thunderous sensation, something like orgasm, something like grace. The colours around him brighten, expand; words take on dazzling new shades; scents are enhanced; he shivers and sobs and the world blisters and cracks like paint, revealing the light of eternity –

The female PC (there's always one) offers him a handkerchief. He takes it and scrubs his face, looking scared and guilty but laughing still, though she, the woman, who is twenty-four and might be pretty out of that uniform, takes his tears as a sign of distress, and puts a hand on his shoulder, feeling strangely maternal –

It's OK, son. It's not your fault.

And that ominous taste at the back of his throat, the taste he associates with childhood, with rotten fruit and petrol and the sickly rose-scent of bubblegum, recedes once more like a bank of cloud, leaving only blue skies in its wake, and he thinks –

At last, I'm a murderer.

Post comment:

chrysalisbaby: *woot woot!* **blueeyedboy** *kicks ass*

Captainbunnykiller: *'Mrs Electric Blue pleasuring herself into the grave . . .' Dude. There's a scene I'd give money to read. How about it, huh?*

Jesusismycopilot: *YOU'RE SICK. I HOPE YOU KNOW THAT.*

blueeyedboy: *I'm aware of my condition, thanks.*

chrysalisbaby: *well i don't care i think ur awesome*

Captainbunnykiller: *Yeah, man. Ignore the troll. Those fucktards wouldn't know good fic if it jumped up and bit them in the ass.*

Jesusismycopilot: *YOU ARE SICK AND YOU WILL BE JUDGED.*

JennyTricks: *(post deleted).*

ClairDeLune: *If these stories upset you, then please don't come here to read them. Thank you, **blueeyedboy**, for sharing this. I know how hard it must be to express these darker feelings. Well done! I hope to read more of this story as it develops!*

9

You are viewing the webjournal of **blueeyedboy**.
Posted at: *23.25 on Wednesday, January 30*
Status: *restricted*
Mood: *unrepentant*
Listening to: *Kansas*: 'Carry On Wayward Son'

No, I don't take it personally. Not everyone appreciates the value of a well-written fic. According to many, I am sick and depraved and deserve to be locked up, or beaten to a pulp, or killed.

So, everyone's a critic, right? I get a lot of death threats. Most are rants from the God squad: *Jesusismycopilot* and friends, who always write in capitals, with little punctuation except for a forest of exclamation points that rises above the main text like the upraised spears of a hostile tribe, and who tell me YOUR SICK! (sic) and THE DAY IS AT HAND! and that Yours Truly will BURN IN H*LL (!!!) WITH ALL THE QUEERS AND PEDOPHILES!

Well, thanks. There are headcases everywhere. A newbie, who calls herself *JennyTricks*, has become a regular visitor, posting comments on all of my fics on a rising scale of outrage. Her style is poor, but she makes up for it in vitriol; leaves no term of abuse unused; promises me a world of hurt if ever she gets her hands on me. I doubt she will, however. The Internet is a safe house, close as the confessional. I never post my details. Besides, their anger gives me a buzz. Sticks and stones, dude; stones and sticks.

But seriously, I love the applause. I even enjoy the occasional hiss.

To provoke a reaction with words alone is surely the greatest victory. That's what my fiction is for. To incite. To see what reactions I can collect. Love and hate; approval and scorn; judgement and anger and despair. If I can make you punch the air, or feel a little sick, or cry, or want to do violence to me – or to others – then isn't that a privilege? To creep inside another mind, to make you do what I *want* you to do –

Doesn't that pay for everything?

Well, the good news is – apart from the fact that my headache is gone – that I now have more time to indulge. One of the advantages of sudden unemployment is the amount of leisure it provides. Time to pursue my interests, both on and offline. Time, as my mother says, to stop and smell the roses.

Unemployment? Well, yes. I've had some trouble recently. Not that Ma knows *that*, of course. As far as my mother is concerned, I still work at Malbry Infirmary, the details unclear, but plausible – at least to Ma, who barely finished school and whose medical knowledge, such as it is, is taken from the *Reader's Digest* and from the hospital soaps she likes to watch in the afternoons.

Besides, in a way, it's almost true. I *did* work at the infirmary – I worked there for nearly twenty years – though Ma never really knew what I did. Technical operations of some kind – also a partial truth of sorts – in a place in which everyone's job description contains either the word *operator* or *technician*; I was until recently one of a team of hygiene technicians operating two shifts a day and attending to such vital responsibilities as: mopping, sweeping, disinfecting, wheeling out the rubbish bins and general maintenance of toilets, kitchens and public areas.

In layman's terms, a cleaner.

My secondary, even more dangerous job – again, at least, until recently – was that of day carer for an elderly man, wheelchair-bound, for whom I used to cook and clean; on good days I'd read, or play music on scratchy old vinyl, or listen to stories I already knew, and later I'd go looking for *her*, for the girl in the bright-red duffel coat –

As of now, I have more time, and much less chance of being caught in the act. My daily routine hasn't changed. I get up in the mornings as usual, dress for work, care for my orchids, park the car in the infirmary car park, pick up my laptop and briefcase, and spend the day at leisure in a series of Internet cafés, catching up on my f-list, or posting my fiction on *badguysrock* away from my mother's suspicious eye. After four I often drop by at the Pink Zebra café, where there is a minimal chance of my running into Ma or her friends, and which offers Internet access for the price of a bottomless pot of tea.

Given my own choice of venue, I think I'd prefer something a little less bohemian. The Pink Zebra is rather too informal for me, with its wide-mouthed American cups, and its Formica-topped tables, and chalked Specials boards and the noise of its many patrons. And the name itself, that word, *pink*, has a most unfortunate pungency that takes me back to my childhood, and to our family dentist, Mr Pink, and of the smell of his old-fashioned surgery with its sugary, sickly odour of gas. But *she* likes it. She would. The girl in the bright red duffel coat. She likes her anonymity among the café's clientele. Of course, that's an illusion. But it's one I'm willing to grant her – for now. One last unacknowledged courtesy.

I try to find a table close by. I drink Earl Grey – no lemon, no milk. That's what my old mentor, Dr Peacock, drank, and I have acquired the taste myself; not entirely usual for a place like the Pink Zebra, that serves organic carrot cake and Mexican spiced hot chocolate, and acts as a refuge for bikers and Goths and people with multiple piercings.

Bethan – the manager – glares at me. Perhaps it's my choice of beverage, or the fact that I'm wearing a suit and tie and therefore qualify as *The Man* – or maybe today it's just my face – the ladder of suture-strips across one cheekbone, the cuts bisecting eyebrow and lip.

I can tell what she's thinking. I shouldn't be here. She's thinking I look like trouble, though it's nothing she can quantify. I'm clean, I'm quiet, I always tip. And yet there's something about me that unsettles her; that makes her think I don't belong.

'Earl Grey, please – no lemon, no milk.'

'Be with you in five minutes, OK?'

Bethan knows all her customers. The regulars all have nicknames, much the same as my friends online, like Chocolate Girl, Vegan Guy, Saxophone Man and so on. I, however, am just OK. I can tell that she would be happier if she could fit me into a category – perhaps

Yuppie Guy, or *Earl Grey Dude* – and knew what to expect of me.

But I prefer to wrong-foot her sometimes: to turn up in jeans occasionally; to order coffee (which I hate), or, as I did a couple of weeks ago, half a dozen pieces of pie, eating them one by one as she watched, clearly itching to say something, but not quite daring to comment. In any case, she is suspicious of me. A man who will eat six pieces of pie is capable of anything.

But you shouldn't judge by appearances. Bethan herself is an irregular choice, with the emerald stud in her eyebrow and the stars tattooed down her skinny arms. A shy, resentful little girl, who compensates now by being vaguely aggressive with anyone who looks at her askance.

Still, it is to Bethan that I owe much of my information. From the café she notices everything. She seldom speaks to me, of course, but I overhear her conversations. With people like me she is cautious, but with her regulars she is cheery, approachable. Thanks to Bethan I can collect all kinds of information. For instance, I know that the girl in the red duffel coat would rather drink hot chocolate than tea; prefers treacle tart to carrot cake; favours the Beatles over the Stones, and plans to attend the funeral at Malbry Crematorium at 11.30 on Saturday.

Saturday. Yes, I'll be there. At least I'll get to see her away from that wretched café. Maybe – just maybe – she owes me that. Closure, as the Americans say. An end to this parade of lies.

Lies? Yes, everyone lies. I've lied ever since I could remember. It's the only thing I do well, and I think we should play to our strengths, don't you? After all, what is a writer of fiction but a liar with a licence? You'd never guess from my writing that I'm as plain-vanilla as they come. Vanilla, at least, on the *outside*; the heart is something different. But aren't we, all of us, killers at heart, tapping out in Morse code the secrets of the confessional?

Clair thinks I should talk to her.

Have you tried telling her how you feel? she suggests in her latest e-mail. Of course, Clair only knows what I want her to know: that for an indeterminate time I have been obsessed with a girl to whom I have hardly spoken a word. But maybe Clair identifies with me rather more than she is aware – or rather, with *blueeyedboy*, whose platonic love for an unnamed girl echoes her own unrequited passion for Angel Blue.

Cap's advice is rather more crude. *Just fuck her and get it over with*, he advises, in the world-weary tone of one trying vainly to hide his own inexperience. *When the novelty wears off, you'll see she's just like all those other bitches, and you'll be able to get back to what matters . . .*

Toxic agrees, and pleads for me to write up the intimate details in my WeJay. *The dirtier the better*, he says. *And by the way, what's her cup size?*

Albertine rarely comments. I sense her disapproval. But *chrysalisbaby* responds to what she sees as my hopeless romance. *Even a bad guy needs someone to love*, she says with awkward sincerity. *You deserve it, blueeyedboy, really you do.* She does not offer herself, not yet, but I sense the longing in her words. Any girl would be lucky, she hints, to earn the love of one such as I.

Poor Chryssie. Yes, she's fat. But she has good hair and a pretty face, and I have led her to believe that I prefer the chubby ones.

The problem is that I play it too well. She now wants to see me on webcam. For the past couple of weeks she has been talking to me through WebJournal, sending me personal messages, including photos of herself.

Y can't i C U? she messages.
Out of the question, I reply.
Y? U ugly? ☺
Yeah. I'm a mess. Broken nose, black eye, cuts and bruises all over me.
I look like I went twelve rounds with Mike Tyson. Trust me, Chryssie.
You'd run a mile.
4 real?? What happened?
Someone took exception to me.
☹ *O!!! U mugged?*
I guess you could call it that.
!!! Oh, fuck, oh, babe, ☹ *i just wanna give U a great big hug.*
Thanks, Chryssie. You're very sweet.
Does it hurt??

Dear Chryssie. I can feel the sympathy coming from her. Chryssie loves to nurture, and I like to feed her fantasy. She's not quite in love with me – no, not yet. But it wouldn't take much to draw her in. It's a little cruel, I know. But isn't that what bad guys do? Besides, she brings these things on herself. All I do is enable them. She's an accident waiting to happen, for which no one could possibly hold me to blame.

Babe, tell me what happened, she says, and today I think maybe I'll humour her. Give a little, take a lot. Isn't that the better deal?

All right then – *babe*. Whatever you say. See what you make of *this* little tale.

10

You are viewing the webjournal of **blueeyedboy** *posting on:*
badguysrock@webjournal.com

Posted at: *14.35 on Thursday, January 31*

Status: *public*

Mood: *amorous*

Listening to: *Green Day:* 'Letterbomb'

Blueeyedboy in love. What? You don't think a killer can fall in love? He has known her for ever, and yet she has never really seen him, not once. He might have been invisible as far as the woman he loves is concerned. But he sees *her*: her hair; her mouth; her small pale face with its straight dark brows; her bright-red coat in the morning mist like something out of a fairy tale.

Red is not her colour, of course – but he doesn't expect her to know that. She doesn't know how he likes to watch through his telephoto lens; noting the details of her dress; the way the wind catches her hair; the way she walks with such precision, marking her passage with near-imperceptible touches. A hand against this wall, here; brushing against this yew hedge, turning her face to catch the scent as she passes the village bakery.

He is not a voyeur, he thinks. He acts for his own protection. His instinct for self-preservation has been honed to a point of such accuracy that he can sense the danger in her, the danger behind the sweet face. It may be the danger he loves, he thinks. The fact that he is walking a dangerous line. The fact that every stolen caress through the lens of his camera is potentially lethal to him.

Or it may just be the fact that she belongs to somebody else.

Until now he has never been in love. It frightens him a little: the intensity of that feeling, the way her face intrudes on his thoughts, the way his fingers trace her name, the way everything somehow conspires to keep her always in his mind –

It changes his behaviour. It makes him contradictory; at the same time more accepting, and less so. He wants to do the right thing, but, so doing, thinks only of himself. He wants to see her, but when he does, flees. He wants it to last for ever, but at the same time longs for it to end.

Zooming closer, he brings her face into mystic, near-monstrous proportions. Now she is a single eye, its colour a hybrid of blue and gold, staring sightlessly through the glass like an orchid in a growing-tank –

But through the eye of love, of course, she always appears in shades of blue. Bruise-blue; butterfly-blue; cobalt, sapphire, mountain-blue. Blue, the colour of his secret soul; the colour of mortality.

His brother in black would have known what to say. *Blueeyedboy* lacks the words. But he dreams of them dancing under the stars, she in a ball dress of sky-blue silk, he in his chosen colours. In these dreams he is beyond words, and he can smell the scent of her hair, can almost feel her texture –

And then comes a sharp knock at the door. *Blueeyedboy* starts guiltily. It annoys him that he does this; he is in his own home, hurting no one, why should he feel this stab of guilt?

He puts away his camera. The knock is repeated; peremptory. Someone sounds impatient.

'Who is it?' says *blueeyedboy*.

A voice, not well-loved, but familiar, comes to him from the other side. 'Let me in.'

'What do you want?' says *blueeyedboy*.

'To talk to you, you little shit.'

Let's call him Mr Midnight Blue. Bigger by far than *blueeyedboy*, and vicious as a mad dog. Today he is in a violent rage that *blueeyedboy* has never seen before, hammering at the front door, demanding to be let in. No sooner are the safety locks released, than he barges his way into the hall and, with no kind of preliminaries, head-butts our hero right in the face.

Blueeyedboy's trajectory sends him smashing into the hallway table; ornaments and a flower vase fly into shrapnel against the wall. He trips and falls at the bottom of the stairs, and then Midnight Blue is on top of him, punching him, shouting at him –

'Fucking keep away from her, you twisted little bastard!'

Our hero makes no attempt to resist. He knows it would be impossible. Instead he just curls into himself like a hermit crab into its shell, trying to shield his face with his arms, crying in fear and hatred, while his enemy lands blow after blow to his ribs and back and shoulders.

'Do you understand?' says Midnight, pausing to recover his breath.

'I wasn't doing anything. I've never even *spoken* to her—'

'Don't give me that,' says Midnight Blue. 'I know what you're trying to do. And what about those photographs?'

'Ph-photographs?' says *blueeyedboy*.

'Don't even think of lying to me.' He pulls them from one of his inside pockets. '*These* photographs, taken by you, developed right here, in your darkroom—'

'How did you get those?' says *blueeyedboy*.

Midnight gives him a final punch. 'Never mind how I got them. If you ever go anywhere near her again, if you talk to her, write to her – hell, if you even *look* at her – I'll make you sorry you were born. This is your final warning—'

'Please!' Our hero is whimpering, his arms thrown up to protect his face.

'I mean it. I'll kill you—'

Not if I kill you first, blueeyedboy thinks, and before he can protect himself, the hateful aroma of rotting fruit fills his throat with its hothouse stench, and a lance of pain drives into his head, and he feels as though he is dying.

'Please—'

'You'd better not lie to me. You'd better not hold out on me.'

'I won't,' he gasps, through blood and tears.

'You'd better not,' says Midnight Blue.

Lying dazed on the carpet, *blueeyedboy* hears the door slam. Warily, he opens his eyes and sees that Midnight Blue has gone. Even so he waits until he hears the sound of Midnight's car setting off down the driveway before slowly, carefully, standing up and going into the bathroom to investigate the damage.

What a mess. What a fucking mess.

Poor *blueeyedboy*; nose broken, lip split, blue eyes blacked and swollen shut. There's blood down the front of his shirt; blood still trickles from his nose. The pain is bad, but the shame is worse, and the worst of it is, this isn't his fault. In this case, he is innocent.

How strange, he thinks, that for all his sins, he should have escaped retribution so far, whereas this time, when he has done nothing wrong, punishment should descend on him.

It's karma, he thinks. *Kar-ma.*

He looks at his reflection, looks at it for a long time. He feels very calm, watching himself, an actor on a small screen. He touches his reflection and feels the answering sting from the abrasions on his face. Nevertheless he feels strangely remote from the person in the looking glass; as if this were simply a reconstruction of some more distant reality; something that happened to someone else many, many years ago.

I mean it. I'll kill you –

Not if I kill you first, he thinks.

And would it be so impossible? Demons are made to be overcome. Maybe not with brute strength, but with intelligence and guile. Already he senses the germ of a plan beginning to form at the back of his mind. He looks at his reflection once more, squares his shoulders, wipes blood from his mouth and, finally, begins to smile.

Not if I kill you first –

Why not?

After all, he has done it before.

Post comment:

chrysalisbaby: *awesome wow was that 4 real?*

blueeyedboy: *As real as anything else I write . . .*

chrysalisbaby: *aw poor* **blueeyedboy** *i just wanna give him a great big hug*

Jesusismycopilot: *BASTARD YOU DESERVE TO DIE.*

Toxic69: *Oh, man. Don't we all?*

ClairDeLune: *This is fantastic,* **blueeyedboy**. *You are finally beginning to come to terms with your rage. I think we should discuss this further, don't you?*

Captainbunnykiller: *Bitchin', dude! This fic pwns. Can't wait to see the payback.*

JennyTricks: *(post deleted).*

JennyTricks: *(post deleted).*

JennyTricks: *(post deleted).*

blueeyedboy: *You're very persistent,* **JennyTricks**. *Tell me – do I know you?*

11

You are viewing the webjournal of **blueeyedboy**.
Posted at: *01.37 on Friday, February 1*
Status: *restricted*
Mood: *melancholy*
Listening to: *Voltaire*: 'Born Bad'

Well, no. It wasn't *quite* like that. But not too far from the truth, all the same. The truth is a small, vicious animal biting and clawing its way towards the light. It knows that if it wants to be born, something – or *someone* – else has to die.

I started life as a twin-set, you know. The other half – who, if he had lived, Ma would have christened Malcolm – was stillborn at nineteen weeks.

Well, that's the official tale, anyway. Ma told me when I was six that I'd swallowed my sibling *in utero* – most probably at some point between the twelfth and the thirteenth weeks – in the course of some dispute over *Lebensraum*. It happens more often than people think. Two bodies, one soul; floating in Nature's developing fluid, fighting for the right to live –

She kept the memory of him alive as an ornament on the mantelpiece – a statuette of a sleeping dog, engraved with his initials. The same piece, in fact, that I broke as a boy, and tried to lie about to protect myself. For which I was thrashed with the piece of electrical cord and told that I was born bad – a killer, even in embryo – that I owed it to both of them to be good, to make something of my stolen life –

In fact, she was secretly proud of me. The fact that I'd swallowed my twin to survive made her believe that I was strong. Ma despised weakness. Hard as tempered steel herself, she couldn't stand a loser. *Life's what you make it*, she used to say. *If you don't fight, you deserve to die.*

After that I often used to dream that Malcolm – whose name appears to me in sickly shades of green – had won the fight and taken my place. Even now I still have that dream: two little ravenous tadpoles, two piranhas side by side, two hearts in a bloodbath of chemicals just clamouring to beat as one. If he had lived instead of me, I wonder, would Mal have taken my place? Would *he* have become *blueeyedboy*?

Or would he have had his own colour? Green perhaps, to go with his name? I try to imagine a wardrobe in green: green shirts, green socks, dark-green V-necked sweater for school. All of it identical to mine (except for the colour, of course), all of it in my size, as if a lens had been placed on the world, painting my life a different shade.

Colours make a difference. Even after so many years, I still follow my mother's colour schemes. Blue jeans, hoodie, T-shirt, socks – even my trainers have a blue star on the side. A black roll-necked sweater, a birthday present from last year, lies unworn in a bottom drawer, and whenever I think to try it on, there's a sudden stab of unreasonable guilt.

That's Nigel's sweater, a sharp voice says, and although I know it's irrational, I still can't bring myself to wear his colour, not even for his funeral.

Perhaps that's because he hated me. He blamed me for everything that went wrong. He blamed me for causing Dad to leave; blamed me for his stretch in jail; for his breakdown; for his ruined life; resented the fact that Ma liked me best. Well, that, at least, was justified. Without a doubt, she favoured me. Or at least, she did at first. Perhaps because of my dead twin; the anguish of her delivery; perhaps because of Mr Blue Eyes, who was, as she said, the love of her life.

But Nigel made sibling rivalry into a major art form. His brothers lived in terror of his uncontrollable rages. His brother in brown escaped the worst, being vulnerable in so many ways. Nigel held him in contempt, a willing slave when it suited him, a human shield against Ma's wrath, the rest of the time a whipping-boy, taking the blame for everyone.

But bullying Bren was too easy. There was no satisfaction to be gained from hitting such a target. You could punch Brendan and make him cry, but no one ever saw him fight back. Perhaps he'd learnt from experience that the best way to deal with Nigel, as with a charging elephant, is to lie still and play dead, hoping to avoid the stampede. And he never seemed to bear a grudge, not even when Nigel tormented him, confirming Ma's belief that Bren was not the sharpest tool in the box, and that if anyone were to give them their fairy-tale ending, then it would be Benjamin.

Well, yes. Ma liked her clichés. Brought up on tales of the Lottery, of younger sons who end up marrying princesses, of eccentric millionaires who leave all their wealth to the sweet little urchin who captures their heart – Ma believed in destiny. She saw these things in black and white. And though Bren submitted without complaint, pre-ferring safe mediocrity to the treacherous burden of brilliance, Nigel, who was no fool, must have felt a certain resentment to find that he had been cast from birth in the role of the ugly stepsister, perpetually the man in black.

And so, Nigel was angry. Angry at Ma; angry at Ben; even angry at poor, fat Brendan, who tried so hard to be quiet and good, and who found increasing solace in food, as if through the comfort of sweet things he might provide himself with some measure of protection in a world too full of sharp edges.

And so when Nigel was playing outside, or riding his bike around the estate, and Bren was sitting watching TV with a Wagon Wheel in each hand and a six-pack of Pepsi at his side, Benjamin was going to work with his Ma, a duster clutched in one chubby hand, eyes wide at the opulence of other people's houses; at their broad stairs and neat driveways, sprawling sound systems and walls of books; at their well-stocked fridges and hallway pianos and shagpile carpets and bowls of fruit on dining-room tables as shiny and broad as a ballroom floor.

'Look at this, Ben,' she would say, pointing at some photograph of a boy or girl in school uniform, grinning gap-toothed from a leather frame. 'That'll be you in a few years' time. That'll be you, at the big school, making me so proud of you—'

Like so many of Ma's endearments, it sounded eerily like a threat. She was in her thirties by then – already worn down to the canvas by the years.

Or so I thought when I was young. Now, looking at her photographs, I see that she was beautiful, perhaps not in the conventional way, but striking with her black hair and dark eyes, and the full lips and high cheekbones that made her look French, though she was British to the bone.

Nigel looked just like her, with his dark espresso eyes. But I was always different: blond hair that faded to brown with time; a thin and rather suspicious mouth; eyes of a curious blue-grey, so large that they almost ate up my face –

Would Mal and I have been identical? Would he have had my blue eyes? Or do I have his, as well as my own, looking for ever inwards?

In oriental languages, or so Dr Peacock used to say, there is no distinction between blue and green. Instead, there is a compound word, something that expresses both shades, and that translates as 'sky-coloured', or 'leaf-coloured'. It made a kind of sense to me. From my earliest infancy, I'd always thought of blue as being primarily 'Ben-coloured', or brown as 'Brendan-coloured', or black as 'Nigel-coloured', without ever stopping to ask myself if others perceived things differently.

Dr Peacock changed all that. He taught me a new way of looking at things. With his maps and his recordings and his books and his cases of butterflies, he taught me to expand my world, to trust in my perception. For that I'll always be grateful to him, even though he let me down. Let us all down, in the end: me, my brothers, Emily. You see, for all his kindness, Dr Peacock didn't care. When he'd had enough of us he simply threw us back on the pile. *Albertine* understands, even though she never makes any reference to that time; pretends, in fact, to be someone else –

Still, recent events may have changed all that. It's time to check on *Albertine*. Although she may not know it yet, I can read all her entries. No restrictions apply to me; public or private, it's all the same. Of course, she doesn't know this. Hidden away in her cocoon, she has no idea how closely I've been watching her. Looks so innocent, doesn't she, with her red coat and her basket? But as my brother Nigel found out, sometimes the bad guys *don't* wear black, and sometimes a little girl lost in the woods is more than a match for the big, bad wolf . . .

PART TWO
black

1

You are viewing the webjournal of **Albertine**.
Posted at: 20.54 on Saturday, February 2
Status: restricted
Mood: black

I've always hated funerals. The noise of the crematorium. The people talking all at once. The clatter of feet on the polished floor. The sickly scent of flowers. Funeral flowers are different from any other kind. They hardly smell like flowers at all, but like some kind of disinfectant for death, somewhere halfway between chlorine and pine. Of course, the colours are pretty, they say. But all I can think of as the coffin goes into the oven at last is the sprig of parsley you get on fish in restaurants: that tasteless, springy garnish that no one ever wants to eat. Something to make the dish look nice; to distract us from the taste of death.

So far, I hardly miss him. I know it's a terrible thing to say. We were friends as well as lovers, and in spite of everything – his black moods, his restlessness, his ceaseless tapping and fidgeting – I cared for him. I know I did. And yet I really don't feel much as his coffin slides into the furnace. Does that make me a bad person?

I think that maybe, yes, it does.

It was an accident, they said. Nigel *was* an appalling driver. Always over the speed limit; always losing his temper, always tapping, rapping, gesturing. As if by his own movements he could somehow compensate for the stolid inactivity of others. And there was always his silent rage: rage at the person in front of him; rage at always being left behind; rage at the slow drivers; rage at the fast drivers, the clunkers, the kids, the SUVs.

No matter how fast you drive, he said – fingers tapping the dashboard in that way that drove me crazy – there's always someone ahead of you, some idiot shoving his back bumper into your face like a randy dog showing its arse.

Well, Nigel. You've done it now. Right at the junction of Mill Road and Northgate, sprawled across two lanes of traffic, overturned like a Tonka toy. A patch of ice, they said. A truck. No one really knew for sure. A relative identified you. Probably your mother, although I have no way of knowing, of course. But it feels like the truth. She always wins. And now she's here, all dressed up, weeping into the arms of her son – her one surviving son, that is – while I stand dry-eyed, at the back of the hall.

There wasn't much left of the car, or of you. Dog food in a battered tin. You see, I am trying to be brutal here. To make myself feel something – *anything* – but this eerie calm at the heart of me.

I can still hear the machinery working behind the curtain; the swish of cheap velvet (asbestos-lined) as the little performance ended. I didn't cry a single tear. Not even when the music began.

Nigel didn't really like classical music. He'd always known what he wanted them to play at his funeral, and they obliged with the Rolling Stones' 'Paint It Black' and Lou Reed's 'Perfect Day', songs that, whilst dark enough in this context, have no power over me.

Afterwards I followed the crowd blindly to the reception room, where I found a chair and sat down away from the mill of people. His mother did not speak to me. I wouldn't have expected her to; but I could sense her presence near by, baleful as a wasps' nest. I do believe she blames me; although it seems hard to imagine how I could have been responsible.

But the death of her son is less of a bereavement to her than an opportunity to parade her grief. I heard her talking to her friends – her voice staccato with outrage:

'*I can't believe she's here,*' she said. '*I can't believe she had the nerve—*'

'*Come on, lovey,*' said Eleanor Vine. I recognized her colourless voice. '*Calm down, it isn't good for you.*'

Eleanor is Gloria's friend as well as her ex-employer. The other two in her entourage are Adèle Roberts, another ex-employer of Mother's, who used to teach at Sunnybank Park, and who everyone assumes is French (because of the accent in her name), and Maureen Pike, the bluff and somewhat aggressive woman who runs the local Neighbourhood Watch. Her voice carries most of all; I could hear her rallying the troops.

'That's right. Settle down. Have another piece of cake.'

'If you think I could eat a thing—'

'Cup of tea, then. Do you good. Keep your strength up, Gloria, love.'

Once more I thought of the coffin, the flowers. By now they would be blackening. So many people have left me this way. When will I start caring?

It all began seven days ago. Seven days ago, with the letter. Until then, we – that is, Nigel and I – existed in a soft cocoon of small daily pleasures and harmless routines; two people pretending to themselves that things are normal – whatever *that* means – and that neither of them is damaged, flawed, possibly beyond repair.

And what about love? That too, of course. But love is a passing ship at best, and Nigel and I were castaways, clinging together for comfort and warmth. He was an angry poet, gazing from the gutter at the stars. I was always something else.

I was born here in Malbry. On the outskirts of this unfashionable Northern town. It's safe here. No one notices me. No one questions my right to be here. No one plays the piano any more, or the records Daddy left behind, or the Berlioz, the terrible *Symphonie fantastique* that still haunts me so. No one talks about Emily White, the scandal and the tragedy. Almost no one, anyway. And all that was so long ago – over twenty years, in fact – that if they think of it at all, it is simply as a coincidence. That one such as I should move into this house – Emily's house – notorious by association, or, indeed, that of all the men in Malbry it should be Gloria Winter's son who found himself a place in my heart.

I met him almost by accident, one Saturday night at the Zebra. Till then I had been almost content, and the house, which had been in need of repair, was finally clear of workmen. Daddy had been dead three years. I'd gone back to my old name. I had my computer; my online friends. I went to the Zebra for company. And if I still sometimes felt lonely, the piano was still there in the back room, now hopelessly out of tune, but achingly familiar, like the scent of Daddy's tobacco, caught in passing down a street, like a kiss from a stranger's mouth –

Then, Nigel Winter came along. Nigel, like a force of Nature, who came and disrupted everything. Nigel, who came looking for trouble, and somehow found me there instead.

There's rarely any unpleasantness at the Pink Zebra. Even on a Saturday, when bikers and Goths sometimes come through on their way to a concert in Sheffield or Leeds, it's nearly always a friendly crowd, and the fact that the place shuts early means that they're usually still sober.

This time was an exception. At ten a group of women – a hen party from out of town – had still not cleared the premises. They'd had a few bottles of Chardonnay, and the talk had turned to scandals past. I pretended not to listen to them; I tried to be invisible. But I could feel their eyes on me. Their morbid curiosity.

'You're her, aren't you?' A woman's voice, a little too loud, divulging in a boozy stage whisper what no one else dared mention. 'You're that What's-her-name.' She put out a hand and touched my arm.

'Sorry. I don't know who you mean.'

'You are, though. I saw you. You've got a Wiki page, and everything.'

'You shouldn't believe what you read on the Net. Most of it's just a pack of lies.'

Doggedly, she went on. 'I went to see those paintings, you know. I remember my mum taking me. I even had a poster once. What was it called? French name. All those crazy colours. Still, it must have been terrible. Poor kid. How old were you? Ten? Twelve? I tell you, if anyone touched one of *my* kids I'd fucking kill the bastard—'

I've always been prone to panic attacks. They creep up on me when

I least expect them, even now, after all these years. This was the first I'd suffered in months, and it took me completely unawares. Suddenly I could hardly breathe; I was drowning in music, even though there was no music playing . . .

I shook the woman's hand from my arm. Flailed out at the empty air. For a second I was a little girl again – a little girl lost among walking trees. I reached for the wall and touched nothing but air; around me, people jostled and laughed. The party was leaving. I tried to hold on. I heard someone call for the bill. Someone asked: *Who had the fish?* Their laughter clattered around me.

Breathe, baby, breathe! I thought.

'Are you OK?' A man's voice.

'I'm sorry. I just don't like crowds.'

He laughed. 'Then you're in the wrong place, love.'

Love. The word has potency.

People tried to warn me at first. Nigel was unstable. He had a criminal past, they said; but after all, my own past could hardly be said to bear scrutiny, and it was so good to be with him – to be with someone real, at last – that I ignored the warnings and plunged straight in.

You were so lovely, he told me later. *Lovely and lost.* Oh, Nigel.

That night we drove out to the moors and he told me all about himself, about his time in prison and the youthful mistake that had sent him there; and then we lay for hours on the heath in the overwhelming silence of the stars, and he tried to make me understand about all those little pins of light scattered across the velvet –

There, I thought. Now for the tears. Though not for Nigel as much as for myself and for that starry night. But even at my lover's funeral, my eyes remained stubbornly dry. And then I felt a hand on my arm and a man's voice said:

'Excuse me. Are you all right?'

I'm very sensitive to voices. Every one, like an instrument, is unique, with its own individual algorithm. His voice is attractive: quiet, precise, with a slight pull on certain syllables, like someone who used to stammer. Not at all like Nigel's voice; and yet I could tell they were brothers.

I said: 'I'm fine. Thank you.'

'"*Fine*",' he repeated thoughtfully. 'Isn't that a useful word? In this case, it means: "I don't want to talk to you. Please go away and leave me alone."'

There was no malice in his tone. Just a cool amusement; maybe even a touch of sympathy.

'I'm sorry,' I began to say.

'No. It's me. I apologize. It's just that I hate funerals. The hypocrisy. The platitudes. The food you'd never think of eating at any other time. The ritual of tiny fish-paste sandwiches and mini jam tarts and sausage rolls—' He broke off. 'I'm sorry. Now I'm being rude. Would you like me to fetch you something to eat?'

I gave a shaky laugh. 'You make it sound so appealing. I'll pass.'

'Very wise.'

I could hear his smile. His charm has a way of surprising me, even now, after all this time, and it makes me feel a little queasy to think that at my lover's funeral I talked – I laughed – with another man, a man I found almost attractive . . .

'I have to say, I'm relieved,' he said. 'I rather thought you'd blame me.'

'Blame you for Nigel's accident? Why?'

'Well, maybe because of my letter,' he said.

'Your letter?'

Once more, I heard him smile. 'The letter he opened the day he died. Why do you think he was driving so recklessly? My guess is he was coming for me. To deliver one of his – *warnings*.'

I shrugged. 'Aren't you the perceptive one? Nigel's death was an *accident*—'

'There's no such thing as an accident as far as our family's concerned.'

I stood up much too fast at that, and the chair clattered back against the parquet floor. 'What the hell does *that* mean?' I said.

His voice was calm, still slightly amused. 'It means we've had our share of bad luck. What did you want? A confession?'

'I wouldn't put it past you,' I said.

'Well, thanks. That puts me in my place.'

I was feeling strangely light-headed by then. Perhaps it was the heat, or the noise, or simply the fact of being so close to him, close enough to take his hand.

'You hated him. You wanted him dead.' My voice sounded plaintive, like a child's.

A pause. 'I thought you knew me,' he said. 'You really think I'm capable?'

And now I thought I could almost hear the first notes of the Berlioz, the *Symphonie fantastique* with its patter of flutes and low caress of strings. Something dreadful was on its way. Suddenly there seemed to be no oxygen in the air I was breathing. I put out a hand to steady myself, missed the back of the chair and stepped out into the open. My throat was a pinprick; my head a balloon. I stretched out my arms and touched only empty space.

'Are you OK?' He sounded concerned.

I tried to find the chair again – I desperately needed to sit down – but I had lost my bearings in the suddenly cavernous room.

'Try to relax. Sit down. Breathe.' I felt his arm around me, guiding me gently towards the chair, and once again I thought of Nigel, and of Daddy's voice, a little off-key, saying:

Come on, Emily. Breathe. Breathe!

'Shall I take you outside?' he said.

'It's nothing. It's fine. It's just the noise.'

'As long as it wasn't something I said—'

'Don't flatter yourself.' I faked a smile. It felt like a dentist's mask on my face. I had to get out. I pulled away, sending my chair skittering against the parquet. If only I could get some air, then everything would be all right. The voices in my head would stop. The dreadful music would be stilled.

'Are you OK?'

Breathe, baby, breathe!

And now the music rose once more, lurching into a major key somehow even more dangerous, more troubling than the minor.

Then his voice through the static said: 'Don't forget your coat, *Albertine*.'

And at that I pulled away and ran, regardless of obstacles, and, finding my voice just long enough to shout – *Let me through!* – I fled once more, like a criminal, pushing my way through the milling crowd and out into the speechless air.

2

You are viewing the webjournal of **blueeyedboy**.
Posted at: *21.03 on Saturday, February 2*
Status: *restricted*
Mood: *caustic*
Listening to: *Voltaire*: 'Almost Human'

So, she finds me almost attractive. That moves me more than words can say. To know that she thinks of me that way – or that she did, for a moment, at least – makes it almost seem worthwhile –

When Nigel came round on the day he died I was developing photographs. My iPod was playing at full blast, which was why I missed the knock at the door.

'B.B.!' Ma's voice was imperious.

I hate it when she calls me that.

'What?' Her hearing is eerily good. 'What are you doing in there? It's been hours.'

'Just sorting out some negatives.'

Ma has a range of silences. This one was disapproving: Ma dislikes my photography, considers it a waste of time. Besides, my darkroom is private; the lock on the door keeps her out. It isn't healthy, so she says; no boy should have secrets from his ma.

'So what is it, Ma?' I said at last. The silence was starting to get to me. For a moment it deepened; grew thoughtful. It is at these moments that Ma is at her most dangerous. She had something up her sleeve, I knew. Something that didn't bode well for me.

'Ma?' I said. 'Are you still there?'

'Your brother's here to see you,' she said.

Well, I'm sure you can guess what happened next. I suppose she felt I deserved it. After all, I had forfeited her protection by keeping secrets from her. It didn't quite happen as it did in my fic, but we have to allow for poetic licence, don't we? And Nigel had a temper, and I was never the type to fight back.

I suppose I could have lied my way out of it, as I have so often before, but by then I think it was too late; something had been set in motion, something that could not be stopped. Besides, my brother was arrogant. So sure of his crude and bludgeoning tactics that he never considered the fact that there might be other, more subtle ways than brute force of winning the battle between us. Nigel was never subtle. Perhaps that's why *Albertine* loved him. He was, after all, so different from her, so open and straightforward; loyal as a good dog.

Is that what you thought, *Albertine*? Is that what you saw in him? A reflection of lost innocence? What can I say? You were wrong. Nigel wasn't innocent. He was a killer, just like me, though I'm sure he never told you that. After all, what would he have said? That for all his pretended honesty, he was as fake as both of us? That he'd taken the role you offered him, and played you like a professional?

The funeral lasted much too long. They always do, and when the sandwiches and the sausage rolls had finally been cleared away, there was still the coming home to endure, and the photographs to be brought out, and the sighs and the tears and the platitudes: as if she'd ever cared for him, as if Ma had cared for anyone in all her life but Gloria Green –

At least it was quick. The Number One, the greatest hit, the all-time favourite platitude, closely followed by such classic tracks as: *At least he didn't suffer*, and *It's wicked, that road, how fast they drive*. The scene of my brother's death now bears a Diana-style floral display – though of somewhat more modest proportions, thank God.

I know. I went on the pilgrimage. My mother, Adèle, Maureen and I; Yours Truly in his colours, Ma regal, all in black, with a veil, reeking of L'Heure Bleue, of course, and carrying, of all things, a stuffed dog with a wreath in its mouth – putting the *fun* into *funeral* –

'I don't think I can bear to look,' she says, face averted, her eagle eye taking in the offerings at the roadside shrine, mentally calculating the cost of a spray of carnations, a begonia plant, a bunch of sad chrysanthemums picked up at a roadside garage.

'They'd better not be from *her*,' she says, quite unnecessarily. Indeed, there is no indication that Nigel's girl has ever even been there, still less that she brought flowers.

My mother, however, is unconvinced. She sends me to investigate and to purge any gift not bearing a card, and then deposits her stuffed dog by the side of the road with a teary sigh.

Flanked by Adèle and Maureen, who each hold an elbow, she totters away on six-inch heels that look like sharpened pencils, and produce a sound that makes my tastebuds cramp, like chalk against a blackboard.

'At least you've got B.B., Gloria, love.'

Greatest Hits, Number Four.

'Yes. I don't know what I'd do without him.' Her eyes are hard and expressionless. At the centre of each one is a small blue pinprick of light. It takes me some time to realize that this is my reflection. 'B.B. would never let me down. He would never cheat on me.'

Did she really say those words? I may have just imagined it. And yet, that is exactly what she considers this betrayal to be. Bad enough, to lose her son to another woman, she thinks. But to lose him to *that* girl, of all girls –

Nigel should have known better, of course. No one escapes from Gloria Green. My mother is like the pitcher plant, *Nepenthes distillatoria*, which draws in its victims with sweetness, only to drown them in acid later when their struggles have exhausted them.

I ought to know; I've been living with her for forty-two years, and the reason I've stayed undigested so far is that the parasite needs a decoy, a lure: a creature that sits on the lip of the plant to persuade all the others there's nothing to fear –

I know. It's hardly a glorious task. But it certainly beats being eaten alive. It pays to be loyal to Ma, you see. It pays to keep up appearances. Besides, wasn't I her favourite, trained in the womb as a murderer?

And, having first disposed of Mal, why should I spare the other two?

I always thought when I was a boy that the justice system was the wrong way round. First, a man commits a crime. Then (assuming he's caught) comes the sentence. Five, ten, twenty years, depending on the crime, of course. But as so many criminals fail to anticipate the cost of repaying such a debt, surely it makes more sense, rather than crime on credit, to pay for one's felony up front, and to do the time *before* the crime, after which, without prosecution, you could safely wreak havoc at your leisure.

Imagine the time and money saved on police investigations and on lengthy trials; not to mention the unnecessary anxiety and distress suffered by the perpetrator, never knowing if he'll be caught, or has got away with it. Under this system I believe that many of the more serious crimes could actually be avoided – as only a very few would accept to spend a lifetime in prison for the sake of a single murder. In fact, it's far more likely that, halfway through the sentence, the would-be offender would opt to go free – still innocent of any crime, though he might have to lose his deposit. Or maybe by then he would have earned enough time to pay for a minor felony – an aggravated assault, perhaps, or maybe a rape or a robbery –

See? It's a perfect system. It's moral, cheap and practical. It even allows for that change of heart. It offers absolution. Sin *and* redemption all in one; cost-free karma at the Jesus Christ superstore.

Which is just my way of saying this: I've already done my time. Over forty years of it. And now, with my release date due –

The universe owes me a murder.

3

You are viewing the webjournal of **blueeyedboy** *posting on:*
badguysrock@webjournal.com
Posted at: *22.03 on Saturday, February 2*
Status: *public*
Mood: *murderous*
Listening to: *Peter Gabriel*: 'Family Snapshot'

His brothers never liked him much. Perhaps he was too different. Perhaps they were jealous of his gift and of all the attention it brought him. In any case, they hated him – well, maybe not Brendan, his brother in brown, who was too thick to genuinely hate anyone, but certainly Nigel, his brother in black, who, the year of Benjamin's birth, underwent such a violent personality change that he might have been a different boy.

The birth of his youngest brother was attended by outbursts of violent rage that Ma could neither control nor understand. As for Brendan, aged three – a placid, stolid, good-natured child – his first words on hearing that he had a baby brother were: *Why, Ma? Send him back!*

Not promising words for Benjamin, who found himself thrown into the cruel world like a bone to a pack of dogs, with no one but Ma to defend him and to keep him from being eaten alive.

But he was her blue-eyed talisman. Special, from the day he was born. The others went to the junior school, where they played on the swings and the climbing frames, risked life and limb on the football pitch, and came home every day with grazes and cuts that Ma seemed never to notice. But with Ben, she was always fretful. The smallest bruise, the slightest cough, was enough to awaken his mother's concern, and the day he came home from nursery school with a bloody nose (earned in a fight over control of the sandpit), she withdrew him from the school and took him on her rounds instead.

There were four ladies on Ma's cleaning round, all of them now coloured blue in his mind. All of them lived in the Village; no more than half a mile from each other, in the long tree-lined alleys between Mill Road and the edge of White City.

Apart from Mrs Electric Blue, who was to die so very unexpectedly some fifteen or twenty years later, there was: Mrs French Blue, who smoked Gauloises and liked Jacques Brel; Mrs Chemical Blue, who took twenty kinds of vitamins and who cleaned the house before Ma arrived (and probably after she left); and finally, Mrs Baby Blue, who collected porcelain dolls, and had a studio under the roof, and was an artist, so she said, and whose husband was a music teacher at St Oswald's, the boys' grammar school down the road, where Ma also went to clean and vacuum the classrooms on the Upper Corridor at four thirty every school day, and to run the big old polisher across what seemed miles of parquet floor.

Benjamin didn't like St Oswald's. He hated the fusty smell of it, the reek of disinfectant and floor polish, the low hum of mould and dried-up sandwiches, dead mice, wormy wood and chalk that got into the back of his throat and caused a permanent catarrh. After a while, just the sound of the name – that gagging sound, *Os-wald's* – would conjure up the smell. From the very start he dreaded the place: he was afraid of the Masters in their big black gowns, afraid of the boys with their striped caps and their blue blazers with the badges on them.

But he liked his mother's ladies. To begin with, anyway.

He's so cute, they said. *Why doesn't he smile? Do you want a biscuit, Ben? Do you want to play a game?*

He found he enjoyed being wooed in this way. To be four years old is to wield great power over women of a certain age. He soon learnt how to exploit this power: how even a half-hearted whimper could cause those ladies real concern, how a smile could earn him biscuits and treats. Each lady had her speciality: Mrs Chemical Blue gave him chocolate biscuits (but made him eat them over the sink); Mrs Electric Blue offered him coconut rings; Mrs French Blue, *langues de chat*. But his favourite was Mrs Baby Blue, whose real name was Catherine White, and who always bought the big red tins of Family Circle biscuits, with their jam sandwiches, chocolate digestives, iced rings, pink wafers – which always seemed especially decadent, somehow, by virtue of their flimsiness, like the flounces on her four-poster bed and her collection of dolls, with their blank and somehow ominous faces staring out from nests of chintz and lace.

His brothers hardly ever came. On the rare occasions that they did, at weekends or holidays, they never showed to advantage. Nigel, at nine, was already a thug: sullen and prone to violence. Brendan, still on the cusp of cute, had also once been privileged, but was now beginning to lose his infant appeal. Besides which he was a clumsy child, always knocking things over, including, on one occasion, a garden ornament – a sundial – belonging to Mrs White, which smashed on to the flagstones and had to be paid for by Ma, of course. For which both he and Nigel were punished – Bren for doing the actual damage, Nigel for not preventing him – after which neither of them came round again, and Benjamin was left with the spoils.

What did Ma make of all this attention? Well, perhaps she thought that someone, somewhere, might fall in love; that in one of those big houses might be found a benefactor for her son. Ben's ma had ambitions, you see; ambitions she barely understood. Perhaps she'd had them all along; or perhaps they were born from those long days polishing other people's silverware, or looking at pictures of their sons in graduation gowns and hoods. And he understood almost from the start that his visits to those big houses were meant to teach him something more than how to beat the dust from a rug or wax a parquet floor. His mother made it clear from the start that he was special; that he was unique; that he was destined for greater things than either of his brothers.

He never questioned it, of course. Neither did she. But he sensed her expectations like a halter round his young neck. All three of them knew how hard she worked; how her back ached from bending and standing all day long; how often she suffered from migraines; how the palms of her hands cracked and bled. From the earliest age, they went shopping with her, and long before they got to school they could add up a grocery list in their heads and know just how little of that day's earnings was left for all their other expenses –

She never voiced it openly. But even unvoiced, they always felt that weight on their backs: the weight of their ma's expectations; her terrifying certainty that they would make her sacrifice worthwhile. It was the price they had to pay, never spoken aloud, but implied; a debt that could never be paid in full.

But Ben was always the favoured one. Everything he did strengthened her hopes. Unlike Bren, he was good at sports, which made him suitably competitive. Unlike Nigel, he liked to read, which fostered her belief that he was gifted. He was good at drawing, too, much to the delight of Mrs White, who had no expectations, who'd always wanted a child of her own, and who fussed over him and gave him sweets; who was pretty and blonde and bohemian, who called him *sweetheart*, who liked to dance; and who laughed and cried for no reason sometimes and who all three boys secretly wished could have been *their* Ma –

And the White house was wonderful. There was a piano in the hall, and a big piece of stained glass above the front door, which on sunny days would cast reflections of red and gold on to the polished floorboards. When his mother was working, Mrs White would show Ben her studio, with its stacked canvases and its rolls of drawing paper, and teach him how to draw horses and dogs, and show him the tubes and palettes of paint, and read out their names, like incantations.

Viridian. Celadon. Chromium. Sometimes they had French or Spanish or Italian names, which made them even more magical. *Violetto. Escarlata. Pardo de turba. Outremer.*

'That's the language of art, sweetheart,' Mrs White would sometimes exclaim. She painted big, sloshy canvases in sugary pinks and ominous purples, upon which she would then superimpose pictures cut out of magazines – mostly heads of little girls – which she would then varnish heavily on to the canvas and adorn with ruffs of antique lace.

Benjamin didn't like them much, and yet it was from Mrs White that he learnt to distinguish between the colours; to understand that his own colour came in a legion of shades; to span the depths between sapphire and ultramarine, to see their textures, know their scents.

'That one's chocolate,' he would say, pointing out a fat scarlet tube with a picture of strawberries on the side.

Escarlata, the label said, and the scent was overwhelming, especially when placed in sunlight, filling his head with happiness and with motes that shone and floated like magic Maltesers up and away into the air.

'How can red be chocolate?'

By then he was nearly seven years old, and still he couldn't really explain. It just was, he told her stoutly, just as Nut Brown (*avellana*) was tomato soup, which often made him feel anxious, somehow, and *verde Veronese* was liquorice, and *amarillo naranja* was the smell of boiled cabbage, which always made him feel sick. Sometimes just hearing their names would do it, as if the sounds contained some kind of alchemy, teasing from the volatile words a joyous explosion of colours and scents.

At first he'd assumed that everyone had this ability; but when he mentioned it to his brothers, Nigel punched him and called him *freak*; and Brendan just looked confused and said, *You can smell the words, Ben?* After which he would often grin and scrunch up his nose whenever Benjamin was around, as if he could sense things the way Ben could, copying him, the way he often did, though never really in mockery. In fact, poor Brendan envied Ben; slow, tubby, frightened Bren, always lagging behind, always doing something wrong.

Ben's gift didn't make any sense to Ma, but it did to Mrs White, who knew all about the language of colours, and who liked scented candles – expensive ones from France – which Ma said was like burning money, but which smelt wonderful, all the same; in violet and smoky sage and boudoir patchouli and cedar and rose.

Mrs White knew someone – a friend of her husband's, in fact – someone who understood these things, and she explained to Ben's mother that Ben might be special, which his Ma had believed all along, of course, but that secretly he had doubted. Mrs White promised to put them in touch with this man, whose name was Dr Peacock, and who lived in one of the big old houses behind St Oswald's playing fields, on the street Ma always called Millionaires' Row.

Dr Peacock was sixty-one, an ex-governor of St Oswald's, the author of a number of books. We sometimes saw him in the Village, a bearded man in a tweed jacket and a floppy old hat, walking his dog. He was rather eccentric, said Mrs White with a rueful smile, and, thanks to some clever investments, was blessed with rather more money than sense –

Certainly Ma didn't hesitate. Being practically tone-deaf herself, she had never paid much attention to the way her son understood sounds and words, which, when she noticed it at all, she attributed to his being *sensitive* – her explanation for most things. But the thought that he might be gifted soon overcame her scepticism. Besides, she needed a benefactor, a patron for her blue-eyed boy, who was already having trouble at school, and needed a fatherly influence.

Dr Peacock – childless, retired, and, best of all, rich – must have seemed like a dream come true. And so she went to him for help, thereby setting in place a series of events, like filters over a camera lens, that coloured the next thirty-odd years in ever-deepening shades.

Of course, she couldn't have known that. Well, how could *any* of them have known what would come of that meeting? And who could have known it would end this way, with two of Gloria's children dead, and *blueeyedboy* helpless and trapped, like those scuttling things at the seaside that day, forgotten and dying in the sun?

Post comment:

ClairDeLune: *This is quite good,* **blueeyedboy**. *I like your use of imagery. I notice you're drawing on personal anecdotes rather more than usual. Good idea! I hope to read more!*

JennyTricks: (*post deleted*).

blueeyedboy: *My pleasure . . .*

4

You are viewing the webjournal of **blueeyedboy** *posting on:*
badguysrock@webjournal.com
Posted at: *01.15 on Sunday, February 3*
Status: *public*
Mood: *serene*
Listening to: *David Bowie:* '*Heroes*'

He'd never met a millionaire. He'd imagined a man in a silk top hat, like Lord Snooty in the comic-books. Or maybe with a monocle and a cane. Instead, Dr Peacock was vaguely unkempt, in a tweedy, bow-tied, carpet-slippery way, and he looked at Ben with milk-blue eyes from behind his wire-rimmed spectacles and said: *Ah. You must be Benjamin*, in a voice like tobacco and coffee cake.

Ma was nervous; dressed to the nines, and she'd made Ben wear his new school clothes – navy trousers, sky-blue sweater, something like the St Oswald's colours, although his own school had no uniform code, and most of the other kids just wore jeans. Nigel and Bren were with them, too – she didn't trust them home alone – both under orders to sit still, shut up, and not to dare touch *anything*.

She was trying to make an impression. Ben's first year at junior school had not been a brilliant one, and by then most of White City knew that Gloria Winter's youngest son had been sent home for sticking a compass into the hand of a boy who had called him a *fucking poofter*, and that only his mother's aggressive intervention had prevented him from being expelled.

Whether that information had reached the Village was yet to be determined. But Gloria Winter was taking no risks, and it was a most angelic Benjamin who now found himself on the steps of the Mansion on that mellow October day, listening to the door-chimes, which were pink and white and silvery, and observing the toes of his sneakers as Dr Peacock came to the door.

Of course he had no real understanding of what a poofter actually was. But there was, he recalled, quite a lot of blood, and even though it wasn't his fault, the fact that he hadn't shown any remorse – had actually seemed to *enjoy* the fracas – quite upset his class teacher, a lady we shall call Mrs Catholic Blue, who (quite publicly, it seemed) subscribed to such amusing beliefs as the innocence of childhood, the sacrifice of God's only son and the watchful presence of angels.

Sadly, her name smelt terrible, like cheap incense and horse shit, which was often distracting in lessons, and which led to a number of incidents, culminating at last in Ben's exclusion; for which his mother blamed the school, pointing out that it wasn't his fault that they weren't able to cope with a gifted child, and promising retribution at the hands of the local newspapers.

Dr Peacock was different. His name smelt of bubblegum. An attractive scent for a little boy, besides which Dr Peacock spoke to him as an adult, in words that slipped and rolled off his tongue like multi-coloured balls of gum from a sweetshop vending machine.

'Ah. You must be Benjamin.'

He nodded. He liked that certainty. From behind Dr Peacock, where a door led from the porch into the hall, a shaggy black-and-white shape hurtled towards our hero, revealing itself to be an elderly Jack Russell dog, which frolicked about them, barking.

'My learned colleague,' said Dr Peacock by way of explanation. Then, addressing the dog, he said: 'Kindly allow our visitors to gain access to the library,' at which the dog stopped barking at once, and led the way into the house.

'Please,' said Dr Peacock. 'Come on in and have some tea.'

They did. Earl Grey, no sugar, no milk, served with shortbread biscuits, now fixed in his mind for ever, like Proust's lime-blossom tea, a conduit for memories.

Memories are what *blueeyedboy* has instead of a conscience nowadays. That's what kept him here for so long, pushing an old man's wheelchair around the overgrown paths of the Mansion; doing his laundry; reading aloud; making toast soldiers for soft-boiled eggs. And even though most of the time the old man had no idea who he was, he never complained, or failed him – not once – remembering that first cup of Earl Grey tea and the way Dr Peacock looked at him, as if he, too, were special –

The room was large and carpeted in varying tones of madder and brown. A sofa; chairs; three walls of books; an enormous fireplace, in front of which lay a basket for the dog; a brown teapot as big as the Mad Hatter's; biscuits; some glass cases filled with insects. Most curious of all, perhaps, a child's swing suspended from the ceiling, at which the three boys stared with silent longing from their place on the sofa near Ma, wanting, but hardly daring, to speak.

'Wh-what are those?' said *blueeyedboy*, indicating a glass case.

'Moths,' said the doctor, looking pleased. 'So like the butterfly in many ways, but so much more subtle and fascinating in design. This one here, with the furry head' – he pointed a finger at the glass – 'is the Poplar hawk-moth, *Laothoe populi*. This scarlet and brown one next to it is *Tyria jacobaeae*, the Cinnabar. And this little chap' – he indicated a ragged brown something that looked like a dead leaf to *blueeyedboy* – 'is *Smerinthus ocellata*, the Eyed Hawk-moth. Can you see its blue eyes?'

Blueeyedboy nodded again, awed into silence not merely by the moths themselves, but by the calm authority with which Dr Peacock uttered the words, then indicated another case, hanging above the piano, in which *blueeyedboy* could see resting a single, enormous lime-green moth, all milk and dusty velvet.

'And this young lady,' said Dr Peacock affectionately, 'is the queen of my collection. The Luna moth, *Actias Luna*, all the way from North America. I brought her here as a pupa, oh, more than thirty years ago, and sat in this room as I watched her hatch, capturing every stage on film. You can't imagine how moving it is, to watch such a creature emerge from the cocoon, to see her spread her wings and fly—'

She can't have gone far, thought *blueeyedboy*. *Just as far as the killing jar –*

Wisely, however, he held his tongue. His ma was getting restless. Her hands clicked together in her lap, shooting cheap fire from her rings.

'I collect china dogs,' she said. 'That makes us both collectors.'

Dr Peacock smiled. 'How nice. I must show you my T'ang figurine.'

Blueeyedboy grinned to himself as he saw the expression on Ma's face. He had no idea what a T'ang figurine looked like, but he guessed it was something as different from Ma's collection of china dogs as the Luna moth was from that creature curled up like a dead leaf over its gaudy, useless eyes.

Ma gave him a dirty look, and *blueeyedboy* understood that sooner or later he would have to pay for making her look foolish. But for now, he knew he was safe, and he looked around Dr Peacock's house with growing curiosity. Apart from the cases of moths, he saw that there were pictures on the walls – not posters, but actual paintings. Aside from Mrs White, with her pink and purple collages, he had never met anyone who owned paintings before.

His eyes came to rest on a delicate study of a ship in faded sepia ink, behind which lay a long, pale beach, with a background of huts and coconut palms and cone-shaped mountains adrift with smoke. It drew him; though he didn't know why. Perhaps the sky, or the tea-coloured ink, or the blush of age that shone through the glass like the bloom on a luscious golden grape –

Dr Peacock caught him staring again. 'Do you know where that is?' he said.

Blueeyedboy shook his head.

'That's Hawaii.'

Ha-wa-ii.

'Maybe you'll get to go there some day,' Dr Peacock told him, and smiled.

And that's how, with a single word, *blueeyedboy* was collected.

Post comment:

Captainbunnykiller: *Man, I think you're losing it. Two posts in as many days, and you haven't murdered anyone* ☺

blueeyedboy: *Give me time. I'm working on it . . .*

ClairDeLune: *Very nice,* **blueeyedboy**. *You show genuine courage in writing down these painful memories! Perhaps you could discuss them more fully at our next session?*

chrysalisbaby: *yay I love this so much (hugs)*

5

You are viewing the webjournal of **blueeyedboy** *posting on:*
badguysrock@webjournal.com
Posted at: *02.05 on Sunday, February 3*
Status: *public*
Mood: *poetic*
Listening to: *The Zombies*: 'A Rose For Emily'

Next he took the three boys out into the rose garden, while their mother drank tea in the library and the dog ran about on the lawn. He showed them his roses and read out their names from the metal tags clipped to the stems. Adelaide d'Orléans. William Shakespeare. Names with magical properties, that made their nostrils tingle and flare.

Dr Peacock loved his roses; especially the oldest ones, the densely-packed-with-petal ones, the flesh-toned, blue-rinse, off-white, old-lady ones that, according to him, had the sweetest scent. In Dr Peacock's garden the boys learnt to tell a moss rose from an Alba, a damask from a Gallica, and Benjamin collected their names as once he had collected the names inscribed on tubes of paint, names that made his head spin, that echoed with more than just colours and scents, from Rose de Recht, a dark-red rose that smelt of bitter choco-late, to Boule de Neige, Tour de Malakoff, Belle de Crécy and Albertine, his favourite, with a musky, pale-pink, old-fashioned scent, like girls in white summer dresses and croquet and iced pink lemonade on the lawn; which, to Ben, smelt of Turkish Delight –

'Turkish Delight?' said Dr Peacock, his eyes alight with interest.
'And this one? Rosa Mundi?'

'Bread.'

'This one? Cécile Brunner?'

'Cars. Petrol.'

'Really?' Dr Peacock said, looking, not angry, as *blueeyedboy* might
have expected, but genuinely fascinated.

In fact, everything about Benjamin was fascinating to Dr Peacock.
It turned out that most of his books were about something he called
synaesthesia, which sounded like something they might do to you in
hospital, but that was actually a *neurological condition*, so he said,
which actually meant that Ma was right, and that Ben had been
special all along.

The boys didn't understand it all, but Dr Peacock said that it was
something to do with the way the sensory parts of the brain worked:
that something in there was cross-wired, somehow, sending mixed
signals from those complex bundles of nerves.

'You mean, like a s-super-sense?' interrupted *blueeyedboy*, thinking
vaguely of Spider-Man, or Magneto, or even Hannibal Lecter (you see
that he was already moving away from the vanilla end of the spectrum
into bad-guy territory).

'Precisely,' said Dr Peacock. 'And when we find out how it works,
then maybe our knowledge will be able to help people – stroke
victims, for instance, or people who have suffered head trauma. The
brain is a complex instrument. And in spite of all the achievements of
science and modern medicine, we still know so little about it: how it
stores and accesses information, how that information is
translated—'

Synaesthesia can manifest in so many ways, Dr Peacock explained
to them. Words can have colours; sounds can have shapes, numbers
can be illuminated. Some people were born with it; others acquired it
by association. Most synaesthetes were visual. But there are other
kinds of synaesthesia, where words can translate as tastes or smells; or
colours be triggered by migraine pain. In short, said Dr Peacock, a
synaesthete might see music; taste sound; experience numbers as
textures or shapes. There was even mirror-touch synaesthesia, in

which, by some extreme of empathy, the subject could actually experience physical sensations felt by *someone else* –

'You mean, if I saw someone getting hit, then I'd be able to feel it too?'

'Fascinating, isn't it?'

'But – how could they watch gangster films, where people get killed and beaten up?'

'I don't think they'd want to, Benjamin. They'd find it too upsetting. It's all about suggestion, you see. This type of synaesthesia would make one very sensitive.'

'Ma says *I'm* sensitive.'

'I'm sure you are, Benjamin.'

By then Benjamin had become increasingly sensitive, not just to words and names, but to voices, too; to their accents and tones. Of course, he'd been aware before of the fact that people had accents. He'd always preferred Mrs White's voice to Ma's, or to the voice of Mrs Catholic Blue, who spoke with a caustic Belfast twang that grated at his sinuses.

His brothers spoke like the boys at school. They said *ta* instead of *thank you*, and *sithee* instead of *goodbye*. They swore at each other in ugly words that stank of the monkey-house at the zoo. His mother made an effort, but failed; her accent came and went depending on the company. It was particularly bad with Dr Peacock – aitches inserted all over the place like needles into a ball of wool.

Blueeyedboy sensed how very hard she worked at trying to impress, and it made him gag with embarrassment. He didn't want to sound like that. He copied Dr Peacock instead. He liked his vocabulary. The way Dr Peacock said: *If you please*; or *Kindly turn your attention to this*; or *To whom am I speaking?* on the phone. Dr Peacock could speak Latin and French and Greek and Italian and German and even Japanese; and when he spoke English he made it sound like a different language, a better one, one that distinguished between *watt* and *what*; *witch* (a green-grey, sour word) and *which* (a sweet and silvery word), like an actor reading Shakespeare. He even spoke like that to the dog, saying: *Kindly desist from chewing the rug*, or *Would my learned colleague like to take a stroll round the garden?* The strangest thing, thought *blueeyedboy*, was that the dog seemed to respond; which made him wonder whether he, too, could be trained to lose his uncouth habits.

From his point of view, Dr Peacock was so impressed with Ben's gift that he promised to tutor the boy himself – as long as he behaved at school – to prepare him for the St Oswald's scholarship exam, in exchange for what he called *a few tests*, and the understanding that anything that transpired from their sessions could be used in the book he was writing, the culmination of a lifetime's study, for which he had interviewed many subjects, though none as young or as promising as little Benjamin Winter.

Ma was overjoyed, of course. St Oswald's was the culmination of all her hopes, of her unvoiced ambitions, of all the dreams she'd ever had. The entrance exam was in three years' time, but she spoke as if it were imminent; promised to save every penny she earned; fussed over Ben more than ever before, and made it very clear that he was being given an incredible chance; a chance that he owed it to her to take –

He was less enthusiastic. He still didn't like St Oswald's. In spite of its navy-blue blazer and tie (just perfect for him, she said), he had already seen enough to be conscious of being unsuitable: unsuitable face, unsuitable hair, unsuitable house, unsuitable *name* –

St Oswald's boys were not called *Ben*. St Oswald's boys were called Leon, or Jasper, or Rufus or Sebastian. A St Oswald's boy can pass off a name like Orlando, can make it sound like peppermint. Even Rupert sounds somehow cool when attached to a navy-blue St Oswald's blazer. Ben, he knew, would be the *wrong* blue, smelling of his mother's house, of too much disinfectant and too little space and too much fried food and not enough books and the harsh, inescapable stink of his brothers.

But Dr Peacock said not to worry. Three years was a long time. Time for him to prepare Ben; to make him into a St Oswald's boy. Ben had *potential*, so he said – a red word, like a stretched rubber band, ready to fly into someone's face –

And so, he accepted. What choice did he have? He was, after all, Ma's greatest hope. Besides, he wanted to please them both – to please

Dr Peacock, most of all – and if that meant St Oswald's, then he was prepared to take up the challenge.

Nigel went to Sunnybank Park, the big comprehensive at the edge of White City. A series of concrete building blocks, with razor wire along the roof, it looked like a prison. It stank like a zoo. Nigel didn't seem to mind. Brendan, nine and also destined for Sunnybank Park, showed no sign of unusual ability. Both boys had been tested by Dr Peacock; neither seemed to interest him much. Nigel he discarded at once; Brendan, after three or four weeks, finding him uncooperative.

Nigel was twelve, aggressive and moody. He liked heavy rock music and films where things exploded. No one bullied him at school. Brendan was his shadow, spineless and soft; surviving only through Nigel's protection, like those symbiotic creatures that live around sharks and crocodiles, safe from predators by virtue of their usefulness to the host. Whereas Nigel was quite intelligent (though he never bothered to do any work), Bren was useless at everything: hopeless at sports, clueless in lessons, lazy and inarticulate, a prime candidate for the dole queue, said Ma, or, at best, a job flipping burgers –

But Ben was destined for better things. Every other Saturday, while Nigel and Brendan rode their bikes or played with their friends out on the estate, he went to Dr Peacock's house – the house that he called the Mansion – and in the mornings sat at a big desk upholstered in bottle-green leather and read from books with hardback covers, and learnt geography from a painted globe with the names written on it in tiny scrolled lettering – *Iroquois*, *Rangoon*, *Azerbaijan* – arcane, obsolete, *magical* names just like Mrs White's paints, that smelt vaguely of gin and the sea, of peppery dust and acrid spices, like an early taste of some mysterious freedom that he had yet to experience. And if you spun the globe fast enough, the oceans and the continents would chase each other so fast that at last all the colours merged into one, into one perfect shade of blue: ocean blue, heavenly blue, Benjamin blue –

In the afternoons they would do other things, like look at pictures and listen to sounds, which was part of Dr Peacock's research, and which Ben found incomprehensible, but to which he submitted obediently.

There were books and books of letters and numbers arranged in patterns that he had to identify. There was a library of recorded sounds. There were questions like: *What colour is Wednesday? What number is green?* – and shapes with intriguing made-up names, but there were never any wrong answers, which meant that Dr Peacock was pleased, and that Ma was always proud of him.

And he *liked* to go to that big old house, with its library and its studio and its archive of forgotten things; records, cameras, bundles of yellow photographs, weddings and family groups and long-dead children in sailor suits with anxious, watch-the-birdie smiles. He was wary of St Oswald's, but it was nice to study with Dr Peacock, to be called *Benjamin*; to listen to him talk about his travels, his music, his studies, his roses.

Best of all, he mattered there. There he was special – a subject, a case. Dr Peacock listened to him; noted down his reactions to various kinds of stimuli; then asked him precisely what he felt. Often he would record the results on his little Dictaphone, referring to Ben as *Boy X*, to protect his anonymity.

Boy X. He liked that. It made him sound impressive, somehow, a boy with special powers – a gift. Not that he *was* very gifted. He was an average pupil at school, never ranking especially high. As for his *sensory gifts*, as Dr Peacock called them – those sounds that translated to colours and smells – if he'd thought about them at all, he'd always just assumed that everyone experienced them as he did, and even though Dr Peacock assured him that this was an aberration, he continued to think of himself as the norm, and everyone else as freakish.

The word serenity *is grey* [says Dr Peacock in his paper entitled 'Boy X and Early Acquired Synaesthesia'], *though* serene *is dark blue, with a slight flavour of aniseed. Numbers have no colours at all, but names of places and of individuals are often highly charged, sometimes overwhelmingly so, often both with colours and with flavours. There exists in certain cases a distinct correlation between these extraordinary sense-impressions and events that Boy X has experienced, which suggests that this type of synaesthesia may be partly associative, rather than merely congenital. However, even in this case a number of interesting physical responses to these stimuli may be*

observed, including salivation as a direct response to the word scarlet, which
to Boy X smells of chocolate, and a feeling of dizziness associated with the
colour pink, which to Boy X smells strongly of gas.

He made it sound so important then. As if they were doing something for science. And when his book was published, he said, both he and *Boy X* would be famous. They might even win a research prize.

In fact Ben was so preoccupied with his lessons at Dr Peacock's house that he hardly ever thought about the ladies from Ma's cleaning round who had wooed him so assiduously. He had more pressing concerns by then, and Dr Peacock's research had taken the place of paintings and dolls.

That was why, six months later, when he finally saw Mrs White one day at the market, he was surprised to see how fat she'd got, as if, after his departure, she'd had to eat for herself all the contents of those big red tins of Family Circle biscuits. *What had happened?* he asked himself. Pretty Mrs White had grown a prominent belly; and she waddled through the fruit and veg, a big, silly smile on her face.

His mother told them the good news. After nearly ten years of trying and failing, Mrs White was finally pregnant. For some reason, this excited Ma, possibly because it meant more hours, but *blueeyedboy* was filled with unease. He thought of her collection of dolls, those eerie, ruffled, not-quite-children, and wondered if she'd get rid of them, now she was getting the real thing.

It gave him nightmares to think of it: all those staring, plaintive dollies in their silks and antique lace abandoned on some rubbish tip, clothes gone to tatters, rain-washed white, china heads smashed open among the bottles and tins.

'Boy or girl?' said Ma.

'A little girl. I'm going to call her Emily.'

Emily. Em-il-y, three syllables, like a knock on the door of destiny. Such an odd, old-fashioned name, compared to those Kylies and Traceys and Jades – names that reeked of Impulse and grease and stood out in gaudy neon colours – whilst hers was that muted, dusky pink, like bubblegum, like roses –

But how could *blueeyedboy* have known that she would one day lead him here? And how could anyone have guessed that both of them would be so close – victim and predator intertwined like a rose growing through a human skull – without their even knowing it?

Post comment:

ClairDeLune: *I really like where this is going. Is it part of something longer?*

chrysalisbaby: *is that 4 real with the colours? how much did U have 2 research it?*

blueeyedboy: *Not as much as you might think ☺ Glad you liked it, Chryssie!*

chrysalisbaby: *aw hunny (hugs)*

JennyTricks: *(post deleted).*

6

You are viewing the webjournal of **Albertine**.
Posted at: 02.54 on Sunday, February 3
Status: restricted
Mood: blank

I cried a river when Daddy died. I cry at bad movies. I cry at sad songs. I cry at dead dogs and TV advertisements and rainy days and Mondays. So – why no tears for Nigel? I know that Mozart's Requiem or Albinoni's Adagio would help turn on the waterworks, but that's not grief; that's self-indulgence, the kind that Gloria Winter prefers.

Some people enjoy the public display. Emily's funeral was a case in point. A mountain of flowers and teddy bears; people wept openly in the streets. A nation mourned – but not for a child. Perhaps for the loss of innocence; for the grubbiness of it all, for their own collective greed, that in the end had swallowed her whole. The Emily White Phenomenon that had caused so much fanfare over the years ended with a whimper: a little headstone in Malbry churchyard and a stained-glass window in the church, paid for by Dr Peacock, much to the indignation of Maureen Pike and her cronies, who felt it was inappropriate for the man to be linked in any way to the church, to the Village, to Emily.

No one really mentions it now. People tend to leave me alone. In Malbry I am invisible; I take pleasure in my lack of depth. Gloria calls me *colourless*; I overheard her once on the phone, back in the days when she and Nigel talked.

I don't see how it can last, she said. *She's such a colourless little thing. I know you must feel sorry for her, but –*

Ma, I do not feel sorry for her!

Well, of course you do. What nonsense—

Ma. One more word and I'm hanging up.

You feel sorry for her because she's—

Click.

Overheard in the Zebra one day: *God knows what he sees in her. He pities her, that's all it is.*

How gently, politely incredulous that one such as I might attract a man through something more than compassion. Because Nigel was a good-looking man, and I was somehow *damaged*. I had a past, I was dangerous. Nigel was open wide – he'd told me all about himself that night as we lay watching the stars. One thing he *hadn't* told me, though – it was Eleanor Vine who pointed it out – is that he always wore black: an endless procession of black jeans, black jackets, black T-shirts, black boots. *It's easier to wash*, he said, when I finally asked him. *You can put everything in together.*

Did he call my name at the end? Did he know I was to blame? Or was it all just a blur to him, a single swerve into nothingness? It all began so harmlessly. We were children. We were innocent. Even *he* was, in his way – *blueeyedboy*, who haunts my dreams.

Maybe it was guilt, after all, that triggered yesterday's panic attack. Guilt, fatigue and nerves, that was all. Emily White is long gone. She died when she was nine years old, and no one remembers her any more, not Daddy, not Nigel, not anyone.

Who am I now? Not Emily White. I will not, *cannot* be Emily White. Nor can I be myself again, now that Daddy and Nigel are gone. Perhaps I can just be *Albertine*, the name I give myself online. There's something sweet about *Albertine*. Sweet and rather nostalgic, like the name of a Proustian heroine. I don't quite know why I chose it. Perhaps because of *blueeyedboy*, still hidden at the heart of all this, and whom I have tried for so long to forget . . .

But part of me must have remembered. Some part of me must have known this would come. For among all the herbs and flowers in my garden – the wallflowers, thymes, clove pinks, geraniums, lemon balm, lavenders and night-scented stocks – I never planted a single rose.

7

You are viewing the webjournal of **blueeyedboy** posting on:
                    badguysrock@webjournal.com
Posted at: *03.06 on Sunday, February 3*
Status: *public*
Mood: *poetic*
Listening to: *Roberta Flack*: 'The First Time Ever I Saw Your Face'

Benjamin was seven years old the year that Emily White was born. A time of change; of uncertainty; of deep, unspoken forebodings. At first he wasn't sure what it meant; but ever since that day at the market, he'd been aware of a gradual shift in things. People no longer looked at him. Women no longer wooed him with sweets. No one marvelled at how much he'd grown. He seemed to have moved a step beyond the line of their perception.

His mother, busier than ever with her cleaning jobs and her shifts at St Oswald's, was often too tired to talk to the boys, except to tell them to brush their teeth and work hard at school. His mother's ladies, who had once been so attentive to Ben, flocking around him like hens around a single chick, seemed to have vanished from his life, leaving him vaguely wondering whether it was something he had done, or if it was simply coincidence that no one (except for Dr Peacock) seemed to want him any more.

Finally he understood. He'd been a distraction; that was all. It's hard to talk to the person who cleans around the back of your fridge, and scrubs around the toilet bowl, and hand-washes your lace-trimmed delicates, and goes away at the end of the week with hardly enough money in her purse to buy even a single pair of those expensive panties. His mother's ladies knew that. *Guardian* readers, every one, who believed in equality, to a point, and who maybe felt a touch of unease at having to hire a cleaner – not that they would have admitted it; they were helping the woman, after all. And compensated in their way by making much of the sweet little boy, as visitors to an open farm may *ooh* and *ahh* over the young lambs – soon to reappear, nicely wrapped, on the shelves as (organic) chops and cutlets. For three years he'd been a little prince, spoilt and praised and adored, and then –

And then, along came Emily.

Sounds so harmless, doesn't it? Such a sweet, old-fashioned name, all sugared almonds and rose water. And yet she's the start of everything: the spindle on which their life revolved, the weathervane that moves from sunshine to storm in a single turn of a cockerel's tail. Barely more than a rumour at first, but a rumour that grew and gained in strength until at last it became a juggernaut; crushing everyone beneath the Emily White Phenomenon.

Ma told them he cried when he heard. How sorry he felt for the poor baby; how sorry, too, for Mrs White – who had wanted a child more than anything and, now that she had her wish at last, had succumbed to a case of the baby blues, refusing to come out of her house, to nurse her child, or even to wash, and all because her baby was blind –

Still, that was Ma all over; exaggerating his sensitivity. Benjamin never shed a tear. *Brendan* cried. It was more his style. But Ben didn't even feel upset; only a little curious, wondering what Mrs White was going to do now. He'd heard Ma and her friends talking about how sometimes mothers harmed their children when under the influence of the baby blues. He wondered whether the baby was safe, whether the Social would take her away, and if so, whether Mrs White would want him back –

Not that he needed Mrs White. But he'd changed a lot since those early days. His hair had darkened from blond to brown; his baby face had grown angular. He was aware even then that he had outgrown his early appeal, and he was filled with resentment against those who had failed to warn him that what is taken for granted at four can be cruelly taken away at seven. He'd been told so often that he was adorable, that he was good – and now here he was, discarded, just like those dolls she had put away when her new, living doll had appeared on the scene –

His brothers showed little sympathy at his sudden fall from grace. Nigel was openly gleeful; Bren was his usual, impassive self. He may not even have noticed at first; he was too busy following Nigel about, copying him slavishly. Neither really understood that this wasn't about wanting attention, either from Ma or from anyone else. The circumstances surrounding Emily's birth had taught them that no one is irreplaceable; that even one such as Ben Winter could be stripped unexpectedly of his gilding. Only his sensory peculiarities now set him apart from the rest of the clan – and even that was about to change.

By the time they got to see her at last, Emily was nine months old. A fluffy thing in rosebud pink, furled tightly in her mother's arms. The boys were at the market, helping Ma with the groceries, and it was *blueeyedboy* who saw them first, Mrs White wearing a long purple coat – *violetto*, her favourite colour – that was meant to look bohemian, but made her look too pale instead, with a scent of patchouli that stung at his eyes, overwhelming the smell of fruit.

There was another woman with her, he saw. A woman of his mother's age, in stonewash jeans and a waistcoat, with long, dry, pale hair and silver bangles on her arms. Mrs White reached for some strawberries, then, seeing Benjamin waiting in line, gave a little cry of surprise.

'Sweetheart, how you've grown!' she said. 'Has it really been so long?' She turned to the woman at her side. 'Feather. This is Benjamin. And this is his mother, Gloria.' No mention of Nigel or Brendan. Still, that was to be expected.

The woman she'd addressed as Feather – *What a stupid name*, thought *blueeyedboy* – gave them a rather narrow smile. He could tell she didn't like them. Her eyes were long and wintry-green, devoid of any sympathy. He could tell she was suspicious of them, that she thought they were common, not good enough –

'You had a b-baby,' said *blueeyedboy*.

'Yes. Her name's Emily.'

'Em-i-ly.' He tried it out. 'C-can I hold her? I'll be careful.'

Feather gave her narrow smile. 'No, a baby isn't a toy. You wouldn't want to hurt Emily.'

Wouldn't? blueeyedboy thought to himself. He wasn't as sure as she seemed to be. What use was a baby, anyhow? It couldn't walk, couldn't talk; all it could do was eat, sleep or cry. Even a cat could do more than that. He didn't know why a baby should be so important, anyway. Surely *he* was more so.

Something stung at his eyes again. He blamed the scent of patchouli. He tore a leaf from a nearby cabbage and crushed it secretly into his hand.

'Emily's a – *special* baby.' It sounded like an apology.

'The doctor says *I'm* special,' said Ben. He smirked at Feather's look of surprise. 'He's writing a book about me, you know. He says I'm remarkable.'

Ben's vocabulary had greatly improved thanks to Dr Peacock's tuition, and he uttered the word with a certain flourish.

'A book?' said Feather.

'For his research.'

Both of them looked surprised at that, and turned to stare at Benjamin in a way that was not entirely flattering. He bridled a little, half-sensing, perhaps, that at last he had snagged their attention. Mrs White was *really* watching him now, but in a thoughtful, suspicious way that made *blueeyedboy* uncomfortable.

'So – he's been – helping you out?' she said.

Ma looked prim. 'A little,' she said.

'Helping out financially?'

'It's part of his research,' said Ma.

Blueeyedboy could tell that Ma was offended by the suggestion that they needed help. That made it sound like charity, which was not at all the case. He started to tell Mrs White that they were helping Dr Peacock, not the other way around. But then Ma shot him a look, and he could see from her expression that he shouldn't have spoken out of turn. She put a hand on his shoulder and squeezed. Her hands were very strong. He winced.

'We're very proud of Ben,' she said. 'The doctor says he has a gift.'

Gift. Gift, thought *blueeyedboy.* A green and somehow ominous word, like radioactivity. *Giffft,* like the sound a snake makes when it sinks its fangs into the flesh. *Gift,* like a nicely wrapped grenade, all ready to explode in your face –

And then it hit him like a slap: the headache, and the stink of fruit that seemed to envelop everything. Suddenly he felt queasy and sick, so sick that even Ma noticed, and relaxed her grip on his shoulder.

'What's wrong now?'

'I d-don't feel so good.'

She shot him a look of warning. 'Don't even think about it,' she hissed. 'I'll give you something to whine about.'

Blueeyedboy clenched his fists and reached for the thought of blue skies, of Feather in a body bag, dismembered and tagged for disposal, of Emily lying blue in her cot with Mrs White wailing in anguish –

The headache subsided a little. Good. The awful smell receded, too. And then he thought of his brothers and Ma lying dead in the mortuary, and the pain kicked back like a wild horse, and his vision was crazed with rainbows –

Ma gave him a look of suspicion. *Blueeyedboy* tried to steady himself against the nearest market stall. His hand caught the side of a packing case. A pyramid of Granny Smiths stood, ready to form an avalanche.

'Anything drops on the floor,' said Ma, 'and I swear I'll make you eat it.'

Blueeyedboy withdrew his hand as if the box might be on fire. He knew that this was his fault; his fault for swallowing his twin; his fault for wishing Ma dead. He was born bad, bad to the bone, and this sickness was his punishment.

He thought he'd got away with it. The pyramid trembled, but did not fall. And then a single apple – he can still see it in his mind, with the little blue sticker on the side – nudged against its companion, and the whole of the front of the fruit stall seemed to slide, apples and peaches and oranges bouncing gleefully against each other, then off the AstroTurf apron and rolling on to the concrete floor.

She waited there until he'd retrieved every single piece of fruit. Some were almost intact; some had been trodden into the dirt. She paid for it at the market stall with an almost gracious insistence. And then, that night, she stood over him with a dripping plastic bag in one hand and the piece of electrical cord in the other, and made him eat it: piece by piece; core and peel and dirt and rot. As his brothers watched through the banisters, forgetting even to snigger as their brother sobbed and retched. To this day, *blueeyedboy* thinks, nothing very much has changed. And the vitamin drink always brings it back, and he struggles to stop himself retching; but Ma never notices. Ma thinks he is delicate. Ma knows he would never do anything to any-one –

Post comment:

chrysalisbaby: *Aw babe that makes me want 2 cry*

Captainbunnykiller: *Forget the tears, man, where's the* blood?

Toxic69: *I concur. Roll out those freakin body bags – and by the way, dude, where's the bedroom action?*

ClairDeLune: *Well done,* **blueeyedboy**! *I love the way you tie these stories in with each other. Without wanting to intrude, I'd love to know how much of this ongoing fic is autobiographical, and how much is purely fictional. The third person voice adds an intriguing sense of distance. Perhaps we could discuss it at Group some day?*

8

You are viewing the webjournal of **blueeyedboy** *posting on:*
badguysrock@webjournal.com
Posted at: *19.15 on Monday, February 4*
Status: *public*
Mood: *pensive*
Listening to: *Neil Young:* 'After The Gold Rush'

After Mrs Electric Blue, he finds it so much easier. Innocence, like virginity, is something you can only lose once, and its departure leaves him with no feeling of loss, but only a vague sense of wonder that it should have turned out to be such a small thing, after all. A small thing, but potent; and now it colours every aspect of his life, like a grain of pure cyan in a glass of water, dyeing the contents deepest blue –

He sees them all in blue now, each potential subject, quarry or mark. *Mark.* As in something to be erased. *Black mark. Laundry mark.* He is very sensitive to words; to their sounds, their colours, their music, their shapes on the page.

Mark is a blue word, like *market;* like *murder.* He likes it much better than *victim,* which appears to him as a feeble eggy shade, or even *prey,* with its nasty undertones of ecclesiastical purple, and distant reek of frankincense. He sees them all in blue now, these people who are going to die, and despite his impatience to repeat the act, he allows some time for the high to wear off, for the colours to drain from the world again, for the knot of hatred that is permanently lodged just

112

beneath his solar plexus to swell to the point at which he *must* act, *must* do something, or die of it –

But some things are worth the wait, he knows. And he has waited a long time for this. That little scene at the market was well over a decade ago; no one remembers Mrs White, or her friend with the stupid name.

Let's call her Ms Stonewash Blue. She likes to smoke a joint or two. At least, she did, when she was young, when she weighed in at barely ninety-five pounds and never, ever wore a bra. Now, past fifty, she watches her weight, and grass gives her the munchies.

So she goes to the gym every day instead, and to t'ai chi and salsa class twice a week, and still believes in free love, though nowadays even that, she thinks, is getting quite expensive. A one-time radical feminist, who sees all men as aggressors, she thinks of herself as *free-spirited*; drives a yellow 2CV; likes ethnic bangles and well-cut jeans; goes on expensive Thai holidays; describes herself as *spiritual*; reads Tarot cards at her friends' parties; and has legs that might pass for those of a thirty-year-old, though the same cannot be said of her face.

Her current squeeze is twenty-nine – almost the same age as *blueeyedboy*. A blonde and cropped-haired androgyne, who parks her motorbike by the church, just far enough away from the Stonewash house to keep the neighbours from whispering. From which our hero deduces that Ms Stonewash Blue is not quite the free spirit she pretends to be.

Well, things have changed since the sixties. She knows the value of networking, and opting out of the rat race somehow seems far less appealing now that her passion for Birkenstocks and flares has given way to stocks and shares –

Not that he is implying that this is why she deserves to die. That would be irrational. But – would the world really miss her, he thinks? Would anyone really care if she died?

The truth, is, no one really cares. Few are the deaths that diminish us. Apart from losses within our own tribe, most of us feel nothing but indifference for the death of an outsider. Teenagers stabbed over drug money; pensioners frozen to death at home; victims of famine or war or disease; so many of us *pretend* to care, because caring is what others expect, though secretly we wonder what all the fuss is really about. Some cases affect us more profoundly. The death of a photogenic child; the occasional celebrity. But the fact is that most of us are more likely to grieve over the death of a dog or a soap opera character than over our friends and neighbours.

So thinks our hero to himself, as he follows the yellow 2CV into town, keeping a safe distance between them. Tonight he is driving a white van, a commercial vehicle stolen from a DIY retailer's forecourt at six fifteen that evening. The owner has gone home for the night, and will not notice the loss before morning, by which time it will be too late. The van will have been torched by then, and no one will link *blueeyedboy* with the serious incident that night, in which a local woman was run down on the way to her salsa class.

The *incident* – he likes that word, its lemony scent, its tantalizing colour. Not quite an accident, but something incidental, a diversion from the main event. He can't even call it a hit-and-run, because no one does any running.

In fact, Ms Stonewash sees him coming, hears the sound of his engine rev. But Ms Stonewash ignores him. She locks the yellow 2CV, having parked it just across the road, and steps on to the pedestrian crossing without a look to left or right, heels clicking on the tarmac, skirt hem positioned just high enough to showcase those more-than-adequate legs.

Ms Stonewash subscribes to the view expressed in the slogan of a well-known line of cosmetics and hair products, a slogan he has always despised and which, to him, sums up in four words all the arrogance of those well-bred female parasites with their tinted hair and their manicured nails and their utter contempt for the rest of the world, for the young man in blue at the wheel of the van, no pale horseman by any means, but did she think Death would call by in person just because she's *worth it?*

He has to stop, she thinks to herself as she steps into the road in front of him. He has to stop at the red light. He has to stop at the crossing. He *has* to stop because I'm *me*, and I'm too important to ignore –

The impact is greater than he expects, sending her sprawling into the verge. He has to mount the kerb in order to reverse over her, and by then his engine is complaining vigorously, the suspension shot, the exhaust dragging on the ground, the radiator leaking steam –

Good thing this isn't my car, he thinks. And he gives himself time for one more pass over something that now looks more like a sack of laundry than anything that ever danced the salsa, before driving away at a decent speed, because only a loser would stay to watch; and he knows from a thousand movie shows how arrogance and vanity are so often the downfall of bad guys. So he makes his modest getaway as the witnesses gather open-mouthed; antelopes at the water-hole watching the predator go by –

Returning to the scene of the crime is a luxury he cannot afford. But from the top of the multi-storey car park, armed with his camera and a long lens, he can see the aftermath of the incident: the police car; the ambulance; the little crowd; then the departure of the emergency vehicle, at far too leisurely a pace – he knows that they need a doctor to declare the victim dead at the scene, but there are instances, such as this one, when any layman's verdict would do.

Officially, Ms Stonewash Blue was pronounced dead on arrival.

Blueeyedboy knows that, in fact, she had expired some fifteen minutes earlier. He also knows that her mouth was turned down just like the mouth of a baby flatfish, and that the police kicked sand over the stain, so that in the morning there would be nothing to show that she'd ever been there, except for a bunch of garage flowers Sellotaped to a traffic sign –

How appropriate, he thinks. How mawkish and how commonplace. Litter on the highway now counts as a valid expression of grief. When the Princess of Wales was killed, some months before this incident, the streets were piled high with offerings, taped to every lamp post, left to rot on every wall, flowers in every stage of decay, composting in their cellophane. Every street corner had its own stack of flowers, mouldering paper, teddy bears, sympathy cards, notes and plastic wrappers, and in the heat of that late summer it stank like a municipal tip –

And why? Who was this woman to them? A face from a magazine;

a walk-on part in a soap opera; an attention-seeking parasite; a woman who, in a world of freaks, just about qualified as normal?

Was she really worth all that? Those outpourings of grief and despair? The florists did well from it, anyway; the price of roses went through the roof. And in the pub later that week, when *blueeyedboy* dared to suggest that perhaps it was somewhat unnecessary, he was taken into a back street by a punter and his ugly wife, where he was given a serious talking-to – not *quite* a beating, no, but with enough slapping and shoving to bring it close – and told he wasn't welcome, and strongly advised to fuck of –

At which point in the story this punter – shall we call him Diesel Blue? – a family man, a respected member of the community, twenty years older than *blueeyedboy* and outweighing him by a hundred pounds – raised one of his loyal fists and smacked our hero right in the mouth, while the ugly wife, who smelled of cigarettes and cheap antiperspirant, laughed as *blueeyedboy* spat out blood, and said: *She's worth more dead than you'll ever be* –

Six months later, Diesel's van is traced through security camera footage to a hit-and-run incident in which a middle-aged woman is killed crossing the road to get to her car. The van, which since has been set on fire, still bears traces of fibre and hair, and although Diesel Blue is adamant that he is not responsible, that the van was stolen the night before, he fails to convince the magistrate, especially in the light of a previous history of drunkenness and violence. The case goes to the criminal court, where, after a four-day trial, Diesel Blue is acquitted, mostly for lack of evidence. The camera footage proves disappointing, failing as it does to confirm the identity of the driver of the van – a figure in a hoodie and baseball cap, whose bulk may be due to an over-sized coat and whose face is never visible.

But to be acquitted in court is not everything. Graffiti on the walls of the house; hostile murmurs in the pub; letters to the local Press; all suggest that Diesel Blue got away with it on a technicality, and when, a few weeks later, his house catches fire (with Diesel and his wife inside), no one grieves especially.

Verdict – accidental death, possibly caused by a cigarette.

Blueeyedboy is unsurprised. He'd had the guy down as a smoker.

Post comment:
Captainbunnykiller: *You are totally sick, dude. I love it!*
chrysalisbaby: *woot woot yay for* **blueeyedboy**
ClairDeLune: *Very interesting. I sense your mistrust of authority. I'd love to hear the story behind this story. Is it also based on real life events? You know I'd love to know more!*
JennyTricks: *(post deleted).*

9

You are viewing the webjournal of **blueeyedboy** *posting on:*
badguysrock@webjournal.com
Posted at: *21.06 on Monday, February 4*
Status: *public*
Mood: *prickly*
Listening to: *Poison:* 'Every Rose Has Its Thorn'

The birth of little Emily White saw a change in *blueeyedboy*'s Ma. She'd always been quick-tempered, but by the end of the summer she seemed perpetually on the brink of some kind of violent eruption. Part of the cause was financial stress: growing boys are expensive, and by unfortunate coincidence, fewer and fewer people in the Village seemed to need any household help. Mrs French Blue had joined the ranks of her ex-employers, and Mrs Chemical Blue, claiming poverty, had reduced her hours to two per week. Perhaps, now Ben was back at school, people felt less charitably inclined to offer work to the father-less family. Or perhaps they'd simply had enough of listening to tales of how talented and special Ben was.

And then, just before Christmas, they ran across Mrs Electric Blue near Tandy's in the covered market, but she didn't seem to notice them, even when Ma spoke to her.

Perhaps Mrs Electric Blue didn't like being seen so close to the market, where there were always people shouting, and torn-off cabbage leaves on the floor, and everything peppered with brown grease, and where people always called you *luv*. Perhaps all that was too common for her. Perhaps she was ashamed of knowing Ma, with her old coat on and her hair scraped back and her three scruffy boys, and her bags full of shopping that she had to carry home on the bus, and her hands with palms all tattooed with dirt from other people's housework.

'Morning,' said Ma, and Mrs Electric Blue just stared, looking weirdly like one of Mrs White's dolls, half-surprised and half-not-quite alive, with her pink mouth pursed and her eyebrows raised and her long white coat with the fur collar making her look like the Snow Queen, even though there wasn't any snow.

It seemed at first as if she hadn't heard. Ben shot her the smile that had once earned him treats. Mrs Electric didn't smile back, but turned away and pretended to look at some clothes that were hanging on a stall near by, although even *blueeyedboy* could see that they weren't at all the kind of clothes she'd wear, all baggy blouses and cheap, shiny shoes. He wondered if he should call her name –

But Ma went red and said: *Come on*, and started to drag him away by the arm. He tried to explain, which was when Nigel punched him, just above the elbow, where it hurts most, and he hid his face in his cry-baby sleeve, and Ma slapped Nigel across the head. And he saw Mrs Electric Blue walk away towards the shops, where a young man – a *very* young man – dressed in a navy pea coat and jeans, was awaiting her impatiently, and would perhaps have kissed her, he thought, had it not been for the presence of the cleaner and her three kids, one of whom was still watching her with that look of reproach, as if he knew something he shouldn't. And that made her walk a little faster, clipping the ground with her high heels, a sound that smells of cigarettes and cabbage leaves and cheap perfume at knock-off prices.

Then, a week later, she let Ma go – making it sound like a generous gesture, saying that she'd imposed too long – which left just two of her ladies, plus a couple of shifts at St Oswald's per week; hardly enough to pay the rent, let alone feed three boys.

So Ma took another job, working on a market stall, from which she would return frozen and exhausted, but carrying a plastic bag filled with half-rotten fruit and other stuff they couldn't sell, which she would serve up in various guises over the course of the week, or worse still, put in the blender to make what she called 'the vitamin drink', which might be made up of such diverse ingredients as cabbage, apple, beetroot, carrot, tomato, peach or celery, but which always tasted to *blueeyedboy* like a sweet-rotten slurry of sludge-green. The tube of paint might be labelled Nut Brown, but shit smells like shit all the same, and it always made him think of the market, so that in time even the word made him retch – *mark-et* – with its barking twin syllables, like an engine that won't start, and all that was because they happened to see Mrs Electric Blue with her fancy-boy in the market that day.

That was why, when they saw her again, six weeks later, in the street, that sickly taste rushed into his mouth, a sharp pain stabbed at his temple, objects around him began to acquire a bevelled, prismic quality –

'Why, Gloria,' said Mrs Electric Blue in that sweetly venomous manner of hers. 'How lovely to see you. You're looking well. How's Ben doing at school?'

Ma gave her a sharp look. 'Oh, he's doing *very* well. His tutor says he's *gifted*—'

It was common knowledge in Malbry that Mrs Electric Blue's son was *not* gifted; that he had tried for St Oswald's, but hadn't got in, then had failed to get into Oxford, in spite of private tutoring. A big disappointment, so they said. Mrs Electric's hopes had been high.

'Really?' said Mrs Electric Blue. She made the word sound like some new and frosty brand of toothpaste.

'Yes. My son's got a tutor. He's trying for St Oswald's.'

Blueeyedboy hid a grimace behind his hand, but not before Ma had noticed.

'He's going to be a scholarship boy.' That was bending the truth a little. Dr Peacock's offer to tutor Ben was payment for his cooperation in his research. His ability remained, as yet, a matter for conjecture.

Still, Mrs Electric Blue was impressed, which was probably Ma's intention.

But now *blueeyedboy* was trying not to be sick as waves of nausea washed over him, flooding him with that market smell, that sludgy-brown stink of the vitamin drink; of split tomatoes gone to white-lipped mush, and half-gone apples (*The brown's the sweetest part,* she'd say), and black bananas and cabbage leaves. It wasn't just the memory, or the sound of her heels on the cobbled street, or even her voice with its high-bred yarking syllables –

It's not my fault, he told himself. *I'm not a bad person. Really, I'm not.*

But that didn't stop the sick smell, or the colours, or the pain in his head. Instead it made it weirdly worse, like driving past something dead in the road and wishing you'd looked at it properly –

Blue is the colour of murder, he thought, and the sick, panicky feeling abated – a little. He thought of Mrs Electric Blue lying dead on a mortuary slab with a tag on her toe, like a nicely labelled Christmas present; and every time he thought of it, the sludgy stink receded again, and the headache dimmed to a dull throb, and the colours around him brightened a little, all merging together to make one blue – oxygen blue, gas-jet blue, circuit-board blue, autopsy blue –

He tried a smile. It felt OK. The rotten-fruit smell had disappeared, although it did come back at regular intervals throughout the whole of *blueeyedboy*'s childhood, as did the phrases his mother spoke that day to Mrs Electric Blue –

Benjamin's a good boy.

We're so proud of Benjamin.

And always with the same, sick knowledge that he was *not* a good boy; that he was crooked in every cell – that, worse still, he *liked* it that way –

And even then, he must have known –

That one day he would kill her.

Post comment:

ClairDeLune: *Very good,* **blueeyedboy!**

chrysalisbaby: *awesome U R so cool*

JennyTricks: (*post deleted*).

JennyTricks: (*post deleted*).

10

You are viewing the webjournal of **blueeyedboy** *posting on:*
badguysrock@webjournal.com
Posted at: *21.43 on Monday, February 4*
Status: *public*
Mood: *deluded*
Listening to: *Murray Head:* 'So Strong'

That year, things went from bad to worse. Ma was mean, money was tight and no one, not even Benjamin, seemed to be able to please her. She no longer worked for Mrs White, and if Mrs White ever came to her stall at the market, Ma made sure someone else served her instead, and pretended not to notice.

Then there were the rumours that had begun to circulate. *Blueeyedboy* was never sure what exactly was being said, but he was aware of the whispers and of the sudden silences that sometimes fell whenever Mrs White approached, and of the way the neighbours looked at him when he was at the market. He thought it might have something to do with Feather Dunne, a gossip and a busybody who had moved into the Village last spring, who had befriended Mrs White and who often helped out with Emily, although why she should scorn *blueeyedboy*'s ma was still a mystery to him. But whatever it was, the poison spread. Soon, everyone seemed to be whispering.

Blueeyedboy wondered if he should try to talk to Mrs White, to ask her what had happened. He'd always liked her best of Ma's ladies, and she had always been nice to him. Surely, if he approached her, she'd

change her mind about letting Ma go, and they could be friends
again –

One day he came home from school early and saw Mrs White's car
parked outside. A surge of relief came over him. They were talking
again, he told himself. Whatever their quarrel had been, it was over.

But when he looked through the window he saw, instead of Mrs
White, Mr White standing there beside the china cabinet.

Blueeyedboy had never had much to do with Mr White. He'd seen
him in the Village, of course, and at St Oswald's, where he worked, but
never like this, never at home, and never without his wife, of course –

He must have come straight from St Oswald's. He was wearing a
long coat and carrying a satchel. A man of middle height and build;
darkish hair turning to grey; small, neat hands; blue eyes behind his
wire-rimmed glasses. A mild, soft-spoken, diffident man, never taking
centre stage. But now Mr White was different. *Blueeyedboy* could feel
it. Living with Ma had given him a special sensitivity to any sign of
tension or rage. And Mr White was angry; *blueeyedboy* could see it in
the way he stood, tensed, immobile, under control.

Blueeyedboy edged closer, making sure to keep well out of sight
under the line of the privet hedge. Through a gap in the branches he
could see Ma, her profile slightly averted, standing next to Mr White.
She was wearing her high-heeled shoes – he could tell, they always
made her look taller. Even so, her head only reached the curve of Mr
White's shoulder. She raised her eyes to his, and for a moment
they stood without moving, Ma smiling, Mr White holding her
gaze.

And then Mr White reached into his coat and pulled out something
that *blueeyedboy* thought at first was a paperback. Ma took it, split the
spine, and then *blueeyedboy* realized that it was a wad of banknotes,
snappy and fresh and unmarked –

But why was Mr White paying Ma? And why did it make him so
angry?

It was then that a thought came to *blueeyedboy*; one of curiously
adult clarity. What if the father he had never known – Mr Blue Eyes
– was Mr White? What if Mrs White had found out? It would explain
her hostility as well as the talk in the Village. It would explain so many

things – Ma's job at St Oswald's, where he taught; her open resentment of his wife; and now this gift of money –

Shielded from view by the privet hedge, *blueeyedboy* craned his neck to see; to detect in this man's features the faintest reflection of his own –

The movement must have alerted him. For a moment their eyes met. Mr White's eyes widened suddenly, and *blueeyedboy* saw him flinch – which was when our hero turned and fled. The question of whether Mr White could have been his father or not was entirely secondary to the fact that Ma would certainly flay him alive if she caught him spying on her.

But as far as he could tell, Mr White said nothing to Ma about seeing a boy at the window. Instead Ma seemed in good spirits, and ceased to complain about money, and as the weeks and months passed without any further disruption, *blueeyedboy*'s suspicions increased, at last becoming a certainty –

Patrick White was his father.

Post comment:

ClairDeLune: *I like the way your stories combine 'real-life' events with fiction. Perhaps you'd like to come back to Group and discuss the process of writing this? I'm sure the others would appreciate an insight into your emotional journey.*

JennyTricks: *(post deleted).*

blueeyedboy: *Jenny, do I know you?*

JennyTricks: *(post deleted).*

blueeyedboy: *Seriously. Do I know you?*

11

Well, if you won't answer me, I'll simply delete your entries. You're on my turf now, *JennyTricks*, and my rules apply. But it feels as if I know you. Could it be that we've met before? Could it be that you're stalking me?

Stalking. Now there's a sinister word. Like part of a plant, a bitter-green stalk that will one day bloom into something sickening. But online, things are different. Online, as fictional characters, we can sometimes allow ourselves the luxury of antisocial behaviour. I'm sick of hearing about how so-and-so *felt so violated* at such-and-such's comments, or how somebody else felt sexually besmirched at some harmless innuendo. Oh, these people with their sensitivities. Excuse me, but writing a comment in capitals *isn't* the same as shouting. Venting a little vitriol isn't the same as a physical blow. So vent away, *JennyTricks*. Nothing you say can touch me. Although I'll admit, I'm curious. Tell me, *have* we met before?

The rest of my online audience shows a pleasing level of appreciation – especially *ClairDeLune*, who sends me a critique (her word) of every single fic I write, with comments on style and imagery. My last attempt, she tells me, is both psychologically intuitive and a breakthrough into a new and more mature style.

Cap, less subtle, as always, pleads for more drama, more anguish, more blood. Toxic, who thinks about sex all the time, urges me to write more explicitly. Or, as he puts it: *Whatever gets your rocks off, dude. Just try to think about mine some time . . .*

As for Chryssie, she just sends me love – adoring, uncritical, slavish love – with a message that says: *Ur made of awesome!* on a banner made up of little pink hearts –

Albertine does not comment. She rarely does on my stories. Perhaps they make her uncomfortable. I hope so. Why post them otherwise?

I saw her again this afternoon. Red coat, black hair, basket over her arm, walking down the hill into Malbry town. I had my camera with me this time, the one with the telephoto lens, and I managed to get a few clear shots from the little piece of waste ground at the top of Mill Road before a man walking his dog forced me to curtail my investigation.

He gave me a suspicious look. He was short, bow-legged, muscular; the type of man who always seems to hate and distrust me on sight. His dog was the same; bandy, off-white; big teeth and no eyes. It growled when it saw me. I took a step back.

'Birds,' I said, by means of explanation. 'I like to come here and photograph birds.'

The man eyed me with open contempt. 'Aye, I'll bet.'

He watched me go with no further comment, but I could feel his eyes in the small of my back. I'll have to be more careful, I thought. People already think I'm a freak – and the last thing I want is for someone to remember later how Gloria Winter's boy was seen lurking around Mill Road with a camera –

And yet, I can't stop watching her. It's almost a compulsion. God knows what Ma would do if she knew. Still, Ma has other fish to fry in the wake (ha!) of Nigel's funeral, though the task of clearing out his flat has fallen to Yours Truly.

Not that there is much to find. His telescope; a few clothes; his computer; half a shelf of old books. Some papers from the hospital in a shoebox under the bed. I'd expected more – a journal, at least – but maybe experience had made him more cautious. If Nigel kept a journal at all, it was probably at Emily's house, where he'd been staying most of the time, and where he could almost certainly rely on its safety from prying eyes.

There is no sign of Nigel's girl here. Not a trace, not a hair, not a photograph. The narrow bed is still unmade, the quilt pulled roughly over the dubious sheet, but she has never slept here. There is no fleeting scent of her, no toothbrush of hers in the bathroom, no coffee cup in the sink bearing the imprint of her mouth. The flat smells of unaired bed, of stale water, of damp, and it will take me less than half a day to clear the contents into the back of a van and to drive it to the refuse site, where anything of value will be sorted and recycled, and the rest consigned to landfill, to the misery of future generations.

It's funny, isn't it, how little a life amounts to? A few old clothes, a box of papers, some dirty plates in the sink? A half-smoked packet of cigarettes, tucked away in a bedside drawer – *she* doesn't smoke, so he kept them here, for those nights when, unable to sleep, he would look out through the skylight with his telescope, trying to see, through the light pollution, the crystal webwork of the stars.

Yes, my brother liked stars. That was pretty much all he liked. Certainly, he never liked *me*. Well, neither of them did, of course, but it was Nigel I feared; Nigel, who had suffered most in the face of Ma's expectations –

Oh, those expectations. I wonder what Nigel made of them. Watching from the sidelines, pallid in his black shirts, bony fists perpetually clenched, so that when he opened up his hands you'd see the little crescents of red that his fingernails had left in his palm, marks he transferred on to my skin whenever he and I were alone –

Nigel's flat is monochrome. Grey sheets under a black-and-white quilt; a wardrobe in shades of charcoal and black. You'd have thought he might have quit that by now, but time has made no difference to my brother's colour scheme. Socks, jackets, sweaters, jeans. Not a shirt, not a T-shirt, not even a pair of underpants that is not the official black or grey –

Nigel was five when Dad left home. I've often wondered about that. Did he remember wearing colours, when he was still the only child? Did he sometimes go to the beach and play on the salty yellow sand? Or did he lie there with Dad at night and point out the constellations? What was he really looking for, scanning the skies with his Junior Telescope (paid for with money from his newspaper round)? Where did his anger come from? Most of all, why was it decreed that *he* should be black, or Ben should be blue? And if our roles had been reversed, would things have turned out differently?

I guess I'll never know now. Maybe I should have asked him. But Nigel and I never really talked, not even back when we were kids. We coexisted side by side, waging a kind of guerrilla war in defiance of Ma's disapproval, each one inflicting as much damage as he could on to the hated enemy.

My brother never knew me, except as the focus of his rage. And the only time I ever found out anything intimate about him, I kept the knowledge to myself, fearing the possible consequences. But if each man kills the thing he loves, must not the opposite also be true? Does each man love the thing he kills? And is love the ingredient that I lack?

I turned on his computer. Skimmed briefly through his favourites. The result was as I'd suspected: links to the Hubble telescope; to images of galaxies; to webcams at the North Pole; to chat rooms in which photographers discussed the latest solar eclipse. Some porn, all of it plain-vanilla; some legally downloaded music. I went into his e-mail – he'd left the password open – but found nothing of interest there. Not a word from *Albertine*; no e-mails, no photographs, no sign that he'd ever known her.

No sign of anyone else, either; no official correspondence, except for the monthly line or two from his therapist; no proof of some clandestine affair; not even a quick note from a friend. My brother had fewer friends than I, and the thought is strangely touching. But now isn't the time to feel sympathy. My brother knew the risks from the start. He shouldn't have got in the way, that's all. It wasn't my fault that he did.

I found the cleanest mug he had and made a cup of tea. It wasn't Earl Grey, but it would do. Then I logged on to *badguysrock*.

Albertine wasn't online. But Chryssie, as always, was waiting for me, her avatar blinking forlornly. Beneath it, an emoticon, coupled with the plaintive message: *chrysalisbaby is feeling sick.*

Well, I'm not entirely surprised. Syrup of ipecac can have some unpleasant side effects. Still, that's hardly my fault, and today I have more pressing concerns.

I glanced quickly through my mailbox. *Captainbunnykiller is feeling good. BombNumber20 is feeling bored.* A meme from Clair entitled: *Try this simple test to know – What kind of a psycho are you?*

Mmm. Cute. And typical Clair, whose knowledge of human psychology – such as it is – is mostly gleaned from cop shows, shows with names like *Blue Murder*, in which feisty female profilers hunt down bed-wetting sociopaths by Getting Inside the Criminal Mind –

So what kind of psycho am I, Clair? Let's look at the results.

> *Mostly Ds. Congratulations! You are a* malignant narcissist. *You are glib, charming, manipulative, and have little or no regard for others. You enjoy notoriety, and are willing to commit acts of violence to satisfy your craving for instant gratification, although secretly you may harbour feelings of inadequacy. You may also suffer from paranoia, and you have a tendency to live in a dream world in which you are the perpetual centre of attention. You need to get professional help, as you are a potential danger to yourself and others.*

Dear Clair. I'm very fond of her. And it's really rather touching that she thinks that she can analyse me. But she has a junior social-worker mentality at best, for all her spit and psychobabble, and besides, she's none too stable herself, as we may discover in due course.

You see, even Clair takes risks online. During what passes for her 'real' work – handing out praise to the talentless and platitudinous comfort to the existentially challenged – she secretly spends hours online updating her fansite on Angel Blue, making banners, searching the Net for pictures, comments, interviews, rumours, guest appearances or any information regarding his current whereabouts. She also writes to him regularly, and has posted on her own website a small collection of his handwritten replies, which are courteous but impersonal, and which only someone truly obsessed would ever take as encouragement . . .

Clair, however, *is* truly obsessed. Thanks to my link to her WeJay, I know that she writes fan fiction about his characters – and sometimes about the man himself – erotic fics that, over the months, are becoming increasingly daring. She also paints portraits of her loved one, and makes cushions on to which she prints his face. Her bedroom at home is filled with these cushions, mostly in pink – her favourite colour – some of them also depicting *her* face next to his, inside a printed heart.

She follows his wife's career, too – an actress to whom he has been happily married for the past five or six years – although recently Clair may have begun to indulge in hopeful speculation. An online friend – who logs on under the name *sapphiregirl* – has informed her of a liaison between Angel's wife and a co-worker on the set of her new film.

This has led to a spate of attacks on Mrs Angel in some of Clair's recent journal posts. Her last post makes her feelings more than clear. She does not want to see Angel hurt; and she is slightly bewildered that a man of his intelligence has not yet come to terms with the fact that his wife is – well, *unworthy*.

The fact that there *was* no such liaison is surely no fault of *sapphiregirl* – these rumours are so easily spread, and how could she possibly have known that Clair would respond so impulsively? It will be interesting to see how Clair reacts if – *when* – Angel's lawyers write to her.

How can I be so sure, you ask? Well, Internet mail can be ignored, but a letter to Mrs Angel's address, and the accompanying box of chocolates (in this case containing an unexpected surprise), all traceable to *ClairDeLune* and posted within five miles of her house – are altogether more sinister.

She will, of course, deny it. But will Angel Blue believe her? And Clair is such a devoted fan: she travels to America to see her idol on the stage; she goes to every convention where she might get a glimpse of him. What might she do on receipt of – let's say, a court order, or even just a rebuke from her man? I suspect her to be volatile – perhaps even slightly deranged. What would it take to make her flip? And wouldn't it be fun to find out?

But for now I have other things on my mind. A man should always clean up after himself. And Nigel is, after all, my mess – my mess, if not my murder.

Does murder run in families? I can almost think it does. Who's next, I wonder? Myself, perhaps, dead of an overdose, maybe, or found beaten to death in an alleyway? A car crash? A hit-and-run? Or will it look like suicide, a bottle of pills by the side of the bath, a blood-stained razor on the tiles?

It could be anything, of course. The killer could be anyone. So play it safe. Don't take any risks. Remember what happened to the other two –

Watch your back, *blueeyedboy*.

12

You are viewing the webjournal of **blueeyedboy** posting on:
                                    badguysrock@webjournal.com
Posted at: *01.22 on Tuesday, February 5*
Status: *public*
Mood: *cautious*
Listening to: *Altered Images: 'Happy Birthday'*

He has always been good at watching his back. Over the years, he has had to learn. Accidents happen so easily, and the men in his family have always been particularly prone to them. It turns out that even his dad, whom *blueeyedboy* had always assumed had simply gone out to buy cigarettes and never bothered to come back, had met with a fatal accident: in his case, a car crash, no one's fault – the kind that the folks at Malbry Infirmary call a *Saturday Night Special*. Too much alcohol; too little patience, maybe a marital crisis and –

– *Wham!*

And so it should come as no surprise that *blueeyedboy* should have turned out this way. No guiding paternal influence; a controlling, ambitious mother; an elder brother who tended to solve all problems with his fists. It's hardly rocket science, is it? And he is more than familiar with the rudiments of psychoanalysis.

Congratulations! You are an Oedipal. Your unusually close relationship with your mother has stifled your ability to grow into an emotionally balanced human being. Your ambivalence towards her emerges in violent fantasies, often sexual in nature.

Well – *duh*, as Cap might say.

Nigel may have missed his dad, but the man meant nothing to *blueeyedboy*. He wasn't even *blueeyedboy's* *real* father – certainly, from his photographs, he sees no resemblance to himself. To Nigel, perhaps: the big, square hands; the black hair falling across the face; the slightly over-pretty mouth, with its hidden threat of violence. Ma often hinted that Peter Winter was possessed of a nasty streak; and if one of them misbehaved, she'd say – whilst wielding that piece of electrical cord – *It's a good thing for you your father's not here. He'd soon sort you out.*

And so the word *father* came to have – shall we say – negative connotations. A loose-lipped, greenish, bilious sound, like the murky water under Blackpool pier, where they used to go on his birthday. *Blueeyedboy* always liked the beach, but the pier itself frightened him, looking as it did like a fossilized animal – a dinosaur maybe – all bones, but still quite dangerous with its muddy feet and broken teeth.

Pier. Peter. *Pierre*, in French. *Sticks and stones may break my bones* –

After seeing Mr White with his ma, our hero's curiosity regarding Patrick White had increased. He found himself watching Mr White whenever he saw him in the Village – walking to St Oswald's with his satchel in one hand and a pile of exercise books in the other; in the park on Sundays with Mrs White and Emily – now two years old and learning to walk – playing games, making her laugh –

It occurred to him that if Mr White were his father, then Emily must be his sister. He imagined himself with a little sister: helping his Ma look after her; reading her stories at bedtime. He began to follow them; to sit in the park where they liked to go, pretending to read a book while he watched –

He hadn't dared ask Ma for the truth. Besides, he didn't need to. He could feel it in his heart. Patrick White *was* his father. Sometimes our hero liked to dream that one day his father would come and take him somewhere far away –

He would have shared, he tells himself. He would have shared him with Emily. But Mr White went out of his way to avoid even having to look at him. A man who, until then, had always greeted him genially in the street; had always called him *young man* and asked how he was doing at school.

It wasn't just because Emily was so much more appealing. There was something in Mr White's face, in his voice whenever our hero approached him; a look of wariness, almost of fear –

But what could Mr White possibly fear from a boy of only nine years old? Our hero had no way of knowing. Was he afraid that *blueeyedboy* might want to harm Emily? Or was he afraid that Mrs White would one day discover his secret?

He started skipping classes at school to hang around St Oswald's. He would hide behind the utility shed and watch the yard as lessons changed: the stream of boys in blue uniforms; the Masters in their flapping black gowns. On Tuesdays it was Mr White who supervised the schoolyard, and *blueeyedboy* would watch him avidly from his hiding-place as he moved across the asphalt, stopping every now and again to exchange a few words with a pupil –

'*String quartet tonight, Jones. Don't forget your music.*'

'*No, sir. Thank you, sir.*'

'*Tuck your shirt in, Hudson, please. You're not on the beach at Brighton, you know.*'

Blueeyedboy remembers one Tuesday, which happened to be his tenth birthday. Not that he expected much in the way of celebration. That year had been especially grim, except for his trips to the Mansion; money was tight; Ma was stressed, and a trip to Blackpool was out of the question – there was too much work to do. Even a birth-day cake, he thought, was probably too much to hope for. Even so, that morning, there seemed to be something special in the air. He was ten years old. The big one-oh. His life was in double digits. Perhaps it was time, he told himself, as he headed towards St Oswald's, to find out the truth about Patrick White –

He found him in the schoolyard, a couple of minutes before the end of School Assembly. Mr White was standing by the entrance to the Middle School Quad, his faded gown slung over his arm, a mug of coffee in one hand. In a minute or two the yard would be filled with boys; now it was deserted, except, of course, for *blueeyedboy*, made instantly conspicuous by dint of his lack of uniform, standing beneath the entrance gate with the school's motto emblazoned on it in Latin – *Audere, agere, auferre* – which, thanks to Dr Peacock, he knows means: *to dare, to strive, to conquer.*

Suddenly, our *blueeyedboy* did not feel very daring. He was desperately sure he would stutter; that the words he so badly wanted to speak would break and crumble in his mouth. And even without the black robe, Mr White looked forbidding: taller and sterner than usual, watching our hero's determined approach, listening to the sound of his shoes on the cobbled courtyard –

'What are you doing here, boy?' he said, and his voice, though soft, was glacial. 'Why have you been following me?'

Blueeyedboy looked at him. Mr White's blue eyes seemed a very long way up. 'M-Mr White—' he began. 'I – I—'

Stuttering begins in the mind. It's the curse of expectation. That's why he was able to speak perfectly normally at certain times, while at others his words turned to Silly String, tangling him uselessly in a web of his own making.

'I— I—' Our hero could feel his face turning red.

Mr White regarded him. 'Look, I don't have time for this. The bell's going to ring any moment now—'

Blueeyedboy made a final effort. He *had* to know the truth, he thought. After all, today was his birthday. He tried to see himself in blue: St Oswald's blue, or butterfly blue. He saw the words like butterflies coming out of his open mouth, and said, with barely a stutter at all –

'Mr White, are you my dad?'

For a moment the silence bound them. Then, just as the morning bell sounded through St Oswald's, *blueeyedboy* saw Patrick White's face change from shock to astonishment, and then to a kind of stunned pity.

'Is *that* what you thought?' he said at last.

Blueeyedboy just looked at him. Around them, the courtyard was filling up with blue St Oswald's blazers. Chirping voices all around, circling like birds. Some of the boys gaped at him, a single sparrow in a flock of budgerigars.

After a moment, Mr White seemed to come out of his stupor.

'Listen,' he said in a firm voice. 'I don't know where you got this idea. But it isn't true. Really, it's not. And if I catch you spreading these rumours—'

'You're *n-not* my f-father?' said *blueeyedboy*, his voice beginning to tremble.

'No,' said Mr White. 'I'm not.'

For a moment the words seemed to make no sense. *Blueeyedboy* had been so sure. But Mr White was telling the truth; he could see it in his blue eyes. But then – why had he given money to Ma? And why had he done it in secret?

And then it fell into place in his mind like the moving parts of a Mouse Trap game. He supposed it had been obvious. Ma was black-mailing Mr White – *blackmail*, a sinister word; the Black and White Minstrels under their paint. Mr White had transgressed, and Ma had somehow found out about it. That would explain the whisperings; the way Mrs White looked at Ma; Mr White's anger, and now his contempt. This man was not his father, he thought. This man had never cared for him.

And now *blueeyedboy* could feel the tears beginning to prick at his eyelids. Terrible, helpless, childish tears of disappointment and of shame. *Please, not in front of Mr White*, he begged of the Almighty, but God, like Ma, was implacable. Like Ma, Our Father sometimes needs that gesture of contrition.

'Are you OK?' said Mr White, reluctantly putting a hand on his arm.

'Fine, thanks,' said *blueeyedboy*, wiping his nose with the back of his hand.

'I don't know how you got the idea that—'

'Forget it. Really. I'm fine,' he said, and very calmly walked away, keeping his spine as straight as he could, although he was a mess inside, although it felt like dying.

It's my birthday, he told himself. *Today, I deserve to be special. Whatever it takes, whatever it costs, whatever punishment God or Ma can possibly inflict on me –*

And that's how, fifteen minutes later, he found himself, not back at school, but at the end of Millionaires' Row, looking towards the Mansion.

*

It was the first time that *blueeyedboy* had been to the Mansion unsupervised. His visits with his brothers and Ma were always strictly controlled, and he knew that if Ma found out what he'd done, she'd make him sorry he'd ever been born. But today he wasn't afraid of Ma. Today, a breath of rebellion seemed to have taken hold of him. Today, for once, *blueeyedboy* was in the mood for a spot of trespass.

The garden was shielded from the road by a set of cast-iron railings. At the far end there was a stone wall, and all around, a blackthorn hedge. On the whole, it didn't look promising. But *blueeyedboy* was determined. He found a space through which to crawl, mindful of the twigs and thorns that snagged at his hair and stuck through his T-shirt, and emerged on the other side of the hedge into the grounds of the Mansion.

Ma always called it 'the grounds'. Dr Peacock called it 'the garden', although there was over four acres of it, orchard and kitchen garden and lawns, plus the walled rose garden in which Dr Peacock took so much pride, the pond and the old conservatory, where pots and gardening tools were kept. Most of it was trees, though, which suited *blueeyedboy* just fine, with alleys of rhododendrons that flared brief glory in springtime and in late summer grew skeletal, encroaching darkly across the path, the perfect cover for anyone wishing to visit the garden unseen –

Blueeyedboy did not question the impulse that had driven him to the Mansion. He couldn't go back to St Oswald's, though, not now, after what had happened. He dared not go back home, of course, and at school he'd be punished for being late. But the Mansion was quiet, and secret, and safe. Simply to be there was enough; to dive into the undergrowth; to hear the summery sounds of the bees high up in the leafy canopy, and to feel the beating of his heart slow down to its natural cadence. He was still so immersed in his agitated thoughts that, walking along an alley of trees, he almost ran into Dr Peacock, who was standing, secateurs in hand, shirtsleeves rolled to the elbow, at the entrance to the rose garden.

'And what brings *you* here this morning?'

For a moment *blueeyedboy* was quite unable to answer. Then he looked past Dr Peacock and saw: the newly dug grave; the mound of earth, the rolled square of turf laid aside on the ground –

Dr Peacock smiled at him. It was a rather complex smile; sad and complicit at the same time. 'I'm afraid you've caught me in the act,' he said, indicating the fresh grave. 'I know how this may look to you, but as we grow older our capacity for sentiment expands to an exponential degree. To you it may look like senility—'

Blueeyedboy stared at him with a perfect lack of comprehension.

'What I mean is,' Dr Peacock said, 'I was just bidding a last goodbye to a very loyal old friend.'

For a moment *blueeyedboy* was still unsure of what he'd meant. Then he remembered Dr Peacock's Jack Russell, over which the old man always made such a fuss. *Blueeyedboy* didn't like dogs. Too eager; too unpredictable.

He shivered, feeling vaguely sick. He tried to remember the name of the dog, but all he could think of was *Malcolm*, the name of his would-have-been-sibling, and his eyes filled with tears for no reason, and his head began to ache –

Dr Peacock put a hand on his arm. 'Don't be upset, son. He had a good life. Are you all right? You're shivering.'

'I don't feel so w-well,' said *blueeyedboy*.

'Really? Well, then, we'd better get you in the house, hadn't we? I'll get you something cool to drink. And then perhaps I should call your mother—'

'No! Please!' said *blueeyedboy*.

Dr Peacock gave him a look. 'All right,' he said. 'I understand. You don't want to alarm her. A fine woman in many ways, but somewhat over-protective. And besides—' His eyes creased in a mischievous smile. 'Am I correct in assuming that on this bright summer morning, the delights of the school curriculum were not enough to keep you indoors when all of Nature's syllabus demanded your urgent attention?'

Blueeyedboy took this to mean that his truancy had been noted. 'Please, sir. Don't tell Ma.'

Dr Peacock shook his head. 'I see no reason to tell her,' he said. 'I was a boy myself, once. Slugs and snails and puppy-dogs' tails. Fishing in the river. Are you fond of fishing, young man?'

Blueeyedboy nodded, even though he'd never tried it; never would.

'Excellent pastime. Gets you outdoors. Of course, I have my gardening—' He glanced over his shoulder at the mound of earth and the open grave. 'Give me a moment, will you?' he said. 'Then I'll fix us both a drink.'

Blueeyedboy watched in silence as Dr Peacock filled in the grave. He didn't really want to look, but he found that he couldn't look away. His chest was tight, his lips were numb, his head was spinning dizzily. Was he really ill, he thought? Or was it the sound of digging, he thought; the tinny rasp of the spade as it bit, the sour-vegetable scent, the crazy thump as each packet of earth clattered into the open grave?

At last Dr Peacock put down the spade, but he did not turn immediately. Instead he stood by the burial mound, hands in pockets, head bowed, for such a long time that *blueeyedboy* wondered if he had been forgotten.

'Are you all right, sir?' he said at last.

At his voice, Dr Peacock turned. He had taken off his gardening hat, and without it the sunlight made him squint. 'How sentimental you must find me,' he said. 'All this ceremony over a dog. Have you ever kept a dog?'

Blueeyedboy shook his head.

'Too bad. Every boy should have one. Still, you've got your brothers,' he said. 'Bet that's lot of fun, eh?'

For a moment, *blueeyedboy* tried to imagine the world as Dr Peacock saw it: a world where brothers were lots of fun; where boys went fishing, kept dogs; played cricket on the green –

'It's my birthday today,' he said.

'Is that so? Today?'

'Yes, sir.'

Dr Peacock smiled. 'Ah. I remember birthdays. Jelly and ice cream and birthday cake. Not that I tend to celebrate nowadays. August the twenty-fourth, isn't it? Mine was on the twenty-third. I'd forgotten until you reminded me.' Now he looked thoughtfully at the boy. 'I think we should mark the occasion,' he said. 'I can't claim to offer much in the way of refreshments, but I do have tea, and some iced buns, and anyway—' At this he grinned, suddenly looking mischievous, like a young boy wearing a false beard and a very convincing old-man's disguise: 'We Virgos should stick together.'

It doesn't sound much, does it? A cup of Earl Grey, an iced bun and the stub of a candle burning on top. But to *blueeyedboy* that day stands out in memory like a gilded minaret against a barren landscape. He remembers every detail now with perfect, heightened precision: the little blue roses on the cup; the sound of spoon against china; the amber colour and scent of the tea; the angle of the sunlight. Little things, but their poignancy is like a reminder of innocence. Not that he ever *was* innocent; but on that day he approached it; and looking back, he understands that this was the last of his childhood, slipping like sand through his fingers –

Post comment:

ClairDeLune: *I'm glad to see you exploring this theme in more detail,
blueeyedboy. Your central character often appears as cold
and emotionless, and I like the way you hint at his hidden
vulnerability. I'm sending you a reading-list of books you
may find useful. Perhaps you'd like to make a few notes
before our next meeting. Hope to see you back here soon!*

chrysalisbaby: *wish i could be there too (cries)*

13

You are viewing the webjournal of **blueeyedboy** *posting on:*
                          badguysrock@webjournal.com
Posted at: *01.45 on Tuesday, February 5*
Status: *public*
Mood: *predatory*
Listening to: *Nirvana*: 'Smells Like Teen Spirit'

After that, Dr Peacock became a kind of hero to *blueeyedboy*. It would have been surprising had he not: Dr Peacock was everything he admired. Dazzled by his personality, hungry for his approval, he lived for those brief interludes, his visits to the Mansion; hanging on to every word Dr Peacock addressed to him –

All *blueeyedboy* remembers now are fragments of benevolence. A walk through the rose garden; a cup of Earl Grey; a word exchanged in passing. His need had not yet turned to greed, or his affection to jealousy. And Dr Peacock had the gift of making them *all* feel special – not just Ben, but his brothers, too; even Ma, who was hard as nails, was not beyond the reach of his charm.

Then came the year of the entrance exam. Benjamin was ten years old. Three and a half years had passed since his first visit to the Mansion. Over that time, many things had changed. He was no longer bullied at school (since the compass incident, the others had learnt to leave him alone), but he was unhappy, nevertheless. He had acquired the reputation of being *stuck-up* – a cardinal sin in Malbry – which, added to his early status as a freak and a queer, amounted to social suicide.

It didn't help that, thanks to Ma, word of his gift had got around. As a result, even the teachers had come to think of him differently – some of them with resentment. A different child is a difficult child, or so thought the teachers at Abbey Road, and, far from being curious, many were suspicious, some openly sarcastic, as if his Ma's expectations and his own inability to conform to the mediocrity of the place were somehow an attack on *them*.

Ma, and her expectations. Grown stronger than ever, of course, now that the gift was official, now that there was a name for it – an *official* name, a syndrome, that smelt of sickness and sanctity, with its furry dark-grey sibilants and its fruity Catholic undertint.

Not that it mattered, he told himself. Another year and he would be free. Free to attend St Oswald's, which Ma had painted in such attractive colours for him that he was almost taken in, and of which Dr Peacock spoke with such affection that he had put his fears aside and thrown himself into the task of becoming what Dr Peacock expected of him: to be the son he'd never had, *a chip*, as he said, *off the old block* –

Sometimes Benjamin wondered what would happen if he failed the entrance exam. But since Ma had long ago come to believe that the exam was merely a formality, a series of documents to sign before he entered the hallowed gates, he knew that his worries were best left unvoiced.

His brothers were both at Sunnybank Park. *Sunnybanker. Rhymes with wanker*, as he used to say to them, which made Brendan laugh but infuriated Nigel, who – when he could catch him – would sometimes pin him between his knees and punch him till he cried, shouting – *Fuck you, you little freak!* – until at last he'd exhausted himself, or Ma heard and came running –

Nigel was fifteen, and hated him. He'd hated him from the very first, but by then his hatred had blossomed. Perhaps he was jealous of the attention his brother received; perhaps it was merely testosterone. In any case, the more he grew, the more he turned his whole being towards making his brother suffer, regardless of the consequences.

Ben was skinny and undersized. Nigel was already big for his age, sheathed in adolescent muscle, and he had all kinds of virtually untraceable ways of inflicting pain – Chinese burns, nips and pinches, sly shin-kicks under the table – though when he got angry, he forgot discretion and, without any fear of retribution, laid into his brother with fists and feet –

Telling tales only made it worse. Nigel seemed oblivious to punishment: it simply fed his resentment. Beatings made him worse. If he was sent to bed hungry, he would force-feed his brothers toothpaste, or dirt, or spiders, carefully harvested in the attic and put aside for just such an eventuality.

Brendan, always the cautious one, accepted the natural order of things. Perhaps he was brighter than they'd thought. Perhaps he feared retribution. He was also ridiculously squeamish, and if Nigel or Ben got a hiding from Ma, he would cry just as much as either of them – but at least he wasn't a threat, and sometimes even shared his sweets with Ben when Nigel was safely out of the way.

Brendan ate a lot of sweets, and now it was really beginning to show. A soft white roll of underbelly hung over the waistband of his donkey-brown cords, and his chest was plump and girly beneath his baggy brown jumpers, and although he and Ben might have had a chance if they'd stood together against Nigel, Brendan never had the nerve. And so Ben learnt to look after himself, and to run when his brother in black was around.

Other things had changed as well. *Blueeyedboy* was growing up. Always prone to headaches, now he began to suffer from migraines, too, which began as strobing lights shot through with lurid colours. After that would come the tastes and smells, stronger than any he'd known before: rotten eggs; creosote; the lurking stink of the vitamin drink; and then, at last, the sickness, the pain, rolling over him like a rock, burying him alive.

He couldn't sleep; couldn't think; could hardly concentrate at school. As if that wasn't bad enough, his speech, which had always been hesitant, had developed into a full-blown stammer. *Blueeyedboy* knew what it was. His gift – his sensitivity – had now become a poison to him. A poison creeping slowly through his body, changing him as it went from healthy, wholesome blood and bone to something with which even Ma found it difficult to sympathize.

She called the doctor in, of course, who at first put down the headaches to growing pains, and then, when they persisted, to stress.

'Stress? What has he got to be stressed about?' she cried in exasperation.

His silence annoyed her even more, and finally led to a series of uncomfortable interrogations, which left him feeling even worse. He quickly learnt not to complain; to pretend that there was nothing wrong with him, even when he was sick with pain and almost ready to collapse.

Instead, he evolved his own system of coping. He learnt which medicine to steal from Ma's cabinet. He learnt how to combat the phantom sensations with magic words and images. He took them from Dr Peacock's maps; from books; from the dark places of his heart –

Most of all, he dreamed in blue. Blue, the colour of control. He had always associated it with power, power like electricity; now he learnt to visualize himself encased in a shell of burning blue, untouchable, invincible. There, he was safe from everything. There, he could replenish himself. Blue was secure. Blue was serene. Blue, the colour of murder. And he wrote down his dreams in the same Blue Book in which he wrote his stories.

But there are other ways than fic to cope with adolescent stress. All you need is a suitable victim, preferably one who can't fight back: a scapegoat who will take the blame for everything you've suffered.

Benjamin's earliest victims were wasps, which he'd hated since he'd been stung in the mouth as he swigged from a half-empty can of Coke left unguarded in the summer sun. From then on, all wasps were guilty. His revenge was to catch them using traps made from jars half-filled with sugar water, and later to impale them on the tip of a needle and watch as each creature struggled and died, pumping its pale stinger in and out and writhing its horribly corseted body like the world's most diminutive pole dancer.

He showed them to Brendan, too, and watched him writhe in discomfort.

'Ah, don't, that's disgusting—' said Bren, his face contorted with dismay.

'Why, Bren? It's only a wasp.'

144

He shrugged. 'I know. But please—'

Ben pulled the needle free of the wasp. The insect, almost severed now, began to turn sticky somersaults. Bren flinched.

'Happy now?'

'It's still m-moving,' Brendan said, his face awry with fear and disgust.

Ben tipped the contents of the jar on to the table in front of Brendan. 'So kill it,' he said.

'Ah, please, Ben—'

'Go on. Kill it. Put it out of its misery, you fat bastard.'

Brendan was almost crying now. 'I c-can't,' he said. 'I just—'

'Do it!' Ben punched him in the arm. 'Do it, kill it, kill it *now*—'

Some people are born to be killers. Brendan was not one of them. And Benjamin revelled sourly in Brendan's stupid helplessness, his whimpering cries as Ben punched him again, his retreat into the corner, arms wrapped around his head. Brendan never tried to fight back. Ben was three years younger, thirty pounds lighter, and still he beat Brendan easily. It wasn't that he hated him; but his weakness was infuriating, making Ben want to hurt him more, to see him squirm like a wasp in a jar –

It *was* a little cruel, perhaps. Brendan had done nothing wrong. But it gave Ben the sense of control that he lacked, and it helped him to manage his growing stress. It was as if by tormenting his brother he could relocate his own suffering; evade the thing that imprisoned him in its cage of scents and colours.

Not that he thought about it much. His actions were purely instinctive, a self-defence against the world. Later, *blueeyedboy* was to learn that this process was called *transference*. An interesting word, coloured a muddy blue-green, that reminds him of the transfers his brothers used to stick on their arms: cheap and messy fake tattoos that stained the sleeves of their school shirts and got them into trouble in class. But somehow, at last, he learnt to cope. First, with the wasp traps, then with the mice, and finally, with his brothers.

And look at your *blueeyedboy* now, Ma. He has exceeded all expectations. He wears a suit to go to work – or at least, to maintain the pretence. He carries a leather briefcase. The word *technician* is in his job title, as is the word *operator*, and if no one knows quite what he does, it is merely because most ordinary people have no idea how complicated these operations can be.

Doctors rely on machines nowadays, Gloria says to Adèle and Maureen, when she meets them on Friday night. *There are millions of pounds invested there in scanners and MRI machines, and* someone *has to operate them –*

Never mind that the closest he has ever come to any one of those clever machines is vacuuming the dust underneath. You see, words *do* have power, Ma: power to camouflage the truth, to colour it in peacock shades.

Oh, if she knew, she'd make him pay. But she won't find out. He's too careful for that. She may have her suspicions, of course – but he thinks he can get away with it. It's just a question of nerve, that's all. Nerve and timing and self-control. That's all a murderer needs, in the end.

Besides, as you know, I've done it before.

Post comment:

JennyTricks: (*post deleted*).

ClairDeLune: *Jenny, don't you ever get tired of coming here to criticize?*
This is intriguing, **blueeyedboy**. *Did you look at the reading-list I sent you? I'd love to know what you thought of it . . .*

14

You are viewing the webjournal of **Albertine**.
Posted at: *01.55 on Tuesday, February 5*
Status: *restricted*
Mood: *awake*

Nothing in my mailbox tonight. Just a *meme* from *blueeyedboy*, tempting me to come out and play. I'm almost certain he's waiting for me; he often logs on at about this time and stays online into the early hours of the morning. I wonder what he wants from me. Love? Hate? Confessions? Lies? Or is it simply the contact he craves, the need to know I'm still listening? In the small hours of the night, when God seems like a cosmic joke and no one seems to be listening, don't we all need someone to touch? Even you, *blueeyedboy*. Watching me, watching you, through a glass darkly, tapping out on this ouija board my letters to the dead.

Is this why he writes these stories of his, posting them here for me to read? Is it an invitation to play? Does he expect me to answer him with a confession of my own?

Tagged by **blueeyedboy** *posting on* **badguysrock@webjournal.com**
Posted at: *01.05 on Tuesday, February 5*
If you were an animal, what would you be? *An eagle soaring over the mountains.*

Favourite smell? *The Pink Zebra café, on a Thursday lunchtime.*
Tea or coffee? *Why have either, when you can have hot chocolate with cream?*
Favourite flavour of ice cream? *Green apple.*
What are you wearing right now? *Jeans, trainers and my favourite old cashmere sweater.*
What are you afraid of? *Ghosts.*
What's the last thing you bought? *Mimosa. It's my favourite flower.*
What's the last thing you ate? *Toast.*
Favourite sound? *Yo-Yo Ma playing Saint-Saëns.*
What do you wear in bed? *An old shirt that belonged to my boyfriend.*
What's your pet hate? *Being patronized.*
Your worst trait? *Evasiveness.*
Any scars or tattoos? *More than I want to remember.*
Any recurring dreams? *No.*
There's a fire in your house. What would you save? *My computer.*
When did you last cry?

Well – I'd *like* to say it was when Nigel died. But both of us know that isn't true. And how could I explain to him that sly, irrational surge of joy that overshadows the bulk of my grief, this knowledge that something is missing in me, some sense that has nothing to do with my eyes?

You see, I *am* a bad person. I don't know how to cope with loss. Death is a heady cocktail of one part sorrow to three parts relief – I felt it with Daddy, with Mother, with Nigel – even with poor Dr Peacock . . .

Blueeyedboy knew – we both knew – that I was just deluding myself. Nigel never stood a chance. Even our love was a lie from the start, sending out its green shoots like those of a cut branch in a vase; shoots, not of recovery, but of desperation.

Yes, I was selfish. Yes, I was wrong. Even from the start I knew that Nigel belonged to someone else. Someone who never existed. But after years of running away, part of me *wanted* to be that girl; to sink into her like a child into a feather pillow; to forget myself – and everything – in the circle of Nigel's arms. Online friendships were no longer enough. All of a sudden I wanted more. I wanted to be normal: to encounter the world, not through a glass, but through my lips and my fingers. I wanted more than the world online; more than a name at my fingertips. I wanted to be understood, not by someone at a keyboard far away, but by someone I could *touch* . . .

But sometimes a touch can be fatal. I should know; it's happened before. Less than a year later, Nigel was dead, poisoned by proximity. Nigel's girl has proved herself just as toxic as Emily White, sending out death with a single word.

Or, in this case, a letter.

15

The letter arrived on a Saturday, as we were having breakfast. By then Nigel was more or less living here, though he still kept his flat in Malbry, and we had established a kind of routine that almost suited both of us. He and I were nocturnal creatures, happiest at night. Thus Nigel came over at ten o'clock; shared a bottle, talked, made love, slept over and left by nine in the morning. At weekends he stayed longer, sometimes till ten or eleven o'clock, which was why he was there in the first place, and why the letter came to him. On a weekday he wouldn't have opened it, and I could have dealt with it privately. I suppose that, too, was part of the plan. But right then I had no idea of the letter bomb about to explode in our unsuspecting faces –

That morning I was eating cereal, which ticked and popped as the milk sank in. Nigel wasn't eating, or even speaking to me much. Nigel hardly ever ate breakfast, and his silences were ominous, especially in the mornings. Sounds orbiting a central silence like satellites around a baleful planet; the creak of the pantry door; the clatter of spoon against coffee jar; the chink of mugs. A second later, the fridge door opened; rattled; slammed. The kettle boiled; a brief eruption followed by a click of military finality. Then, the clack of the letter box and the stolid double-thump of the post.

Most of my mail is junk mail, though I rarely get mail of any kind. My bills are paid by direct debit. Letters? Why bother. Greetings cards? Forget it.

'Anything interesting?' I said.

For a moment Nigel said nothing at all. I heard the unfolding of paper. A single sheet, unfurled with a dry rasp, like the unsheathing of a sharpened knife.

'Nigel?'

'What?'

He jiggled his foot when he was annoyed; I could hear it against the table leg. And now there was something in his voice; something flat and hard, like an obstacle. He tore the used envelope into halves, then he fingered the single sheet. Stropped it on his thumb, like a blade –

'It isn't bad news, or anything?' I did not speak of what I dreaded most, though I could feel it hanging over me.

'For fuck's sake. Let me read,' he said. Now the obstacle was within my reach; like a sharp-edged table-top in an unexpected place. Those sharp edges never miss; they have a gravity all of their own, pulling me every time into their orbit. And there were so many sharp edges in Nigel; so many zones of restricted access.

It wasn't his fault, I told myself; I would not have had him otherwise. We completed each other in some strange way: his dark moods and my lack of temperament. I am wide open, as he used to say; there are no hidden places in me, no unpleasant secrets. All the better; because deceit, that essentially female trait, is the thing that Nigel despised most of all. Deceit and lies, so alien to him – so alien, he thought, to me.

'I have to go out for an hour or so.' His voice sounded oddly defensive. 'Will you be OK for a while? I have to go to Ma's house.'

Gloria Winter, née Gloria Green, sixty-nine years old and still clutching at the remains of her family with the tenacity of a hungry remora. I knew her as a voice on the line; a rimshot Northern accent; an impatient drumming on the receiver; an imperious way of cutting you off like a gardener pruning roses.

Not that we've ever been introduced. Not officially, anyway. But I know her from Nigel; I know her ways; I know her voice on the telephone and her ominous range of silences. There are other things, too, that he never told me, but that I know only too well. The jealousy; the rancour; the rage; the hatred mixed with helplessness.

He rarely spoke of her to me. He rarely even mentioned her name. Living with Nigel, I soon understood that some subjects were best left alone, and this included his childhood, his father, his brothers, his past and most especially Gloria, who shared, along with her other son, a talent for bringing out the worst in Nigel.

'Can't your brother deal with this?'

I heard him stop on the way to the door. I wondered if he were turning round, fixing me with his dark eyes. Nigel rarely mentioned his brother, and when he did it was all bad. *Twisted little bastard* was about the best I'd heard so far – Nigel never had much objectivity when it came to discussing his family.

'My brother? Why? Has he spoken to you?'

'Of course not. Why would he?'

Another pause. I felt his eyes on the top of my head.

'Graham Peacock's dead,' he said. His voice was curiously flat. 'An accident, by the sound of it. Fell out of his wheelchair during the night. They found him dead in the morning.'

I didn't look up. I didn't dare. Suddenly everything seemed enhanced; the taste of coffee in my mouth; the sound of the birds; the beat of my heart; the table at my fingertips with all its scars and scratches.

'This letter's from your brother?' I said.

Nigel ignored the question: 'It says that the bulk of Peacock's estate – valued at something like three million pounds—'

Another silence. 'What?' I said.

That strangely uninflected voice was somehow more disturbing than rage. 'He's left it all to you,' he said. 'The house, the art, the collections—'

'Me? But I don't even know him,' I said.

'The twisted little *bastard*.'

No need for me to ask who he meant; that phrase was reserved for his brother. So very like him in so many ways, and yet, whenever his name arose, I could almost believe that Nigel could kill a man; could beat him to death with fists and feet . . .

'This must be a mistake,' I said. 'I've never met Dr Peacock. I don't even know what he looks like. Why would he leave his money to me?'

'Well – maybe because of Emily White.' Nigel's voice was colourless.

And now the coffee tasted like dust; the birds fell silent; my heart was a stone. That name had silenced everything – except for the buzz of feedback that began right at the base of my spine, erasing all of the past twenty years in a surge of deadly static . . .

I know I should have told him then. But I'd hidden the truth for so long; believing that Nigel would always be there; hoping for the perfect time; not knowing that *this* time was all we had –

'Emily White,' said Nigel.

'Never heard of her,' I said.

16

When dealt one of life's terrible blows – the death of a parent, the end of a relationship, the positive test result, the guilty verdict, the final step off the tall building – there comes a moment of light-headedness, almost of euphoria, as the string which tethers us to our hopes is cut and we bounce off in another direction, briefly powered by the momentum of release.

The penultimate movement of the *Symphonie fantastique* – 'The March to the Scaffold' – has a similar moment, when the condemned arrives within view of the gallows, and the minor key shifts into a triumphant major, as if at the sight of a friendly face. I know how it feels: that lurch of deliverance, the feeling that the worst has already happened and that the rest is merely gravity.

Not that the worst *had* happened – not yet. But the clouds were gathering. By the time that letter arrived, Nigel had less than an hour to live; and the last thing he ever said to me were the four little syllables of her name, Emily White, like a musical sting performed by the ghost of Beethoven . . .

And Dr Peacock was dead at last. Ex-Master of St Oswald's School, eccentric, genius, charlatan, dreamer, collector, saint, buffoon. Unrelenting in death as in life; somehow it did not surprise me to learn that once more, with the kindest intent, he had torn my life apart.

Not that he could have harmed me. Not intentionally, anyway. Emily always loved him: a large, heavy man with a soft beard and a strangely childlike manner, who read from *Alice in Wonderland* and played old, scratchy records on a wind-up gramophone while she sat on the swing in the Fireplace House and talked about music and painting and poetry and sound. And now the old man was dead at last, and there was no escaping him, or the thing we had helped set in motion.

I don't really know how old Emily was when she first went to the Fireplace House. All I know is that it must have been some time after the Christmas concert, because that is where my memory shorts out for good; one moment I'm there, with the music all around me like some fabulous velvet, the next . . .

Feedback and white noise. A long rush of static, broken occasionally by a sudden burst of perfect sound, a phrase, a chord, a note. I try to make sense of it, but I cannot; too much of it is hidden. Of course there were witnesses; from them I can, if I wish, piece together the variations, if not the fugue. But I trust them less than I trust myself – and besides, I've worked hard to forget all that. Why should I try to remember it now?

When I was a child, and the worst happened – toys broken, affection denied, the small but poignant sorrows of childhood recalled through the mist of adult grief – I always sought refuge in the garden. There was a tree where I loved to sit; I remember its texture, its elephant hide, the sappy, plush scent of dead leaves and moss. Nowadays, when I'm lost and confused, I head for the Pink Zebra. It's the safest place in my world; an escape from myself, a sanctuary. Everything here seems expressly designed to fit my unique requirements.

To begin with, its comfortable size, with every table against a wall. Its menu lists all my favourites. Best of all, unlike the genteel Village, it has no affiliations or pretensions. I am not invisible here, and although that could have its dangers, it's good to be able to walk in and to have people talk *to* you and not *at* you. Even the voices are different here: not reedy like Maureen Pike's or breathy and sour like

Eleanor Vine's or affected like Adèle Roberts's, but rich with the tones of jazz clarinet and sitar and steel drums, with lovely calypso rhythms and lilts, so that just sitting here is almost as good as music.

I headed there that Saturday after Nigel had gone. That name on his lips had unsettled me, and I needed a place to think things out. Somewhere noisy. Somewhere safe. The Zebra was always a refuge for me; always filled with people. Today there were more than usual, all waiting outside the café door; their voices surging around me like animals at feeding-time. Saxophone Man's Jamaican accent. The Fat Girl, with her breathy tone. And orchestrating everything, Bethan, with her Irish lilt, cheery, speaking to everyone, pulling it all together:

'Hey, what's going on? You're late. You should have been here ten minutes ago.'

'Hello, darlin'! What'll it be?'

'You got any more of that chocolate cake?'

'Hang on, I'll have a look for you.'

Thank goodness for Bethan, I told myself. Bethan, my coat of camouflage. I don't think Nigel really understood. He resented all the time I spent at the Pink Zebra; wondered how I could so often prefer the company of strangers to his own. But to understand about Bethan, you have to be able to penetrate the many disguises with which she surrounds herself: the voices, the jokes, the nicknames, the cheery Irish cynicism that hides something closer to the bone.

Underneath all that there's someone else. Someone damaged and vulnerable. Someone trying desperately to make sense of something sad and senseless . . .

'There you are, darlin'. Try that for size. Hot chocolate, with cardamom cream.'

The chocolate is one of my favourites. Served with milk in a tall glass, with coconut and marshmallows, or dark, with a clash of chilli.

'Listen to this. Creepy Dude came in to the Zebra the other day. Sat down just where you're sitting. Ordered the lemon meringue pie. I watched him eat it from over there, then he came back to the counter and ordered another. I watched him eat that, then when he'd finished, he called me over and ordered more pie. Honest to God, darlin', your man must have et six pieces of pie in under half an hour. The Fat Girl was sitting right there opposite him, and I thought her eyes were going to pop out of her head, so I did.'

I sipped my chocolate. It was tasteless. But the warmth was comforting. I carried on the conversation without really paying attention to it, against a wall of background noise as meaningless as waves on a shore.

'Hey, babe, lookin' good—'

'Two espressos, Bethan, please.'

'Six pieces of pie. Imagine that. I've been thinking that maybe he's on the run, that he's shot his lover and he's planning to jump off Beachy Head before the police catch up with him, because six pieces of pie – Jesus God! – now there's a man with nothing to lose—'

'And I told her, I said, "I'm not 'avin' *that*—"'

'Be with you in a minute, babe.'

Sometimes in a noisy room you can pick out the sound of a single voice – sometimes even a single word – that clatters against the wall of sound like an out-of-tune violin in an orchestra.

'Earl Grey, please. No lemon, no milk.'

His voice is unmistakable. Soft and slightly nasal, perhaps, with a peculiar emphasis on the aspirates, like a theatre actor, or maybe a man who once stuttered. And now I could hear the music again, the opening chords of the Berlioz, never very far from my thoughts. Why it had to be *that* piece, I don't know; but it's the sound of my deepest fear, and it sounds to me like the end of the world.

I kept my own voice steady and low. No need to disturb the customers. 'You've really done it now,' I said.

'I have no idea what you're talking about.'

'I'm talking about your letter,' I said.

'What letter?'

'Don't bullshit me,' I said. 'Nigel got a letter today. Given the mood he was in when he left, and given the fact that I only know one person capable of winding him up to that level—'

'I'm glad you think so.' I heard his smile.

'What did you tell him?'

'Not much,' he said. 'But you know my brother. Impulsive. Always getting the wrong idea.' He paused, and once more I heard his smile.

'Perhaps he was shaken by the news of Dr Peacock's legacy. Perhaps he just wanted Ma to be sure that he knew nothing about it—' He took a sip of his Earl Grey. 'You know, I thought you'd be pleased,' he said. 'It's still a magnificent estate. Perhaps the property's a little rundown. Still, nothing that can't be fixed, eh? Then there's the art. The collections. Three million pounds is conservative. I'd estimate it at closer to four—'

'I don't care,' I hissed at him. 'They can give it to someone else.'

'There isn't anyone else,' he said.

Oh yes there is. There's Nigel. Nigel, who trusted me –

How fragile are these things we build. How tragically ephemeral. In contrast, the house is solid as stone; as tiles and beams and mortar. How could we compete with stone? How could our little alliance survive?

'I have to admit,' he said mildly, 'I thought you might show some gratitude. After all, Dr Peacock's estate is likely to bring you a tidy sum – more than enough to get out of this place and buy yourself somewhere decent.'

'I like my life as it is,' I said.

'Really? I'd kill to get out of here.'

I picked up my empty chocolate cup; turned it round and round in my hands. 'So how *did* Dr Peacock die? And how much did he leave *you?*'

A pause. 'That wasn't very kind.'

I lowered my voice to a hiss. 'I don't care. It's over. Everyone's dead—'

'Not quite.'

No, I thought. *Well – maybe not.*

'So you *do* remember.' I heard his smile.

'Not much. You know how old I was.'

Old enough to remember, he means. He thinks I should remember more; but for me now most of those memories exist only as fragments of Emily, some at best contradictory, others, frankly impossible. But I know what everyone else knows: that she was famous; she was unique; college professors wrote theses on what they had begun to call *The Emily White Phenomenon.*

Memory [says Dr Peacock in his thesis 'The Illuminated Man'], is, at best, an imperfect and highly idiosyncratic process. We tend to think of the mind as a fully functioning recording machine, with gigabytes of information – aural, visual and tactile – within easy recall. This could not be further from the truth. Although it is true that in theory, at least, I should be able to remember what I had for breakfast on any particular morning of my life, or the precise wording of a Shakespeare sonnet I had to study as a child, it is more probable that without recourse to drugs or deep hypnosis – both methods being, in any case, highly questionable, given the level of suggestibility in the subject – those particular memories will remain inaccessible to me and will finally degrade, like electrical equipment left in the damp, causing short-outs and cross-wiring until finally the system may default into alternative or backup memory, complete with sense-impressions and internal logic, which may in fact be drawn from a completely different set of experiences and stimuli, but which provides the brain with a compensatory buffer against any discontinuity or obvious malfunction.

Dear Dr Peacock. He always took so long to make a point. If I try hard I can still hear his voice, which was plush and plummy and just a little comic, like the bassoon in *Peter and the Wolf*. He had a house near the centre of town, one of those big, deep old houses with high ceilings, and worn parquet floors, and wide bay windows, and spiky aspidistra, and the genteel smell of old leather and cigars. There was a fireplace in the parlour, a huge thing with a carved overmantel and a clock that ticked; and in the evenings he would burn logs and pine cones in the giant hearth and tell stories to anyone who cared to walk in.

There was constant traffic at the Fireplace House. Students (of course); colleagues; admirers; vagrants on the scrounge for a bite to eat and a cup of tea. Everyone was welcome, as long as they behaved themselves; and as far as I knew, no one had ever abused Dr Peacock's good nature, or caused him any embarrassment.

It was the kind of house where there is something for everyone. There was always a bottle of wine to hand, and a pot of tea standing on the hearth. There was food, too: usually bread and some kind of soup, several fat fruitcakes weighted with plums and brandy, and an enormous barrel of biscuits. There were several cats, a dog called Patch, and a rabbit that slept in a basket under the parlour window.

In the Fireplace House, time stood still. There was no television, no radio, no newspapers or magazines. There were gramophones in every room like great open lilies with tongues of brass; there were shelves and cupboards of records, some small, some as wide as serving dishes, scored close with ancient voices and yawning, scratchy, vinegary strings. There were marbles and bronzes on wobbly tables; strings of jet beads; powder compacts half-filled with fragrant dust; books with autumn pages; globes; fiddly collections of snuffboxes, miniatures, cups and saucers, clockwork dolls. That was home to Emily White, and to think that now I could join her there, a perpetual child in a house of forgotten things, free to do anything I liked . . .

Except, of course, to leave.

I thought I'd managed to get away. To make a new life for myself with Nigel. But I know that was all an illusion now; a game of smoke and mirrors. Emily White never got away. Nor did Benjamin Winter. How could I hope to be different? And do I even understand from what I'm trying to escape?

Emily White?

Never heard of her.

Poor Nigel. Poor Ben. And it hurts, doesn't it, *blueeyedboy*? To be eclipsed by a brighter star, to be ignored and left in the dark, without even a name of your own? Well, now you know how I felt. How I've always felt. How I *still* feel –

'That's all in the past,' I said. 'I hardly remember it any more.'

He poured another cup of Earl Grey. 'It'll all come back eventually.'

'And if I don't *want* it all to come back?'

'I don't believe you'll have the choice.'

Perhaps he was right about that, at least. Nothing ever vanishes. Even after all these years, Emily still shadows me. Now there's an admission, *blueeyedboy*. I'm sure you can see the irony. But the tenor of our relationship is closer in some ways than friendship. Maybe because of the screen that divides us, so like the screen of the confessional.

Perhaps that's what drew me to *badguysrock*. It's a place for people like me, I suppose; a place to confess, if needs be; to tell those stories that ought to be true, even if they are really not. As for *blueeyedboy* – well, I'll admit he draws me too. We fit together so well, he and I; folded together like tissue paper in an album of old photographs, our lives touch in so many ways that we might almost be lovers. And the fiction he writes is so much more true than the fiction on which I have built my life.

I heard his mobile phone beep. In retrospect I think it was the first of those texts of condolence; the messages from his WeJay announcing that his brother was dead.

'Sorry. Got to go,' he said. 'Ma's got lunch on the table. But try to think about what I said. You can't outrun the past, you know.'

When he had gone I considered his words. Perhaps he was right, after all. Perhaps even Nigel would understand. After so many years of seeing the world through a glass darkly, perhaps it was time to face myself; to take back my past and *remember* . . .

But all I can really be sure of now is the impending static in the air, and the first movement of the Berlioz, the 'Rêveries – Passions', gathering like clouds.

PART THREE

white

1

You are viewing the webjournal of **Albertine** *posting on:*
                        badguysrock@webjournal.com
Posted at: *21.39 on Thursday, February 7*
Status: *public*
Mood: *tense*

Her first recorded memory is of a chunk of potter's clay. Bland as butter, later drying to a rough scale on her arms and elbows, it smells of the river behind her house, of the rain on the pavements, of the cellar where she must never, *ever* go, where her mother keeps the winter potatoes in their little coffins, growing their long blind eyes up to the light.

Blue clay, her mother says. She squishes it between starfish fingers. *Make something, Emily. Make a shape.*

The clay is soft; beneath her hands it feels like slippery skin. She brings it to her mouth; it tastes like the side of the bathtub when she puts her tongue against it: warm, soapy, a little sour. *Make a shape*, her mother says; and the little girl's hands begin to explore the piece of slippery blue clay, to stroke it like a wet puppy, to fondle and find the shape inside.

But that's nonsense, of course. She doesn't remember the piece of clay. In fact, there are no memories at all of those years that she can altogether trust. She has learnt by imitation; she can reel off every word. And she knows that there *was* a piece of clay; for years it stood in the studio, hard and dense as a fossilized head.

Later, it sold to a gallery, nicely mounted and cast in bronze. Rather overpriced, perhaps; but there's always a market for that kind of thing. Murder memorabilia, hangman's nooses, pieces of bone; the trappings of notoriety, sold to collectors everywhere.

She had hoped for a better memorial. But this, she thinks, will have to do. For want of proper memories, she will take the clay head cast in bronze, and the letters chiselled into the brass nearly thirty years ago.

First Impressions (the inscription says).

Emily White, aged 3.

Post comment:

blueeyedboy: **Albertine,** *I'm speechless. You have no idea how much this means to me. Will there be more of this? Please?*

Albertine: *Maybe. If you want it so badly . . .*

2

You are viewing the webjournal of **Albertine** posting on:
badguysrock@webjournal.com
Posted at: 22.45 on Thursday, February 7
Status: public
Mood: determined

Her mother was an artist. Colours were her whole life. Emily White learnt to crawl on the floor of her mother's workshop; before she could speak she already knew the powdery smell of the watercolours and the chalks, the metallic scent of the acrylics, the smoky reek of the oils. Her mother smelt of turpentine; the child's first word was 'paper'; her first playthings were the rolls of parchment kept under the desk; she remembered their fascinating crinkle, their dusty smell.

As her mother worked Emily learnt to know the sounds of her progress: the fat sloshing of the background brushes; the scratching of nibs; the soft *hishh* of pastels and sponges; the *scree* of scissors; the scrubbing of pencils on art paper.

These were the rhythms of her mother; sometimes accompanied by small sounds of irritation or satisfaction, sometimes by pacing, most often by a running commentary of colour and shade. By the time she was a year old, Emily had still not learnt to walk, but could name all the colours in her mother's box of paints. Their names rang out like chimes in her head: *damson, umber, ochre, gold; madder, violet, crimson, rose.*

Violet was her favourite; the tube had been squeezed almost empty, then curled up like a party favour to eke out the rest. White was full, but only because the tube was new; black was dry and seldom used, pushed to the back of the paintbox among the hairless brushes and cleaning-rags.

'Pat, she's a slow developer. Einstein was the same.' That must be a false memory, she thinks, like so many from those early days: her mother's voice high above her, Daddy's tentative reply.

'But sweetheart, the doctor—'

'Damn the doctor! She can name every colour in the box.'

'She's just repeating what you tell her.'

'She is *not!*'

A familiar high note quivers in her mother's voice, a vinegary note that catches at her sinuses and makes her eyes water. She does not know its name – not yet, though later she will know it as F sharp – but she can pick it out on Daddy's piano. But that's a secret even from her mother; the hours spent together at the old Bechstein, Daddy with his pipe in his mouth, Emily sitting in his lap with her small hands just touching the keyboard as he plays the *Moonlight Sonata* or *Für Elise* and her mother thinks she is in bed.

'Catherine, please—'

'She can see *perfectly!*'

The smell of turpentine intensifies. It is the smell of her mother's distress, and of her terrible disappointment. She scoops the child up in her arms – Emily's face pressed into the front of her overalls – and as she turns, Emily's feet drag across the work-bench, scattering tubes and pots and paintbrushes, *rat-tat-tat* over the parquet floor.

'Catherine, listen—' Her father's voice, as always, is humble, almost apologetic. As always, he smells faintly of Clan tobacco, though officially he never smokes in the house. 'Catherine, please—'

But she is not listening. Instead she holds the child and moans: 'You can see, can't you, Emily, my darling? *Can't* you?'

It *must* be a false memory. Emily was barely a year old; surely she could not have understood or remembered anything so well. And yet she seems to recall it so clearly: her bewildered tears, her mother's cries, and her father's mumbled counterpoint. The smell of the studio and the paint from her mother's overalls sticking her fingertips together, and all the time that high F sharp tremor in her mother's voice, the note of her thwarted expectations, like a persistent harmonic on an over-tightened string.

Daddy knew almost from the first. But he was a meek, reflective little man, a foil to her mother's rages. Even as a small child Emily sensed that she thought him inferior; that he had disappointed her. Perhaps because of his lack of ambition; perhaps because it had taken him ten years to give her the child she longed for. He was a music teacher at St Oswald's; he played several instruments, but the piano was the only one her mother tolerated in the house, and the rest were sold, one by one, to pay for her treatments and therapies.

It was no real sacrifice, Daddy said. After all, he had access to all his department's resources. It was only fair; Emily's mother suffered from headaches, and Emily was a restive infant, apt to wake at the slightest noise. As a result he transferred his records and his music to the school; he could always listen to them at lunchtimes or Break, and besides, school was where he spent most of his time.

You have to understand what it was like for her.

That's Daddy speaking; always making excuses, always ready to stand in her defence, like a tired old knight in the service of a mad queen who has lost her empire. It took Emily a long time to understand the cause of Daddy's subservience. Daddy had been unfaithful once, with a woman who meant nothing to him, but to whom he had given a child. And now he owed Catherine a debt – a debt that could never be repaid – which meant that for the rest of his life he would always accept second place, never complaining, never protesting, never seeming to hope for anything more than to serve her, to give her what she wanted, to redeem the irredeemable.

Babe, you have to understand.

They managed on his salary; she took it as her natural right to pursue her artistic ambitions while Daddy worked to keep them both. From time to time a little gallery sold one of her mother's collages. Little by little her mother's ambition shifted. She was born before her time, she said. Future generations would know her. What might have turned her inwards made her fiercely determined; she threw her heart into having a baby, long after Daddy's small expectations had ceased.

Finally, Emily came. *Oh, the plans we made* – that's Daddy talking, though I doubt whether he was allowed any part in the planning of Emily's young life – *The dreams we had for you, Emily.* For seven and a half months Emily's mother became almost domesticated: knitted bootees in pastel colours; played whale music for a stress-free delivery; wanted a natural birth but took gas at the final moment. So that it was Daddy who counted Emily's fingers and toes, holding his breath at the squalling amazement at his fingertips; the hairless monkey with its eyes squinched shut and its tiny fists clenched.

Darling, she's perfect.

Oh, my God –

But she was nearly two months premature. They gave her too much oxygen; the process detached her retinas. No one noticed straight away; in those days it was enough to know that Emily had all her limbs. When later her blindness became more apparent, Catherine denied it.

Emily was a *special* child, she said. Her gifts would take time to develop. Her mother's friend Feather Dunne – an amateur astrologer – had already predicted a brilliant future: a mystical union between Saturn and the Moon confirmed that she was exceptional. When the doctor became impatient, Emily's mother removed herself to an alternative therapist, who recommended eyebright, massage and colour therapy. For three months she lived in a haze of incense and candles; lost interest in her canvases; never even combed her hair.

Daddy suspected post-natal depression. Catherine denied it, but veered periodically from one extreme to the other: one day protective, refusing to allow him near; the next sitting unresponsive, heedless of the bundle at her side that squalled and squalled.

Sometimes it was worse than that, and Daddy had to turn to the neighbours for help. There had been a mistake, said Catherine; the hospital had mixed up the babies; had somehow given away her perfect baby for this damaged one.

Look at it, Patrick, she would say. *It doesn't even look like a baby. It's hideous. Hideous.*

She told Emily that when she was five. There could be no secrets between them, she said; they were part of each other. *Besides, love is a kind of madness, isn't it, darling? Love is a kind of possession.*

Yes, that was her voice; that was Catherine White. *She feels things more than the rest of us,* so Emily's father used to say, as if in apology for apparently feeling so much less. And yet it was Daddy who kept things going, during her breakdown and afterwards; Daddy who paid the bills, who cooked and cleaned; who changed and fed; who every day guided Catherine gently into her abandoned studio and showed her the brushes and paints and her baby crawling among the rolls of paper and the crunchy curls of wood.

One day she picked up a paintbrush, inspected it for a moment, then put it down again; but it was the first interest she had shown for months, and Daddy took it as a sign of improvement. It was: by the time Emily was two years old, her mother's creative passion had returned; and although now it was channelled almost exclusively through the child, it was no less ardent than before.

It began with that head in blue clay. But clay, though interesting enough, did not retain her attention for long. Emily wanted new things; she wanted to touch, to smell, to feel. The studio had become too small to contain her; she learnt to follow walls into other rooms; to find the good place under the window where the sun shone; to use the tape-recorder to listen to stories; to open up the piano and to play the notes one-fingered. She loved to play with her mother's tin of loose buttons; to push her hands deep inside; to slither them out on to the floor and arrange them by size, shape and texture.

In every way but one, you see, Emily was an ordinary child. She loved stories, which her father would record for her; she loved to walk in the park; she loved her parents; she loved her dolls. She had a small child's small, infrequent tantrums; she enjoyed her visits to the farm in Pog Hill, and dreamed of getting a puppy.

By the time Emily learnt to walk, her mother had almost accepted her blindness. Specialists were expensive, and their conclusions were inevitably variations on the same theme. Her condition was irreversible; she responded only to the brightest of direct lights, and then only a very, very little. She could not distinguish shapes; could barely recognize movement, and had no awareness of colour.

But Catherine White was not to be defeated. She flung herself into Emily's education with all the energy she had once given to her work. First, clay, to develop spatial awareness and encourage creativity. Next, numbers, on a large wooden abacus with beads that clicked and clacked. Then letters, using a Braille slate and an embossing machine. Then, on Feather's advice, 'colour therapy', designed, so she said, to stimulate the visual parts of the cortex by image association.

'If it can work for Gloria's boy, then why can't it work for Emily?'

This was the phrase she used every time Daddy tried to protest. It didn't matter that Gloria's boy was a different case entirely; all that mattered to Catherine White was that Ben – or *Boy X*, as Dr Peacock called him, with typical pretentiousness – had somehow acquired an extra sense; and if the son of a cleaner could do it, then why not little Emily?

Little Emily, of course, had no idea what they were talking about. But she wanted to please; she was eager to learn, and the rest just followed naturally.

The colour therapy worked, to a point. Although the words themselves held no more meaning for Emily than the names of the colours in her paintbox, *green* brings back the memory of summer lawns and cut grass. *Red* is the scent of Bonfire Night; the sound of crackling wood; the heat. *Blue* is water; silent; cool.

'Your name is a colour, too, Emily,' said Feather, who had long, tickly hair that smelt of patchouli and cigarette smoke. 'Emily White. Isn't that lovely?'

White. Snow white. So cold it is almost hot at the fingertips, freezing, burning.

'Emily. Don't you love the pretty snow?'

No, I don't, Emily thinks. Fur is pretty. Silk is pretty. Buttons are pretty in the tin, or rice, or lentils slipping *frrrrrrpp* through the fingers. There's nothing pretty about snow, which hurts your hands and makes the steps slippery. Anyway, white isn't a colour. White is the ugly *brrrrr* you get between radio stations, when the sound breaks up and there's nothing left but noise. White noise. White snow. Snow White, half-dead, half-sleeping under glass.

When she was four, Daddy suggested that Emily might go to school. Maybe in Kirby Edge, he said, where there was a facility. Catherine refused to discuss it, of course. With Feather's help, she said, her teaching had already worked a near-miracle. She had always known Emily was an exceptional child; she was not to waste her gifts in a school for blind children where she would be taught rug-making and self-pity, nor in a mainstream school where she would always be second-rate. No, Emily was to continue to receive tuition from home, so that when she eventually regained her sight – and there was no doubt at all in Catherine's mind that this would happen some day – she would be ready to face whatever the world chanced to offer her.

Daddy protested as strenuously as he could. It was not nearly enough; Feather and Catherine barely heard him. Feather believed in past lives, and thought that if the correct parts of Emily's brain were stimulated, then she would regain her visual memory; and Catherine believed . . .

Well, you know what Catherine believed. She could have lived with an ugly child; even a deformed child. But a blind child? A child with no understanding of colours?

Colours, colours, colours. Green, pink, gold, orange, purple, scarlet, blue. Blue alone has a thousand variations: cerulean, sapphire, cobalt, azure; from sky-blue to deepest midnight, passing through indigo and navy, powder-blue to electric-blue, forget-me-not, turquoise and aqua and Saxe. You see, Emily could understand the *notation* of colours. She knew their terms and their cadences; she learnt to repeat the notes and arpeggios of their seven-tone scale. And yet the *nature* of colours still eluded her. She was like a tone-deaf person who has learnt to play the piano, knowing that what he hears is nothing like music. But she could perform; oh yes; she could.

'See the daffodils, Emily.'

'Pretty daffodils. Sunny yellow-golden daffodils.' As a matter of fact, they felt ugly to the touch; cold and somehow *meaty*, like slices of ham. Emily much preferred the fat silky leaves of the lamb's tongue, or the lavenders with their nubbly flower-heads and sleepy smell.

'Shall we paint the daffodils, sweetheart? Would you like Cathy to help you?'

The easel was set up in the studio. There was a big paintbox on the left, with the colours labelled in Braille. Three pots of water stood to the right, and a selection of brushes. Emily liked the sable brushes best. They were the best quality, and soft as the end of a cat's tail. She liked to run them along the place just underneath her lower lip, a place of such sensitivity that she could feel every hair on a paintbrush, and where the nap of a piece of velvet ribbon was the most exquisitely discerned. The paper – thick, glossy art paper with its new, clean-bedclothes smell – was fastened to the easel with bulldog clips, and was sectioned into squares like a chessboard, by means of wires stretched across the paper. That way, Emily could be sure of not straying outside the picture, or confusing sky with trees.

'Now for the trees, Emily. Good. That's good.'

Trees are tall, Emily thinks. Taller than my father. Catherine lets her touch them, puts her face to their rough sides, like hugging a beardy man. There's a smell, too, and a hint of movement, far away but still connected, still touching somehow. 'It's windy,' Emily suggests, trying hard. 'The tree's moving in the wind.'

'Good, darling! Very good!'

Splosh, splash. Now the white, no-colour paper is green. She knows this because her mother hugs her. Emily feels her trembling. There is a note in her voice, too – not F sharp this time, but something less shrill and teary – and something in Emily swells with pride and happiness, because she loves her mother; she loves the smell of turpentine because it is the smell of her mother; she loves the painting lessons because they make her mother proud – although later, when it is over and she creeps back to the studio and tries in vain to understand *why* it makes her so happy, Emily can feel only the tiniest roughening and crinkling of the paper, like hands after washing-up. That's all she can feel, even with her lower lip. She tries not to feel too disappointed. There must be something there, she thinks. Her mother says so.

Post comment:
blueeyedboy: *That was beautiful,* **Albertine**.
Albertine: *Glad you liked it,* **blueeyedboy** . . .

3

You are viewing the webjournal of **blueeyedboy** *posting on:*
badguysrock@webjournal.com
Posted at: *04.16 on Friday, February 8*
Status: *public*
Mood: *creative*
Listening to: The *Moody Blues*: 'The Story In Your Eyes'

Poor Emily. Poor Mrs White. So close and yet so far apart. What had started with Mr White and our hero's abortive quest for his father had broadened into a kind of obsession with the whole of the household: with Mrs White, her husband, and most of all, with Emily, the little sister he might have had if things had turned out differently.

And so, all through that summer, the summer of his eleventh year, *blueeyedboy* followed them in secret, ritually noting their comings and goings; their clothes; the things they liked to do; their haunts, in the cloth-backed Blue Book that served him as a journal.

He followed them to the sculpture park where little Emily liked to play; to the open farm with its piglets and lambs; to the pottery workshop café in town, where for the price of a cup of tea you could buy and shape a lump of clay, to be baked in the oven the same day, then painted and taken home to take pride of place on some mantelpiece, in some cabinet.

The Saturday of the blue clay, Emily was four years old. *Blueeyedboy* had spotted her with Mrs White, walking slowly down the hill into Malbry, Emily in a little red coat that made her look like an unseasonal Christmas bauble, her little dark head bobbing up and down, Mrs White in boots and a blue print dress, her long blonde hair trailing down her back. He followed them all the way into town, keeping close to the hedges that lined the road. Mrs White never noticed him, not even when he ventured close, shadowing her blue silhouette with the doggedness of a junior spy.

Blueeyedboy, junior spy. He liked the stealthy sound of the phrase, its pearly string of sibilants, its secret hint of gunsmoke. He followed them into Malbry town centre, and into the pottery workshop, where Feather was waiting at a table for four, a cup of coffee in front of her, a half-smoked cigarette between her elegant fingers.

Blueeyedboy would have liked to have joined them there, but Feather's presence daunted him. Since that first day at the market, he had sensed that she didn't like him somehow, that she thought he wasn't good enough for Mrs White or Emily. So he sat at a table behind them, trying to look casual, as if he had money to spend there and business of his own to conduct.

Feather eyed him suspiciously. She was wearing a brown ethnic-print dress and a lot of tortoiseshell bangles that clattered as she moved the hand holding the half-smoked cigarette.

Blueeyedboy avoided her gaze and pretended to look out of the window. When he dared to look back again, Feather was talking quite loudly to Mrs White, elbows on the table, occasionally tapping a little cone of cigarette ash into her empty teacup.

The pretty waitress came up to him. 'Are you all together?' she said.

Blueeyedboy realized that she had assumed that he had come in with Mrs White, and before he could stop himself, he'd said yes. Against the sound of Feather's voice, his small deception went unnoticed, and in a few moments the waitress had brought him a Pepsi and a lump of clay, with the kindly instruction to call for her if ever he needed anything more.

He was not sure what he'd intended to make. A dog for Ma's collection, perhaps; something to put on the mantelpiece. Something – anything – to draw her away, even for an instant, from the Mansion, Dr Peacock's work, and aspects of synaesthesia.

He watched them over his Pepsi, looking askance at Emily with her starfish hands splayed around her lump of blue clay. Feather was encouraging her, saying: *Make something, darling. Make a shape.* Mrs White was leaning forward, tensed with hope and expectancy, her long hair hanging so close to the clay that it looked as if it might stick there.

'What's it going to be? A face?'

There came a sound from Emily that might have been acquiescence.

'And those are the *eyes*, and there's the *nose*—' said Feather, sounding ecstatic, though *blueeyedboy* couldn't see anything much to provoke such rapt excitement.

Emily's hands moved on the clay, gouging a hole here and there, exploring with her fingertips, scraping her nails around the back to form the semblance of hair. Now he could see it *was* a head, though primitive and misshapen, with bat's ears and a ludicrous pseudo-scientist's brow that dwarfed the other features. The eyes were shallow thumbprints; barely even visible.

But Feather and Mrs White crowed in delight, and *blueeyedboy* drew closer to them, trying to see what it was in their eyes that made it so remarkable.

Feather gave him a dirty look. He pulled away from the table at once. But Mrs White had noticed him, and instead of pleased recognition, he saw a look of alarm in her eyes, as if she thought he might hurt Emily, as if he could be dangerous –

'What are *you* doing here?' she said.

He gave a shrug. 'N-nothing.'

'Where are your brothers? Your mother?'

He shrugged. Faced with his long-pursued quarry at last, he found that speech had abandoned him, leaving nothing but broken syllables and a stammer that rendered him helpless.

'You're following me,' said Mrs White. 'What do you want?'

Again, he shrugged. He couldn't have explained it to her even if they had been alone, and Feather's presence by her side made it even less possible. He twisted on the seat of his chair, feeling trapped and foolish, with the taste of the vitamin drink in his throat, and his forehead like a squeezed balloon –

Feather narrowed her eyes at him. 'You know this counts as harassment,' she said. 'Catherine could call the police.'

'He's only a boy,' said Mrs White.

'Boys grow up,' said Feather darkly.

'What do you want?' said Mrs White again.

'I-I just w-wanted to s-see E-Emily,' said *blueeyedboy*, feeling nauseous. He looked at the lump of untouched clay and the half-drunk Pepsi at his side. He hadn't intended to order them. He had no money to pay for them. And now here was Mrs White's friend talking about calling the police –

He really meant to tell her the truth. But now he hardly knew what that was. He had thought that when he spoke to her he would know what it was that he wanted to say. But now, as the vegetable stink increased and the ache in his head intensified, he knew that what he wanted from her was something far closer to the bone; a word that came clothed in shades of blue . . .

Late that night, alone in his room, he took out the Blue Book from under his bed and, instead of his journal, began to write a story.

Post comment:

ClairDeLune: *Interesting, how this fic explores the evolution of the creative process. If you don't mind, I'd like to circulate this to some of my other students – or maybe we could discuss it here?*

4

You are viewing the webjournal of **blueeyedboy**.
Posted at: *22.40 on Friday, February 8*
Status: *restricted*
Mood: *ominous*
Listening to: *Jarvis Cocker:* 'I Will Kill Again'

Eleanor Vine called round early tonight while Ma was getting ready to go out, and took the opportunity to take Yours Truly to task again. It seems that my continuing absence from our writing-as-therapy group has been noted and commented upon. She doesn't attend herself, of course – too many people; too much dirt – but I guess Terri must have talked.

People talk to Eleanor. She seems to invite confidences, somehow. And I can see how it's killing her that she has known me all this time and still has no more knowledge of me than when I was four years old –

'You really should go back, you know,' she says. 'You need to get out more. Make new friends. Besides, you owe it to your Ma—'

Owe it to Ma? Don't make me laugh.

I adjusted my iPod earpiece. It's the only way I can deal with her. Through it, in his rasping voice, Jarvis Cocker confided to me what, if given half a chance, he would do to someone like Eleanor –

She gave me a look of fish-eyed reproach. 'I hear there's someone who's missing you.'

'Really?' I feigned innocence.

'Don't be coy. She likes you.' She gave me a nudge. 'You could do worse.'

'Yeah. Thanks, Mrs Vine.'

Interfering old trout. As if that collection of fucktards and losers could ever throw up a live one. I know who she means; I'm not interested. In my earpiece Cocker's voice shifted registers, now soaring plaintively towards the octave:

And don't believe me if I claim to be your friend
'Cos given half the chance I know that I will kill again . . .

But Eleanor Vine is persistent as glue. 'You could be a nice-looking young man, once those bruises have disappeared. You don't want to be selling yourself short. I've seen you hanging around that girl, and you know as well as I do that if your Ma knew, there'd be hell to pay.'

I flinched at that. 'I don't know what you mean.'

'That girl in the Pink Zebra. The one with all the tattoos,' she said.

'Who, Bethan?' I said. 'She hates me.'

Eleanor raised an eyebrow that was mostly skin and wire. 'On first-name terms, then, are we?' she said.

'I hardly ever speak to her, except to order Earl Grey.'

'That's not what *I've* heard,' said Eleanor.

That'll be Terri, I told myself. She sometimes goes into the Zebra. In fact, I think she follows me. It's getting quite hard to avoid her.

'Bethan's not my type,' I said.

Eleanor seemed to calm down after that, the roguish expression returning to her sharp and avid features. 'So – you'll think about what I said, then? A girl like our Terri won't wait around for ever. You're going to have to do something soon—'

I gave a sigh. 'All right,' I said.

She gave me an approving look. 'I knew you'd see sense. Now – I have to go. I know your Ma's got her salsa class. But keep me up to date, won't you? And remember what they always say—'

I wondered what cliché she would use this time. *Faint heart never won fair lady?* Or: *Best strike while the iron's hot?*

As it was, she didn't have the chance, because Ma came in just at that moment, all in black, with sequins. Her dancing shoes had six-inch heels. I didn't envy her partner.

'Eleanor! What a surprise!'

'Just having a chat with B.B.,' she said.

'That's nice.' I thought Ma's eyes narrowed a little.

'I'm surprised he doesn't have a girlfriend,' said Eleanor, with a sideways glance. 'If I were twenty years younger,' she said, addressing her words to my mother now, 'I swear I'd marry him myself.'

I considered Mrs Vine in blue. It suited her.

'Really,' said Ma.

I suppose she means well, I told myself, even though she has no idea what she's dealing with. She's only trying to do what's best, as Ma always tries to do what's best for me. But *Our Terri*, as she calls her, is hardly the stuff of fantasy. Besides, I have no time for romance. I have other fish to fry.

Mrs Vine gave me something that I guessed was meant to be a smile. 'Can you drop me off at home? I'd walk, but I know you'll be driving your ma, and—'

'Yes,' I said. 'You have to go.'

5

You are viewing the webjournal of **blueeyedboy** posting on:
badguysrock@webjournal.com
Posted at: 23.49 on Saturday, February 9
Status: public
Mood: clean
Listening to: Genesis: 'One For The Vine'

He calls her Mrs Chemical Blue. Hygiene and neatness are her concern; something that, in fifteen years, has gone beyond reason – or even a joke. Biscuits eaten over the sink; windows washed daily; dusting ten, twenty times a day; ornaments on the mantelpiece rearranged every quarter of an hour. She was always house-proud – *and what an odd word,* he thinks to himself, recalling what he knows of that house, and the way she used to watch his Ma at work, thin hands clenched in fearful distress, her face rigid with anxiety that a dishtowel might be left disastrously unaligned, or a mat slightly askew to the door, or a speck of dust left on a rug, or even a knick-knack out of place.

Mr Chemical Blue has long gone, taking their teenage son with him. Perhaps she regrets it a little, sometimes; but children are so messy, she thinks, and she never could make him understand how hiring a cleaner only complicated things; caused her, not less, but more work; meant something else to supervise, another person in the house, another set of fingerprints – and although she knew no one was to blame, she found their presence unbearable – yes, even that sweet little boy – until finally they had to go –

183

Since then, of course, it has worsened. With no one to keep her under control, obsession has taken over her life. No longer content with her spotless house, she has progressed to compulsive hand-washing and near-toxic doses of Listerine. Always slightly neurotic, fifteen years of alcohol and antidepressants have taken their toll on her personality so that now, at fifty-nine years old, she is nothing but twitches and tics, a nervous system out of control, thinly upholstered in wan flesh.

No one would miss her, he tells himself. In fact, it would probably be a relief. An anonymous gift to her family: to her son, who visits twice a year and who can hardly bear to see her like this; to her husband, who has moved on, and whose guilt has grown like a tumour; to her niece, who lives in despair of her perpetual interference and her well-meant but disastrous attempts to fix her up with a nice young man.

Besides, she, too, deserves to die; if only for the waste of time, for sunny days spent indoors, for words unspoken, for smiles unnoticed, for all the things she could have done if only she could have settled for *less* –

Only gossip sustains her now. Gossip, rumour and speculation, disseminated via telephone lines on to the parish grapevine. Behind her lace curtains, she sees all. Nothing goes unnoticed to her; no lingering speck of human dirt. No crime, no secret, no petty aberration goes unreported. Nothing escapes examination. No one evades judgement. Does she ever sometimes wish that she could put it all aside, throw open the door and breathe the air? Does she sometimes wonder whether her obsessive attention to cleanliness does not hide a different kind of dirt?

She may have done so, long ago. But now all she can do is watch. Like a crab in its shell, like a barnacle, battened tight against the world. What does she do in there all day? No one is allowed to enter the house unless they leave their shoes outside. Teacups are disinfected before and after use. Groceries are delivered to the front porch. Even the postman deposits the mail, not through the door, but into a metal box by the gate, to be retrieved furtively, and at speed, by Mrs Chemical Blue, wearing Marigolds, her pale eyes wide

184

with the daily unease of traversing six feet of unsanitized space . . .

It's a challenge he cannot resist. To erase her like a difficult stain; to oust her like a parasite; to winkle her out of her shell and force her into the open again.

But in the end, it's easy. It requires only subterfuge and some small expense. A hired white minivan, bearing the insignia of an imaginary firm; a baseball cap and a dark-blue jumpsuit with the same firm's logo embroidered on the top pocket; sundry items ordered via the Internet, paid on a borrowed credit card and delivered to a PO box in town; plus a clipboard to give him authority, and a glossy illustrated brochure (wholly produced on his desktop PC) extolling the virtues of an industrial cleaning product of such efficiency that it has only now been granted a licence for (strictly limited) domestic use.

He explains all this through a crack in the door, from which Mrs Chemical Blue's eye watches him with a jellyfish glaze. For a moment, fear outstrips her desire; and then she caves in, as he knows she will, and invites the nice young man inside.

This time, he really wants to watch. So he wears a mask for the crucial part, bought from an Army surplus store. The gas, purchased from a US website claiming to deal with unwanted parasites, remains officially untested on humans, as yet – although a local dog has already contributed to his research, with very promising results. Mrs Chemical Blue should last longer, he thinks; but given her poor immunity and the nervous rise and fall of her chest, he is fairly sure of the outcome.

Still, he expects to feel something more. Guilt, perhaps; even pity. Instead he feels only scientific curiosity mixed with that childlike sense of wonder at the smallness of it all. Death is no big deal, he thinks. The difference between life and its opposite can be as small as a blood clot, as insignificant as a bubble of air. The body is, after all, a machine. He knows a little about machines. The greater the number of moving parts, the greater the chance of things going wrong. And the body has so many moving parts –

Not for long, he tells himself.

The agonal phase (this being the term used by clinicians to describe the visible part of life's attempt to detach itself from protoplasm too compromised to sustain it) lasts for slightly less than two minutes according to his Seiko watch. He tries to observe dispassionately, to avoid the twitching hands and feet of the dying woman on the floor and to try to determine the goings-on behind those peculiar jellyfish eyes, the final, barking gasps for breath –

For a moment the sound makes him queasy, as for a fleeting moment (is there any other kind?) a phantom taste accompanies it – a taste of rotten fruit and dead cabbage – but he forces himself to ignore it by concentrating on Mrs Chemical Blue, whose agonal phase is coming to an end, her floating eyes beginning to glaze, her lips now a shade between cyan and mauve.

In the end, he does not know enough about anatomy to be absolutely certain of the true cause of death. But as Hippocrates used to say: *Man is an obligate aerobe.* Which probably means, he later concludes, that Mrs Chemical Blue died because her aerobically obligated cells failed to receive enough oxygen, thereby resulting in lethal shock.

In other words, therefore, *not my fault.*

His latex gloves have left no prints on the well-polished surfaces. His boots are new, right out of the box, and leave no telltale traces of mud. A window left open will disperse the smell from the offending canister, which he will toss into a skip as he passes the municipal dump before returning the van – minus its logo – to the firm from which he hired it. Her death will look like an accident – a seizure, a stroke, a heart attack – and even if they suspect foul play, there's nothing to make them suspect him.

He burns the jumpsuit and the workman's cap on the bonfire of leaves in his back yard, and the scent of that burning – like Bonfire Night – reminds him of toffee and candyfloss and the turning of fairground wheels in the dark; things that his mother always denied him, though his brothers went to the fair, coming home sticky-fingered and stinking of smoke, and queasy from the carnival rides, while he remained safely indoors, where nothing bad could happen to him.

Today, however, he is free. He rakes the heart of the bonfire and feels its heat against his face; and he feels a surge of sudden release –

And he knows he's going to do it again. He even knows who the next one will be. He breathes in that scent of bonfire smoke, thinks of her face, and smiles to himself –

And all around him, the colours flare like fireworks exploding in the sky.

Post comment:

ClairDeLune: *We need to talk about this,* **blueeyedboy.** *I think the way in which your fiction is developing sheds interesting insights on your family relationships. Why don't you message me later today? I'd really like to discuss it with you.*

JennyTricks: (*post deleted*).

blueeyedboy: *Hello again. Do I know you?*

JennyTricks: (*post deleted*).

JennyTricks: (*post deleted*).

JennyTricks: (*post deleted*).

blueeyedboy: *Please, Jenny. Do I know you?*

6

You are viewing the webjournal of **blueeyedboy**.
Posted at: *14.38 on Sunday, February 10*
Status: *restricted*
Mood: *sleepless*
Listening to: *Van Morrison:* 'Wild Night'

Lots of love to my journal today. Mostly in response to my fic, which Clair believes is a breakthrough in style, Toxic assures me *pwns ass*, Cap summarizes as *fuckin' resplendent, man*, and Chryssie, who is still sick, thinks is *awesome (and really hott!)*.

Well, sick she may be, but Chryssie is happy. She has lost six pounds this week – which means, according to her online calorie counter, that, assuming she keeps to her present rate, she will achieve her weight loss goal by this August, rather than July of next year – and she sends love and virtual hugs to her friend *azurechild*, who has always been so supportive.

Clair, however, is upset. She has received an e-mail from Angel Blue. Or rather, from a representative, telling her to cease her correspondence with Angel forthwith, and threatening legal action.

Poor Clair is hurt and indignant. She has never sent any offensive letters or suspicious packages, either to Angel or to his wife. Why would she? She worships Angel. She respects his privacy. She is certain his wife is behind all this. Angel is too nice, she says, to do this to someone who has become, over the months, a friend.

Mrs Angel's jealousy is proof of what she has long since suspected:

that Angel's marriage is in crisis; or may even have been a sham from the start. Her online pleas to Angel Blue have begun to attract an audience. Some post to tell her to get a life. Some encourage her to pursue her dream. Some have tales of their own to tell of disappointment, love and revenge. One correspondent, *Hawaiianblue*, urges her to hold fast, to gain her man's attention by force, to show him some token of her love that no one could possibly mistake –

And *Albertine* has been posting fic. I take this as a good sign; now that she has in some way recovered from the shock of my brother's death, she has been online every day.

During their time together, of course, her presence was far less regular. Sometimes several weeks would pass without her even logging on. As webmaster, I can track her movements: how many times she visits the site; what she posts there; what she reads.

I know that she follows everything I write, even the comments. She reads Clair's entries, too, and Chryssie's – I know she is concerned about Chryssie's dieting. She doesn't talk to Cap much – I sense he makes her uncomfortable – but *Toxic69* is a regular correspondent, perhaps because of his handicap. To some, these online friendships can take on a disproportionate significance, especially for those of us for whom the world on screen is more real, more tangible than what lies outside.

Today, she wanted to talk to me. Perhaps it was because of Nigel's funeral, or my last fic. She may have found it disturbing. In fact, I was rather hoping she would. In any case, she came to me, via our private messaging service. Hesitant, shaken, slightly indignant, a child in need of comforting.

Where do you get these stories you write? Why do you have to tell them here?

Ah. The perennial question. Where do stories come from? Are they like dreams, shaped by our subconscious? Do goblins bring them in the night? Or are they all simply forms of the truth, mirror versions of what could have been, twisted and plaited like corn dollies into a plaything for children?

Perhaps I have no choice, I type. It's closer to the truth than she thinks.

A pause. I'm used to her silences. This one goes on a little too long, and I know that she is somehow distressed.

You didn't like my last fic.

It isn't a question. The silence grows. Alone of all my online tribe, *Albertine* has no icon. Where all the others display an image – Clair's picture of Angel Blue, Chryssie's winged child, Cap's cartoon rabbit – she keeps to the default setting: a silhouette in a plain blue square.

The result is oddly disconcerting. Icons and avatars are part of the way we interact. Like the shield designs of mediaeval times, they serve both as a defensive tool and as the image of ourselves we show to the world, cheap escutcheons for those of us with no honour, no king, no country.

So how does *Albertine* see herself?

Time passes, lingering, ticking off the seconds like an impatient schoolmistress. For a while I am sure she has gone.

Then at last she replies. *Your story disturbed me a little,* she says. *The woman reminds me of someone I know. A friend of your mother's, actually.*

Funny, how fact and fic intertwine. I say as much to *Albertine*.

Eleanor Vine's in hospital. She was taken ill late last night. Something to do with her lungs, I heard –

Really? What a coincidence.

If I didn't know any better, she says, *I could almost believe you were somehow involved.*

Could you really? I had to smile.

It sounds just a touch sarcastic to me. But in the absence of facial expressions, there is no way of knowing for sure. If this had been Chryssie or Clair, then she would have followed her comment with a symbol – a smile, a wink, a crying face – to eliminate ambiguity. But *Albertine* does not use emoticons. Their absence makes conversation with her curiously expressionless, and I am never entirely sure if I have understood her fully.

Do you feel guilty, blueeyedboy?

Long pause.

Truth or dare?

Blueeyedboy hesitates, weighing the joy of confiding in her against the danger of saying too much. Fiction is a dangerous friend; a smokescreen that could dissipate and blow away without warning, leaving him naked.

Finally he types: *Yes.*

Maybe that's why you write these things. Maybe you're assuming guilt for something you're not really guilty of.

Hm. What an interesting idea. *You don't think I'm guilty of anything?*

Everyone's guilty of something, she says. *But sometimes it's easier to confess to something we haven't done than to face up to the truth.*

Now she's trying to profile *me.* I told you she was clever.

So – why do you come here, Albertine? What do you think you're guilty of?

Silence, then, for so long that I'm almost sure she has broken the connection. The cursor blinks, relentlessly. The mailbox *bips.* Once. Twice.

I wonder what I would do now if she simply told the truth. But nothing's ever that easy. Does she even know what she did? Does she *know* that it all started then, at the concert in St Oswald's Chapel, a word that conjures up for me the Christmassy colours of stained glass and the scent of pine and frankincense?

Who are you really, *Albertine*? Plain-vanilla or bad guy at heart? A killer, a coward, a fraudster, a thief? And when I reach the centre of you, will I know if there's anyone home?

And then she replies, and quickly logs off before I can comment or ask for more. In the absence of icons or avatars, I cannot be sure of her motives, but I sense that she is running away, that I have finally touched her somehow –

Truth or dare, Albertine? What have you come here to confess?

Her message to me is just four words long. It simply says:

I told a lie.

7

You are viewing the webjournal of **blueeyedboy** *posting on:*
                    badguysrock@webjournal.com
Posted at: 04.38 on Monday, February 11
Status: *public*
Mood: *confiding*
Listening to: *Hazel O'Connor*: 'Big Brother'

Everyone does it. Everyone lies. Everyone colours the truth to fit: from the fisherman who exaggerates the length of the carp that got away, to the politician's memoir, transmuting the metal of base experience into the gold of history. Even *blueeyedboy's* diary (hidden under his mattress at home) was far more wish-fulfilment than fact, detailing with pathetic hopefulness the life of a boy he could never be – a boy with two parents, a boy with friends, a boy who did ordinary things, who went to the seaside on his birthday, a boy who loved his Ma – knowing that the bleaker truth was hiding there under the surface, patiently waiting to be exposed by some casual turn of the tide.

Ben failed the St Oswald's entrance exam. He should have seen it coming, of course, but he'd been told so many times that he would pass that everyone took it for granted, like crossing a friendly border, nothing more than a token gesture to ensure his passage into St Oswald's, and subsequently, his success –

It wasn't that the paper was hard. In fact, he found it quite easy – or would have done, if he'd finished it. But that place, with its smells, unmanned him; and the cavernous room filled with uniforms; and the lists of names tacked to the wall; and the cheesy, hostile faces of the other scholarship boys.

A panic attack, the doctor said. A physical reaction to stress. It began with a nervous headache, which, halfway through the first paper, rapidly grew into something more: a turbulence of colour and scent that drenched him like a tropical storm and bludgeoned him into unconsciousness, there on St Oswald's parquet floor.

They took him to Malbry Infirmary, where he pleaded to be given a bed. He knew his scholarship had sailed, and that Ma was going to be furious, and that the only way to avoid real trouble was by getting the doctors on his side.

But once again, his luck was out. The nurse called Ma straight away, and the teacher who had accompanied him – a Dr Devine, a thin man whose name was a murky dark green – told her what had happened to him.

'You'll let him retake the exam, though?' Ma's first anxious thought was of the longed-for scholarship. To make things worse, by then Ben was feeling fine, with hardly a trace of a headache left. Her berry-black eyes locked briefly on his; long enough, at least, to convey that he was in a world of hurt.

'I'm afraid not,' said Dr Devine. 'That's not St Oswald's policy. Now, if Benjamin were to sit the common exam—'

'You mean he won't get the scholarship?' Her eyes were narrowed almost to slits.

Dr Devine gave a little shrug. 'I'm afraid the decision isn't mine. Perhaps he could try again next year.'

Ma started forward. 'You don't understand—'

But Dr Devine had had enough. 'I'm sorry, Mrs Winter,' he said, heading for the infirmary door. 'We can't make exceptions for just one boy.'

She kept her calm until they got home. Then she unleashed her rage. First with the piece of electrical cord, then afterwards with her fists and feet, while Nigel and Brendan watched like caged monkeys from the upstairs landing, their faces pressed silently against the bars.

It wasn't the first time she'd beaten him. She'd beaten them all at some time or another – mostly Nigel, but Benjamin too, and even stupid Brendan, who was too scared of everything to ever put a foot wrong – it was her way of keeping them under control.

But this time it was something else. She'd always thought him exceptional. Now, it seemed, he was *just one boy*. The knowledge must have come as a shock, a terrible disappointment to her. Well, that's what *blueeyedboy* thinks now. In fact, he must have known even then that his mother was going insane.

'You lying, malingering little *shit!*'

'No, Ma, please,' whimpered Ben, trying to shield his face with his arms.

'You blew that exam on purpose, Ben! You let me down on purpose!' She grabbed him with one hand by the hair and forced his arm away from his face in readiness for another blow.

He closed his eyes and reached for the words, the magic words to tame the beast. Then came inspiration –

'Please. Ma. It's not my fault. Please, Ma. I love you—'

She stopped. Fist raised like a gauntlet of gems, one eye levelled malignantly.

'What did you say?'

'I love you, Ma—'

Back then, when Ben had gained some ground, he needed to consolidate his position. He was already shaken, already in tears. It didn't take much to summon the rest. And as he clung to her, snivelling, his brothers still watching from the top of the stairs, it struck him that he was good at this, that if he played his cards right, he might just survive. Everyone has an Achilles heel. Ben had just found his mother's.

Then, from behind the bars of the staircase he saw Brendan's eyes go wide. For a moment Brendan held his gaze, and he was suddenly convinced that Bren, who never read anything, had read his mind as easily as he might read a Ladybird book.

His brother looked away at once. But not before Ben had seen that look; that look of understanding. Was it really so obvious? Or had he just been wrong about Bren? For years he had simply dismissed him as a fat and useless waste of space. But how much did Benjamin really know about his backward brother? How much had he taken for granted? He wondered now if he'd made a mistake; if Bren wasn't brighter than he'd thought. Bright enough to have seen through his act. Bright enough to present a threat –

He freed himself from Ma's embrace. Bren was still waiting on the stairs, looking scared and stupid once more. But Benjamin knew he was faking it. Beneath that drab plumage his brother in brown was playing some deeper game of his own. He didn't know what it was – not yet. But from that moment, Benjamin knew that one day he might have to deal with Bren –

Post comment:

Albertine: *Are you sure you know where you're going with this?*

blueeyedboy: *Quite sure. Are you?*

Albertine: *I'm following you. I always have.*

blueeyedboy: *Ah! The snows of yesteryear . . .*

8

You are viewing the webjournal of **Albertine** posting on:
badguysrock@webjournal.com
Posted at: 20.14 on Monday, February 11
Status: public
Mood: mendacious

Yes, that's where it starts. With a little white lie. White, like the pretty snow. Snow White, like in the story – and who would think snow could be dangerous, that those little wet kisses from the sky could turn into something deadly?

It's all about momentum, you see. Just as that one little, thoughtless lie took on a momentum of its own. A stone can set off an avalanche. A word can sometimes do the same. And a lie can become the avalanche, bringing down everything in its path, bludgeoning, roaring, smothering, reshaping the world in its wake, rewriting the course of our lives.

Emily was five and a half when her father first took her to the school where he taught. Until then it had been a mysterious place (remote and beguiling as all mythical places) which her parents sometimes discussed over the dinner-table. Not often, though: Catherine disliked what she called 'Patrick's shop-talk' and frequently turned the conversation to other matters just as it became most interesting. Emily gathered that 'school' was a place where children came together – to learn, or so her father said, though Catherine seemed to disagree.

'How many children?'

Buttons in a box; beans in a jar. 'Hundreds.'

'Children like me?'

'No, Emily. Not like you. St Oswald's School is just for boys.'

By now she was reading avidly. Braille books for children were hard to find, but her mother had created tactile books from felt and embroidery, and Daddy spent hours every day carefully transcribing stories – all typed in reverse, using the old embossing machine. Emily could already add and subtract as well as divide and multiply. She knew the history of the great artists; she had studied relief maps of the world and of the solar system. She knew the house inside and out. She knew about plants and animals from frequent visits to the children's farm. She could play chess. She could play the piano, too – a pleasure she shared with her father – and her most precious hours were spent with him in his room, learning scales and chords and stretching her small hands in a vain effort to span an octave.

But of other children she knew very little. She heard their voices when she played in the park. She had once petted a baby, which smelt vaguely sour and felt like a sleeping cat. Her next-door neighbour was called Mrs Brannigan, and for some reason she was inferior – perhaps because she was Catholic; or perhaps because she rented her house, whilst theirs was bought and paid for. Mrs Brannigan had a daughter a little older than Emily, with whom she would have liked to play, but who spoke with such a strong accent that the first and only time they had spoken, Emily had not understood a word.

But Emily's father worked in a place where there were hundreds of children, all learning maths and geography and French and Latin and art and history and music and science; as well as fighting in the yard, shouting, talking, making friends, chasing each other, eating dinners in a long room, playing cricket and tennis on the grass.

'I'd like to go to school,' she said.

'You wouldn't.' That was Catherine, with the warning note in her voice. 'Patrick, stop talking shop. You know how it upsets her.'

'It doesn't upset me. I'd like to go.'

'Perhaps I could take her with me one day. Just to see—'

'*Patrick!*'

'Sorry. Just – you know. There's the Christmas concert next month, love. In the school chapel. I'm conducting. She likes—'

'Patrick, I'm not listening!'

'She likes music, Catherine. Let me take her. Just this once.'

And so, just once, Emily went. Perhaps because of Daddy; but mostly because Feather was in favour of the plan. Feather was a staunch believer in the healing powers of music; besides, she had recently read Gide's *La Symphonie Pastorale*, and felt that a concert might boost Emily's flagging colour therapy.

But Catherine didn't like the idea. I think now that part of it was guilt; the same guilt that had pushed her to remove all traces of Daddy's passion for music from the house. The piano was an exception; even so, it had been relegated to a spare room, where it sat amongst boxes of forgotten papers and old clothes, where Emily was not supposed to venture. But Feather's enthusiasm tipped the balance, and on the evening of the concert they all walked down towards St Oswald's, Catherine smelling of turpentine and rose (*a pink smell*, she tells Emily, *pretty pink roses*), Feather talking high and very fast, and Emily's father guiding her gently by the shoulder, taking care not to let her slip in the wet December snow.

'OK?' he whispered, as they neared the place.

'Mm-mm.'

She had been disappointed to hear that the concert was not to take place in the school itself. She would have liked to see Daddy's place of work; to have entered the classrooms with their wooden desks, smelt the chalk and the polish; heard the echo of their footsteps against the wooden floors. Later, she was allowed those things. But this event was to take place in the nearby chapel, with the St Oswald's choristers, and her father *conducting*, which she understood to mean guiding, somehow; showing the singers the way.

It was a cold, damp evening that smelt of smoke. From the road came the sounds of cars and bicycle bells and people talking, muffled almost to nothing in the foggy air. In spite of her winter coat she was cold; her thin-soled shoes squelching against the gravel path, and droplets of moisture in her hair. Fog makes the outside feel smaller, somehow; just as the wind expands the world, making the trees rustle and soar. That evening Emily felt very small, squashed down almost to nothing by the dead air. From time to time someone passed her – she felt the swish of a lady's dress, or it might have been a Master's gown – and heard a snatch of conversation before they were once more swept away.

'Won't it be crowded, Patrick? Emily doesn't like crowds.' That was Catherine again, her voice tight as the bodice of Emily's best party dress, which was pretty (and pink) and which had been brought from storage for one last outing before she outgrew it completely.

'It's fine. You've got front-row seats.'

As a matter of fact Emily didn't mind crowds. It was the *noise* she didn't like: those flat and blurry voices that confused everything and turned everything around. She took hold of her father's hand, rather tightly, and squeezed. A single pump meant I *love you*. A double-pump, I *love you, too*. Another of their small secrets, like the fact that she could almost span an octave if she bounced her hand over the keys, and play the lead line of *Für Elise* while her father played the chords.

It was cool inside the chapel. Emily's family didn't attend church – though their neighbour, Mrs Brannigan, did – and she had been inside St Mary's once, just to hear the echo. St Oswald's Chapel sounded like that; their steps *slap-slapped* on the hard, smooth floor, and all the sounds in the place seemed to go *up*, like people climbing an echoey staircase and talking as they went.

Daddy told her later that it was because the ceiling was so high, but at the time she imagined that the choir would be sitting above her, like angels. There was a scent, too; something like Feather's patchouli, but stronger and smokier.

'That's incense,' said her father. 'They burn it in the sanctuary.'

Sanctuary. He'd explained that word. A place to go where you can be safe. Incense and Clan tobacco and angels' voices. Sanctuary.

There was movement all around them now. People were talking, but in lower voices than usual, as if they were afraid of the echoes. As Daddy went to join the choristers and Catherine described the organ and pews and windows for her, Emily heard *wishwishwish* from all around the hall, then a series of settling-down noises, then a hush as the choir began to sing.

It was as if something had broken open inside her. *This*, and not the piece of clay, is Emily's first memory: sitting in St Oswald's Chapel with the tears running down her face and into her smiling mouth, and the music, the lovely music, surging all around her.

Oh, it was not the first time that she had ever heard music; but the homely *rinkety-plink* of their old piano, or the tinny transistors of the kitchen radio, could not convey more than a particle of this. She had no name for what she could hear, no terms with which to describe this new experience. It was, quite simply, an awakening.

Later her mother tried to embellish the tale, as if it needed embellishment. She herself had never really enjoyed religious music – Christmas carols least of all, with their simple tunes and mawkish lyrics. Something by Mozart would have been much more suitable, with its implication of like calling to like, though the legend has a dozen variations – from Mozart to Mahler and even to the inevitable Berlioz – as if the complexity of the music had any bearing on the sounds themselves, or the sensations they evoked.

In fact the piece was nothing more than a four-part a cappella version of an old Christmas carol.

> *In the bleak midwinter,*
> *Frosty wind made moan,*
> *Earth stood hard as iron,*
> *Water like a stone;*

But there is something unique about boys' voices; a tremulous quality, not entirely comfortable, perpetually on the brink of losing pitch. It is a sound that combines an almost inhuman sweetness of tone with a raw edge that is nearly painful.

She listened in silence for the first few bars, unsure of what she was hearing. Then the voices rose again:

> *Snow had fallen, snow on snow,*
> *Snow on snow –*

And on the second *snow* the voices grazed *that* note, the high F sharp that had always been a point of mysterious pressure in her, and Emily began to cry. Not from sorrow or even from emotion; it was simply a reflex, like that cramping of the tastebuds after eating something very sour, or the gasp of fresh chilli against the back of the throat.

Snow on snow, snow on snow they sang, and everything in her responded. She shivered; she smiled; she turned her face to the invisible roof and opened her mouth like a baby bird, half-expecting to *feel* the sounds like snowflakes falling on her tongue. For almost a minute Emily sat trembling on the edge of her seat, and every now and then the boys' voices would rise to that strange F sharp, that magical ice-cream-headache note, and the tears would spill once more from her eyes. Her lower lip tingled; her fingers were numb. She felt as if she were touching God –

'Emily, what is it?'

She could not reply. Only the sounds mattered.

'Emily!'

Every note seemed to cut into her in some delicious way; every chord a miracle of texture and shape. More tears fell.

'Something's wrong.' Catherine's voice came from a great distance. 'Feather, please. I'm taking her home.' Emily felt her starting to move; tugging at her coat, which she had been using as a cushion. 'Get up, sweetheart, we shouldn't have come.'

Was that satisfaction in her voice? Her hand on Emily's forehead was feverish and clammy. 'She's burning up. Feather, give me a hand—'

'No!' whispered Emily.

'Emily, darling, you're upset.'

'Please—' But now her mother was picking her up; Catherine's arms were around her. She caught a fleeting smell of turpentine behind the expensive perfume. Desperately she searched for something, some magic, to make her mother stop: something that would convey the urgency, the imperative to stay, to *listen* . . .

'Please, the music—'

Your mother doesn't care much for music. Daddy's voice; remote but clear.

But what *did* Catherine care for? What for her was the language of command?

They were half-out of their seats now. Emily tried to struggle; a seam ripped under the arm of her too-tight dress. Her coat, with its fur collar, smothered her. More of the turpentine smell, the smell of her mother's fever, her madness.

And suddenly Emily understood, with a maturity far beyond her years, that she would never visit her father's school, never go to another concert, just as she would never play with other children in case they hurt or pushed her, never run in the park in case she fell.

If they left now, Emily thought, then her mother would *always* have her way, and the blindness, which had never really troubled her, would finally drag her down like a stone tied to a dog's tail, and she would drown.

There must be words, she told herself; magic words, to make her mother stay. But Emily was five years old; she didn't know any magic words; and now she was moving down the aisle with her mother on one side and Feather on the other, and the lovely voices rolling over them like a river.

In the bleak midwinter,
Lo-ooong ago –

And then it came to her. So simple that she gasped at her own audacity. She *did* know magic words, she realized. Dozens of them; she had learnt them almost from the cradle, but had never really found a use for them until now. She knew their fearsome energy. Emily opened her mouth, stricken with a sudden, demonic inspiration.

'The colours,' she whispered.

Catherine White stopped mid-stride. 'What did you say?'

'The colours. Please. I want to stay.' Emily took a deep breath. 'I want to *listen to the colours.*'

Post comment:
blueeyedboy: *How brave of you to post this,* **Albertine**. *You know I'll have to reciprocate . . .*

9

Listen to the colours. Oh, please. Don't tell me she was innocent; don't tell me that, even then, she didn't know exactly what she was doing. Mrs White knew all about *Boy X* and his synaesthesia. She knew Dr Peacock would be near by. Easy enough to feed her the line; easier still to believe it when Emily responded by starting to hear the colours.

Ben was in his first year at school. Imagine him then: a chorister, all scrubbed and clean and ready to go in his blue St Oswald's uniform under the frilled white cassock.

I know what you're thinking. He failed the exam. But that was just the scholarship. With money she had set aside, as well as with help from Dr Peacock, Ma had managed to get him into St Oswald's after all, not as a scholar, but as a fee-paying pupil, and here he was in the front row of the school choir, hating every moment of it. And if they didn't already have good enough cause to despise him, he knew that the other boys in his form would never leave him alone after this, not to mention Nigel, who had been dragged along most reluctantly, and who would take it out on him later, he knew, in gibes and kicks and punches.

In the bleak midwinter,
Frosty wind made moan –

He'd prayed in vain for puberty to break his voice and release him. But whilst the other boys in his class were already thickening like palm trees, reeking of teenage civet, Ben remained slim and girlish and pale, with an eerie, off-key treble voice.

Earth stood hard as iron,
Water like a stone –

He could see his mother three rows back, listening for the sound of his voice, and Dr Peacock, behind her; and Nigel, going on seventeen, sprawled and scowling across the bench; and sweaty and malodorous Bren, looking terribly uncomfortable with his lank hair and his pursed-up face, like the world's most enormous baby.

Blueeyedboy tried not to look; to concentrate on the music, but now he caught sight of Mrs White, just a few seats away from him, with Emily by her side – Emily, in her little red coat and her dress of rose-pink, with her hair in bunches and her face illuminated with something half-distress, half-joy –

For a moment he thought her eyes caught his; but the eyes of the blind are like that, aren't they? Emily couldn't see him. Whatever he did, however he tried – Emily never would. And yet, those eyes drew him, skittering from side to side like marbles in a doll's head, like a couple of blue-eye beads, reflecting ill-luck back to the sender.

Blueeyedboy's head was beginning to spin, throbbing in time to the music. A headache was coming; a bad one. He searched for the means to protect himself, imagining a capsule of blue, hard as iron, cold as stone, blue as a block of Arctic ice. But the pain was inescapable. A headache that would escalate until it wrung him like a rag –

It was hot in the choir stalls. Red-faced in their white smocks, the choristers sang like angels. St Oswald's takes its choir seriously: the boys are drilled in obedience. Like soldiers, they are trained to stand and keep their position for hours on end. No one complains. No one dares. *Sing your hearts out, boys, and smile!* bugles the choirmaster during rehearsals. *This is for God and St Oswald's. I don't want to see a single boy letting down the team.*

But now Ben Winter was looking pale. Perhaps the heat; the incense; perhaps the strain of keeping that smile. Remember, he was delicate; Ma always said so. More sensitive than the other two; more prone to illness and accidents –

The angel voices rose again, sweeping towards the crescendo.

Snow had fallen, snow on snow –

And that was when it happened. Almost in slow motion; a thud: a movement in the front row; a pale-faced boy collapsing unseen on to the floor of the chapel; striking his head on the side of a pew, a blow that would require four stitches to mend, a crescent moon on his forehead.

Why did no one notice him? Why was Ben so wholly eclipsed? No one saw him – not even Ma – for just as he fell, a little blind girl in the crowd suffered a kind of panic attack, and all eyes turned to Emily White, Emily in the rose-coloured dress, flailing her arms and shouting out: *Please. I want to stay. I want to –*

Listen to the colours.

Post comment:
Albertine: *Nice comeback,* **blueeyedboy.**
blueeyedboy: *Glad you liked it,* **Albertine.**
Albertine: *Well,* liked *is maybe not the word –*
blueeyedboy: *Nice comeback,* **Albertine** . . .

10

You are viewing the webjournal of **Albertine** *posting on:*
badguysrock@webjournal.com
Posted at: *23.49 on Monday, February 11*
Status: *public*
Mood: *raw*

Listen to the colours. Maybe you remember the phrase. Glib coming from the mouth of an adult, it must have seemed unbearably poignant from that of a five-year-old blind girl. In any case, it did the trick. *Listen to the colours.* All unknowing, Emily White had opened up a box of magic words, and was drunk with their power and her own, issuing commands like a diminutive general, commands which Catherine and Feather – and later, of course, Dr Peacock – obeyed with unquestioning delight.

'What do you see?'

Diminished chord of F minor. The magic words unfurl like wrapping-paper, every one.

'Pink. Blue. Green. Violet. So pretty.'

Her mother claps her hands in delight. 'More, Emily. Tell me more.'

A chord of F major.

'Red. Orange. Ma-gen-ta. Black.'

It was like an awakening. The infernal power she had discovered in herself had blossomed in an astonishing way, and music was suddenly a part of her curriculum. The piano was brought out of the spare room and re-tuned; her father's secret lessons became official, and Emily was allowed to practise whenever she liked, even when Catherine was working. Then came the local newspapers, and the letters and gifts came pouring in.

The story had plenty of potential. In fact, it had all the ingredients. A Christmas miracle; a photogenic blind girl; music; art; some man-in-the-street science, courtesy of Dr Peacock, and a lot of controversy from the art world that kept the papers wondering on and off for the next three years or so, caught up in speculation. The TV eventually caught on to it; so did the Press. There was even a single – a Top Ten hit – by a rock band whose name I forget. The song was later used in the Hollywood film – an adaptation of the book – starring Robert Redford as Dr Peacock and a young Natalie Portman as the blind girl who sees music.

At first Emily took it for granted. After all, she was very young, and had no basis for comparison. And she was very happy – she listened to music all day long; she studied what she loved most, and everyone was pleased with her.

Over the next twelve months or so Emily attended a number of concerts, as well as performances of *The Magic Flute*, the *Messiah* and *Swan Lake*. She went to her father's school several times, so that she could get to know the instruments by feel.

Flutes, with their slender bodies and intricate keys; pot-bellied cellos and double basses; French horns and tubas like big school canteen-jugs of sound; narrow-waisted violins; icicle bells; fat drums and flat drums; splash cymbals and crash cymbals; triangles and timpani and trumpets and tambourines.

Sometimes her father would play for her. He was different when Catherine was not there: he told jokes; he was exuberant, dancing Emily round and round to the music, making her dizzy with laughter. He would have liked to have been a professional musician: clarinet, and not piano, had been his preferred instrument, but there was little call for a classically trained clarinet player with a lurking passion for Acker Bilk, and his small ambitions had gone unvoiced and unnoticed.

But there was another side to Catherine's conversion. It took Emily months to discover it; longer still to understand. This is where my memories lose all cohesion; reality merges with myth so that I cannot trust myself to be either accurate or truthful. Only the facts speak for themselves; and even they have been so much disputed, queried, mis-reported, misread that only scraps remain of anything that might show me how it really was.

The facts, then. You must know the tale. In the audience that evening, sitting three rows from the front, at the end, was a man called Graham Peacock. Sixty-seven years old; a well-known local person-ality; a noted gourmet; a likeable eccentric; a generous patron of the arts. That evening in December, during a recital of Christmas songs in St Oswald's Chapel, Dr Peacock found himself party to an incident that was to change his life.

A small girl – the child of a friend of his – had suffered a kind of panic attack. Her mother began to carry her out, and in the scuffle that ensued – the child struggling valiantly to stay, the mother trying with equal fortitude to remove her – he heard the child speak a phrase that struck at him like a revelation.

Listen to the colours.

At the time Emily barely understood the significance of what she had said. But Dr Peacock's interest left her mother in a state of near-euphoria; at home, Feather opened a bottle of champagne, and even Daddy seemed pleased, though that might just have been because of the change in Catherine. Nevertheless he did not approve; later, when the thing had begun, his was the only dissenting voice.

Needless to say, no one listened. The very next day little Emily was summoned to the Fireplace House, where every possible test was run to confirm her special talents.

Synaesthesia [writes Dr Peacock in his paper 'Aspects of Modularity'] *is a rare condition where two – or sometimes more – of the five 'normal' senses are apparently fused together. This seems to be related to the concept of modularity. Each of the sensory systems has a corresponding area, or module, of the brain. While there are normal interactions between modules (such as using vision to detect movement), the current understanding of human perception cannot account for the stimulation of one module inducing brain activity in a different module. However, in a synaesthete, this is precisely the case.*

In short, a synaesthete may experience any or all of the following: shape as taste, touch as scent, sound or taste as colour.

All this was new to Emily, if not to Feather and Catherine. But she understood the idea – they all knew about *Boy X*, after all – and from what she'd heard of his special gift, it was not too far removed from the word associations and art lessons and colour therapies she had learnt from her mother. She was five and a half at the time; eager to please; even more so to perform.

The arrangement was simple. In the mornings Emily would go to Dr Peacock's house for her music lesson and her other subjects; and in the afternoons she would play the piano, listen to records, and paint. That was her only duty, and as she was allowed to listen to music as she performed it, it was no great burden. Sometimes Dr Peacock would ask her questions, and record what she said.

Emily, listen. What do you see?

A single note picked out on the clunky old piano in the Fireplace House. G is indigo, almost black. A simple triad takes it further; then a chord – G minor, with a diminished seventh in the bass – resolves in a velvety violet caress.

He marks the result in his notebook.

Very good, Emily. That's my good girl.

Next comes a series of soft chords; C sharp minor; D diminished; E flat minor seventh. Emily points out the colours, marked in Braille on the paintbox.

To Emily it feels almost like playing an instrument, her hands on the little coloured keys; and Dr Peacock notes it down in his scratchy little notepad, and then there is tea by the fireplace, with Dr Peacock's Jack Russell, Patch II, snuffling hopefully after biscuits, tickling Emily's hands, making her laugh. Dr Peacock speaks to his dog as if he, too, is an elderly academic; which makes Emily laugh even more, and which soon becomes part of their lessons together.

'Patch II would like to enquire,' he says in his bassoony voice, 'whether today Miss White feels inclined to peruse my collection of recorded sounds—'

Emily giggles. 'You mean listen to records?'

'My furry colleague would appreciate it.'

On cue, Patch II barks.

Emily laughs. 'OK,' she says.

Over the thirty months that followed, Dr Peacock became an increasingly large part of all their lives. Catherine was deliriously happy; Emily was an apt pupil, spending three or four hours at the piano every day, and suddenly there was a much-needed focus to all of their lives. I doubt Patrick White could have stopped it, anyway, even if he had wanted to; after all, he too had a stake in the affair. He, too, wanted to believe.

Emily never asked herself why Dr Peacock was so generous. To her he was simply a kind and funny man who spoke in long and ponderous phrases and who never came to see them without bringing some gift of flowers, wine, books. On Emily's sixth birthday he gave her a new piano to replace the old, battered one on which she had learnt; throughout the year there were concert tickets, pastels, paints, easels, canvas, sweets and toys.

And music, of course. Always music. Even now that hurts most of all. To think of a time when Emily could play every day for as long as she liked, when every day was a fanfare, and Mozart, Mahler, Chopin, even Berlioz would line up like suitors for her favour, to be chosen or discarded at whim . . .

'Now, Emily. Listen to the music. Tell me what you hear.'

That was Mendelssohn, *Lieder ohne Worte*, Opus 19, Number 2, in A minor. The left-hand part is difficult to master, with its tight blocks of semi-quavers, but Emily has been practising, and now it's almost perfect. Dr Peacock is pleased. Her mother, too.

'Blue. Quite a dark blue.'

'Show me.'

She has a new paintbox now, sixty-four colours arranged like a chessboard, almost as broad as the desk-top. She cannot see them, but knows them by heart; arranged in order of brightness and tone. F is violet; G is indigo; A is blue; B is green; C is yellow; D is orange; E is red. Sharps are lighter; flats darker. Instruments, too, have their own colours within the orchestral palette: the woodwind section is often green or blue; the strings, brown and orange; the brass, red and yellow.

She picks up her thick brush and daubs it in the paint. She is using watercolours today, and the scent is chalky and grannyish, like Parma violets. Dr Peacock stands to one side, Patch II curled up at his feet. Catherine and Feather stand on the opposite side, ready to pass Emily anything she may need. A sponge; a brush; a smaller brush, a sachet of glitter powder.

The *Andante* is a leisurely abstract, like a day at the seaside. She dabbles her fingers in the paint and strokes them across the smooth untreated paper so that it contracts into ridges, like shallow-water sand, and the paint melts and slides into the gullies her fingers have left. Dr Peacock is pleased; she can hear the smile in his bassoony voice, although much of what he says is incomprehensible to her, swept aside by the lovely music.

Sometimes, other children come by. She remembers a boy, rather older than she is, who is shy, and stammers, and doesn't talk much, but sits on the sofa and reads. In the parlour there are sofas and chairs, a window seat and (her favourite) a swing, suspended from the ceiling on two stout ropes. The room is so large that Emily can swing as high as she likes without hitting anything; besides, everyone knows to keep out of her way, and there are no collisions.

Some days she does not paint at all; instead she sits on her swing in the Fireplace House and listens to sounds. Dr Peacock calls it the Sound Association Game, and if Emily works hard, he says, there will be a present at the end. All she has to do is sit on the swing, listen to the records and tell him the colours she can see. Some are easy – she already has them sorted in her mind like buttons in a box – others not. But she likes Dr Peacock's sound machines, and the records, especially the old ones, with their long-dead voices and wind-up scratchy gramophone strings.

Sometimes there is no music at all, but just a series of sound effects, and these are hardest of all. But Emily still tries her best to satisfy Dr Peacock, who writes down everything she says in a series of cloth-backed notebooks, sometimes with such force that his pencil goes through the paper.

'Listen, Emily. What do you see?'

The sound of a thousand Westerns; a gun fires, a bullet ricochets against a canyon wall; *Gunsmoke*; Bonfire Night and charred potatoes. 'Red.'

'Is that all?'

'Madder red. With a trail of crimson.'

'Good, Emily. Very good.'

It's really very easy; all she has to do is let her mind go. A penny dropped; a man whistling off-key; a single thrush; a door-knocker; the sound of one hand clapping. She goes home with her pockets crammed with sweets. Dr Peacock clack-clacks up his findings every night on a typewriter with a Donald Duck voice. His papers have names like 'Induced Synaesthesia', 'The Colour Complex' and 'Out of Sight, Out of Mind'. His words are like the gas the dentist gives her when he has to drill a tooth; she slides away under its shivery caress, and all the perfumes of the Orient cannot save her.

Post comment:

blueeyedboy: *Oh, yes!*

Albertine: *You mean you want more?*

blueeyedboy: *If you can bear it, then so can I . . .*

11

You are viewing the webjournal of **Albertine** posting on:
badguysrock@webjournal.com
Posted at: 01.45 on Tuesday, February 12
Status: public
Mood: culpable

Most of this, of course, is speculation. Those memories are not mine; they belong to Emily White. As if Emily could be a reliable witness to anything. And yet her voice – her plaintive treble – calls to me from over the years. *Help me, please! I'm still alive! You people buried me alive!*

'Red. Dark red. Oxblood, with purple streaks.'

Chopin's Nocturne Number 2 in E flat major. She has a good ear for music, and at six years old she can already pick out most of the chords, although the fretful double-rows of chromatics are still beyond the skill of her stubby fingers. This does not trouble Dr Peacock. He is far more interested in her painting skills than in any musical talent.

According to Catherine, he has already framed and hung half a dozen of Emily's canvases on the walls of the Fireplace House – including her *Toreador*; her *Goldberg Variations*; and (her mother's favourite) her *Nocturne in Violet Ochre*.

'There's so much energy in them,' says Catherine, in a trembling voice. 'So much experience. It's almost mystic. The way you take the colours from the music and bring them on to the canvas – do you know, Emily? I envy you. I wish I could see what you see now.'

No child could fail to be flattered by such praise. Her paintings make people happy; they earn her rewards from Dr Peacock and the approval of his many friends. She understands that he is planning another book, much of it based on his recent findings.

She knows that she is not the only person he has befriended in his search for synaesthetes. In his book *Beyond Sense*, he explains, he has already written at length about the case of a teenage boy, referred to throughout simply as *Boy X*, who appeared to exhibit signs of olfactory-gustatory acquired synaesthesia.

'What does that mean?' Emily says.

'He experienced things in a special way. Or, at least, he said he could. Now concentrate on the notes, please—'

'What kind of things did he see?' she says.

'I don't think he saw anything.'

Until Emily's appearance on the scene, *Boy X* had been Dr Peacock's pet project. But between a young blind prodigy who can hear colours (and paint them), and a teenage boy with an affinity to smells, there could be no real competition. Besides, the boy was a free-loader, said Catherine; willing to fabricate any number of phoney symptoms to gain attention. The mother was even worse, she said; any fool could see that she'd put her son up to it in the hope of getting her hands on Dr Peacock's money.

'You're too trusting, Gray,' she said. 'Anyone else would have spotted them a mile off. They saw you coming, dear. They had you fooled.'

'But my tests clearly show that the boy responds—'

'The boy responds to *money*, Gray. And so does his mother. A few quid here, a tenner there. It all builds up, and before you know it—'

'But Cathy – she works on the *market*, for God's sake – she's got three kids, the father's nowhere to be seen. She needs someone—'

'So what? So do half the mothers on the estate. Are you going to pay this boy for the rest of his life?'

Under pressure, Dr Peacock admitted that he had already contributed to the boy's school fees, plus a thousand pounds into a trust fund – *For college, Cathy, the lad's quite bright* –

Catherine White was furious. It wasn't her money, but she resented it as much as if it had been stolen from her own pocket. Besides, it was almost cruel, she said, to have led the boy to expect so much. He'd probably have been happy enough, if no one had tried to give him ideas. But Dr Peacock had encouraged him, had made him into a malcontent.

'That's what you get, Gray,' she said, 'trying to play Pygmalion. Don't expect gratitude from the boy – in fact, you're doing him a disservice, leading him to believe that he can sponge off you instead of getting a proper job. He could even end up being dangerous. Give money to these people, and what do they do? They buy drink and drugs. Things get out of hand. It wouldn't be the first time that some poor benevolent soul has been murdered in his bed by the very people he's trying to help—'

And so on. Finally, following heated discussions between Dr Peacock and Catherine, *Boy X* ceased his visits to the Fireplace House, never to return.

Catherine was magnanimous in victory. *Boy X* had been a mistake, she said. Paid handsomely for his cooperation in Dr Peacock's experiments, it was only natural that a person of his type should try to exploit the situation. But now here was the real thing, that rarest of phenomena: a blind-from-birth true synaesthete, reborn to sight again through music. It was a fabulous story, and deserved to stand alone. There was to be no one to undermine the uniqueness of the Emily White Phenomenon.

Post comment:

blueeyedboy: *Ouch! That was rather below the belt –*
Albertine: *I'll stop whenever you've had enough . . .*
blueeyedboy: *Do you really think you can?*
Albertine: *I don't know,* **blueeyedboy.** *The question is: can you?*

12

You are viewing the webjournal of **blueeyedboy** *posting on:*
badguysrock@webjournal.com
Posted at: *01.56 on Tuesday, February 12*
Status: *public*
Mood: *sorry*
Listening to: *Mark Knopfler:* 'The Last Laugh'

That marked the end for Benjamin. He'd sensed it almost immediately, that subtle shift in emphasis, and though it took some time to die, like a flower in a vase, he knew that something had ended for him that night in St Oswald's Chapel. The shadow of little Emily White had eclipsed him almost from the start: from her story, which was sensational, to the undeniable media appeal of the blind girl, whose super-sense was to make her a national superstar.

Now Ben's long days at the Mansion dwindled to an hourly session; time that he shared with Emily, sitting quietly on the couch while Dr Peacock showed her off as if she were some collector's piece – a moth, perhaps, or a figurine – expecting Ben to admire her, to share in his enthusiasm. Worse still, Brendan was there again (to keep an eye on him, Ma said, while she went to work at the market); his gawping, grinning brother in brown with his greasy hair and hangdog look, who rarely spoke, but sat and stared, filling Ben with such hate and shame that sometimes he wanted nothing more than to run away and to leave Bren alone – awkward, boorish, out of place – in that house of delicate things.

Catherine White put a stop to that. It wasn't right for those boys to be there, not without supervision. There were too many valuable things in that house; too many temptations. Benjamin's visits dwindled once again, so that now he dropped by just once a month, and waited with Bren on the front steps until Mrs White was ready to leave, hearing piano music drift out across the lawn, laden with the scent of paint, so that every time *blueeyedboy* hears that sound – be it a Rachmaninoff prelude or the intro to 'Hey Jude' – it brings back the memory of those days and the sorry little lurch of the heart that he felt when he glanced through the parlour window and saw Emily sitting on the swing, pendulum-ing back and forth like a happy little bird –

At first, all he did was watch her. Like everyone else, he was dazzled by her, content to simply admire her ascent, much as Dr Peacock must have watched the Luna moth as she struggled out of the chrysalis, in awe and admiration, coloured, perhaps, with a little regret. She was so pretty, even then. So effortlessly lovable. There was something about the trusting way in which she held her father's hand, face turned up towards him like a flower to the sun; or the monkeyish way in which she would scramble on to the piano stool, one leg tucked in, a sock at half-mast, half-eerie, half-enchanting. She was like a doll that had come to life, all porcelain and ivory, so that Mrs White, who had always liked dolls, could dress her daughter all year round in bright little outfits and matching shoes right out of an old-fashioned storybook.

As for our hero, *blueeyedboy* –

Puberty had hit him hard, with pimples on his back and face, and a half-broken voice that, even now, retains a slightly uneven tone. His childhood stammer had got worse. He lost it later, but that year it got so bad that on some days he could hardly speak. Smells and colours intensified, bringing with them migraines that the doctor promised would fade with time. They never did. He has them still, although his coping strategies have become somewhat more sophisticated.

After the Christmas concert, Emily seemed to spend most of her time at the Mansion. But with so many other people there, *blueeyedboy* rarely spoke to her; besides which, his stammer made him self-conscious, and he preferred to remain in the background, unregarded and unheard. Sometimes he would sit on the porch outside with a comic or a Western, content to be in her orbit, quietly, without fuss. Besides, reading was a pleasure seldom allowed Yours Truly at home, where Ma was always in need of help, and his brothers never left him alone. Reading was for sissies, they said, and whatever he chose – be it *Superman*, *Judge Dredd* or even just the *Beano* – would always incur the ridicule of *blueeyedboy's* brother in black, who would pester him relentlessly – *Look at the pretty pictures! Aww! So what's your super-power, then?* – until *blueeyedboy* was by turns shamed and coerced into doing something different.

Midweek, between visits to the Mansion, he would sometimes walk past Emily's house in the hope of seeing her playing outside. Occasionally, he saw her in town, but always with her mother: standing to attention like a good little soldier, sometimes flanked by Dr Peacock, who had become her protector, her mentor, her second father. As if she needed *another* one, as if she didn't already have everything.

It probably sounds like he envied her. That isn't altogether true. But somehow he couldn't stop thinking about her, studying her, watching her. His interest gathered momentum. He stole a camera from a second-hand shop, and taught himself to take pictures. He stole a long lens from the same shop, almost getting caught that time, but managing to get away with his trophy before the fat man at the counter – surprisingly speedy for all his bulk – finally gave up the pursuit.

When his mother told him at last that he was no longer welcome at the Mansion, he didn't quite believe her. He'd become so accustomed to his routine – sitting quietly on the couch, reading books, drinking Earl Grey tea, listening to Emily's music – that to be dismissed after all this time felt like an unfair punishment. It wasn't his fault – he'd done nothing wrong. It was surely a misunderstanding. Dr Peacock had always been so kind; why would he turn against him now?

Later, *blueeyedboy* understood. Dr Peacock, for all his kindness, had been just another version of his mother's ladies, who'd been so friendly when he was four, but who had so quickly lost interest. Friendless, starved of affection at home, he'd read too much into those affable ways: the walks around the rose garden; the cups of tea; the sympathy.

In short, he'd fallen into the trap of mistaking compassion for caring.

Calling round that evening in the hope of finding out the truth, Yours Truly was met, not by Dr Peacock, but by Mrs White, in a black satin dress with a string of pearls round her long neck, who told him that he shouldn't be there; that he was to leave and never come back, that he was trouble, that she knew his type –

'Is that what Dr Peacock says?'

Well, that was what he *meant* to say. But his stammer was worse than ever that day, closing his mouth with clumsy stitches, and he found he could hardly say a word.

'B-but why?' he asked her.

'Don't try to pretend. Don't think you can get away with it.'

For a moment, shame overwhelmed him. He didn't know what he had done, but Mrs White seemed so sure of his guilt, and his eyes began to sting with tears, and the stink of Ma's vitamin drink in his throat was almost enough to make him gag –

Please don't cry, he told himself. *Not in front of Mrs White.*

She gave him a look of burning contempt. 'Don't think you can get around me like that. You ought to be ashamed of yourself.'

Blueeyedboy was. Ashamed and suddenly angry; and if he could have killed her then, he would have done it without hesitation or remorse. But he was only a schoolboy, and she was from a different sphere, a different class, to be obeyed, no matter what – his mother had trained her sons well – and the sound of her words was like a spike being driven into the side of his head –

'Please,' he said, without stammering.

'Go away,' said Mrs White.

'Please. Mrs White. C-can't we be friends?'

She raised an eyebrow. 'Friends?' she said. 'I don't know what you're talking about. Your mother was my cleaner, that's all. Not even a very good one. And if you think that gives you the right to harass me and my daughter, then think again.'

'I wasn't ha-ha—' he began.

'And what do you call those photographs?' she said, looking him straight in the face.

The shock of it dried his tears at once.

'Ph-photographs?' he said shakily.

Turns out Feather had a friend who worked in the local photo shop. The friend had told Feather, who'd told Mrs White, who'd demanded to see the relevant prints and had taken them straight to the Mansion, where she'd used them to prove her argument that befriending the Winters had been a mistake, one from which Dr Peacock should distance himself without delay –

'Don't think you haven't been seen,' she said. 'Creeping around after Emily. Taking pictures of us both—'

That wasn't true. He never shot *her*. He only ever shot Emily. But he couldn't say that to Mrs White. Nor could he beg her not to tell Ma –

And so he left, dry-eyed with rage, tongue stapled to the roof of his mouth. And as he looked over his shoulder for one last glimpse of the Mansion, he saw a movement in one of the upper windows. He moved away almost at once; but *blueeyedboy* had had time to see Dr Peacock, watching him, warding him off with a sheepish smile –

That was where it really began. That's where *blueeyedboy* was born. Later that night he crept back to the house, armed with a can of peacock-blue paint, and, almost paralysed with fear and guilt, he scrawled his rage on the big front door, the door that had been cruelly shut in his face, and then, alone in his room again, he took out the battered Blue Book to draw up another murder.

Post comment:

Albertine: *Oh please, not another murder. I really thought we were getting somewhere.*

blueeyedboy: *All right, but – you owe me one . . .*

13

You are viewing the webjournal of **blueeyedboy** *posting on:*
badguysrock@webjournal.com

Posted at: *02.05 on Tuesday, February 12*
Status: *public*
Mood: *crushed*
Listening to: *Don Henley*: 'The Boys Of Summer'

It only started out as that. A journal of his fictional life. There is a kind of innocence in those early entries, hidden away between the lines of cramped, obsessive handwriting. Sometimes he remembers the truth: the daily disappointments; the rage; the hurt; the cruelty. The rest of the time he can almost believe that he was really *blueeyedboy* – that what was in the Blue Book was real, and Benjamin Winter and Emily White just figments of some other person's imagination. The Blue Book helped him stay sane; in it he wrote his fantasies; his secret vengeance against all those who hurt and humiliated him.

As for little Emily –

He watched her more than ever now. In secret, in envy, in longing, in love. Over the months that followed his expulsion from the Peacock house, he followed Emily's career, her life. He took hundreds of photographs. He collected newspaper clippings of her. He even befriended the little girl who lived next door to Mrs White, giving her sweets and calling on her in the hope of a glimpse of Emily.

For some time Dr Peacock had worked to keep Emily's identity secret. In his papers she was simply *Girl Y* – a fitting replacement to *Boy X* – until such time as he and her parents chose to launch her into the world. But *blueeyedboy* knew the truth. *Blueeyedboy* knew what she was. A Luna moth in a glass case, just waiting to fly from the chrysalis straight into the killing jar –

He went on taking photographs, though he learnt to do it with greater stealth. He got two after-school jobs – a newspaper round, a couple of nights washing dishes at a local café – and with his wages he bought himself a second-hand enlarger, a stack of photographic paper and some trays and chemicals. Using books from the library, he learnt to develop the photographs himself, eventually converting the cellar, which his mother never used, into a little darkroom.

He felt like someone who had missed the winning lottery number by a single digit – and it didn't help that Ma never failed to make him feel that somehow it had all been *his* fault, that if he'd been smarter, quicker, better, then it could have been one of her boys scooping up the attention, the praise.

That year, Ma made it clear to her sons that all of them had let her down. Nigel, for failing so miserably to keep the other two in line; Brendan, for his stupidity; but most especially Benjamin, on whom so many hopes had been placed, but who had failed his Ma in every way. At the Mansion; at home; but most of all at St Oswald's. Ben's schooling at that exclusive establishment had proved the greatest setback of all, confounding Ma's expectations that her son was destined for great things. In fact, he'd hated it from the start, and only his relationship with Dr Peacock had prevented him from saying so.

But now everything about it was inimical to him: from the boys, who, just like the ones from the estate, called him *freak* and *loser* and *queer* (albeit in more refined accents), to the pretentious names of the buildings themselves – names like Rotunda and Porte-Cochère – names that tasted of rotten fruit, plummy with self-satisfaction and ripe with the odour of sanctity.

Like the vitamin drink, St Oswald's was meant to be good for his health; to help him achieve his potential. But after three miserable years there, where to some extent he had tried to fit in, he still wanted Dr Peacock's house, with the fireplace and the smell of old books. He missed the Earth globes with their magical names; and most of all he missed the way Dr Peacock used to talk to him, as if he really *cared* –

No one at St Oswald's cared. It was true that no one bullied him – well, not the way his brother did – but all the same he could always feel that undercurrent of contempt. Even the Masters had it, although some were better than others at concealing it.

They called him by his surname, *Winter*, like an Army cadet. They drilled him with tables and irregular verbs. They gave huge, dramatic sighs at his displays of ignorance. They set him to copying lines.

I will keep my schoolbooks in immaculate condition. (Nigel always found them, however well he hid them away.) *My uniform represents the school. I will wear it always with pride.* (This was when Nigel had scissored his tie, leaving nothing but a stub.) *I will at least pretend to pay attention when a senior Master enters the room.* (This from the ever-sarcastic Dr Devine, who came into his form-room one morning to find him asleep at his desk.)

The worst of it was that he really tried. He tried to excel at his schoolwork. He wanted his teachers to be proud of him. Whereas some boys failed through laziness, he was acutely aware of the hated privilege of attending St Oswald's Grammar School, and he tried very hard to deserve it. But Dr Peacock, with his fine disregard for the curriculum, had coached him in only the subjects he himself valued – art, history, music, English literature – neglecting maths and the sciences, with the result that Ben had lagged behind ever since his first term at school and, in spite of all his efforts, had never recovered the deficit.

When Dr Peacock withdrew from their lives, Benjamin had expected Ma to withdraw him from the grammar school. In fact he prayed for it fervently, but the one time he dared mention the matter to her, she whacked him with the length of electrical cord.

'I've already put too much into you,' she said, as she folded the cord away. 'Far too much, in any case, to let you drop out at this stage.'

After that, he knew better than to complain. He sensed another shift in things as adolescence claimed him. His brothers were growing up fast, and Ma, like an October wasp sensing the coming of winter, had turned vicious overnight, making her sons the target of her frustrations. Suddenly they were all under fire, from the way they spoke to the length of their hair, and blueeyedboy realized with growing dismay that Ma's devotion to her sons had been part of a long-term investment plan that now was expected to bear fruit.

Nigel had left school some three months ago, and the urge to make Ben suffer had begun to take second place to finding a flat, a girl, a job, an escape – from Ma, from his brothers, from Malbry.

Now he seemed suddenly older, more distant, more given to dark moods and silences. He'd always been moody and withdrawn. Now he became almost a recluse. He'd bought himself a telescope, and on cloudless nights he took to the moors, coming home in the early hours, which was no bad thing as far as Ben was concerned, but which made Ma anxious and irritable.

If Nigel's escape was in the stars, Brendan had found another route. At sixteen he already outweighed Ben by fifty pounds, and, far from losing his puppy fat, now supplemented his confectionary habit with alarming amounts of junk food. He too had a part-time job, at a fried-chicken place in Malbry town centre, where he could snack all day if he liked, and from which he returned on weekday nights with the Bargain Bucket Meal Deal, which, if he wasn't hungry then, he would have cold for breakfast the following morning, along with a quart of Pepsi, before setting off for Sunnybank Park, where he was in his final year. Ma had hoped that he would at least stay on until his A-levels, but nothing Ma could say or do had any effect on Ben's voracious brother, who seemed to have made it his mission in life to eat his way out of her custody. Ben reckoned it was only a matter of time before Brendan failed his exams and dropped out, then moved away altogether.

Benjamin felt some relief at this. Ever since the St Oswald's entrance exam, he'd had a growing suspicion that Bren was keeping tabs on him. It wasn't anything Ben had said; just the way he looked at him. Sometimes he suspected Bren of following him when he went out; sometimes when he went to his room he was sure his things had been moved about. Books he'd left under his bed would migrate, or vanish for a day or two, then reappear somewhere else. It didn't really make sense, of course. What did Brendan care about books? And yet it made him uneasy to think of someone else going through his things.

But Bren was the least of his worries by then. So much had been invested in him. So much money; so much hope. And now that the returns were about to pay off, there could be no question of retreat. His mother would not submit to the humiliation of hearing the neighbours say that Gloria Winter's boy had dropped out of school –

'You'll do what I tell you and like it,' she said. 'Or I swear I'll make you pay.'

I'll make you pay was Ma's refrain throughout the whole of that year, it seemed. And so, throughout the whole of that year, her sons ran in fear of Gloria.

Blueeyedboy knew he deserved it, at least; *blueeyedboy* knew that he was bad. *How* bad, no one understood. But his mother made it clear to him that there was to be no going back: that to disappoint her at this stage would result in the worst kind of punishment.

'You owe it to me,' Ma said, with a glance at the green ceramic dog. 'What's more, you owe it to *him*. You owe it to your brother.'

Would Malcolm have been a success if he had lived? *Blueeyedboy* often asked himself that. It made him nervous to think of it. As if he were living two lives at once. One for himself, and one for Mal, who would never have the chances he'd had. Fear gnawed at him like a rat in a cage. What if he failed her? What would she do?

His escape from it all was in writing. He kept the Blue Book in the darkroom, where neither Ma nor his brothers would find it, and every night, when things got too bad, he would spin his fear into stories. Always from the point of view of a bad guy, a villain, a murderer –

His victims were many, his methods diverse. No simple shootings for *blueeyedboy*. His style may have been questionable, but his imagination was limitless. His victims died in colourful ways: caught in complex torture machines; buried in wet sand up to their necks; snared in fiendish death traps.

He used the Blue Book as a record of his fictional killings, along with a few actual experiments: Ben had recently moved on from wasps to moths, and later to mice, which were quite easy to obtain, using a simple bottle trap, and whose trapped and fluttering heartbeats –

amplified by the resonant glass – echoed the frantic rhythm of his own.

The trap was made from a milk bottle, in which Ben would place a quantity of bait. It was his way of selecting victims; of isolating the guilty from the innocent. The mouse climbs into the bottle, eats the bait, but is unable to climb back up the frictionless wall. It dies quite quickly – of exhaustion and shock – its little pink feet pedalling against the glass as if on an invisible wheel.

The point is, though: they *chose* to die. They chose to enter the baited trap. Their deaths were therefore *not his fault* –

But all that was about to change.

Post comment:
JennyTricks: (*post deleted*).
blueeyedboy: *Jenny? How I've missed you . . .*

14

You are viewing the webjournal of **Albertine** posting on:
badguysrock@webjournal.com
Posted at: 03.12 on Tuesday, February 12
Status: public
Mood: restless

A lie has a rhythm of its own. Emily's began with a rousing overture; mellowed into a solemn andante; elaborated on several themes and variations; and finally emerged into a triumphant scherzo, to standing ovations and lengthy applause.

It was her grand opening. Her formal presentation to the media. *Girl Y* had served her purpose; now she was ready to take the stage. She was three weeks shy of her eighth birthday; she was clever and articulate; her work was practice-perfect and ready to stand up to scrutiny. As part of the fanfare, the Press had been informed; there was to be an auction of her paintings in a small gallery off Malbry's Kingsgate; Dr Peacock's new book was about to come out, and suddenly, or so it seemed, the whole world was talking about Emily White.

> *This small figure* [said the *Guardian*], *with her bobbed brown hair and wistful face, hardly strikes one as a typical prodigy.* [Why? you wonder. What did they expect?] *In fact at first sight she seems very much like any other eight-year-old, but for the way her eyes skid and skitter, giving this writer the uncomfortable impression that she can see deep into his soul.*

The writer was an ageing journalist called Jeffrey Stuarts, and if he had a soul at all, she never caught a sniff of it. His voice was always a trifle too loud, with a percussive attack like dried peas in a bowl – and his smell was Old Spice aftershave trying too hard to overwhelm an under-scent of sweat and thwarted ambition. That day he was all affability.

> *It hardly seems conceivable* [he goes on to say] *that the canvases that sing and soar from the walls of this tiny gallery off Malbry's Kingsgate can be the unaided work of this shy little girl. And yet there is something eerie about Emily White. The small pale hands flutter restlessly, like moths. The head is cocked just a little to one side, as if she hears something the rest of us do not.*

As a matter of fact she was simply bored.

'Is it true,' he asked, 'that you can actually *see* the music?'

Obediently she nodded; behind him she could hear Dr Peacock's plush laughter above a twittering of white noise. She wondered where her father was; listened for his voice and thought for a second she heard it, all snarled up in the growing cacophony.

'And all these paintings – they actually *represent* what you see?'

Again, she nodded.

'So, Emily. How does it feel?'

> *I may be over-dramatizing, but I feel that there is something of the blank canvas about her; an other-worldly quality that both captivates and repels. Her paintings reflect this; as if the young artist has somehow gained access to another plane of perception.*

Oh, my. But the man enjoyed his alliteration. There was much more in the same vein; Rimbaud was mentioned (inevitably); Emily's work was compared to that of Münch and Van Gogh, and it was even suggested that she had experienced what Feather liked to call *channelling*, which meant that she had somehow tuned into some open frequency of talent (possibly linked to artists long-dead) to produce these astonishing paintings.

At first glance [writes Mr Stuarts], *all her canvases seem to be abstracts. Big, bold blocks of colour, some so highly textured as to be almost sculpture. But there are other influences here that surely cannot be coincidental. Emily White's* Eroica *has a look of Picasso's* Guernica; Birthday Bach *is as busy and intricate as a Jackson Pollock, and* Starry Moonlight Sonata *bears more than a passing resemblance to Van Gogh. Could it be, as Graham Peacock suggests, that all art has a common basis in the collective unconscious? Or is this little girl a conduit to something beyond the sensitivity of ordinary mortals?*

There was more – much more – in this vein. A digested version found its way into the *Daily Mirror* under the headline: BLIND GIRL'S SUPER-SENSE. The *Sun* ran it too, or something very similar, flanked with a photo of Sissy Spacek taken from the film *Carrie*. Shortly afterwards a more extended version was published in a journal called *Aquarius Moon*, alongside an interview with Feather Dunne. The myth was well on its way by then; and although on that particular day there were no signs of the knives that would soon come out in response, I think that even so the attention made her uneasy. Emily hated crowds; hated noise, and all the people who came and went, their voices pecking at her like hungry chickens.

Mr Stuarts was talking to Feather now; Emily could hear her throaty patchouli-dark voice saying something about how *differently able* children were often ideal hosts for benevolent spirits. To her left was her mother, sounding just a little drunk; her laughter too loud in the smoke and the noise.

'I always knew she was an exceptional child,' Emily heard above the noise. 'Who knows? Maybe she's the next step on the evolutionary ladder. One of the Tomorrow Children.'

The Tomorrow Children. God, that phrase. Feather used it in her *Aquarius Moon* interview (for all I know she may have coined it herself), and it alone spawned a dozen theories of which Emily remained mercifully ignorant – at least until the final collapse.

Now it only jarred, and she stood up from her chair and began to move towards the open door, following the smooth line of the wall, feeling soft air on her upturned face. It was warm outside; she could feel the evening sun against her eyelids and smell magnolia from the park across the road.

A *white smell*, said her mother's voice in her mind. *Magnolia white.* To Emily it sounded soft and chocolatey, like a Chopin nocturne, like *Cinderella*, a scent of magic. The heat from within the gallery was oppressive by comparison; the voices of all those people – guests, academics, journalists, all talking at once and at the tops of their voices – pushing at her like a hot wind. She'd never had an exhibition before. She'd never even had a proper birthday party. She sat down on the gallery step – there was a cast-iron railing, and she pressed her hot cheek against its pockmarked surface and lifted her face towards the white smell.

'Hello, Emily,' someone said.

She turned towards the sound of his voice. He was standing a dozen feet away. A boy – older than she was, she thought; maybe as old as sixteen. His voice sounded oddly flat and tight, like an instrument playing in the wrong register, and Emily could hear caution in it, combined with interest, and something close to hostility.

'What's your name?'

'B.B.,' he said.

'That's not a name,' Emily said.

His shrug was implicit in his tone. 'It's what they call me at home,' he said. There was a rather lengthy pause. Emily could feel him wanting to speak, and sensed he was staring at her. She wished he would either ask his question, or go away and leave her alone. The boy did neither, but just stood there, opening his mouth and then closing it again, like a shop door on a busy day.

'Watch out,' she said. 'You're catching flies.'

She heard his teeth click together. 'I thought you were supposed to be b-blind.'

'I am, but I can *hear* you all right. You make a noise when you open your mouth. Your breathing changes—' Emily turned away, feeling suddenly impatient. Why did she bother explaining things? He was just another tourist, here to see the freak. In a moment, if he dared, he'd ask her about the colours.

When he did, it took Emily a moment to understand what he was saying. The stammer she'd already noticed in his voice had intensified; not, she realized, through nerves, but from some real conflict that knotted his words into a tangle that for a few seconds even he could not undo.

'You can really *h-* you can *h-h-* you can *hear* c-c—' Emily could hear the frustration in his voice as he struggled with the words. 'You can really hear c-colours?' he said.

She nodded.

'So. What colour am I?'

She shook her head. 'I can't explain. It's like a kind of extra sense.'

The boy laughed. Not a happy sound. 'Malbry smells of shit,' he said in a fast and toneless voice. 'Dr Peacock smells of bubblegum. Mr Pink smells of dentist's gas.' Emily noticed that he hadn't stuttered once throughout this speech, the longest she'd heard him make so far.

'I don't understand,' she said, puzzled.

'You don't know who I am, do you?' he said, with a touch of bitterness. 'All those times I watched you play, or sit in your s-swing in the living-room—'

The penny dropped. 'You're him? *You're Boy X?*'

For a long time he said nothing. Perhaps he'd nodded – people forget – and then he just said: 'Yes. That's me.'

'I remember hearing about you,' she said, not wanting him to know that her mother thought he was a fake. 'Where did you go? After Dr Peacock—'

'I didn't go anywhere,' he said. 'We live in White City. The bottom end of the village. Ma works on the m-market. S-selling f-fruit.'

There was a long silence. This time she couldn't hear him struggling to speak, but she could feel his eyes on her. It was uncomfortable; it made her feel indignant and a little guilty at the same time.

'I fucking hate fruit,' he said.

There was another long pause, during which she closed her eyes and wished the boy would go away. Mother was right, she told herself. He wasn't like her. He wasn't even friendly. And yet . . .

'What's it like?' She had to ask.

'What, selling fruit?'

'That – thing you do. The taste-smell-word thing. I don't know the name.'

There was a long silence as, once more, he struggled to explain. 'I don't d-*do* anything,' he said at last. 'It's like – it's just *there*, somehow. Like yours, I guess. I see something, I hear something, and then I get a feeling. Don't ask me why. Weird things. And *it hurts*—'

Another pause. Inside the gallery the sound of voices had dimmed; Emily guessed that someone was getting ready to make a speech.

'You're lucky,' said B.B. 'Yours is a gift. It makes you special. Mine, I'd do without it any day. It hurts, I get these headaches *here*—' He placed a hand on her temple, and another one at the nape of her neck. She felt a tremor go through him then, as if he were actually in pain.

'Plus everyone thinks you're m-mad, or worse, that you're faking it to get attention. I mean, do *you* think I'm faking it?'

For a second she faltered. 'I don't know—'

That laugh again. 'Well, there you go.' Suddenly the pent-up anger Emily had heard in his voice was overlaid with a tremendous weariness. 'At the end, even *I* thought I'd been faking it. And Dr Peacock – don't blame him. I mean, they say it's a gift. But what's it *for*? Yours I can understand. Seeing colours when you're blind. Painting music. It's like a b-bloody miracle. But mine? Imagine what it's like for me, every d-day—' Now he was stuttering again. 'Some d-days it's so bad I can hardly think, and what's it for? What's it even *for*?'

He stopped, and Emily could hear him breathing harshly. 'I used to think there was a cure,' he said finally. 'I used to think that if I did the tests, then Dr Peacock would find a cure. But there isn't a way. It gets everywhere. It gets into everything. TV. Films. You can't get away. From it. From *them*—'

'The smells, you mean?'

He paused. 'Yeah. The smells.'

'What about me?' Emily said. 'Do I have a smell?'

'Sure you do, Emily,' he said, and now she could hear the tiniest hint of a smile in his voice. '*Emily White* smells of roses. That rose that grows by the wall at the edge of the doctor's garden. *Albertine*, that was its name. That's what your name smells like to me.'

Post comment:
JennyTricks: *(post deleted).*
blueeyedboy: *(post deleted).*
JennyTricks: *(post deleted).*
Albertine: *Why, thank you . . .*

15

You are viewing the webjournal of **blueeyedboy**.
Posted at: 04.29 on Tuesday, February 12
Status: restricted
Mood: good
Listening to: Genesis: 'The Lady Lies'

I knew from that moment she was faking it. Not quite eight years old, and yet already she was cleverer than any of those others: the ones in charge of the media hype; the ones who thought they'd created her.

What's it like? That – thing you do.

She was so beautiful, even then. Skin like vanilla ice cream, that smooth dark hair and those sibyl's eyes. Good breeding makes for good skin. Her breeding went right down to the bone: forehead, cheekbones, wrists and neck, collarbones chiselled and lovely. But –

What's it like? That thing you do?

She would never have asked me otherwise. Not if she'd been telling the truth. These things we feel – these things we *sense* – are deeply embedded inside us, like razor blades in a bar of soap: sharp, inexplicable edges that cut as keenly as beauty.

That lie of hers confirmed it; but already I knew she belonged with me. Both of us soulmates in deceit; both of us bad guys, for ever, at heart. There was no point in my asking her when – or if – I could see her again. It would have been difficult enough with an ordinary child to arrange the kind of clandestine meeting that I had in mind – with this now-famous blind girl, I didn't stand a chance.

That was when the dreams began. No one had really explained to me about hormones, or growing up, or sex. For a woman with three teenage sons, Ma had proved curiously prudish on the subject, and when the relevant time had come, I'd learnt most of the truth from my brothers, a bike-shed education at best, which did not entirely prepare me for the magnitude of the experience.

I'd been a late developer. But that spring I caught up with a vengeance. I grew three inches taller, my skin cleared, and suddenly I was acutely and uncomfortably aware of myself, of the intensity of all my sensations – which seemed, if anything, even stronger than before – to the way I awoke in the mornings with a hard-on that sometimes took hours to subside.

My emotions veered from plummeting misery to absurd elation; all my senses were enhanced; I wanted desperately to be in love, to touch, to kiss, to feel, to *know* –

And through it all were those dreams: vivid, plosive, passionate dreams that I wrote down in my Blue Book, dreams that filled me with shame and despair and a dreadful, lurking sense of joy.

Nigel had told me some months before that it might soon be time for me to do my own laundry. I saw what he meant now, and took his advice, airing my room and washing my bedsheets three times a week in the hope of dispersing the civet smell. Ma never commented; but I felt her disapproval grow, as if it were somehow my fault that I was leaving my boyhood behind.

Ma was looking old, I thought, hard and sour as an under-ripe apple; and there was a sense of desperation in her now, in the way she watched me at the dinner-table, telling me to sit up, to eat properly, to stop *slouching*, for God's sake –

At her insistence I had stayed in school, and had so far managed to conceal the fact that I was lagging far behind. But by Easter the public exams loomed close, and I was failing in most of my subjects. My spelling was awful; maths made my head ache, and the more I tried to concentrate, the more the headaches assaulted me, so that even the sight of my school clothes laid out on the back of a chair was enough to bring it on; torture by association.

There was no one to whom I could go for help. My teachers – even the more well-disposed among them – were inclined to take the view that I just wasn't cut out for academic work. I could hardly explain to them the true reason for my anxiety. I could hardly admit to them that I was afraid of Ma's disappointment.

And so I hid the evidence. I faked my mother's signature on a variety of absence notes. I hid my school reports; I lied; I forged my end-of-term results. But she must have suspected something was wrong, because she began a covert investigation – she must have known that I would lie – first contacting the school by phone to find out what story I'd told, and then making an appointment with my form-teacher and the Head of Year. In which she learnt that since Christmas I had barely attended school at all, due to a prolonged bout of flu which had led to my missing the exams –

I remember the night of that meeting. Ma had cooked my favourite meal – fried chilli chicken and corn on the cob – which I suppose should have alerted me that something serious was afoot. I should have noticed her clothes, too – the dark-blue dress and those high-heeled shoes – but I guess I'd become complacent. I never suspected that I was being lulled into a false sense of security, and I had no inkling of the reprisals that were about to descend on my unsuspecting head.

Maybe I was careless. Maybe I'd underestimated Ma. Or maybe someone saw me in town with my stolen camera –

Anyway, my mother knew. She knew, she watched and she bided her time; then, when she'd spoken to the Head of Year and my teacher, Mrs Platt, she came back home in her interview clothes and cooked me my favourite dinner, and when I'd finished eating it, she left me on the sofa and turned the television on, and then she went into the kitchen (I presumed it was to wash the dishes), and then she came back silently and the first thing I knew was the scent of L'Heure Bleue and her voice in my ear, hissing at me –

'You little *shit*.'

I turned abruptly at the sound, and that was when she hit me. Hit me with the dinner-plate; hit me right in the face with it, and for a second I was torn between the shock of the impact against my eyebrow and cheekbone and simple dismay at the mess of it – at the chicken grease and corn kernels in my face and in my hair, more dismayed at that than the pain, or the blood that was running into my eyes, colouring the world in shades of *escarlata* –

Half-dazed I tried to back away; hit the couch with the small of my back, sending a glassy pain up my spine. She hit me again, in the mouth this time, and then she was on top of me, punching and slapping and screaming at me –

'You lying little shit, you cheating little *bastard*!'

I know you think I could have fought back. With words, if not with my fists and feet. But for me there were no magic words. No specious declaration of love could ward off my mother's fury, and no declaration of innocence could stem the tide of her violent rage.

It was that rage that frightened me – the mad, ballistic anger of her – far, far worse than those punches and slaps, and the sludgy stink of the vitamin drink that was somehow a terrible part of it all, and the way she screamed those things in my ears. Until finally I was crying – *Ma! Please! Ma!* – curled up in a corner beside the couch with my arms wrapped around my head, and blood in my eyes, and blood in my mouth, and that weak and fearful baby-blue word, like the helpless cry of a newborn, punctuating every blow, until the world went by degrees from blood-red to blue-black, and the outburst was finally over.

Afterwards, she made it clear how badly I'd disappointed her. Sitting on the couch with a cloth held up to my cut mouth and another to my eyebrow, I listened to my long list of crimes, and sobbed as I heard the sentence passed.

'I'm going to keep my eye on you, B.B.'

I spy. My mother's eye, like the watchful Eye of God. I felt it like a fresh tattoo, like a graze on my bare skin. Sometimes I see it in my mind: and it's bruise-blue, hospital-blue, faded prison-overall-blue. It marks me, inescapably – the mark of my mother; the mark of Cain, the mark that can never be erased.

Yes, I had disappointed her. First, she told me, with my lies – as if by telling the truth I might have spared myself all this. Then with my many failures: failure to excel at school; failure to be a good son; failure to live up to what she'd always expected of me.

'Please, Ma.' My ribs hurt; later we found out that two of them were broken. My nose, too, was broken – you can see it isn't quite straight – and if you look closely at my lips you can still see the scars, tiny silvery threadneedle scars, like someone's schoolboy stitching.

'You've got no one to blame but yourself,' she said, as if all she'd given me was a maternal slap, something to get my attention. 'And what about that girl, eh?'

The lie was automatic. 'What girl?'

'Don't you look so innocent—' She gave a thin-lipped, vinegary smile, and a finger of ice went down my back. 'I know what you've been up to. Following that blind girl.'

Had Mrs White spoken to her? Had Ma got into my darkroom? Had one of her friends mentioned seeing me with a camera?

But she knew. She always does. The photographs of Emily; the graffiti on Dr Peacock's front door; the weeks of playing truant from school. And the Blue Book, I thought in sudden alarm – could it be that she'd found that, too?

Now my hands began to shake.

'Well, what have you got to say for yourself?'

There was no way I could explain it to her. 'Please, M-Ma. I'm s-sorry.'

'What is it with you and that blind girl? What have you two been doing?'

'Nothing. Really. Nothing, Ma. I've never even t-talked to her!'

She gave me one of her freezing smiles. 'So – you've *never* talked to her? Never – not once – in all this time?'

'Just once. Once, in front of the gallery—'

My mother's eyes narrowed abruptly, I saw her hand move upwards, and I knew she was going to slap me again. The thought of those aggressive hands anywhere near my mouth again was suddenly unbearable, and I flinched away defensively and said the first thing that came into my mind:

'Emily's a f-fake,' I said. 'She doesn't hear any colours. She doesn't even know what they are. She's making it up – she told me so – and everybody's c-cashing in—'

Sometimes it takes a new idea to stop a charging juggernaut. She looked at me with those narrowed eyes, as if she were trying to see through the lie. Then, very slowly, she lowered her hand.

'*What* did you say?'

'She makes it up. She tells them what they want to hear. And Mrs White set her up to it—'

The silence simmered around her awhile. I could see the idea taking root in her, supplanting her disappointment, her rage.

'She *told* you that?' she said at last. 'She told you she was making it up?'

I nodded, feeling braver now. My mouth still hurt, and my ribs were sore, but now there was a taste of victory behind that of my suffering. In spite of what my brothers believed, invention at short notice had always been a talent of mine; and now I used it to free myself from my mother's terrible scrutiny.

I told her the lot. I fed her the line. All the things you've ever read about the Emily White affair: every rumour; every gibe; every piece of vitriol. All of that began with *me* – and, like the speck of irritant at the heart of the oyster that hardens to become a pearl, it grew, and bore fruit, and was harvested.

You knew I was a bad guy. What you don't yet know is *how* bad: how there and then I set the course towards this final, fatal act; how little Emily White and I came to be fellow-travellers on this road –

This tortuous road to murder.

16

You are viewing the webjournal of **Albertine** posting on:
badguysrock@webjournal.com
Posted at: 08.37 on Wednesday, February 13
Status: public
Mood: despondent

It all began to decline right then, the night of that first exhibition. It took some time for me to realize it, but that was when the Emily White Phenomenon began to take on a disquieting turn. It seemed nothing more than a ripple at first, but especially after the success of Dr Peacock's book, there were more and more people ready to take notice, to believe the worst, to scorn, to envy or to sneer.

In France, a country fond of its child prodigies, *L'Affaire Emily* had attracted more than its share of attention. One of Emily's first patrons – an old Paris friend of Dr Peacock – sold several of her paintings from his gallery on the Left Bank. *Paris-Match* had seized the story, as had *Bild* magazine in Germany, and all of England's tabloid press – not to mention Feather's piece in *Aquarius Moon*.

But then came the scandal. The swift decline. Exposure by the media. Less than six months after that triumphant launch, Emily's career was already foundering.

I never saw it coming, of course. How could I possibly have known? I didn't read papers or magazines. Gossip and rumours passed me by. If there was something in the air, I was too self-absorbed to notice; so deep inside my masquerade that I barely saw what was happening.

Daddy knew – he'd known from the start – but he couldn't stop the avalanche. Accusations had been made. Investigations were under way. The papers were filled with conflicting reports, a book was being launched, there was even a film – but one thing was clear to everyone. The bubble had burst. The wonder had gone. The Emily White Phenomenon was well and truly over. And so, with nothing left to lose, like the Snow Child in the fairy tale, we melted away, Daddy and I, leaving no trace of ourselves behind.

At first it seemed like a holiday. *Just until we get back on our feet.* An endless succession of B & Bs. Bacon for breakfast, birdsong at dawn, fresh clean sheets on strange, narrow beds. A holiday from Malbry, he said; and for the first few weeks I believed him, following like a tame sheep until finally we came to rest in a remote little place near the Scottish border, where no one, he said, would recognize us.

I didn't miss my mother at all. I know that must sound terrible. But to have Daddy all to myself like this was such an unusual pleasure that Malbry and my old life seemed to me like something that had happened to someone else, to quite a different girl, long ago. And when finally it became clear to me that something was wrong, that Daddy was slowly losing his mind, that he would never get back on his feet, I covered for him as best I could, until at last they came for us.

He'd always been a quiet man. Now, depression claimed him. At first I'd thought it was loneliness, and I'd tried my best to make it up to him. But as time passed, he grew more remote, more couched in his eccentricities, dependent on his music to such an extent that he forgot to eat, forgot to sleep, telling the same old stories, playing the same old pieces again on the piano in the hall, or on the cracked old stereo, *Für Elise* and *Moonlight Sonata*, and of course the Berlioz, the *Symphonie fantastique* and especially 'The March to the Scaffold' – while I did my best to care for him, and he slipped into silence.

Eighteen months later, he had his first stroke. Lucky I'd been there, they said; lucky I'd found him when I had. It was a mild one, the doctor said; affecting just his speech and his left hand. They didn't seem to understand how important his hands were to Daddy – it was the way he spoke to me when he couldn't express himself with words.

But that was the end of our hideaway. At last, the world had discovered us. They took us to different places – Daddy to a care centre near Malbry, me to another kind of home, where I endured for the next five years without a moment's realization that *someone* had to be paying the bills; that someone was looking out for us, and that Dr Peacock had tracked us down.

Later I learnt of the correspondence between them; of Dr Peacock's repeated attempts to make contact; of Daddy's refusal to answer him. Why did Dr Peacock care? Perhaps it was from a feeling of guilt; or loyalty to an old friend; or pity for the little girl caught up in the tragedy.

In any case, he paid our bills, watched over us from afar, while the house still stood empty, unused and unloved, boxed-up like an unwanted gift, packed to the rafters with memories.

I turned eighteen. I found my own place. There in the centre of Malbry: a tiny cube on a fourth floor, with a living-room-slash-bedroom, a kitchenette and a half-tiled bathroom that smelt of damp. I visited Daddy every week – sometimes he even knew who I was. And though for a while I was sure I'd be recognized, finally I understood. No one cared about Emily White. No one even remembered her.

But nothing ever disappears. Nothing ever really ends. For all the safety and love that Nigel gave me, I realize now – if a little late – that all I had done in following him was to substitute one golden cage for a different set of bars.

But now, at last, I am free of them all. Free of my parents, free of the doctor, free of Nigel. So who am I now? Where do I go? And how many others have to die before I am free of Emily?

Post comment:
blueeyedboy: *Very moving,* **Albertine**. *I sometimes ask myself the same thing –*

PART FOUR

smoke

1

You are viewing the webjournal of **blueeyedboy**.
Posted at: *15:06 on Wednesday, February 13*
Status: *restricted*
Mood: *mellow*
Listening to: *Voltaire*: 'Blue-eyed Matador'

I slept till long after midday today. Told Ma I'd taken some time off work. I don't sleep much at the best of times. But recently I've been averaging only two or three hours a night, and the latest quid pro quo with *Albertine* must have taken more out of me than I'd thought. Still, it was worth it, don't you think? After twenty silent years, suddenly she wants to talk.

Can't say I really blame her. Traditionally, raising the dead has always had serious consequences. In her case, inevitably, the tabloids will come out in droves. Money, murder and madness always make for excellent Press. Can she survive the exposure? Or will she remain in hiding here; in tacit, furtive acceptance of a past that never happened?

When I'd showered and changed my clothes I went to look for *Albertine*. The Pink Zebra café on Mill Road; it's where she goes when she feels the need to be someone else. It was six o'clock. She was sitting alone at the counter, with a cup of hot chocolate and a cinnamon bun. Underneath her red coat, I saw, she was wearing a sky-blue dress.

Albertine *in blue*, I thought. *This may just be my lucky day.*

'May I join you?'

245

She gave a start at the sound of my voice.

'If you'd rather not socialize, I promise I won't say a word. But that hot chocolate looks wonderful, and—'

'No. Please. I'd like you to stay.'

Grief always gives her face a kind of emotional nakedness. She held out her hand. I took it. A thrill ran through me; a tremor that moved from the soles of my feet right up into the roots of my hair.

I wonder if she felt it too; her fingertips were slightly cold, her small hand not quite steady in mine. There's something almost childlike about her, a kind of passive acceptance that Nigel must have taken for vulnerability. I, of course, know better; but, as she must know, I'm a special case.

'Thank you.' I took a seat next to her. Ordered Earl Grey and whichever pastry was highest in calories. I hadn't eaten for twenty-four hours, and I was suddenly ravenous.

'Lemon meringue pie?' She smiled. 'That seems to be your favourite.'

I ate the pie, and she drank her hot chocolate, leaving the cinnamon bun untouched. The process of eating makes a man look strangely inoffensive, somehow; all weapons laid down in a common purpose.

'How are you coming to terms with it?' I said, when the pie was finished.

'I don't want to talk about that,' she said.

At least she didn't pretend she didn't know what I was talking about. A few days more and she won't have the choice any more. All it will take is a word to the Press, and the story will be out, whether she likes it or not.

'I'm sorry, *Albertine*,' I said.

'It's over, B.B. I've moved on.'

Well, *that* was a lie. No one moves on. The wheel just keeps on turning, that's all, creating the illusion of momentum. Inside it, we are all rats; running in growing desperation towards a painted blue horizon that never gets any closer.

'Lucky you, moving on. At least being dead gives closure.'

'What's that supposed to mean?' she said.

'Well, everyone sides with the victim, of course. Deserving or not,

246

everyone mourns as soon as the mark is safely dead. But what about the rest of us? The ones with problems of our own? Being dead is pretty straightforward. Even my brothers managed that. But living with guilt is something else. It's not easy being the bad guy—'

'Is *that* what you are?' she said mildly.

'I think we've both established that.'

The ghost of a smile crossed her face, like a wisp of cloud on a summer's day. 'What happened between you and Nigel?' she said. 'He never talked about you much.'

Didn't he? Good. 'Does it matter now?'

'I just want to understand. What was it between you two?'

I shrugged. 'We had issues.'

'Don't we all?'

I laughed at that. 'Our issues were different. The whole of our family was different.'

Her eyes skittered for a moment. She has remarkably beautiful eyes; blue as a fairy tale, flecked with gold. Mine are grey in comparison; chilly, they tell me; changeable.

'Nigel didn't tell me much about any of his family,' she said, locating her cup of hot chocolate and bringing it carefully to her lips.

'As I mentioned, we weren't close.'

'It wasn't that. I know families. He couldn't stay away, somehow. As if there were something keeping him here—'

'That would be Ma,' I told her.

'But Nigel *hated* his mother—' She stopped. 'I'm sorry. I know you're devoted to her.'

'Is that what he told you?' My voice was dry.

'I just assumed – well, you live with her.'

'Some people live with cancer,' I said.

Albertine hardly ever smiles. I think she finds it difficult to understand those tiny facial variables, the difference between a smile and a frown, a grimace of pain. Not that her face is expressionless. But social conventions are not for her, and she does not express what she does not feel.

'So why do you stay?' she said at last. 'Why don't you get away, like Nigel?'

'Get away?' I gave a sharp laugh. 'Nigel didn't get away. He ended up half a mile from home. And with the girl next door, no less. You think that counts as getting away? But then, you're hardly an expert. You both ended up in the same gutter, but at least Nigel was looking up at the stars.'

She was silent for such a long time that I wondered if I'd gone too far. But she is tougher than she looks.

'I'm sorry,' I told her. 'Was that too direct?'

'I think I'd like you to go now.' She put down her cup of chocolate. I could hear the tension in her voice, still under control for the moment, but almost ready to escalate.

I stayed where I was. 'I'm sorry,' I said. 'But Nigel wasn't an innocent. He was playing a game with you. He knew who you were, who you used to be. And he knew that when Dr Peacock died he'd have his ticket out of here.'

'You're lying!'

'No, not this time,' I said.

'Nigel hated liars,' she said. 'That was why he hated you.'

Ouch. That was cruel, Albertine.

'No, he hated me because I was Ma's favourite. He was always jealous of me. Anything I wanted, *he* had to have. Perhaps that's why he wanted you. *And* Dr Peacock's money, of course.' I glanced at the still-untouched cinnamon bun. 'Aren't you going to eat that?'

She ignored me. 'I don't believe you. Nigel would never have lied to me. He was the straightest person I know. That's why I loved him.'

'*Loved* him?' I said. 'You never did. What you loved was being some-one else.' I took a bite of the cinnamon bun. 'As for Nigel – who knows? Maybe he wanted to tell you the truth. Maybe he thought you needed time. Or maybe he was enjoying the feeling of power it gave him over you—'

'What?'

'Oh, please. Don't be disingenuous. Some men enjoy being in control. My brother was a control freak – and he had a temper, of course. An uncontrollable temper. I'm sure you must be aware of that.'

'Nigel was a good man,' she said in a low voice.

'There's no such thing,' I told her.

'He was! He was _good!_' Now her voice distressed the air in jagged patterns of green and grey. Soon, I knew, they would bring that scent; but I let the silence roll awhile.

'Sit down. Just for a moment,' I said, and guided her hands towards my face.

For a moment she resisted me. Perhaps it was too much intimacy. But then she must have changed her mind, because at that moment she closed her eyes and put her hands against my face, with cool fingertips that explored me from brow to chin, gently taking in the sutures under my left eye; the still-swollen bruise on my cheekbone; the cut lip, the broken nose –

'Nigel did this?' Her voice was small.

'What do _you_ think?'

Now her eyes were open again. God, but they were beautiful. No grief in them now, nor anger, nor love. Just beauty, blank and blameless.

'Nigel was always unstable,' I said. 'I suppose he must have told you that. That he was prone to acts of violence? That he murdered his brother, no less?'

She winced. 'Of course he told me. He said it was an accident.'

'But he told you all about it, right?'

'He got in a fight over twenty years ago. That doesn't make him a murderer.'

'Oh, please,' I interrupted. 'What does it matter how long ago? No one changes. It's a myth. There's no road to Damascus. No path to redemption. Not even the love of a good woman – assuming such a thing exists – can wash the blood from a killer's hands.'

'Stop it!' Her own hands were shaking. 'Can't we just leave this alone?' she said. 'Can't it just stay in the past, for once?'

The _past?_ Don't give me that, _Albertine._ You, of all people, should understand that the past is never over. We drag it behind us everywhere, like a can tied to a stray dog's tail. Try to outrun it, it just makes more noise. Until it drives you crazy.

'He never told you, did he?' I said. 'He never said what happened that day?'

'Don't. Please. Leave me alone.'

I could tell from the tone of her voice that she'd given me all she could today. Better than I'd expected, in fact; and besides, the essential part of a game is always knowing when to fold. I paid my bill with a twenty-pound note, leaving it tucked under my plate. She did not respond, or even look up, as I said goodbye to her and left. The last I saw of her as I opened the door and stepped out into the darkness was the fleeting flash of colour as she reached for her red duffel coat hanging behind the counter, and the crescent moon of her profile eclipsed behind the screen of her open hands –

Truth hurts, doesn't it, *Albertine*? Lies are so much safer. But murderers run in our family, and Nigel was no exception. And who would have thought that nice young man could have ever done such a terrible thing? And who would have thought that a little white lie could snowball into murder?

2

It was an accident, they said. A cracked skull, the result of a fall down-stairs. Not even the main stairs, as it turned out, but the six stone steps at the front door. Somehow he'd come off the ramp that I'd built, or maybe he had tried to stand, as sometimes he did occasionally; to stand up miraculously and walk across the misty white lawn like Jesus on the water.

That was over three weeks ago. Lots of things have happened since then. My brother's death; the loss of my job; my dialogue with *Albertine*. But don't think I ever forgot. Dr Peacock was always on my mind. Old enough to have been forgotten by almost everyone he'd known; old enough to have outlived his fame, even his notoriety. A pathetic old man, half-blind and confused, who told the same stories again and again and barely recognized my face –

He wrote me into his will, you know. How ironic is that? You'll find me at the end of the list, under *miscellaneous other*. I guess a man who can leave thirty thousand pounds to the animal shelter that supplied his dogs can well afford a couple of grand for the guy who used to clean up for him, and cook his mushy old-man's meals, and wheel him around the garden.

A couple of grand. Less, with tax. Not nearly enough to qualify as a motive. But it's rather nice to be, if not exactly *recognized*, then at least given *some* acknowledgement for all the work I did for him, for my tireless good cheer, for my honesty –

Did he recall my tenth birthday? The candle on the iced bun? I don't suppose so – why should he care? I was nobody; nothing to him. If that day still survived within his damaged memory, it would have been as the day he buried poor old Rover, or Bowser, or Jock, or whatever the hell the dog's name was. To pretend to myself that he might have cared for me, for *blueeyedboy*, is ludicrous. I was simply a project to him, not even the main act of the show. Still, I can't help wondering –

Did he know his murderer? Did he try to call for help? Or was it all just a blur to him, a heap of broken images? Personally, I like to think that, right at the end, he understood. That as he died, his senses returned for just long enough for him to know just *how* he was dying, and *why*. Not everyone gets to know those things. Not everyone gets that privilege. But I like to think that maybe he did, and that the last thing he ever saw, the picture that followed him into eternity, was a familiar face, a more-than-familiar pair of eyes –

The police came round to the house, of course. Eleanor Vine directed them there, though I still have no idea how she found out I was working at the Mansion. For a woman who spent most of her time shut up in her house, cleaning the floors, she seemed to have an uncanny knack for revealing embarrassing secrets. In this case, however, I realized, with some relief, that my cover was only partially blown: she knew I was working for Dr Peacock, but not about my hospital job, though she may have had her suspicions by then, and exposure might have been just a matter of time.

Did she believe I was involved? If so, she was disappointed. There were no handcuffs, there was no interrogation, no trip to the police station. Even the questions they asked me had a tired quality. After all, there was no sign of violence. The victim had merely suffered a fall. The death – the *accidental* death – of one old man (even if he had been famous once) was hardly a matter for much concern.

My mother took it badly, though. It wasn't the thought that I might have killed Dr Peacock, but just the fact that I'd been in the house, had worked in that house for eighteen months without her even suspecting it – and worse, that *Eleanor* had known –

'How could you?' she said, when they had gone. 'How could you set foot in that house again, after everything that's happened?'

There was no point my denying what I'd done. But as any seasoned liar knows, a half-truth can screen a thousand lies. And so I confessed. I'd had no choice. I'd had to take on extra work. It was part of the hospital's outpatient scheme. The fact that I'd got that particular case was nothing but coincidence.

'You could have talked your way out of it. You could talk your way out of a locked *room*—'

'It isn't as easy as that, Ma—'

She slapped me then, across the mouth. One of her rings cut my lip. Probably the tourmaline. Its taste was Campari soda with an aluminium chaser of blood.

Tourmaline. Tour. Malign. It sounds like a place of imprisonment, an evil tower from a Perrault fairy tale, and its smell is the same as St Oswald's, a reek of disinfectant and dust and polish and cabbage and chalk and boys.

'Don't you dare patronize me. Don't think I don't know what you're up to.'

My mother has a sixth sense. She always knows when I've done something wrong; when I'm *thinking* of doing something wrong.

'You wanted to see him, didn't you? After everything he's done to us. You wanted his fucking *approval*.' Her camelbacked foot in its slingback heel began to tap a quick, irregular rhythm against the leg of the sofa. The sound of it made my throat go dry, and the vegetable stink of it was enough to make me want to gag.

'Please, Ma.'

'Didn't you?'

'Please, Ma, it's not my fault—'

She is surprisingly quick with her hands. I was expecting the second blow, and still it caught me by surprise, knocking me sideways into the wall. The cabinet with the china dogs shivered once, but nothing fell.

'Then whose fault *is* it, you little shit?'

I put a hand to my cut lip. I knew she hadn't even begun; her face was almost expressionless, but her voice was charged like a battery. I took a step closer to the cabinet. I figured she wouldn't risk anything so close to her china dogs.

When she's dead, I thought to myself, *I'm going to take every single one of those fucking dogs out into the back yard and stamp on them with my engineer boots.*

She saw me looking. 'B.B., come *here!*'

Just as I thought, I told myself. She wanted me clear of that cabinet. She'd acquired a new ornament, I saw; an Oriental specimen. I put out my hand and rested it very gently against the pane.

'Don't do that,' my mother snapped. 'You'll leave fingerprints on the glass.'

I could tell she wanted to hit me again. But she didn't – not then – because of those dogs. Still, I couldn't stay there all day. I turned towards the parlour door, hoping to make it upstairs to my room, but Ma grabbed hold of the door-handle and, with one hand in the small of my back, yanked the door open into my face –

After that, it was easy. Once I was down, her feet did the rest, her feet in those fucking sling-backed heels. By the time she was done I was snivelling, and my face was laddered with scratches and cuts.

'*Now* look at you,' Ma said – the violent outburst over now, but still with a trace of impatience, as if this were something I'd brought on myself, some unrelated accident. 'You're a mess. What on earth were you playing at?'

I knew there was no point in trying to explain. Experience has taught me that when Ma gets like this, it's better to stay quiet and hope for the best. Later, she'll fill in the gaps with some kind of plausible story; a fall down the stairs, an accident. Or maybe this time I was mugged, or beaten up on my way from work. I should know. It's happened before. And those sharp little breaks in her memory are getting increasingly frequent, more so since my brother's death.

I tested my ribs. None seemed broken. But my back hurt where she'd kicked me, and there was a deep cut across my eyebrow where the edge of the door had struck. Blood drenched the front of my shirt, and I could already feel one of my headaches coming, arpeggios of coloured light troubling my vision.

'I suppose you'll need stitches now,' said Ma. 'As if I didn't already have enough to do today. Oh, well.' She sighed. 'Boys will be boys. Always up to something. Lucky I was here, eh? I'll come with you to the hospital.'

OK, so I lied. I'm not proud of the fact. It was Ma, and not Nigel, who messed up my face. Gloria Green; five foot four in her shoes, sixty-nine and built like a bird –

You'll be fine in no time, love, said the pink-haired nurse as she fixed me up. Stupid bitch. As if she cared. I was just a patient to her. *Patient. Penitent.* Words that smell of citrus green and sting like a mouthful of needles. And I have been so patient, Ma, patient for so very long.

I had to quit my job after that. Too many questions; too many lies; too many snares in which to be caught. Having discovered one subterfuge, Ma could so easily have checked me out and exposed the pretence of the past twenty years –

Still, it's a short-term setback. My long-term plan remains unchanged. Enjoy your china dogs, Ma. Enjoy them while you still can.

I suppose I ought to feel pleased with myself. I'm getting away with murder. A smile, a kiss, and – *Whoops! All gone!* – like a malignant conjuring trick. You don't believe me? Check it out. Search me from all angles. Look for hidden mirrors, for secret compartments, for cards up my sleeve. I promise you I'm totally clean. And yet, it's going to happen, Ma. Just you watch it blow up in your face.

These were my thoughts as I lay there on the hospital trolley, thinking about those china dogs and how I was going to stomp them into powder the minute – the *second* – Ma was dead. And as soon as I let the thought take shape without the comforting blanket of fic, it was almost as if a nuke had gone off inside my skull, tearing into me, wringing me like a wet rag and cramping my jaw in a silent scream –

'I'm sorry, sweetheart. Did that hurt?' The pink-haired nurse, all three of her, swam briefly across my consciousness like a shoal of tropical fish.

'He gets these headaches,' said Ma. 'Don't worry. It's only stress.'
'I can get the doctor to prescribe something—'
'No. Don't bother. It'll pass.'

That was nearly three weeks ago. Forgotten, if not quite forgiven, perhaps, the stitches removed, the bruises now veering from purple and blue to an oil-slick palette of yellows and greens. The headache took three days to subside, during which time Ma fed me home-made soup and watched by my bed as I shivered and moaned. I don't think I said anything aloud. Even in my delirium, I think I was cleverer than that. In any case, by the end of the week, things were back to normal again, and *blueeyedboy* was, if not quite off the hook, then at least back in the net for another spell.

Meanwhile, on the bright side –

Eleanor Vine is most unwell. Taken ill last Saturday, she remains in hospital, on a respirator. Toxic shock, so Terri says, or maybe some kind of allergy. I can't say I'm particularly surprised – with the number of pills Eleanor takes, apparently at random, something like this had to happen some day. Still, it's an odd coincidence that a fic posted in my WeJay should have taken on such a life of its own. It's not the first time this has happened, either; it's almost as if, by some voodoo, I have acquired the ability to delete from the world all those who hurt or threaten me. A stroke of the keys – and *pfft! Delete.*

If only it were as easy as that. If this were simply a matter of wishful thinking, then my troubles would have been over more than twenty years ago. It began with the Blue Book – that catalogue of my hopes and dreams – and followed on into cyberspace, on to my WeJay, and *badguysrock*. But of course it's only fiction. And although it may have been Catherine White in my fic – or Eleanor Vine, or Graham Peacock, or any of those parasites – there was only ever one face in my mind: battered and bleeding, bludgeoned to death, strangled with piano wire; electrocuted in the bath; poisoned; drowned; decapitated, dead in a hundred different ways.

One face. One name.

I know. It's unforgivable. To wish for my mother's death in this way – to *long* for it, as one might long for a cool drink on a hot day, to wait with racing heart for the sound of her key in the front door, to hope that today might be the one –

Accidents happen so easily. A hit-and-run; a fall down the stairs; a random act of violence. Then there are the health issues. At sixty-nine, she is already old. Her hands are thick with arthritis; her blood pressure is sky-high. Cancer runs in the family: her own mother died at fifty-five. And the house itself is filled with potential hazards: over-loaded electrical sockets; loose carpet runners; plant pots balanced precariously on bedroom window-ledges. Accidents happen all the time; but never, it seems, to Gloria Green. It's enough to drive a boy to despair.

And yet I continue to live in hope. Hope, the most spiteful of all the demons in Pandora's little box of tricks –

3

It's February the 14th, Valentine's Day, and love, true love, is in the air. That's why I've left that envelope on the corner of the china cabinet next to the chocolates and flowers. *Not* roses, thank God, nor even orchids, but a nice arrangement nonetheless, lavish enough to be expensive, though not enough to be vulgar.

The card itself is selected with care: no jokey cartoons, no sexual innuendo, no promises of undying affection. Ma knows me better than that. It's the gesture that matters; the triumph that she will feel on her next outing with – for instance – Maureen, Eleanor, or Adèle, whose son lives in London and who rarely even telephones.

We do not fool ourselves, Ma and I. But still the game goes on. We've played the game a long, long time; this game of stealth and strategy. Each of us has had our share of victories and defeats. But now comes the chance to own the field – which is why right now I can't afford to take unnecessary risks. She's suspicious enough of me as it is. Unstable, too, and growing worse. It was bad enough when my brothers were here, but now I am the only one, the last, and she keeps me like one of her china dogs, on display from all angles –

She expresses surprise at the gifts and the card. This, too, is part of the game. If there had been no Valentine, she would have made no comment, but in a few days there would have been consequences. And so it pays to observe the conventions, to play along, to remember the stakes. That's why I've made it this far, of course. By always giving the devil his due.

Online, my friends remember me, too. There are six virtual Valentine's cards, innumerable pictures and banners, including one from Clair, hoping to see me soon, she says, and hoping I find love this year –

Why, how sweet of you, *ClairDeLune*. As it happens I hope so, too. But you have other concerns today – not least, the e-mail you sent from your hotmail account to Angel Blue, bearing a message of undying love, as well as the extra little surprise delivered to his New York address.

I knew that password would come in useful. And, as it happens, I've changed it now, from *clairlovesangel* to *clairhatesangie*, Angie being Mrs Angel Blue. It's cruel, I know. It may cause grief. But as we enter this new phase together, I have become increasingly impatient of time spent away from my main focus. I no longer need my army of mice. Their squeaking has become tiresome. They were a pleasant diversion once. And I needed them to build up this place, to bait my virtual bottle trap, my own private pitcher plant.

But now that *Albertine* and I are entering the final phase of the game, the last thing I want is her wasting her time. Time to concentrate on what really matters; to move in for the tête-à-tête –

And so, of today, all of *badguysrock* has become our private battleground. *Site under construction*, it says, which ought to keep most of our visitors out, while I send out my personal Valentines to deal with the more persistent ones.

Clair's you already know about. Chryssie's takes a different form; that of a dieting challenge – *lose 10lbs in only 3 days!* – a drop in the ocean for Chryssie, of course, but it should keep her out of my hair for a while.

As for Cap, a careless word dropped in his name on a gang message board, followed up by an e-mail inviting him to meet a friend at a certain place, at a certain time, in one of Manhattan's less pleasant districts –

Meanwhile, what of *Albertine*? I hope I haven't upset her. She's very sensitive, of course; recent events must have shaken her. She isn't answering her phone, which implies that she is screening calls. And maybe she lacks the energy, today of all days, when the nation honours a festival, which, though riddled with the pox of merchandising, purports to celebrate true love –

Somehow I don't see Nigel as the type. Then again, I wouldn't. It's hard to visualize one's childhood tormentor as the kind of person who would buy a bunch of red roses, make up a playlist of love songs, or send a Valentine's card to a girl.

Maybe he was, though. Who can say? He may have had hidden depths. He was certainly moody enough as a boy – spending hours alone in his room, looking at his maps of the sky, writing his verses, and listening to rock music that ranted and railed.

Nigel Winter, the poet. Well – you wouldn't have thought it to look at him. But I found some of his poetry, in a book at the bottom of his wardrobe, among the clothes in charcoal and black. A Moleskine notebook – slightly worn – in my brother's colour.

I couldn't help it. I stole the book. Removed myself from the scene of the crime to scrutinize it at leisure. Nigel didn't notice at first; and later, when he discovered the loss, he must have known that there could have been any number of places in which he might have mislaid a small, unobtrusive black notebook. Under his mattress; under the bed; under a fold of carpet. I played the innocent as I watched him search the house in stealth; but I'd hidden the notebook safely away in a box at the back of the garage. Nigel never mentioned to either of us what it was he was looking for, though his face was dark with suspicion as he questioned us – obliquely, and with uncommon restraint.

'Did you go into my stuff?' he said.

'Why? Did you lose something?'

He gave me a look.

'Well?'

He hesitated. 'No.'

I shrugged, but I was grinning inside. Whatever was in that book, I thought, must be something very important. But rather than attract attention to something he clearly wanted to hide, my brother played indifference, hoping perhaps that the notebook would lie for ever undisturbed –

As if. As soon as I could, I retrieved it from its hiding-place. It looked like an astronomy notebook at first; but in between the lists of figures, of sightings of planets and shooting stars and lunar eclipses, I found something else: a journal like mine, but of poetry –

> *The sweet curve of your back,*
> *Your neck – my fingers walk*
> *A dangerous line.*

Poetry? Nigel? Gleefully I read on. Nigel, the poet. What a joke. But my brother was full of contradictions, as well as being almost as cautious as I, and I learnt that behind his sullen façade there lay a few surprises.

The first was that he favoured haikus, those deceptively simple little rhymeless poems of only seventeen syllables. If anything, I would have expected Nigel to have gone for blowsy verses, thumping rhymes, sonnets with rhythms that thundered and rang, bludgeoning blocks of blank verse –

The second surprise was that he was in love – desperately, fiercely in love. It had been going on for months – ever since he'd bought the telescope, in fact, which hobby gave him the perfect excuse to come and go at night as he pleased.

That in itself was amusing enough. I hadn't seen Nigel as the type for romance. But the third surprise was the greatest of all – the thing that killed my amusement cold and made my heart quicken with delayed fear.

I flicked back through the notebook again, my fingers suddenly cold and numb, a cottony, chemical taste in my mouth. Of course, I'd always known that to be caught in possession of Nigel's book might have had serious consequences. But as I read further I understood the terrible risk I'd taken. Because this was something far more incriminating than just a few poems and scribblings. And if Nigel

261

suspected that I was the thief, I'd earn myself more than a beating. If anyone ever found out what I knew –

For that, my brother would kill me.

4

You are viewing the webjournal of **blueeyedboy**.
Posted at: 21.30 on Thursday, February 14
Status: restricted
Mood: disappointed
Listening to: Blondie: 'Picture This'

No Valentine yet from *Albertine*. I wonder, *did* he love her? Did they lie side by side in bed, his arm thrown carelessly around her shoulders, her face pressed into the curve of his neck? Did he wake to find her there, and wonder at his good fortune? Did he sometimes forget who he was, imagine that through love of her, some day he could be someone good?

But love is a treacherous animal, a shape-shifter by nature, making the poor man king for a day; transforming the most volatile into paragons of stability; a crutch for the weak, a shield for the craven – at least, until the buzz wears off.

He got it badly. I knew he would. My erstwhile tormentor, who used to force-feed me spiders, had finally, fatally, fallen in love. And with the least likely candidate, in one of those random encounters that even I could not have foreseen.

> The sweet curve of your back,
> Your neck –

I suppose you could have called her attractive. Not at all my type, of

263

course; but Nigel had always been perverse, and the boy who had spent his childhood trying to escape one older woman had fallen straight into the clutches of another. Her name was Tricia Goldblum; and she was an ex-employer of Ma's. An elegant fifty-something; ice-blonde; and with that air of helplessness that makes them irresistible. Still, there's no accounting for taste, is there? And I suppose she must have felt flattered. Mrs Electric Blue, as was, now divorced from her husband and free to indulge her predilection for nice young men.

Does that sound familiar yet? They always say to write what you know. And fiction is a tower of glass built from a million tiny truths, grains of sand fused together to make a single, gleaming lie –

He'd never really known her from the days when Ma worked as a cleaner. Perhaps he'd encountered her once or twice in one of the cafés or shops in town. But he'd never had reason to speak to her, to understand her, as I had. And as for that day at the market, the day I remembered so vividly –

As far as I was able to tell, Nigel had no memory of it at all. Perhaps that was why he chose her – Malbry's Mrs Robinson, whose furtive collection of young men had coloured her reputation, not blue, but scarlet in the eyes of such folk as Catherine White, Eleanor Vine and, most judgemental of all, Gloria Green.

Not that Nigel cared about *that* at the time. Nigel was besotted. But Mrs Goldblum valued discretion, and their affair was conducted in secret at first, with Mrs Goldblum calling the shots. Still, of course, that journal of his was enough to tell me everything: how cleverly she had reeled him in; even her penchant for sex toys was there, among the haikus and star charts.

My first impulse, of course, was to tell Ma, who had hated Mrs Goldblum ever since she'd abandoned us, and whose venom was no less lethal for having been stored away. But then I seriously believed that Nigel would have killed me. I knew his temper; and I guessed that Nigel in love, like Nigel at war, was capable of anything.

And so I nursed my discovery until such time as it could be of use. I never told Ma, never mentioned it, not even obliquely, to either of them. I was alone with my secret, a hoard of stolen banknotes that I could never spend without incriminating myself.

But enough of that for the moment. We'll get to that in due course. Suffice it to say that as time passed, the Moleskine diary revealed its use. And now I realized how easily, with the help of a few judicious props, I could set a bottle trap, which hopefully would set me free –

5

You are viewing the webjournal of **blueeyedboy**.
Posted at: *22.15 on Thursday, February 14*
Status: *restricted*
Mood: *malevolent*
Playing: *Pulp*: 'I Spy'

When Nigel was released from jail, I'd expected him, now he was free, to try again, to rebuild his life, to do all those things he'd always planned, to take the chance he'd been given, and run. But Nigel was never predictable; he was more than usually perverse, seeking out the opposite of whatever he was expected to do. And something in my brother had changed. Not something you could quantify, but something that I recognized. Like a ship in the Sargasso Sea, he had become entangled; enmeshed in himself, swallowed up by the pitcher plant that was Malbry, and our mother.

Oh, yes. Our mother. In spite of it all, he came back home – not to the house, but to Malbry; to Ma. Certainly he had no one else. His friends – such as they were – had moved on. All he had was his family.

My brother was twenty-five by then. He had no money, no prospects, no job. He was taking stabilizing drugs, though he was far from stable. And he blamed me for what had happened to him – blamed me unfairly, but doggedly – although even a headcase like Nigel should have been able to see that it wasn't my fault that he had committed murder –

All that didn't come out at once, of course. But Nigel had never

266

liked me, and now he liked me even less. I suppose he had good reason. To him, I must have seemed a success. By then I was studying – or so he believed – at Malbry Polytechnic, as was, though its status was upgraded a year later to that of a university, much to Ma's satisfaction. I still had money from my part-time job at the electrical shop, though, since I was a student, Ma allowed me to keep all of my salary. The Emily White affair was over, and Ma and I had already moved on.

To look at, Nigel hadn't changed much. His hair was longer than before, and sometimes it was greasy. He had a new tattoo on his arm – a single Chinese character, the symbol for 'courage' in basic black. He was thinner, and somehow smaller, too, as if part of him had been worn away like the end of a pencil eraser. But he still wore black all the time, and he liked the girls as he always had, although, as far as I ever knew, he never kept with the same one for more than a couple of weeks or so, as if trying to keep himself in check; as if he was afraid, somehow, that the rage that had killed a man might some day spring out at someone else.

At first he had no contact with Ma. No surprise, after what he had done. He moved into a flat in town, found himself a job there, and over the next few years lived alone – not happy, perhaps, but free.

And then, somehow, she reeled him back in. That freedom was just an illusion. One day I came home to find him there, sitting with Ma in the parlour, looking like a dead man, and along with that sneaking *Schadenfreude* I felt a sinking sense of doom.

No one escapes the pitcher plant. Not Nigel, not me, not anyone.

It was not a true rapprochement. But over the next eighteen years or so, we saw Nigel three or four times a year. At Christmas; on Ma's birthday; at Easter; on *my* birthday – and every time he came round, he would sit in the same place in the parlour, and stare at the shelf of china dogs – Mal's statuette had been repaired, of course, and had now been joined by a similar one, in the shape of a sleeping puppy.

And every time Nigel visited, he would stare at those fucking china dogs and drink tea from Ma's visitors' cups and listen to her carry on about how much the church had raised this year, and how the hedge needed clipping. And every other Sunday night he would phone at precisely eight thirty (which was when Ma's soaps were over), and stay on until she had finished with him, while the rest of the time he tried to make sense of what was left of his life with therapy and Prozac, working days and spending the nights in his attic flat watching stars that seemed increasingly remote each time, or cruising the streets in his black Toyota and waiting for someone, for *something* . . .

And then, along came *Albertine*. She should never have been there, of course. She didn't belong in that new café, the oddly named Pink Zebra, with its gassy, soporific scent and primary-school colours. And she certainly didn't belong with Nigel, who should have been out of the picture by then, but who had messed up his escape.

Maybe I ought to have stopped it then. I knew she was dangerous. But Nigel had already brought her home, like a little stray cat from out of the cold. Nigel was in love, he said. Needless to say, he had to go –

And though it *looked* like an accident, you and I know better, of course. I swallowed him, as I swallowed Mal, as I swallowed all of my brothers. Swallowed them down like the vitamin drink – *One, two, three, gone!* – and the taste may be sour, but the victory is sweeter than a summer rose –

6

You are viewing the webjournal of **blueeyedboy** *posting on:*
                         badguysrock@webjournal.com
Posted at: *23.25 on Thursday, February 14*
Status: *public*
Mood: *baroque*
Listening to: *The Rolling Stones:* 'Paint It Black'

Let's call him Mr Midnight Blue. A man of moods and mysteries. A poet and a lover, she thinks; a gentle man with a head full of stars. The truth is, she's living in fantasy. A fantasy in which two lost souls may find each other by happenstance, and be saved from themselves through true love –

What a joke. Poor girl. In fact her man is a headcase with blood on his hands; a liar; a coward; an arrogant thug. What's more, though she thinks he has chosen her, the truth is *she* was chosen for *him*.

You think that isn't possible? People are just like cards, you know. *Pick a card. Any card.* And the trick is to make the mark believe that the card he has picked was his choice, his own particular Queen of Spades –

He drives a black Toyota. He uses it to cruise the streets, as he used to do, in the days before. Still thinks of it as *before* and *after* – as if such a cataclysmic event could change the predestined orbit of a man's life, like two planets in collision, which then go off their separate ways.

Of course, that isn't possible. There is no way to cheat Fate. His crime has become a part of him, like the shape of his face, and the scar on his hand that runs across his heart line, the only physical reminder of that nasty interlude. A shallow cut that healed fast; unlike his victim, poor bastard, who died of a cracked skull a fortnight later.

But of course, Midnight Blue doesn't think of himself as a murderer. It was an accident, he says; an altercation that got out of hand. He never meant to do it, he says – as if that could somehow raise the dead, as if it makes a difference that he acted on impulse, that he was misled, that he was only twenty-one –

His lawyer was inclined to agree. Cited his mental state, which was poor; claimed there were special circumstances, and finally tried for a verdict of misadventure. A piebald word, half-red, half-black, that smells distinctly fishy to me, and sounds almost as if it could be a name: Miss Adventure, like *Boy X*, a comic-book adventuress –

Can any sentence compensate for the loss of a human life? *I'm sorry. I didn't mean it.* All those snivelling, wretched excuses. A five-year stretch – much of it spent in the quilted comfort of a psychiatric ward – discharged Midnight Blue's debt to society – which doesn't mean to say he was cured; or that he didn't deserve to die –

Reader, I killed him. I had no choice. That black Toyota was just too alluring. And I wanted something poetic this time: something to mark the victim's death with a final, triumphant fanfare.

There is a CD deck under the dashboard, on which he likes to play music as he drives. Midnight Blue favours loud bands, rock music that rants and rails. He likes his music noisy, his vocals raucous, the squeal of guitars; likes to feel the deep punch of the bass in his eardrums and that kick of response in his lower belly, like something there could still be alive.

Some might say that, at his age, he ought to have turned down the volume by now; but Midnight Blue knows that rebellion is something born from experience, a lesson learnt the hard way, wasted on adolescents. Midnight Blue has always been a kind of existentialist; brooding on mortality; taking out on the rest of the world the fact that he is going to die.

A small glass jar under the seat is *blueeyedboy*'s contribution. The rest is all from Midnight Blue: for he is the one who turns up the sound; turns on the heater; drives home in his usual way, by his usual route, at his usual speed. Inside the open jar, a single wasp makes its way sluggishly towards freedom.

A wasp, you say? At this time of year? They are not impossible to find. Under the roof there are often nests, left over from summer, in which the insects lie dormant, waiting for the temperature to rise. Not so hard to climb up there, to ease one out of its padded cell, to transfer it into a glass jar and wait –

The car begins to warm up. Slowly the insect comes to life in an amplified burr of synths and guitars. It crawls towards the source of heat; its stinger begins to pump in time to the rhythm of the bass and drums. Midnight Blue does not hear it. Nor does he see it crawling up the back of the car seat and on to the window, where it slowly unfolds its wings and begins to stutter against the glass –

Two minutes later, the wasp is alert. A combination of music, warmth and light has fully awakened it at last. It takes flight for a moment, hits the glass, rebounds and stubbornly tries again. And then it flies into the windscreen, just at the moment when Midnight Blue approaches the junction, driving with his usual impatience, cursing the other road users, the road, tapping out his frustration on the padded dashboard –

He sees the wasp. It's instinctive. He raises a hand towards his face. The insect, sensing the movement, veers a little closer. Midnight Blue strikes out, keeping one hand on the steering wheel. But the wasp has nowhere to go. It flies back into the windscreen, where it buzzes balefully. Midnight Blue, panicked now, fumbles for the window controls. He misses, and hits the volume instead, bumping up the sound and –

Wham! The volume kicks up from merely loud to an ear-buzzing burst of decibels; a sudden cataclysm of sound that shocks the steering wheel from his hand, sends it jerking spastically, and as Midnight Blue fights for control he slams right across the two lanes, his car tyres squealing soundlessly across the hard shoulder to hell, to the sound of a wailing wall of guitars –

I like to think he thought of me. Right at that moment, when his head smashed through the windscreen, I like to think he saw something more than just a cartoon trail of stars or the shadow of the Reaper. I'd like to think he saw a familiar face, that he knew in

271

that flashgun moment of death *who* had murdered him, and why.

Then again, maybe he didn't. These things are so ephemeral. And Midnight Blue died instantly, or at least within seconds of impact, as the car turned into a fireball, consuming everything inside.

Well – maybe the wasp made it out alive.

It didn't even sting the guy.

Post comment:

Captainbunnykiller: *And he's* back!!!

Toxic69: *You rock!*

chrysalisbaby: *woot woot*

JennyTricks: *(post deleted).*

JennyTricks: *(post deleted).*

JennyTricks: *(post deleted).*

JennyTricks: *(post deleted).*

blueeyedboy: **Albertine?** *Is that you?*

JennyTricks: *(post deleted).*

blueeyedboy: **Albertine?**

7

You are viewing the webjournal of **Albertine**.
Posted at: *22:46 on Friday, February 15*
Status: *restricted*
Mood: *awake*

It's only fiction, he protests. He never murdered anyone. And yet, there they are – his confessions in fic. Too close to be lies, too vile to be real; Valentines from the other side, picture postcards from the dead.

It *is* only fiction, isn't it? How could it possibly be anything else? This virtual life is so nicely secure, battened against reality. These virtual friends, too, are safely confined behind this screen, this mouse mat. No one expects to encounter the truth in these worlds we build for ourselves. No one expects to feel it this way, through a glass, darkly.

But *blueeyedboy* has a special way of shaping the truth to his purpose. He does the same with people, too: winds them up like clock-work toys and sends them crashing into . . .

Walls? Articulated lorries on a busy main road?

Reader, I killed him. What dangerous words. What am I meant to do with them? Does he believe what he's telling me, or is he just trying to mess with my mind? Nigel drove a black Toyota. And I know the style in which he drove, and his fear of wasps, and his favourite tracks, and the CD deck under the dashboard. Most of all, I remember how much that letter troubled him, and how he set off to his mother's house to deal with his brother once and for all . . .

Blueeyedboy has been trying to reach me all day. There are five unopened e-mails from him waiting in my inbox. I wonder what he wants from me. Confessions? Lies? Declarations of love?

Well, this time I won't react. I refuse. Because that's what he wants. A dialogue. He's played this game so many times. He admits that he is manipulative. I've watched him do it with Chryssie and Clair. He likes to subject them to mind games, to push them into declaring themselves. Thus, Chryssie is besotted with him; Clair thinks she can heal him; Cap wants to *be* him, and as for myself . . .

What *do* you want of me, *blueeyedboy*? What kind of reaction do you expect? Anger? Scorn? Confusion? Distress? Or could this be something more than that, some declaration of your own? Could it be that, after watching the world through a glass for so long, you finally, desperately want to be *seen*?

At ten o'clock the Zebra shuts. I'm always the last one out of the door. I found him waiting for me outside, under the shelter of the trees.

'Walk you home?' said *blueeyedboy*.

I ignored him. He followed me. I could hear his footsteps behind me, as I've heard them so many times.

'I'm sorry, *Albertine*,' he said. 'Obviously I shouldn't have posted that fic. But you wouldn't answer my e-mails, and—'

'I don't care what you write,' I said.

'That's the spirit, *Albertine*.'

We walked in silence for a while.

'Did I tell you I collect orchids?'

'No.'

'I'd like to show them to you some day. The *Zygopetala* are particularly fragrant. Their scent can fill a whole room. Perhaps I could offer you one as a gift. By way of an apology—'

I shrugged. 'My house plants never survive.'

'Neither do your friends,' he said.

'Nigel's death was an accident.'

'Of course it was. Like Dr Peacock's and Eleanor Vine's—'

I felt my heart give a sick lurch.

'You didn't know?' He sounded surprised. 'She passed away the other night. *Passed away*. What a strange expression. Makes her sound like a parcel. Anyway, she's dead meat. Poor Terri will be inconsolable.'

We walked in silence after that, crossing Mill Road by the traffic lights, listening as the trees came alive over our heads in the rising wind. No snow this year – in fact it is unusually mild, and the air has a milky quality, as if a storm were coming. We passed by the silent nursery school; the shuttered and empty bakery; the Jacadees' house, with its scent of fried garlic and yams and roasting chillies.

At last we paused at the garden gate. By then it felt almost companionable: victim and predator side by side, close enough to touch.

'Can you still do it?' I said at last. 'That – you know – that thing you do.'

He gave a short, percussive laugh. 'It's not a skill you lose,' he said. 'In fact, it gets easier every time.'

'Like murder,' I said.

He laughed again.

I fumbled for the catch on the gate. Around me, the milky, troubled air smelt of fresh earth and rotting leaves. I struggled with myself to keep calm, but I could feel myself slipping away, becoming someone else, as I do every time he looks at me.

'You aren't going to ask me in? Very wise. People might talk.'

'Another time, perhaps,' I said.

'Whenever you want, *Albertine*.'

As I moved towards the house I could feel him watching me, sensed his eyes on the back of my neck as I fumbled for the door key. I can always tell when I am being watched. People give themselves away. He was too silent, too motionless, to be doing anything else but staring.

'I know you're there,' I said, without turning round.

Not a word from *blueeyedboy*.

I was almost tempted to ask him in, then, just to hear his reaction. He thinks I am afraid of him. In fact, the opposite is true. He is like a little boy playing with a wasp in a jar: fascinated, but terribly afraid that at some point the trapped creature will escape its confinement and take revenge. It's hard to believe, isn't it, that something so small could inspire such unease? And yet, Nigel, too, was afraid of wasps.

Such a little thing, you'd think, to drive a man into a panic. A blob of fuzz; a drone of wings; armed with nothing more than a sting and a tiny amount of irritant.

You think I don't see how you're playing me. Well, maybe I see more than you think. I see your self-hatred. I see your fear. Most of all, I see what you want, deep down in your secret heart. But what you *want* and what you *need* are not necessarily the same. Desire and compulsion are two different things.

I know you're still out there, watching me. I can almost feel your heart. I can tell how fast it's beating now, like that of an animal caught in a trap. Well, I know how *that* feels. To have to pretend I'm someone else; to live every moment in fear of the past. I've lived this way for over twenty years, hoping to be left alone . . .

But now I'm ready to show myself. At last, from this dried-up chrysalis, something is about to emerge. So – if you're as guilty as you say, you'd better run, while there's still time. Run, like the helpless rat you are. Run as far and as fast as you can –

Run for your life, *blueeyedboy*.

8

I told you before. Nothing ends. Nothing really begins either, except in the kind of story that starts with *Once upon a time, long, long ago,* and in which, in blatant defiance of the human condition, they all live happily ever after. My tastes are rather more humble. I'd settle for out-living Ma. Oh, and the chance to stamp on those dogs. That's all I've ever wanted. The rest of them – my brothers, the Whites, even Dr Peacock – are simply the icing on the cake; a cake long past its sell-by date, and sour under the frosting.

But before I can hope for forgiveness, I have to make the confession. Perhaps that's why I'm here, after all. This screen, like that of the confessional, serves a double purpose. And yes, I'm aware that the fatal flaw in most of our fictional bad guys is that common desire to confess; to strut; to reveal to the hero his master plan, only to be foiled at last –

That's why I'm not going public on this. Not yet, anyway. All of these restricted posts are accessible only by password. But maybe later, when it's done and I'm sitting on a beach somewhere, drinking Mai Tais and watching the pretty girls go by, I'll mail you the password; I'll give you the truth. Maybe I owe you that, *Albertine*. And maybe one day you'll forgive me for everything I did to you. Most likely you won't. But that's OK. I've been living with guilt for a long time. A little more won't kill me.

Things *really* began to fall apart the summer that followed my brother's death. A long and turbulent summer, all dragonflies and thunderstorms. I was still only seventeen, a month from my eighteenth birthday, and the weight of my mother's attention now sat like a permanent thundercloud over my life. She had always been demanding. Now that my brothers were out of the way, she was viciously critical of every little thing I did, and I dreamed of running away, like Dad –

Ma had been through a difficult patch. The business with Nigel had done something to her. Nothing you would have noticed at first; but living with her as I did, I knew that all was not right with Gloria Green. It had started with lethargy at first; a slow, dull state of recovery. She would sit staring into space for hours; would eat whole packets of biscuits; would talk to people who weren't there; or sleep away whole afternoons before going to bed at eight or nine . . .

Grief sometimes does that to you, Maureen Pike explained to me. Of course, Maureen was in her element then, coming to see us every day, bringing home-made cakes and sound advice. Eleanor, too, offered support, recommending St John's Wort and group therapy. Adèle brought gossip and platitudes. *Time heals all things. Life must go on.*

Tell *that* to the cancer ward.

Then, as the summer waned, Ma had entered another phase. The lethargy had given way to a manic kind of activity. Maureen explained the phenomenon, which she said was called *displacement*; and welcomed it as necessary to the healing process. At that time, Maureen's daughter was doing a degree in psychology, and Maureen had embraced the world of psychoanalysis with the same self-important, lolloping zeal she gave to church fêtes, Junior Fun Days, collections for the elderly, her book group, her work at the coffee shop and ridding Malbry of paedophiles.

In any case, Ma was busy that month: working five days on the market stall, cooking, cleaning, making plans, ticking off time like an impatient schoolmistress – and, of course, keeping an eye on Yours Truly.

I'd had an easy time until then. For nearly a month, enshrouded with grief, she'd barely even noticed me. Now she made up for that in spades: questioning my every move; making the vitamin drink twice a day and worrying about everything. If I coughed, she assumed I was at death's door. If I was late, I'd been murdered or mugged. And when she wasn't fretting over all the things that might happen to me, she was rigid with fear over what I might *do* – that I'd find myself in trouble, somehow, that she'd lose me to drink, or drugs, or a girl –

But there was no escape for *blueeyedboy*. Three months had passed since the incident when Ma had hit me with the plate, and after Nigel failed her, Ma's obsession with success had grown to monstrous proportions. I'd missed my school exams, of course; but an appeal by Ma (on compassionate grounds) had earned me a review of my case. Malbry College was where she believed I should continue my studies. She had it all planned out for me. A year to re-sit those exams; and then I could start afresh, she said. She'd always dreamed of one of her boys entering the medical profession. I was her only hope, she said; and with a ruthless disregard for my wishes – indeed, for my ability – she began to mark out my future career.

I tried to argue with her at first. I had no qualifications. Besides, I wasn't cut out for medicine. Ma was saddened, but took it well – or so I thought in my innocence. I'd expected an outburst at the very least; one of Ma's violent attacks. What I got was a week of redoubled affection and lavishly home-cooked dinners – always my favourites – which she laid on the table with the virtuous air of a long-suffering guardian angel.

Soon after that I fell violently ill, with acute stomach cramps and a fever that brought me to my knees. Even to sit up in bed was to precipitate the most awful spasms of pain and vomiting, and to stand – still less to walk – was wholly out of the question. Ma cared for me with a tenderness that might have made me suspicious if I hadn't been suffering so much. Then, after almost a week, she reverted suddenly to type.

I'd been getting better. I'd lost pounds in weight; I was weak, but at last the pain had gone, and I was able to eat simple food in small quantities. A cup of noodle soup; some bread; a tablespoonful of plain rice; soldiers dipped in egg yolk.

She must have been worried by then, of course. Ma was no doctor; she had no concept of dosage, and the violence of my reaction must have been alarming. Waking up a few nights before from a sleep that was part delirium, I'd heard her talking to herself, arguing fiercely with someone not there:

It serves him right. He needs to learn.

But he's in pain. He's sick –

He'll live. Besides, he should have listened to me –

What had she put in those lavish meals? Ground glass? Rat poison? Whatever it had been, it had worked fast. And the day I was finally able to sit up in bed, even to stand, Ma came in, not with a tray, but with an application form – a form from Malbry College, which she had already filled in for me.

'I hope you've had time to think,' she said in a suspiciously cheery voice. 'Lying in bed doing nothing all day, letting me fetch and carry for you. I hope you've had time to think about everything I've done for you. Everything you owe me—'

'Please. Not now. My stomach hurts—'

'No, it doesn't,' she said. 'In a day or two you'll be good as new, eating me out of house and home, like the ungrateful little bastard you are. Now, have a look at these papers.' Her expression, which had begun to darken, once more took on that look of relentless cheeriness. 'I've been looking at those courses again, and I think you should do the same.'

I looked at her. She was smiling at me, and I felt a pang of guilt in my stomach for letting the thought even cross my mind –

'What was wrong with me?' I said.

I thought her eyes flickered. 'What do you mean?'

'Do you think it was something I ate?' I went on. 'You didn't get sick at all, did you, Ma?'

'I can't afford to get sick,' she said. 'I've got you to look after, haven't I?' Then she moved in close to me and fixed me with her espresso eyes. 'I think it's time you got up now,' she said, shoving the papers into my hand. 'You've got a lot of work to do.'

That time I knew better than to protest. I signed up without a word for three subjects I knew nothing about, knowing I could change them later. I was already an accomplished liar; rather than actually take the courses and risk my mother finding out when I failed, I waited until the beginning of term and secretly changed my subject choices to something more suited to my personal talents, then found myself a part-time job in an electrical shop a few miles away, and let her believe I was studying.

After that, it was simply a question of forging my certificates – easy, on a computer – after which I hacked into the Malbry *Examiner*'s computer files and added a single name – my own – to a soon-to-be-published list of results.

I've tried to do my own cooking ever since. But there's always the vitamin drink, of course, which Ma prepares with her own hands, and which keeps me well – or so she says, with a kind of sly innuendo. Every eighteen months or so I come down with a sudden, violent illness characterized by terrible stomach cramps, and my mother cares for me lovingly, and if these bouts of sickness always seem to coincide with moments of tension between Ma and myself, that's just because I am sensitive, and these things have an effect on my health.

I never got away, of course. Some things are inescapable. Even London is too far to go – Hawaii, an impossible dream.

Well, maybe not *quite* impossible. That old blue lamp is still alight. And although it has taken more time than even I imagined it would, I begin to sense that at long last my patience is about to be rewarded.

Patience, too, is a game, of course, a game of skill and endurance. *Solitaire*, the Americans call it, a far less optimistic name, tinged with the grey-green of melancholy. Well, a solitary game it may be; but in my case that's surely a blessing. Besides, in a game that one plays with oneself, can anyone be said to lose?

9

You are viewing the webjournal of **blueeyedboy**.
Posted at: *23.49 on Saturday, February 16*
Status: *restricted*
Mood: *trapped*
Listening to: *Boomtown Rats: 'Rat Trap'*

'You've got a lot of work to do.'

I'd assumed at first that she meant school. In fact, school was only a part of it. My mother's plans ran deeper than that. It began just after my illness, and hers, in the last days of September, and I remember it all in greys and blues, with a thundery light that hurt my eyes, and a heat that pressed down on to my head, giving me a penitent's slouch, a habit that I never quite lost.

When the police called round for the first time, I assumed it was because of something I'd done. The camera I'd stolen, perhaps; the graffiti on Dr Peacock's door; or maybe finally someone had guessed how I'd disposed of my brother.

But I was not arrested. Instead I sweated it out of doors while Ma entertained in the parlour, bringing out the good biscuits, and the visitors' teacups that usually took pride of place in the cabinet under the china dogs. Then, after what seemed like an interminable wait, the two officers – a man and a woman – came out looking very serious, and the woman said: 'We need to talk.' And I could have passed out with terror and guilt, except that Ma was watching me with that look of expectant pride, and I knew that

282

it wasn't something I'd done, but something she *expected of me* –

Of course, you know what that was. Ma never lets anything go. And what I'd revealed about Emily the day Ma hit me with the plate had festered and borne fruit in her mind, so that now, at last, it was ready for use.

She fixed me with her berry-black eyes. 'I know you don't want to tell them,' she said in a voice like a razor blade hidden inside a toffee apple. 'But I've brought you up to respect the law, and everyone knows it's not your fault—'

For a moment I didn't understand. I must have looked scared, because the policewoman put her arm around me and whispered. 'That's right, son. It's not your fault—' And then I remembered what I'd written that night on Dr Peacock's door, and all the components fell in place like the pieces of a Mouse Trap game, and I understood what my mother had meant –

You've got a lot of work to do.

'Oh, please,' I whispered. 'Please, no.'

'I know you're afraid,' my mother said – in that voice that sounded sweet, but was not. 'But everybody's on your side. No one's going to blame you.' Her eyes, as she spoke, were like steel pins. Her hand on my arm looked gentle, but the next day there would be bruises. 'All we want is the truth, B.B. Just the truth. How hard can that be?'

Well, what could I do? I was alone. Alone with Ma, trapped and afraid. I knew that if I called her bluff, if I disgraced her publicly, she'd find a way to make me pay. So I played the game, telling myself that it was just a white lie; that *their* lies had been much worse than mine; that in any case, I had no choice –

The policewoman's name was Lucy, she said. I guessed her to be very young, maybe just out of training school, still fired with hopeful ideals and convinced that children have no reason to lie. The man was older, more cautious; less likely to show sympathy; but even so, he was gentle enough, allowing her to question me, making notes in his notepad.

'Your mother says you've been ill,' she said.

I nodded, not daring to say it aloud. Beside me, Ma, like a granite cliff face, one arm around my shoulders.

'She says you were delirious. Talking and shouting in your sleep.'

'I guess,' I said. 'It wasn't too bad.'

I felt my mother's bony fingers tighten on my upper arm. 'You say that now you're better,' she said. 'But you don't know the half of it. Until you've got children of your own, you can't imagine how it feels,' she said, without releasing my arm. 'To see my boy in such a bad way, crying like a baby.' She flashed me a brief, unsettling smile. 'You know I lost my other boy,' she said, with a glance at Lucy. 'If anything happened to B.B. now, I think I might go crazy.'

I saw the two officers exchange glances.

'Yes, Mrs Winter. I know. It must have been a terrible time.'

Ma frowned. 'How *could* you know? You're not much older than my son. Do *you* have any children?'

Lucy shook her head.

'Then don't presume to empathize.'

'I'm sorry, Mrs Winter.'

For a moment, Ma was silent, staring vacantly into space. She looked like an unplugged fruit machine; for a second I wondered if she'd had a stroke. Then she went on in a normal voice – at least what passes for normal with her.

'A mother knows these things,' she said. 'A mother senses everything. I knew there was something wrong with him. He started to talk and cry in his sleep. And that's when I began to suspect that something funny was going on.'

Oh, she was clever. She fed them the line. Fed it to them like poisoned bait, watching as I wriggled and squirmed. And the facts were indisputable. Between the ages of seven and thirteen, Ma's youngest son Benjamin had enjoyed a special relationship with Dr Graham Peacock. As payment for helping in his research, the doctor had befriended him, had taken charge of his schooling, had even offered financial aid to Ma, a single parent –

Then suddenly, without warning, Ben had ceased to cooperate. He had become introverted and secretive; had started doing badly at school; had begun to misbehave; above all, he had flatly refused to go back to the Mansion, giving no good reason for his behaviour, so that Dr Peacock had withdrawn his support, leaving Ma to fend alone.

She should have suspected there and then that something had gone seriously wrong, but anger had blinded her to her son's needs, and when, later, graffiti had been scrawled on the door of the Mansion, she had simply seen it as another proof of his growing delinquency. Ben had denied the vandalism. Ma had not believed him. It was only now that she realized what that gesture had really been; a cry for help; a warning –

'What did you write on the door, B.B.?' Her voice was chequered with menace and love.

I looked away. 'Please, M-ma. It was so long ago. I d-don't really think—'

'B.B.' Only I could hear the change in her voice: the vinegary, sour-vegetable tone that brought back the reek of the vitamin drink. Already my head was beginning to throb. I reached for the word that would drive it away. A word that sounds vaguely French, somehow, that makes me think of green summer lawns and the scent of cut grass in the meadows –

'Pervert,' I whispered.

'What?' she said.

I said it again, and she smiled at me.

'And why did you write that, B.B.?' she said.

'Because he is.' I was still feeling trapped, but behind the fear and the guilt of it all there was something almost pleasurable: a sense of perilous ownership.

I thought of Mrs White, and of the way she had looked that day on the steps of the Mansion. I thought of the pity on Mr White's face, that day in St Oswald's schoolyard. I thought of Dr Peacock's face peering through the curtains, and his sheepish smile as I crept away. I thought of the ladies who had spoiled and petted me as a child, only to scorn me when I grew up. I thought of my teachers at school, and my brothers, who'd treated me with such contempt. Then I thought of Emily –

And I saw how easy it would be to take revenge on all those people, to make them pay attention to me, to make them suffer as I had. And for the first time since my earliest childhood, I was conscious of an exhilarating sensation. A feeling of power; an energy rush; a force; a current; a surge; a charge.

Charge. Such an ambivalent word, with its implications of power and blame, attack and detention, payment and cost. And it smells of burnt wiring and solder, and its colour is like a summer's sky, thundery and luminous.

Don't think I'm trying to absolve myself. I told you I was a bad guy. No one forced me to do what I did. I made a conscious decision that day. I could have done the right thing. I could have pulled the plug on it all. Told the truth. Confessed the lie. I had the choice. I could have left home. I could have escaped the pitcher plant.

But Ma was watching, and I knew that I would never do those things. It wasn't that I was afraid of her – although I was, most terribly. It was simply the lure of being in charge – of being the one to whom eyes turned –

I know. Don't think I'm proud of this. It's not exactly my greatest moment. Most crimes are annoyingly petty, and I'm afraid mine was no exception. But I was young, too young in any case to see how cleverly she had handled me, guiding me through a series of hoops to a reward that would ultimately reveal itself to be the worst kind of punishment.

And now she was smiling – a genuine smile, radiating approval. And, at that moment, I wanted it, wanted to hear her say: *well done,* even though I hated her –

'Tell them, B.B.,' she said, pinning me with that brilliant smile. 'Tell them what he did to you.'

10

The first thing that happened after that was that Emily was taken into protective care. Just as a precaution, they said; just to ensure her safety. Her reluctance to incriminate Dr Peacock was seen as proof of long-term abuse rather than simple innocence, and Catherine's rage and bewilderment when faced with the accusations was seen as further evidence of some kind of collusion. Something had clearly been going on. At best, a cynical fraud. At worst, a large-scale conspiracy.

And now came Yours Truly's testimony. It had started so harmlessly, I said. Dr Peacock had been very kind. Private lessons, cash now and then – that was how he'd reeled us in. And that was how he'd approached Catherine White, a woman with a history of depression, ambitious and easily flattered, so eager to believe that her child was special that she'd managed to blind herself to the truth.

The books in Dr Peacock's library did much to support my claim, of course. Biographies of literature's most notorious synaesthetes. Nabokov; Rimbaud; Baudelaire; De Quincey – self-confessed drug-users, homosexuals, paedophiles. Men whose pursuit of the sublime took precedence to the petty morality of their day. The material seized as evidence was not directly incriminating, but the police are no great connoisseurs of art, and the sheer volume of material in Dr Peacock's collection was enough to convince them that they had the right man. Class photographs of St Oswald's boys taken whilst he was a governor. Volumes of Greek and Roman art; engravings of statues of naked young men. A first edition of Beardsley's *Yellow Book*; a collection of Ovenden prints from *Lolita*; a pencil drawing of a young male nude (attributed to Caravaggio); a lavishly illustrated copy of *The Perfumed Garden*; books of erotic poetry by Verlaine, Swinburne, Rimbaud and the Marquis de Sade –

'You showed this stuff to a seven-year-old?'

Dr Peacock tried to explain. It was part of the boy's education, he said. And Benjamin was interested; he wanted to know what he was –

'And what *was* he, according to you?'

Once more, Dr Peacock struggled to enlighten his audience. But while Boy X had been fascinated by case studies of synaesthetes, of music and migraines and orgasms that manifested themselves in trails of colour, the police seemed far more interested in finding out precisely what he and Boy X had talked about during all those private lessons. Whether he'd ever been tempted to touch Benjamin; whether he'd ever given him drugs; whether he'd ever spent time alone with him – or his brothers.

And when Dr Peacock finally broke, and vented his rage and frustration, the officers looked at each other and said: 'That's a nasty temper you've got. Did you ever strike the boy? Slap him, correct him in any way?'

Numbly, the doctor shook his head.

'And what about the little girl? It must have been frustrating, having to work with such a young child. Especially when you've been used to teaching boys. Was she ever uncooperative?'

'Never, said Dr Peacock. 'Emily's a sweet little girl.'

'Eager to please?'

He nodded.

'Eager enough to fake a result?'

The doctor denied it vehemently. But the damage was already done. I had painted a more than plausible picture. And if Emily failed to confirm his tale, then that was simply because she was young, confused, and in denial of the way in which she had been used –

They tried to keep it from the Press. Might as well try to stop the tide. The wave of speculation broke just in the wake of the film's release. By the end of that year Emily White was national news; and then, just as suddenly, infamous.

The tabloid headlines came out in force. The *Mail*: *ABUSE CLAIMS IN SUPER-SENSE CASE*. The *Sun*: *SEE EMILY PLAY!* Best of all, from the *Mirror*: *EMILY – WAS SHE A FAKE?*

Jeffrey Stuarts, the journalist who had followed Emily's case throughout, living with the family, attending sessions at the Mansion, answering the sceptics with the keenness of a true fanatic, saw what was coming and quickly changed course, hastily rewriting his book – to be entitled *The Emily Experiment* – to include, not only rumours of sleaze at the Mansion, but strong hints of a darker truth behind the Emily Phenomenon.

The hard, ambitious mother; the weak, ineffectual father; the influential New Age friend; the child-victim, trained to perform; the predatory old man, consumed by his obsessions. And, of course, Boy X. Redeemed by what he'd had to endure, he was in it to the hilt. The guileless victim. The innocent. Once again, the blue-eyed boy.

Of course, it never went to court. It never even made it to the magistrate. Whilst still under investigation, Dr Peacock suffered a heart attack that landed him in intensive care. The case was postponed indefinitely.

But just the faintest whiff of smoke was enough to convince the public. Trial by tabloid is swift and sure. Within three months, it was over. *The Emily Experiment* went straight to the top of the best-seller lists. Patrick and Catherine White agreed to a trial separation. Investors withdrew their money; galleries ceased to display Emily's work. Feather moved in with Catherine, while Patrick removed himself to a hostel just outside Malbry.

It wasn't a permanent move, he said. It was simply to give them a little space. A twenty-four-hour police guard was stationed outside the Mansion in the wake of several arson attempts. And the papers were all over Catherine. A row of photographers flanked the house, snapping up anyone who crossed the threshold.

Graffiti appeared on the front door. Hate mail came by the sackful. The *News of the World* ran a picture of Catherine, in tears, with a story (confirmed by Feather, to whom they paid five thousand pounds) that she had suffered a mental breakdown.

Christmas brought little improvement, though Emily was allowed home for the day. Before that the child had remained in the custody of the Social Services, who, failing to detect any signs of abuse, interrogated her kindly but relentlessly until even she began to wonder if she, too, wasn't losing her mind.

Try to remember, Emily.

I know the technique. I know it well. Kindness is a weapon, too, a padded cartoon goofy-stick that batters away at the memory, turning it all into candyfloss.

It's all right. It's not your fault.

Just tell us the truth, Emily.

Imagine what it was like for her. Everything was going wrong. Dr Peacock was under investigation. Her parents were suddenly living apart. People kept asking her questions, and although they kept saying it wasn't her fault, she couldn't help thinking that somehow it was. That somehow, that little snow-white lie had turned into an avalanche –

Listen to the colours.

She wanted to say it was all a mistake, but of course, it was far too late for that. They wanted a demonstration: a once-and-for-all display of her gift, well away from the influence of Dr Peacock or her mother, a performance to confirm or refute for ever the claim that she was a fake, a pawn in their game of deception and greed.

And that was how, in January, on a snowy morning in Manchester, she found herself with her easel and paints, on a sound stage surrounded by cameras, with hot lights battening down on her head and the sound of the *Symphonie fantastique* pouring out of the speakers. And right at that moment the miracle happens and *Emily hears the colours* –

It is by far her most famous work. *Symphonie fantastique in*

Twenty-four Conflicting Colours looks something like a Jackson Pollock and something like a Mondrian, with that huge, grey shadow in the far corner reaching into the illuminated canvas like the hand of Death in a field of bright flowers . . .

So says Jeffrey Stuarts, at least, in the follow-up to his best-selling book: *The Emily Enigma*. That, too, raced to the top of the charts, although it was clearly a rehash of the previous one, with an afterword to include the events that followed its publication. After that, of course, the experts pursued the story, with professionals in every associated field from art to child psychology warring with each other to prove their conflicting theories.

Each camp had its adherents, be they cynics or believers. The child psychologists saw Emily's work as a symbolic expression of her fear; the paranormal camp as a harbinger of death; the art experts saw in the change of style a confirmation of what many had already secretly suspected: that Emily's synaesthesia had been a pretence from the start and that Catherine White, and not Emily, had been the creative influence behind such works as *Nocturne in Scarlet Ochre* and *Starry Moonlight Sonata*.

Symphonie fantastique is altogether different. Created in front of an audience on a piece of canvas eight feet square, it almost writhes with energy, so that even a dullard like Jeffrey Stuarts was able to feel its ominous presence. If fear has a colour, then this is it: menacing strings of red, brown and black overlaid with occasional violent patches of light, and that clanging square of blue-grey like the trapdoor to an oubliette –

To me, it smells of Blackpool pier, and my mother, and the vitamin drink. To Emily, it must have been the first step through a looking glass into a world in which nothing was sane, nothing was certain any more.

They tried to hide the truth from her. On compassionate grounds, the experts said. To tell her the truth at such a young age, especially in such circumstances, could prove traumatic in the extreme. But we heard it through the grapevine even before it hit the stands: that Catherine White was in hospital following a failed suicide attempt. And suddenly it seemed that every reporter in the world was heading straight for Malbry, the sleepy little Northern town where everything seemed to be happening, and where the clouds were still gathering for one more cosmic thunderstorm –

11

Clair e-mailed me again today. Apparently, she is missing me. And the fic I posted on Valentine's Day has caused more concern than usual. She urges me to return to the fold, to discuss my feelings of alienation and to face up to my responsibilities. The tone of her e-mail is neutral enough; but I sense her disapproval. Maybe she is feeling sensitive; or maybe she feels that my fiction provokes an inappropriate response in subjects such as Toxic and Cap, whose predilection for violence needs no further encouragement.

> *You need to come back to Group* [she says]. *Talking online is no substitute. I'd rather see you face to face. Besides, I'm not sure these stories of yours are really very helpful. You need to confront these exhibitionist tendencies of yours and face up to reality –*

Bip! Delete message.

Now she's gone.

That's the beauty of e-mail, Clair. That's why I'd rather meet online than in your little drawing-room with its nice, non-threatening prints on the walls and its scent of cheap pot-pourri. And at the writing group, you're in charge, whereas *badguysrock* belongs to me. Here, I ask the questions; here I am in complete control.

No, I think I'd rather stay and pursue my interests in the comfort and seclusion of my own room. I like myself so much better online. I can express so much more. It was here, and not at that awful school, that I received my classical education. And from here I can crawl into your mind, scent out your little secrets, expose your petty weaknesses, just as you try to find out mine.

Tell me – how *is* Angel Blue these days? I'm sure you must have heard from him. And Chryssie? Still sick? Well, that's too bad. Shouldn't you be talking to *her*, Clair, instead of cross-examining me?

The e-mail *bips*. New message from Clair.

> *I really think we should talk soon. I know you find our discussions*
> *uncomfortable, but I'm getting really worried about you. Please e-mail me*
> *back to confirm!*

Bip! Delete message.

Whoops, all gone.

If only deleting Clair were as easy.

Still, I have other concerns right now, not least how I stand with *Albertine*. It's not that I hope for forgiveness. Both of us have come too far for that. But her silence is disquieting; and it is all I can do to prevent myself from calling by at her house today. Still, I don't think that would be wise. Too many potential witnesses. Already, I suspect we are being watched. All it would take is a word to Ma, and the house of cards would come tumbling down.

And so half an hour before closing time, I found myself back at the Zebra. My masochistic side so often drives me to that place, that safe little world of which Yours Truly is definitely *not* a part. In passing I noticed, to my annoyance, that Terri was sitting by the door. She looked up hopefully as I came in; I did my best to ignore her. So much for discretion, I thought. Like her aunt, she is an eager observer; a gossip, in spite of her diffidence; the kind of person who stops at the scene of a car crash, not to help, but to participate in the collective misery.

Saxophone Man with the dreadlocks was sitting close by with a pot of coffee at his elbow; he gave me a look designed to convey his contempt for such as I. Maybe Bethan has mentioned me. From time to time she does, you know, in a vain attempt to prove to herself how much she now detests me. *Creepy Dude*, she calls me. I'd hoped for something more imaginative.

I sat down in my usual place; ordered Earl Grey, no lemon, no milk. She brought it on a flowered tray. Lingered just long enough for me to suspect her of having something on her mind, then came to a decision; sat down squarely beside me, looked into my eyes and said:

'What the hell do you *want* from me?'

I poured out the tea. It was fragrant and good. I said: 'I have no idea what you're talking about.'

'Hanging around here all the time. Posting those stories. Raking things up—'

I had to laugh. 'Me? Raking things up? I'm sorry, but when the details of Dr Peacock's will come out, everything you do is going to be news. That isn't my fault, *Albertine*.'

'I wish you wouldn't call me that.'

'You chose it yourself,' I pointed out.

She shrugged. 'You wouldn't understand.'

Well, that's where you're wrong, Albertine. I understand it all too well. The heart's desire to be someone else, to take on a new identity. In a way I've done it myself –

'I don't want his money,' she said. 'I only want to be left alone.'

I grinned. 'Hope *that* works out for you.'

'You talked him into it, didn't you?' Her eyes were dark with anger now. 'Working there, you had the chance. He was old, suggestible. You could have told him anything.'

'Believe me, Bethan, if I had, don't you think I'd have done it for myself?' I let the thought sink in for a while. ''Dear old Dr Peacock. Still trying, after all these years, to make amends. Still half-convinced he could raise the dead. With Patrick gone, there was only you left. Nigel must have been over the moon—'

She looked at me. 'Not *that* again. I tell you, Nigel didn't care about that.'

'Oh, please,' I said. 'Love may be blind, but you'd have to be *really* stupid to think that someone like Nigel wouldn't have cared that his girlfriend was about to inherit a fortune—'

'You told him about Dr Peacock's will?'

'Who knows? I may have let something slip.'

'When?' Her voice was paper-thin.

'Eighteen months ago, maybe more.'

Silence. Then: 'You bastard,' she hissed. 'Are you trying to make me believe that this was a set-up from the start?'

'I don't care what you believe,' I said. 'But I'm guessing that he was protective. He didn't like you living alone. He hadn't mentioned marriage yet, but if he had, you would have said yes.' I paused. 'How am I doing so far?'

She fixed me with eyes the colour of murder. 'You know, this is pointless,' she said. 'You're never going to sell me this. Nigel didn't *care* about money.'

'Really? How romantic,' I said. 'Because according to the credit-card statements I came across when I cleared out his flat, when Nigel died he was badly in debt. To the tune of nearly ten thousand pounds – it can't have been easy, making ends meet. Maybe he got impatient. Maybe he got desperate. Dr Peacock was old and sick, but his illness was far from terminal. He could have lived another ten years—'

Now her face was colourless. 'Nigel didn't kill Dr Peacock,' she said, 'any more than you could have done. He wouldn't do a thing like that—' Her voice was wavering. It hurt me to cause her such distress, but she needed to know. To understand.

'Why couldn't he, Bethan? He's done it before.'

She shook her head. 'That was different.'

'Is *that* what he said?'

'Of course it was!'

I grinned.

She stood up abruptly, sending her chair clattering. 'Why on earth does it *matter?*' she cried. 'All that was such a long time ago, so why do you always keep bringing it up? Nigel's *dead*, it's *over* now, so why can't you just leave me alone?'

Her distress was strangely moving, I thought. Her face was bleak and beautiful. The emerald stud in her eyebrow winked at me like an open eye. Suddenly, all I wanted was for her to hold me, to comfort me, to tell me the lies that everyone secretly most wants to hear.

But I had to go on. I owed it to her. 'It's never over, Bethan,' I said. 'There's no going back from murder. Especially when it's a relative – and Benjamin was only sixteen—'

She eyed me with hatred, and now, for the first time, I could almost believe her capable of the act that had already deleted two of Gloria Winter's boys permanently from existence.

'Nigel was right,' she said at last. 'You *are* a twisted bastard.'

'That hurt my feelings, *Albertine*.'

'Don't play the innocent, Brendan.'

I shrugged. 'That's hardly fair,' I said. 'It was *Nigel* who murdered Benjamin. I was lucky I wasn't there. If things had been different, it could have been me.'

PART FIVE

mirrors

1

You are viewing the webjournal of **blueeyedboy**.
Posted at: 23.40 on Tuesday, February 19
Status: restricted
Mood: tired
Listening to: Cyndi Lauper: 'True Colours'

All right. You can call me Brendan. Does that make you happy now? *Now* do you think you know me? We choose our names, our identities; just as we choose the lives we lead. I have to believe that, *Albertine*. The alternative – that these things are allocated at birth, or even before, *in utero* – is far too appalling to contemplate.

Someone once told me that seventy per cent of all praise received in the course of an average lifetime is given before the age of five. At five years old, almost anything – eating a mouthful of food; getting dressed; drawing a picture in crayon – can earn the most lavish compliments. Of course, that stops eventually. In my case, when my brother was born – my brother in blue, that is – Benjamin.

Clair, with her love of psychobabble, sometimes speaks of what she calls *the reverse halo* effect; that tendency we all have to assign the colours of villainy on the basis of a single flaw: such as having swallowed a sibling, perhaps, or collected a bucket of sea creatures and left them to die in the scorching sun. When Ben was born, my halo reversed; and henceforth *blueeyedboy* was stripped of all his former privileges.

I saw it coming. At three years old, I already knew that the squalling blue package Ma had brought home would bring me nothing but misery. First came her decision to allocate colours to her three sons. That's where it started, I realize, although she may not have known it then. But that's how I became Brendan Brown – the dull one, neither fish nor fowl – eclipsed on one side by Nigel Black and on the other by Benjamin Blue. No one noticed me any more – unless, of course, I did something wrong, in which case the piece of electrical cord was only too quick to be deployed. No one thought I was special enough to merit any attention.

Still, I've managed to change all that. I've reclaimed my halo – in Ma's eyes, at least. As for you, *Albertine* – or must I call you Bethan now? You always saw more than the others did. You always understood me. You never had the slightest doubt that I, too, was remarkable, that beneath my sensitivity beat the heart of a future murderer. Still –

Everyone knows it wasn't my fault. I never laid a hand on him. In fact, I wasn't even there. I was watching Emily. *All* those times I watched her, followed her to the Mansion and back, felt Dr Peacock's welcoming hug, flew with her on her little swing, felt her mother's hand in mine, heard her say: *Well done, sweetheart* –

My brother never did those things. Perhaps he never needed to. Ben was too busy feeling sorry for himself to take an interest in Emily. *I* was the one who cared for her; took pictures of her from over the hedge; shared the scraps of her strange little life.

Perhaps that was why I loved her then; because she had stolen Benjamin's life just as he had stolen mine. My mother's love; my gift; my chance; all of them passed to Benjamin, as if I'd simply held them in trust until the better man came along.

Ben, the blue-eyed boy. The thief. And what did he do with his big chance? He pissed it away in resentment because somebody else got a bigger break. Everything: his intelligence; his place at St Oswald's; his chance at fame; even his time at the Mansion. All thrown to the winds because Benjamin didn't just want a slice of the cake, he wanted the bloody bakery. Well, that's what it looked like to Brendan Brown, left with only the few crumbs he managed to steal from his brother's plate –

But now, the cake belongs to me. The cake, as well as the bakery.
As Cap would say: *Pure pwnage, man* –
   I got away with murder.

2

You are viewing the webjournal of: **blueeyedboy** posting on:
                                    badguysrock@webjournal.com
Posted at: 23.47 on Tuesday, February 19
Status: public
Mood: vulnerable
Listening to: Johnny Cash: 'Hurt'

They call him Mr Brendan Brown. Too dull to be gifted; too dull to be seen; too dull even for murder. Shit-brown; donkey-brown; boring, butthead, bastard-brown. All his life he has tried to be blind, an unwilling spectator to everything, watching through interlaced fingers as the action unrolls without him, wincing at the slightest blow, the smallest hint of violence.

Yes, Brendan Brown is sensitive. Action movies frighten him. Wildlife documentaries are out; as are horror movies, video games, cowboy films or combat scenes. He even feels for the bad guy. Sports, too, are a discomfort to him, with their risk of injuries and collisions. Instead he watches cookery shows, or gardening shows, or travelogues, or porn, and dreams of other places; feels printed sunlight on his face –

It's squeamishness, his mother says. *He feels things more than the others do.*

Perhaps he does, thinks Brendan Brown. Perhaps he feels things differently. Because if he watches someone in pain, it makes him so uncomfortable that sometimes he is physically sick, and he cries in frightened confusion at the things the images make him feel –

His brother in blue is aware of this, and makes him watch his experiments with flies and wasps, and then with mice; shows him pictures to make him squirm. Dr Peacock calls it *mirror-touch synaesthesia*, and it presents – in his case, at least – as a kind of pathological sensitivity, in which the optical part of the brain some-how mirrors the physical, so that he can experience what others feel – be it a touch, or a taste, or a blow – as clearly as if it were done to himself.

His brother in black despises him, scorns him for his weakness. Even his mother ignores him now: the middle child, the quiet one, caught between Nigel, the black sheep, and Benjamin, the blue-eyed boy –

Brendan hates his brothers. He hates the way they make him feel. One is angry all the time, the other smug and contemptuous. And Brendan feels for them – too much – whether or not he wants to. They itch; he wants to scratch. They bleed; and Brendan obediently bleeds for them. Truth told, it isn't empathy. It's only a mindless physical response to a series of visual stimuli. He wouldn't care if they both died – as long as they did it far away, where he didn't have to watch it.

Sometimes, when he's alone, he reads. Slowly at first, and in private: books about travel and photography; poems and plays; short stories, novels and dictionaries. The printed word is different from what he sees around him. In his mind, the action unfolds without his body's involvement. He reads in the cellar late at night by the light of the bare bulb; the cellar that, lacking a room of his own, he has secretly converted into a darkroom. Here he reads books that his teachers wouldn't believe he had the wit to understand; books that, if his mates at school were to catch him reading, would make him a target for every joke, for every bully that came along.

But here, in his darkroom, he feels safe; there's no one here to laugh at him when he follows the words with his finger. No one to call him retarded when he reads the words aloud. No, this is Brendan's private place. Here he can do as he pleases. And sometimes, when he's alone, he has dreams. Dreams of dressing in something other than brown, of having people notice him, of showing his true colours.

But that's the problem, isn't it? All his life he has been Brendan Brown; doomed to be dull, to be stupid. In fact, he was never stupid.

He simply hid it very well. At school, he did the minimum work, to protect himself from ridicule. At home, he has always pretended to be stolid and unimaginative. He knows that he is safer that way, now that Ben has taken his place, has robbed him of Ma's affection, has swallowed him, as he himself swallowed Mal, in the desperate struggle for dominance –

It isn't fair, thinks Brendan Brown. He, too, has blue eyes. He, too, has special skills. His shyness and his stammer leads them all to assume that he is inarticulate. But words have tremendous power, he knows. He wants to learn how to handle them. And he is good with computers. He knows how to process information. He is fighting his dyslexia with the aid of a special programme. Later, under cover of his part-time job at the fast-food place, he joins a creative-writing class. He isn't very good at first, but he works hard; he wants to learn. Words and their meanings fascinate him. He wants to know more about them. He wants to strip the language down to the very motherboard.

Most importantly, he is discreet. Discreet and very patient. To nail his colours to the mast would be to declare his intentions. Brendan Brown knows better than this. Brendan values camouflage. That is why he has survived this far. By blending into the background; by letting other people shine; by standing on the sidelines to watch while the opposition destroys itself –

Sun Szu says in *The Art Of War: All warfare is based on deception.* Well, if there's anything our boy knows, it's how to deceive and obfuscate.

> *Hence, when able to attack, we must seem unable; when using our forces, we must seem inactive; when we are near, we must make the enemy believe we are far away; when far away, we must make him believe we are near.*

He chooses his moment carefully. He has never been impulsive. Unlike Nigel, who could always be relied upon to act first and think later (if he thought at all), responding to triggers so obvious that even a child could have played him –

If your opponent is of choleric temper, seek to irritate him.

Easily done, where Nigel is concerned. A well-placed word could do it. In this case it leads to violence; to a chain reaction that no one can stop and which ends with the death of his brother in blue and the arrest of his brother in black, and Badass Brendan, free of them both and whiter than the driven snow –

Item One: a black Moleskine notebook.

Item Two: some photographs of his brother in black cavorting with Tricia Goldblum, aka Mrs Electric Blue – some of them nicely intimate, taken with a long lens from the back of the lady's garden and developed in stealth in the darkroom, which no one, not even Ma, knows about –

Put them both together, like nitrogen and glycerine, and –

Wham!

In fact, it was almost too easy. People are so predictable. Nigel was especially, with his moods and his violent temper. Thanks to the reverse-halo effect (Nigel *always* hated Ben), all our hero had to do was to wind him up and put him in place, and the rest was a foregone conclusion. A casual word in Nigel's ear, suggesting that Ben was spying on him; the mention of a secret cache; then planting the evidence for Nigel to find under his brother's mattress, and after that the only thing our boy had to do was to remove himself from the premises while the sordid business of murder unfurled.

Ben denied all knowledge, of course. *That* was the fatal mistake. Brendan knew from experience that the only way to avoid serious hurt is to confess to the crime immediately, even when you're innocent. He'd learnt that lesson early on – thereby earning himself the convenient reputation of being a hopeless liar, whilst taking the blame for a number of things for which he was not responsible. In any case, Ben had no time to explain. Nigel's first blow cracked his skull. After that – well, suffice it to say that Benjamin never stood a chance.

Of course, our hero wasn't there. Like Macavity, the Mystery Cat, he has mastered the difficult technique of eclipsing himself from unpleasantness. It was Brendan's Ma who found her son, who called the police and the ambulance, and then who kept watch at the hospital, and who never cried, not even once, not even when they told her that the damage was irreversible, that Benjamin would never wake up –

Manslaughter, they called it.

Interesting word – *man's laughter* – coloured in shades of lightning-blue and scented with sage and violet. Yes, he sees Ben's colours now. After all, he took his place. It all belongs to Brendan now – his gift; his future; his colours.

It took a little time to adjust. At first our hero was sick for days. His stomach felt like a bottomless pit; his head ached so much that he thought he would die. In one sense, he feels he deserved it. Another part of him grins inside. It's like an evil magic trick. He is innocent of any crime, and yet secretly guilty of murder.

But something is missing nevertheless. Violence is still beyond him. Which is somewhat unfortunate, given the extent of his rage. Without this poison gift, he thinks, anything would be possible. His thoughts are clear and objective. He has no conscience to trouble him. The most terrible things are in his mind, only a blink away from execution. But his body rejects the scenario. Only in fic can he act with impunity. Only then can he be truly free. In life, that surge of victory must always be paid for in the end; paid for in sickness and suffering, just as bad thoughts must be paid for in full –

She still has that piece of electrical cord. Of course, she doesn't use it now. Instead she uses her fists; her feet; she knows that he will never fight back. But he dreams of that piece of electrical cord, and of the china dogs that gape so vapidly from the glass case. The cord would fit snugly around her throat six or seven times at least; after which, the glass case and the china dogs wouldn't stand a fucking chance –

The thought makes him suddenly edgy again. It brings a taste to the back of his throat. It's a taste he ought to know by now: a brackish taste that makes him gag; that makes his mouth go starchy with fear and his heart lurch like a landed fish.

A voice from downstairs. 'Who's there?' she calls.

He gives a sigh. 'It's me, Ma.'

'What are you doing? It's time for your drink.'

He switches off the computer and reaches for his headphones. He likes to listen to music. It gives a different context to things. He wears his iPod all the time, and he has long since mastered the art of *seeming* to listen to what she says, while in his head something else is playing, the secret soundtrack to his life.

He goes downstairs. 'What's that, Ma?'

He watches her mouth moving soundlessly. In his head, the Man in Black sings in a voice so old and broken that he might already be dead. And Brendan feels so empty inside, consumed by such an emptiness, a craving that nothing can satisfy – not food, not love, not murder – like the snake that set out to swallow the world, and ended up by swallowing itself.

And he knows, deep down, that his time has come. Time to take his medicine. Time to do what he has longed to do for the past forty years – practically all of his life. To nail his colours to the mast and to turn and face his enemy. What has he got to lose, after all? His vitamin drink? His empire of dirt?

Post comment:
JennyTricks: (*post deleted*).
Albertine: (*post deleted*).
JennyTricks: (*post deleted*).
blueeyedboy: Albertine?

3

So that's how a mirror-touch synaesthete got away with murder. A neat trick, you have to admit, which I carried off with my usual flair. Mirrors are very versatile. You can levitate; make things disappear; put swords through the naked lady. Yes, sometimes there are headaches. But *blueeyedboy* has helped me with that. Didn't I say I preferred myself when I was writing as someone else? *Blueeyedboy* has no empathy. He rarely feels for anyone. His cold, dispassionate view of the world is a welcome foil for my tenderness.

Tenderness? I hear you say. Well, yes. I'm *very* sensitive. A mirror-touch synaesthete feels everything he witnesses. As a boy, it took me some time to realize that others did not function this way. Until Dr Peacock arrived on the scene, I'd assumed I was perfectly normal. These things sometimes run in families, I'm told; though even in identical twins the way in which the condition manifests itself is often completely different.

In any case, my brother Ben had no wish to share the limelight. The first time we went to the Mansion, he warned me that if I gave as much as a hint to Dr Peacock that I was not the everyday citizen, the vanilla flavour I seemed to be, then there would be consequences of the most unpleasant kind. At first, I defied the warning. If only because of that sepia print, the picture of Hawaii, and the way Dr Peacock spoke to me, and the thought that I might be remarkable –

I stood my ground for two whole weeks. Nigel was openly scornful – as if Brendan Brown could do anything – and Benjamin watched me resentfully, awaiting his chance to take me down. Even then, he was devious. A casual word or two to Ma; a hint that I was jealous of him; more hints that I was faking my gift and simply copying my brother.

Face it: I never had a chance. I was fat and ungainly; dyslexic; a joke; a stutterer; a disaster at school. Even my eyes were that chilly blue-grey whereas Ben's were a luminous, summery shade that made people want to love him. Of course they believed him. Why wouldn't they?

With the help of the piece of electrical cord, Ma extracted a full confession. In a way I think we were both relieved. I'd known I couldn't compete with Ben. And as for Ma – she'd known from the start; she'd known I couldn't be special. How dare I try to discredit Ben? How dare I tell such lies to her? I snivelled and howled my apologies while my brother watched with a smile on his face, and after that, all it took was the threat of a complaint to Ma to make me his obedient slave.

That was the last time I tried to tell anyone about my gift. Once more, Ben had eclipsed me. I tried to go back to being Brendan Brown, safely less-than-average. But something in Ma had shifted. Perhaps it was the reverse-halo effect. Perhaps the Emily White affair. In any case, from that moment forth, I became the whipping-boy, the butt of her frustration. When Dr Peacock stopped working with Ben, I found that she held me somehow to blame. The year Ben failed at St Oswald's, I was the one who was punished – and yes, I *had* been planning to drop out of school, but both of us knew that if Ben had done well, then no one would have thought twice about me.

Food became my great escape – food, and later, Emily. I ate, not out of hunger or greed, but to cushion myself against a world where everything was dangerous; where every word was a false friend; where even to watch TV was a risk, and every scene a sharp edge just waiting for me to run into it.

Nowadays, I've learnt to cope. Music helps a little; and fic; and now, thanks to the Internet, I have found a means to enjoy my gift. The world online is a medium for every possible kind of porn. And of course, for a mirror-touch synaesthete, that's as good as the real thing. A touch, a kiss, and sometimes I can almost forget that it isn't me on that screen at all, that I am just an observer, a spy, and that the real action is going on somewhere else.

Medium. What an interesting word. It describes at the same time what I *was* – the middle child, the average Joe – and what I am now, a speaker in tongues, a living mouthpiece for the dead.

They say you only have one life. Look online, and you'll see that's not true. Try Googling your name one day, and see how many others share it. All those people who might have been you: the charity case; the sportsman; the almost-famous actor; the one on Death Row; the celebrity chef; the one who shares your birthday – all of them shadows of what might have been if things had been slightly different.

Well, I had the chance to be different. To step out of my own life and into one of my shadows. Wouldn't anyone do the same? Wouldn't *you*, if you had the chance?

4

Of course, Ma grieved for Benjamin. In silence, at first – an ominous calm that at first I took for acceptance. Then came the other symptoms; the rage; the forays into insanity. I'd hear her in the middle of the night, dusting the china dogs downstairs or simply walking around the house.

Sometimes she sobbed: *It wasn't your fault.* Sometimes she mistook me for my brother, or ranted at me for my failures. Sometimes she screamed: *It should have been you!* Sometimes she woke me in the night, sobbing – *Oh B.B, I dreamed you'd died* – and it took me some time to understand that we were interchangeable, and that Benjamin Blue and *blueeyedboy* were often, to Ma, one and the same –

Then came the fallout. Inevitably. After the shock came the backlash, and suddenly I was the target once more for all kinds of expectations. With both of my brothers gone from the scene, my role had altered drastically. *I* was now Ma's blue-eyed boy. I was now her only hope. And she felt that I owed it to her to try again, to go back to school; perhaps to study medicine – to do all the things that *he* should have done, and that only I could now achieve.

At first I tried to defend myself. I wasn't cut out for medicine. I'd failed every science subject at Sunnybank Park, and I'd barely scraped through O-level maths. But Ma was having none of it. I had a responsibility. I'd been lazy and slack for far too long; now it was time for me to change . . .

Well, you know what happened then. I fell mysteriously sick. My belly was filled with writhing snakes, pouring their venom into my guts. By the end of it all, I'd lost so much weight that I looked like a clown in my old clothes. I flinched at loud noises, cringed at bright lights. And sometimes I barely remembered the terrible, marvellous thing that I'd done, or where Ben finished and Brendan began –

Well, that's only natural, isn't it? My memories are so nebulous, sneakily substituting second-hand smoke into this game of mirrors. I was feverish; I was in pain; I don't know what I said to her. I don't remember anything – lies, confessions, promises – but when I was fully recovered, and I left my bed for the first time, I knew that something about me had changed. I was no longer Brendan Brown, but something else entirely. And, truth be told, I no longer knew with any kind of certainty whether I had swallowed Ben, or whether he had swallowed *me* –

Of course I don't believe in ghosts. I scarcely believe in the living. And yet, that's just what I became, a shadow of my brother. When the Emily scandal broke, I reinvented his story. I already had his gift, of course, thanks to my own condition. Which made it so much easier to make them believe that I was telling the truth.

I started to wear Ben's colour, his clothes. At first just for practicality's sake, because my own clothes were too big. I didn't wear blue all the time. A sweatshirt here, a T-shirt there. Ma didn't seem to notice. The scandal surrounding Emily White had made me into a hero; people bought me drinks in pubs; girls suddenly found me attractive. I'd started at Malbry College that term. I let Ma believe I was studying medicine. My teenage skin had finally cleared; I'd even lost my stammer. Best of all, I was still losing weight. With my brothers gone, I seemed to have lost that ravenous need to consume, to collect, to swallow everything in sight. What started with Mal had ended with Ben. At last, my craving was satisfied.

5

You are viewing the webjournal of **blueeyedboy**.
Posted at: *21.56 on Tuesday, February 19*
Status: *restricted*
Mood: *wistful*
Listening to: *Judy Garland:* 'Somewhere Over The Rainbow'

Well, Clair – you got your way. I finally went back to Group today. With everything going so nicely to plan, I think I can allow myself a little harmless distraction. Besides, this may be the last time –

It's a little powder-beige box of a room with a spider plant on a shelf by the door and a picture of Angel Blue on the wall. The chairs are orange, and have been arranged in a circle so that no one feels inferior. In the middle of the circle is a small table on which there is a flowered tray with a teapot, some cups, a plate of biscuits (Bourbon creams – which I hate, by the way), some lined A4 paper, a bundle of pens and the obligatory box of tissues.

Well, don't expect any tears from me. *Blueeyedboy* never cries.

'Hello! It's so great to see you,' said Clair. (She always says that to everyone.) 'How are you feeling?'

'OK, I guess.'

I'm rather less articulate in real life than I am online. One of the many reasons that I still prefer to stay at home.

'What happened to your face?' she said. She'd already forgotten my fic, of course – or decided it had to be all in my head.

I shrugged. 'I had an accident.'

She gave me a look of fake sympathy. She looks like her mother, Maureen Pike; especially now that she's reaching that age. Forty-one, forty-two; and suddenly it all moves south, no, not to Hawaii, but to some bleaker territory, a place of dry gulches and fallen rocks and holy rolling wilderness. A far cry, indeed, from *ClairDeLune*, who posts erotic fic on my site and who claims to be only thirty-five. Still, as you must have guessed, who we are on *badguysrock* can differ wildly from our real-life selves. As long as it stays a fantasy, who really cares which role we adopt? Cowboy or Indian, black hat or white, no one makes a judgement.

And yet, these games we like to play are linked to an underlying layer of truth – an untapped stratum of desire. We are what we dream. We know what we want. We know that we are *worth* it –

And if what we want is wickedness? If what we want is iniquity?

Well, maybe we are worth that, too. And the wages of sin is –

'Tea?' Clair indicated the flowered tray.

Tea. The poor man's Prozac. 'No, thanks.'

Terri, who takes her tea black and always ignores the biscuits – but who will eat a whole tub of chocolate-chip ice cream the moment she gets home – patted the chair beside her.

'Hi, Bren,' she simpered.

'Fuck off,' I told her.

I ran my eyes over the rest of the group. Yes, they were all there. Half a dozen assorted headcases; plus would-be writers; soapbox queens; failed poets (is there any other kind?); all desperate for a chance to be heard. But only one of them matters to me. Bethan, with the Irish eyes, watching me so hungrily –

Today she was wearing a sleeveless grey top that showed the stars tattooed down her arms. *That Irish girl of Nigel's*, Ma calls her, refusing even to mention the name. *The one with all those nasty tattoos.*

Nasty is my mother's word for those things over which she has no control. My photographs. My orchids. My fic. In fact, I rather like Bethan's tattoos, which help to hide the silvery scars that she has had since adolescence, and which criss-cross her arms like spiders' webs. Is *that* what Nigel saw in her? That passion for stars that echoed his own? That furtive, perpetual sense of distress?

In spite of her garish appearance, Bethan hates to be stared at. Perhaps that's why she hides herself beneath so many layers of deception. Tattoos, piercings, identities. As a child, she was docile and shy; mousy; almost invisible. Well, that's Catholicism for you, I suppose. A perpetual war between repression and excess. No wonder Nigel fell for her. She was that rare individual: someone more damaged than he was.

'Stop staring at me, Brendan,' she said.

I wish she wouldn't call me that. *Brendan* has a sour smell, like something damp in the cellar. It makes my mouth go fuzzy-felt dry, and its colour is – well, you know what it is. *Bethan* is no better, with its snuffy scent of church incense. I preferred her as *Albertine*; colourless, immaculate –

Clair intervened. 'Now, Bethan, please. You know what we said. I'm sure Bren didn't mean to stare.' She gave me one of her syrupy looks. 'And seeing as you're here, Bren, why don't we start with you today? I hear you've been going out more. That's good.'

I gave a shrug.

'Where have you been going, Bren?'

'Around. You know. Out. Town.'

She gave a wide, approving smile. 'That's really great to hear,' she said. 'And I'm so glad you're writing again. Is there anything you'd like to read for us today?'

I shrugged again.

'Now, don't be shy. You know we're here to help you.' She turned towards the rest of the group. 'Everyone, would you please show Bren how special he is to all of us? How much we want to help him?'

Oh no. Not the fucking group hug. Anything but that. Please.

'I do have a little something—' I said, more to divert their attention than because of any need to confess.

Clair's eyes were fixed upon me now, hungry and expectant. It's the look she gets on her face sometimes when she's telling us about Angel Blue. And I *do* look rather like him, of course – that, at least, was not a lie – which means, thanks to the halo effect, that Clair has a soft spot for me, and a tendency to believe what I say.

'Really? Can we hear it?' she said.

I looked across at Bethan once more. I used to think she hated me, and yet, perhaps she's the only one who really understands what it is to live every moment with the dead, to speak with the dead, to sleep with the dead –

'We'd love to hear it, Bren,' said Clair.

'Are you sure that's what you want?' I said, still directing my gaze towards Bethan. She was watching intently, her blue eyes narrowed like gas flames.

'Of course,' said Clair. 'Don't we, everyone?'

Nods all around the circle. I noticed that Bethan stayed perfectly still.

'It may be a little – edgy,' I said. 'Another murder, I'm afraid.' I smiled at Clair's expression and at the way the others leaned forward, just like pugs at feeding time. 'Sorry about that, guys,' I said. 'You're going to think that's all I do.'

6

You are viewing the webjournal of **blueeyedboy**, *posting on:*
badguysrock@webjournal.com
Posted at: *22.31 on Tuesday, February 19*
Status: *public*
Mood: *clean*
Listening to: *The Four Seasons:* 'Bye Bye Baby'

He calls her Mrs Baby Blue. She thinks she is an artist. Certainly, she looks like one: her dirt-blonde hair is artistically tousled; she wears paint-spattered jumpsuits and long strings of beads and likes to burn scented candles, which help the creative process, she says (plus they get rid of the smell of paint).

Not that she has accomplished much. No, all her creative passion has gone into raising her daughter. A child is like a work of art, and this one is perfect, she tells herself; perfect and talented and good –

He has been watching her from afar. He thinks how beautiful she is, with her neat little bob and her blanched-almond skin and her little red coat with the pointed hood. She looks nothing like her mother. Everything about her is self-contained. Even her name is beautiful. A name that smells of roses.

Her mother, on the other hand, is everything he most dislikes. Inconstant; pretentious; a parasite, feeding off her daughter, living through her, stealing her life with her expectations –

Blueeyedboy despises her. He thinks of all the harm she has done – to him, to both of them – and he wonders: *Would anyone really care?*

All things considered, he thinks maybe not. The world would be cleaner without her.

Cleaner. What a wonderful word. In blue, it maps out what he does, what he is and what he will achieve, in one. *Cleaner.*

The perfect crime comes in four stages. Stage One is obvious. Stage Two takes time. Stage Three is a little harder, but by now he is getting used to it. Five murders, counting Diesel Blue, and he wonders if he can call himself a serial killer yet, or if he first needs to refine his style.

Style is important to *blueeyedboy.* He wants to feel there's a poetry, a greater purpose in what he does. He would like to do something intricate: a dissection; a beheading; something dramatic, eccentric and strange. Something that will make them shiver; something that will set him apart from the rest. Most importantly, he would like to watch; to see the expression in her eyes; to have her know at last who he is –

He knows from his observation that when she is alone in the house, Mrs Baby Blue likes to take long baths. She stays in the bath for an hour at least, reading magazines – he has seen the telltale watermarks in the bundles of papers she puts out for recycling. He has seen the flicker of candles against the frosted window glass and caught the scent of her bath oil as the water rushes into the drain. Baby Blue bathtime is sacrosanct. She never answers the telephone; never even answers the door. He knows this. He has tried it. She doesn't even lock herself in –

He waits in the garden. He watches the house. Waits for the glow of candles and the sound of water in the pipes. Waits for Mrs Baby Blue; and then, very quietly, lets himself in.

The house has been redecorated. There are new paintings on the walls – abstracts for the most part – a scarlet and brown Axminster carpet in the hall.

Axminster. Ax. Minster. A red word. What does it mean? Axe-murderer. Axe. Minster. Murder in the Cathedral. The thought distracts him for a moment, makes him feel dizzy and remote, brings that taste into his mouth again, that fruity, rotting sweetness that heralds the worst of his headaches. He concentrates on the colour blue; its soothing properties, its calm. Blue is the blanket he reaches for whenever he feels alone or afraid; he closes his eyes, clenches his fists and thinks to himself –

It's not my fault.

When he opens them, the taste and the headache are both gone. He looks around the silent house. The layout is as he remembers it; there's the same lurking scent of turpentine; and those china dollies, *not* thrown away, but under glass in the parlour, all starey-eyed and sinister among their faded ringlets and lace.

The bathroom is tiled in aqua and white. Mrs B is reclining, eyes closed, in the water. Her face is a startling turquoise – some beauty mask, he conjectures. There is a copy of *Vogue* on the floor. Something smells of strawberries. Mrs B favours bath bombs that leave a sparkly residue: a layer of stardust on her skin.

Stellatio: the act of unconsciously transferring bath-bomb glitter on to another person without their knowledge or consent.

Stellata: the tiny fragments of sparkly stuff that find their way into his hair, his skin; three months later, he's still finding those bright flecks around the house, signalling his guilt in Morse code.

He watches her in silence. He could do it now, he tells himself; but sometimes the urge to be seen is too strong; and he wants to see the look in her eyes. He lingers for a moment; and then, some sense alerts her to him. She opens her eyes – for a moment there is no shock at all, just a wide, blank amazement, like that of those dollies in the hall – and then she is sitting up, a surge of water pulling at her, making her heavy, making her slow, and the smell of strawberries is suddenly overwhelming, and the glittery water splashes his face, and he is leaning into the bathtub, and she's punching at him with her helpless fists, and he grabs her by her soapy hair and pushes her under the surface.

It is surprisingly easy. Even so, he dislikes the mess. The woman is covered with glittery stuff that transfers on to his skin. The scent of synthetic strawberry intensifies. She heaves and struggles beneath his weight, but gravity is against her, and the weight of the water holds her down.

He waits for several minutes, thinking of those pink wafers in the tins of Family Circle, and another scent emerges from the lightning chain of words – *Wafer. Communion. Holy Ghost.* He allows himself to relax; gives his breathing time to slow down, then carefully, methodically, he goes about his housework.

No prints will be found at the scene – he is wearing latex gloves, and has politely removed his shoes in the hall, like a good little boy on a visit. He checks the body. It looks OK. He mops the spilled water from the bathroom floor and leaves the candles burning.

Now he strips off his wet shirt and jeans, balls them up in his gym bag, puts on the clean clothes he has brought. He leaves the house as he found it – takes the wet clothes home with him and puts them in the washing machine.

There, he thinks. *All gone.*

He waits for discovery – no one comes. He has managed it again. But this time, he feels no euphoria. In fact he feels a sense of loss; and that harsh and cuprous dead-vegetable taste, so like that of the vitamin drink, creeps into his throat and fills his mouth, making him gag and grimace.

Why is this one different? he thinks. Why should he feel her absence now, when everything is so close to completion, and why should he feel he has thrown away – to use his Ma's habitual phrase – the baby with the bath water?

Post comment:

ClairDeLune: *Thank you for this,* **blueeyedboy**. *It was wonderful to hear you read this in Group. I hope you won't leave it so long next time! Remember we're all there for you!*

chrysalisbaby: *wish i could have heard U read* ☺

Captainbunnykiller: *Bitchin' – LOL!*

Toxic69: *This is better than sex, man. Still, if you could find your way to writing a bit of both, some day –*

7

You are viewing the webjournal of **blueeyedboy**.
Posted at: 23.59 on Tuesday, February 19
Status: restricted
Mood: lonely
Listening to: Motorhead: 'The Ace Of Spades'

Well, of course, one has to allow for poetic licence. But sometimes fiction is better than life. Maybe that's how it *should* have been. Murder is murder – be it by poison, by proxy, by drowning or by the thousand paper-cuts of the Press. Murder is murder, guilt is guilt, and under the fic beats a telltale truth as red and bloody as a heart. Because murder changes everyone – victim, culprit, witness, suspect – in so many unexpected ways. It's a Trojan, which infects the soul, lying dormant for months and years, stealing secrets, severing links, corrupting memories and worse, and finally emerging at last in a system-wide orgy of destruction.

No, I don't feel any remorse. Not for Catherine's death, at least. It was instinct that led me to act as I did; the instinct of a baby bird struggling for survival. Ma's response, too, was instinctive. I was, after all, the only child. I had to succeed, to be the best; discretion was no longer an option. I'd accepted Ben's inheritance. I read his books. I wore his clothes. And when the Peacock scandal broke, I told my brother's story – not as it really happened, of course, but how Ma had imagined it, revealing my brother once and for all as the saint, the victim, the star of the show –

Yes, I do feel sorry for that. Dr Peacock *had* been kind to me. But I had no choice. You know that, right? To refuse would have been unthinkable; I was already caught in the bottle trap, a trap of my own making, and I was fighting for my life by then, the life I'd stolen from Benjamin.

You understand, *Albertine*. You took a life from Emily. Not that I hold it against you. Quite the opposite, in fact. A person who knows how to take a life can always take another. And as I think I said before, what really counts – in murder, as in all affairs of the heart – is not so much knowledge as desire.

Well – may I still call you *Albertine*? *Bethan* never suited you. But the roses that grew up your garden wall – *Albertine*, with their wistful scent – were just the same variety as the ones that grew at the Mansion. I suppose I must have told you that. You always paid attention. Little Bethan Brannigan, with her bobbed brown hair and those slate-blue eyes. You lived next door to Emily, and in a certain kind of light you could almost have been her sister. You might even have been a friend to her, a child of her own age to play with.

But Mrs White was a terrible snob. She despised Mrs Brannigan, with her rented house and her Irish twang and suspiciously absent husband. She worked at the local primary school – in fact, she'd once taught my brother, who dubbed her Mrs Catholic Blue, and poured contempt on her beliefs. And though Patrick White was more tolerant than either Benjamin or Ma, Catherine kept Emily well away from the Irish girl and her family.

But you liked to watch her, didn't you? The little blind girl from over the wall who played the piano so beautifully; who had everything you didn't have, who had tutors and presents and visitors and who never had to go to school? And when I first spoke to you, you were shy; a little suspicious, at least at first, then flattered at the attention. You accepted my gifts first with puzzlement, then finally with gratitude.

Best of all, you never judged me. You never cared that I was fat. You never cared that I stammered, or thought of me as second-rate. You never asked a thing of me, or expected me to be someone else. I was the brother you'd never had. You were the little sister. And it never once occurred to you that you were just an excuse, a stooge; that the main attraction was somewhere else –

Well, now you know how I felt. We don't always get what we want in life. I had Ben, you had Emily; both of us on the sidelines; extras; substitutes for the real thing. Still, I became quite fond of you. Oh, not in the way I loved Emily, the little sister I should have had. But your innocent devotion was something I'd never encountered before. It's true that I was nearly twice your age; but you had a certain quality. You were engaging, obedient. You were unusually bright. And, of course, you desperately longed to be whatever it was that I wanted of you –

Oh, *please*. Don't be disgusting. What kind of a pervert do you take me for? I liked to be with you, that was all, as I liked being close to Emily. Your mother never noticed me, and Mrs White, who knew who I was, never tried to intervene. On weekdays I'd call round after school, before your mother came home from work, and at weekends I'd meet you somewhere, either at the playground on Abbey Road or at the end of your garden, where we were less likely to be seen, and we'd talk about your day and mine; I'd give you sweets and chocolates, and I'd tell you stories about my Ma, my brothers, myself and Emily.

You were an excellent listener. In fact, I sometimes forgot your age and spoke to you as an equal. I told you about my condition – my gift. I showed you my cuts and bruises. I told you about Dr Peacock, and all the tests he'd performed on me before he chose my brother. I showed you some of my photographs, and confessed to you – as I could not to Ma – that all I'd ever wanted in life was to fly as far as Hawaii.

Poor little lonely girl. Who else did you have but me? Who else was there in your life? A working mother, an absent father, no grand-parents, no neighbours, no friends. Except for Yours Truly, what did you have? And what wouldn't you have done for me?

Don't ever let them tell you that an eight-year-old child can't feel this way. Those pre-adolescent years are filled with anguish and revolt. Adults try to forget this; to fool themselves into thinking that children feel less strongly than they; that love comes later, with puberty, a kind of compensation for the loss of a state of grace –

Love? Well, yes. There are so many kinds. There's *eros*: simplest and most transient of all. There's *philia*: friendship; loyalty. There's *storge*:

the affection a child gives its parents. There's *thelema*: the desire to perform. Then there's *agape*: platonic love; for a friend; for a world; love for a stranger you've never met; the love of all humanity.

But even the Greeks didn't know everything. Love is like snow: there are so many words, all unique and untranslatable. Is there a word for the love you feel for someone you've hated all your life? Or the love for something that makes you sick? Or that sweet and aching tenderness for the one you're going to kill?

Please believe me, *Albertine*. I'm sorry for all that happened to you. I never wanted you to be hurt. But madness is catching, isn't it? Like love, it believes the impossible. Moves mountains; deals in eternity; sometimes even raises the dead.

You asked me what I wanted of you. Why I couldn't just leave it alone. Well, *Albertine*, here it is. You are going to do for me what I can never do for myself. The single act that can set me free. The act I've been planning for over twenty years. An act I could never carry out, but which *you* could perform so easily –

Pick a card. Any card.

The trick is to make the mark believe that the card he has picked was his own choice, instead of the one that was chosen for him. Any card. My card. Which happens to be –

Haven't you guessed?

Then pick a card, *Albertine*.

326

8

You are viewing the webjournal of **Albertine**.
Posted at: *23.32 on Tuesday, February 19*
Status: *restricted*
Mood: *tense*

He's playing games with me, of course. That's what *blueeyedboy* does best. We've played so many games, he and I, that the line between truth and fiction has become permanently blurred. I ought to hate him, and yet I know that whatever he *is*, whatever he *does*, I am in part responsible.

Why is he doing this to me? What does he hope to achieve this time? Everyone in this story is dead – Catherine; Daddy; Dr Peacock; Ben; Nigel, and, most importantly, Emily. And yet as he read his story out loud I felt my throat begin to constrict, my nerves to jangle, my head to spin, and soon the chords of the Berlioz would start to tighten in my mind –

'Bethan? Are you all right?' he said. I could hear the little smile in his voice.

'I'm sorry.' I stood up. 'I have to go.'

Clair looked slightly impatient behind her sympathetic façade. I'd interrupted the story, of course, and everyone else was riveted.

'You don't look terribly well,' said Bren. 'I hope it wasn't something I said—'

'Fuck you,' I told him, and made for the door.

He gave me a rueful shrug as I passed. Strange that, after all he has

327

done, I should feel that sorry little skip of the heart every time he looks at me. He's crazy, and false, and deserves to die, yet there's still something inside me that wants to believe, that still tries to find excuses for him. All that was such a long time ago. We were different people then. And both of us have paid a price, have left a part of ourselves behind, so that neither of us can ever be whole, or escape the ghost of Emily.

For a time, I thought I *had* escaped. Perhaps I might even have managed if he hadn't been there to remind me. Every day in every way, taunting me with his presence until suddenly it all comes out, and the box of delights is broken, and all the demons are free at last, scourging the air with memories.

Funny, where these things can lead us. If Emily had lived, would we have been friends? Would *she* have worn that red coat? Would she have lived in *my* house? Would Nigel have fallen for *her* that night at the Zebra, instead of me? Sometimes I feel I'm in Looking Glass Land, living a life that's not quite mine, a second-hand life that never quite fitted.

Emily's life. Emily's chair. Emily's bed. Emily's house.

But I like it there; it feels right somehow. Not like my old house from so long ago, which is now home to the Jacadees, and which rings with the noise of their cheery lives and the spices of their kitchen. Somehow I couldn't have stayed there. No, Emily's house was the place for me, and I have barely allowed it to change, as if she might come back some day and claim her rightful property.

Perhaps that's why Nigel never settled there, preferring to keep to his flat in town. Not that he really remembered her – he missed that business entirely – but I suppose Gloria disapproved, as indeed she disapproved of everything about me. My hair; my accent; my body art; but most of all my proximity to whatever had happened to Emily White, a mystery only half-resolved, in which her son was also enmeshed.

I don't believe in ghosts, of course. *I'm* not the one who's crazy. But all my life I've seen her here: tapping her way round Malbry; walking in the park; by the church; vivid in her bright-red coat. I've seen her; I've *been* her in my mind. How could it have been otherwise? I've been living Emily's life for longer than I have my own. I listen to her music.

I grow her favourite flowers. I visited her father every Sunday afternoon, and right until the end he nearly always called me Emily.

Still, the time for nostalgia is long past. My journal now serves a
new purpose. Confession is good for the soul, they say, and over time
I have acquired the habit of the confessional. It's so much easier this
way, of course; there is no priest, no penance. Only the computer
screen and the absolution of the *Delete* key. *The moving finger writes,
and, having writ,* can be erased at the touch of a hand; unwriting the
past, deleting blame, making the sullied spotless again –

Blueeyedboy would understand. *Blueeyedboy*, with his online games.
Why does he do it? Because he can. And equally, because he *can't.*
And also, of course, because Chryssie believes in happy-ever-after;
because Clair buys Bourbon biscuits instead of Family Circle;
and because Cap is a fucktard who wouldn't know tough if it jumped
up and tore out what's left of his guts –

I know. I'm beginning to sound like him now. I suppose it comes
with the territory. And besides, I've always been very good at mimick-
ing other people. It is, you might say, my only skill. My one successful
party piece. But this is no time for complacency. This is the time to be
most aware. Even at his most vulnerable, *blueeyedboy* is dangerous. He
is far from stupid, and he knows how to hit back. Nigel – poor Nigel
– is a case in point, deleted just as effectively as if *blueeyedboy* had hit
a key.

That's how he does it. That's how he copes. He said as much in his
story. That's how a mirror-touch synaesthete orchestrated the death of
one brother, by using another as proxy. And that's how he managed to
kill Nigel, with the help of an insect in a jar. And if I am to believe
him now, that's how he caused those *other* deaths, shielding himself
from the consequences by watching it all in reverse, through his fic,
like Perseus slaying the Gorgon.

I've thought of going to the police. But it sounds so absurd, doesn't it? I
can imagine their faces now; their looks of sympathetic amusement. I
could show them his online confessions – if that's what they really are –
and I'd be the one to look crazy, lost in a world of fantasy. Like a stage
magician as he prepares to saw the lady in half, *blueeyedboy* scrupulously
invites us to check that there has been no subterfuge.

Look, no tricks. No hidden trapdoor. There's nothing hidden up his sleeve. His crimes are public, for all to see. To speak up now would simply be to turn the spotlight on myself; to add another scandalous strand to a tale already barbed with lies. I imagine my life with Nigel placed under their scrutiny; I can already see the Press coming like starving rodents out of their holes, swarming over everything, and every little scrap of my life torn up and nibbled at and used to line their filthy nests.

I walked home via the Fireplace House. I knew it so well from his stories. In fact I'd only seen it once, in secret, when I was ten years old. I remembered the garden, all roses, and the bright green lawns, and the big front door, and the fish pond with its fountain. Of course I'd never been inside. But Daddy had told me everything. Over twenty years later, I found my way back with eerie, unsurprising ease. Class had finished at eight o'clock, and a murky dark had fallen, smelling of smoke and sour earth, bracketing the houses and cars in a halo of streetlight-orange.

The house was shut, as I'd thought it would be, but the front gate opened easily and the path had been recently weeded and cleared. Bren's work, I told myself. He has always hated disorder.

Security lights came on as I passed. White spotlights against the green. I could see my giant shadow against the wall of the rose garden, pointing like a finger down the path and across the lawn.

I tried to imagine the house as my own. That gracious house, those gardens. If Emily had lived, I thought, they would have belonged to her now. But Emily had not lived, and the fortune had gone to her family, or at least what was left of it – to her father, Patrick White – and then, at last, from Daddy to me. I wish I could refuse the gift. But it's too late: wherever I go, Emily White will follow me. Emily White and her circus of horrors: the gloaters, the haters, the stalkers, the Press . . .

The upstairs windows were boarded up. Across the fading front door someone had recently sprayed in blue paint: *ROT IN HELL U PERVERT*.

Nigel? No, surely not. I don't believe Nigel would have harmed the old man, whatever the provocation. And as for Bren's *other* suggestion

– that Nigel had never loved me at all, that it had all been because of the money –

No. That's *blueeyedboy* playing games again, trying to poison everything. If Nigel had lied to me, I would have known. And yet I can't help wondering – what was in that letter he got? The letter which sent him off in such a rage? Could Brendan have been blackmailing him? Had he threatened to reveal his plans? Could Nigel really have been involved in something that led to murder?

Click.

A small, but quite familiar sound. For a moment I stood listening, the sound of my blood like surf in my ears, my skin a-prickle with nervous heat. *Could they have found me already?* I thought. Was this the exposure I'd feared?

'Is anyone there?'

No answer. The trees *hisshed* and whispered with the wind.

'Brendan!' I called. 'Bren? Is that you?'

Still nothing moved. There was silence. And yet I could feel him watching me as I've felt him watch me so often before, and the hackles stood up at the back of my neck, and my mouth was suddenly sour and dry.

Then I heard it again. *Click.*

The shutterclick sound of a camera, so dreadfully innocuous, weighted with menace and memories. Then the furtive sound of his retreat, almost inaudible, back through the bushes. He is very quiet, of course. But I can always hear him.

I took a step towards the sound, parted the bushes with my hands.

'Why are you following me?' I said. 'What is it you want, Bren?'

I thought I heard him behind me then, a furtive sound in the undergrowth. I made my voice seductive now, a velvet cat's-paw of a voice, to coax an unsuspecting rat. 'Brendan? Please. We need to talk.'

There was a piece of rock at my feet by the edge of the border. I hefted it. It felt good. I imagined myself bringing it down on his head as he hid there in the bushes.

I stood there, holding the rock in my hand, looking out for a sign of him. 'Brendan? Are you there?' I said. 'Come out. I want to talk to you—'

Once more I heard a rustling, and this time I reacted. I took a step, spun round, and then, as hard as I could, I pitched the rock towards the source of the rustling sound. There came a thud and a muffled cry – and then a terrible silence.

There. You've done it, I told myself.

It didn't feel real; my hands were numb. My ears were filled with white noise. *Was this all I had to do? Is it so easy to kill a man?*

And then it hit me; the horror, the truth. Murder *was* easy, I realized; as easy as throwing a casual punch; as easy as lifting up a stone. I felt empty, amazed at my emptiness. Could this really be all there was?

Then came the opening chords of grief; a swell of love and sickness. I heard a dreadful wounded cry, which for a moment I took to be his voice, but later understood was my own. I took a step towards the place where I'd thrown the rock at Brendan. I called his name. There was no reply. He could be hurt, I told myself. He could be alive, but unconscious. He could be faking it; lying in wait. I didn't care; I had to know. *There*, behind the rose hedge – the briars tore my hands bloody.

And then came a movement behind me. He must have been very silent. He must have crawled on his hands and knees between the herbaceous borders. As I turned I caught a glimpse of his face, his look of pain and disbelief.

'Bren?' I called. 'I didn't mean—'

And then he was running away through the trees, a flash of blue parka against the green. I heard him slip on the dead leaves, sprint across the gravel path, vault over the garden wall and jump down into the alleyway. My heart was pounding furiously. I was shaking with adrenalin. Relief and bitterness warred in me. I hadn't crossed the line, after all. I was not a murderer. Or could it be that the fateful line was not the act, but the *intent*?

Of course, that's academic now. I've shown my hand. The game is on. Like it or not, if he gets the chance, he will try to kill me.

9

You are viewing the webjournal of **blueeyedboy**.
Posted at: *00.07 on Wednesday, February 20*
Status: *restricted*
Mood: *hurt*
Listening to: *Pink Floyd:* 'Run Like Hell'

Bitch. You got me. Right on the wrist – I'm lucky it isn't broken. If you'd hit me in the head – as you undoubtedly meant to – it would have been goodnight, sweet prince, or pick the cliché of your choice.

I have to say I'm a little surprised. I didn't mean any harm, you know. I was only taking photographs. I certainly hadn't expected you to react quite so aggressively. Fortunately I know that garden very well. I know how to move between the beds, and where to watch unnoticed. I knew how to make my escape, too – as I had so many times before – over the wall into the street, with my hurt wrist pressed hard against my stomach and tears of pain half-blinding me, so that everything seemed garlanded with dirty-orange rainbows.

I ran home, trying to tell myself that I *wasn't* running home to Ma, and got back just as she was finishing up in the kitchen.

'How was class?' she called through the door.

'Fine, Ma,' I told her, hoping to get upstairs before she saw me. Mud on my trainers; mud on my jeans; my wrist beginning to swell and throb – that's why I'm still typing with one hand – and my face a map of where I'd been; of places Ma had warned me against –

'Did you talk to Terri?' she said. 'I'm sure she's upset about Eleanor.'

Surprisingly, Ma has taken it well. Far better than I had expected. Spent most of today looking at hats and choosing hymns for the funeral. Ma enjoys her funerals, of course. She relishes the drama. The trembling hand; the tearful smile; the handkerchief pressed to the lipsticked mouth. Tottering by with Adèle and Maureen, each supporting an elbow:

Gloria's such a survivor.

She stopped me halfway up the stairs. Looking down I could see the top of her head; the parting in her black hair that over time has grown from a narrow path into a four-lane motorway. Ma dyes her hair, of course; it's one of the things I'm not supposed to know about, like the Tena pads in the bathroom, and what happened to my father. But *I'm* not allowed to have secrets from *her*, and she levelled the force of her scrutiny on to my guilty profile as I stood like a deer in the headlights, waiting for the hammer to fall.

But when she spoke, I found that Ma still sounded surprisingly cheery. 'Why don't you have a nice bath?' she said. 'Your dinner's in the oven. There's some of that chilli chicken you like, and some home-made lemon pie.' No mention of the mud on the stairs, or even the fact that I was half an hour late.

Sometimes that's the worst part. I can live with her when she's evil. It's when she's *normal* that it hurts, because that's when the guilt comes creeping back, bringing the headache, the sickness. It's when she's normal that I can feel the bulbs of arthritis in her hands and the way her back aches when she stands up, and that's when I remember what it was like in the old days, before my brother was born, in the days when I was her *blueeyeedboy* –

'I'm not really hungry right now, Ma.'

I expected her to react to that. But this time Ma just smiled and said: 'All right, B.B., you get some rest,' and went back into the kitchen. I was surprised (and oddly disturbed) to be let off the hook so easily; but still, it's good to be back in my room, with a glass of wine and a sandwich, and an ice-pack on my injured hand.

The first thing I did was log on. *Badguysrock* was deserted, although my inbox was filled with messages, mostly from Clair and Chryssie. Nothing from *Albertine*. Oh, well. Perhaps she is feeling shaken. It isn't easy to face the fact that you're capable of murder. But she was always so keen to believe in absolutes. In actual fact the line between good and evil is so blurred as to be almost indistinguishable; and it's only long after you've crossed it that you become aware that it even existed at all.

Albertine, oh *Albertine*. I feel very close to you today. Through the throbbing of my wrist, I can feel the beat of your heart. I wish you all the best, you know. I hope you find what you're looking for. And when it's over, I hope you can find a little place in your heart for me, for *blueeyedboy*, who understands far more than you imagine –

10

You are viewing the webjournal of **Albertine**.
Posted at: *23.32 on Wednesday, February 20*
Status: *restricted*
Mood: *impatient*

Not a word from *blueeyedboy*. Not that I expected one – not so soon, anyway. I'm guessing he'll lie low for a while, like an animal driven to earth. I'm guessing three days before he comes out. The first, to check out the area. The second, to establish a plan of action. The third, to finally make his move. Which is why I made *my* move today – emptying my bank account, setting my things in order, packing away my belongings in preparation for the inevitable.

Don't think this is going to be easy for me. These things are never straightforward. Even less so for him, of course; but his methods are chosen to fool his uniquely cross-wired brain into thinking his actions are not his fault, while the victim walks straight into the trap carefully laid out for them.

What will it be, I wonder? Having now made my intentions so clear, I cannot expect him to make an exception in my case. He'll try to kill me. He has no choice. And his feelings for me – such as they are – are founded on guilt and nostalgia. I've always known what I was to him. A shade; a ghost; a reflection. A substitute for Emily. I knew that, and I didn't care; that was how much he meant to me.

But people are lines of dominoes: one falls, then all the others follow. Emily and Catherine; Daddy, Dr Peacock and me. Nigel and

Bren and Benjamin. Where it begins is seldom clear; we own only part of our personal story.

It doesn't seem fair, does it? We all imagine our lives as a story in which we ourselves take centre stage. But what about the extras? What about the substitutes? For every leading role there exist a multitude of expendables, hanging around in the background, never in the spotlight, never speaking a line of dialogue, sometimes not even making the final edit, ending their lives as a single frame on the cutting-room floor. Who cares when an extra bites the dust? Who owns the story of *their* life?

For me it begins at St Oswald's. I can't have been more than seven years old, but I do remember what happened in remarkably vivid detail. Every year my mother and I would go to the Christmas concert in the chapel at St Oswald's at the end of the long winter term. I liked the music, the carols, the hymns, and the organ like a hydra with its shining tongues of brass. She liked the solemnity of the Masters in their black gowns, and the sweetness of the choristers with their angel smocks and candles.

I saw things with such clarity then. The memory loss came afterwards. One moment I was in sunlight; the next in chequered shadows, with only a few flecks of brilliance left to prove that the memories had ever been there. But that day, everything was clear. I remember all of it.

It begins with a little girl crying in the row just in front of me. That was Emily White, of course. Two years younger than I was, and already stealing the limelight. Dr Peacock was there, as well – a large, kind-looking, bearded man with an affable voice like a French horn, whilst elsewhere – another small drama played out, unseen by the major protagonists.

It wasn't much of a drama. Just a blue-eyed boy in the choir pitching forward on to his face. But there was a minor commotion; the music wavered, but did not stop, and a woman – the boy's mother, I assumed – rushed forward into the stalls, her high shoes skidding on the polished floor, her face a lipstick blur of dismay.

My own mother looked disapproving. *She* wouldn't have rushed forward. She would never have made such a fuss – especially not here, in chapel, with everyone so ready to judge and to spread those hateful rumours.

'Gloria Winter. I should have known—'

It was a name I'd heard before. She'd told me the boy had caused trouble at school. In fact, the whole family was bad news: godless, wicked and profane.

Irredeemable, she'd said. It was the word Mother reserved for the worst kind of sinners: rapists, blasphemers, matricides.

Gloria was holding her son. He had cut his head on the side of the pew. Blood – a surprising amount of it – spattered his chorister's surplice. Behind her, two boys, one in black, one in brown, stood by like extras in a game. The black one looked sullen; even bored. The one in brown – a clumsy-looking boy with long, lank hair over his eyes and an oversized sweatshirt that emphasized, rather than hid, his gut – looked distressed, almost dazed.

He put a shaking hand to his head. I wondered if he'd fallen, too.

'What do you think you're playing at? Can't you see I need help?' Gloria Winter's voice was sharp. 'B.B., get a towel, or something. Nigel, call an ambulance.'

Nigel, at sixteen; an innocent. I wish I could say I remembered him. But frankly, I never noticed him; my attention was all on Bren. Perhaps because of the look in his eyes: that trapped and helpless expression. Perhaps because I sensed, even then, a kind of bond between us. First impressions matter so much; they shape us for what comes later.

He raised his hand to his head again. I saw his expression, a rictus of pain as if he'd been hit by something falling from the sky, and then he stumbled against the step and fell to his knees almost at my feet.

My mother had already moved to help, guiding Gloria through the crowd.

I looked down at the boy in brown. 'Are you all right?'

He stared at me in open surprise. To tell the truth, I'd surprised myself. He was so much older than I. I rarely spoke to strangers. But there was something about him that moved me, somehow: an almost childlike quality.

'Are you all right?' I repeated.

He had no time to answer me. Gloria turned impatiently, one arm still supporting Benjamin. It struck me then how tiny she was: wasp-waisted in her pencil skirt, stiletto heels barely grazing the floor. My mother disliked stiletto heels – which she called *slutilloes* – and which, she claimed, were responsible for a variety of conditions ranging from chronic back pain to hammer toes and arthritis. But Gloria moved like a dancer, and her voice was as sharp as those six-inch heels as she snapped at her ungainly son:

'Brendan, get over here right now, or, God help me, I'll wring your fucking *neck*—'

I saw my own mother flinch at that. The F-word was strictly out-lawed in our house. And coming from the boy's mother, too – I couldn't help but feel sympathy. He scrambled clumsily to his feet, his face now flushing a dull red. And I could see how troubled he was, how scared and self-conscious and filled with hate.

He wishes she were dead, I thought, with sudden, luminous certainty.

It was a dangerous, powerful thought. It lit up my mind like a beacon. That this boy should wish his mother dead was almost beyond imagining. Surely this was a mortal sin. It meant that he would burn in hell; that he was damned for eternity. And yet, I was drawn to him somehow. He looked so lost and unhappy. Maybe I could save him, I thought. Maybe he was redeemable . . .

11

You are viewing the webjournal of **Albertine**.
Posted at: *02.04 on Thursday, February 21*
Status: *restricted*
Mood: *anxious*

Let me explain. It's not easy. As a child I was very shy. I was bullied at school. I had no friends. My mother was religious, and her disapproval weighed upon every aspect of my life. She showed me little affection, making it clear to me from the start that only Jesus deserved her love. I was my mother's gift to Him; a soul for His collection, and though I was far from perfect, she said, with His grace and my efforts I might one day be good enough to meet the Saviour's exacting standards.

I don't remember my father at all. Mother never spoke of him, though she wore a wedding ring, and I was left with the vague impression that he had disappointed her, and that she had sent him away, as I too would be sent away if I failed to be good enough.

Well, I tried. I said my prayers. I did my chores. I went to Confession. I never spoke to strangers, or raised my voice, or read comic-books, or took a second slice of cake if Mother invited a friend to tea. But even so, it was never enough. I always fell short of perfection, somehow. There was always a fault in my stubborn clay. Sometimes it was my carelessness; a tear in the hem of my school skirt; a smear of mud on my white socks. Sometimes it was bad thoughts. Sometimes, a song on the radio – Mother detested rock music and called it *Satan's flatulence* – or a passage from a book I'd read. There were so many dangers, Mother said; so many pits on the road to hell. But she tried, in her fashion; she always tried. It wasn't her fault I turned out this way.

There were no toys or dolls in my room, just a blue-eyed Jesus on the cross and a plaster angel (slightly cracked) that was meant to drive away bad thoughts and make me feel safe at night.

In fact, it made me nervous. Its face, neither male nor female, looked like a dead child's. And as for the blue-eyed Jesus, with his head thrown back and his bleeding ribs, he looked neither kind nor compassionate, but angry, tortured and frightening – and why not, I asked myself? If Jesus died to save us all, why wouldn't He be angry? Wouldn't He be furious at what He'd had to endure for our sakes? Wouldn't He want vengeance somehow – for the nails, and the spear, and the crown of thorns?

If I die before I wake, I pray, dear Lord, my soul to take –

And so at night I would lie sleepless for hours, terrified to close my eyes in case the angels took my soul, or, worse still, that Jesus Himself would rise from the dead and come for me, ice-cold and smelling of the grave, and hiss in my ear:

It should have been you.

Bren was dismissive of my fears, and indignant that Mother encouraged them.

'I thought my Ma was bad enough. But yours is a fucking fruitcake.'

I sniggered at that. The F-word again. I'd never dared to use it. But Bren was so much older than I; so very much more daring. Those stories he told me about himself – stories of cunning and secret revenge – far from being horrified, I felt a sneaking admiration. My mother believed in humility, Bren in getting even. This was an entirely new concept to me – accustomed as I was to one kind of creed, I was secretly both thrilled and appalled to hear the Gospel of Brendan.

The Gospel of Brendan was simple. Hit back as hard and as low as you can. Forget about turning the other cheek; just get the first punch in and run away. If in doubt, blame someone else. And never confess to *anything*.

Of course I admired him. How could I not? His words made a great deal of sense to me. I was slightly anxious for his soul, but secretly it seemed to me that if Our Saviour had adopted some of Brendan's attitude instead of being *quite* so meek, it might have been better for everyone. Brendan Winter kicked ass. Bren would never let himself be bullied or intimidated. Bren never lay awake in bed, paralysed by fear. Bren hit back at his enemies with the force of angels.

Well, none of that was strictly true. I realized *that* soon enough. Bren told me things as they *ought* to have been, and not precisely as they *were*. Still, I liked him better that way. It made him – if not quite innocent, then at least redeemable. And that's what I wanted – or thought I did. To save him. To fix what was broken inside. To shape him like a piece of clay into the face of innocence.

And I liked to listen. I liked his voice. When he was reading his stories to me, he never used to stutter. Even his tone was different – quiet and cynically humorous, like a woody cor anglais. The violence never troubled me; besides, it was fiction. What harm could it do? The Brothers Grimm had written far worse: babies devoured by ogres, by wolves; mothers deserting their children; sons sent into exile or killed, or cursed by wicked witches.

The moment I first saw him I knew that Bren had a problem with his mother. I'd seen Gloria in the Village, though we didn't have much to do with her. But I knew her through Bren, and hated her – not for my own sake, but for his.

Slowly, I came to know her more: the vitamin drink, and the china dogs, and the piece of electrical cord. Sometimes Bren showed me the marks she had left: the scratches, welts and bruises. He was so much older than I was, and yet on these occasions I felt as if *I* were the grown-up. I comforted him. I listened to him. I gave him unconditional love, sympathy and admiration. And it never once occurred to me that while I thought I was shaping *him*, he was really shaping *me* . . .

12

You are viewing the webjournal of **Albertine**.
Posted at: *13.57 on Thursday, February 21*
Status: *restricted*
Mood: *melancholy*

Brendan Winter and I became friends five months after the concert. I was going through a difficult time; Mother was always busy at work, and at school I was bullied more than ever. I didn't really understand why. There were other fatherless children in Malbry. Why was I so different? Perhaps it was my fault, I thought, that my Dad had gone away. Perhaps he'd never wanted me in the first place. Maybe neither of my parents had.

That was when Brendan turned up again. I recognized him immediately. Mother was busy, as always. I was alone in the garden. And Emily was in her house, playing the piano – something by Rachmaninov, something sweet and melancholy. I could hear her through the window, which was open, and around which a tangle of roses were in bloom. It looked like a fairy-tale window to me, in which a princess ought to appear: Sleeping Beauty, or Snow White, or maybe the Lady of Shalott.

Brendan was no Lancelot. He was wearing brown cords, and a beige canvas jacket that made him look like a padded envelope. He was carrying a satchel. His hair was longer than before, almost covering his face. He passed by the house, heard the music and stopped, not ten feet away from the garden gate. He hadn't seen me; I was on my swing under the weeping willow tree. But I saw his face as he heard her play, the little smile that touched his mouth. He took out a camera from his satchel, a camera with a long lens; and with a deftness that looked out of place, he clicked off a dozen shots of the house – *clickclickclick*, like dominoes falling – before slipping the camera back into his satchel almost without breaking step.

I left my place on the swing. 'Hey.'

He turned, looking hunted; then seemed to relax when he saw who I was.

'Hey, I'm Bethan,' I said.

'B-Brendan.'

I leaned my elbows on the gate. 'Brendan, why were you taking pictures of the Whites' house?'

He looked alarmed at that. 'Please. If you t-tell anyone, I'll get into trouble. I – just like taking pictures, that's all.'

'Take a picture of me,' I said, showing my teeth like the Cheshire Cat.

Bren looked round, then grinned. 'OK. Just as long as you promise, B-Bethan. Not a word to anyone.'

'Not even Mother?'

'*Especially* not Mother.'

'All right, I promise,' I told him. 'But why do you like taking pictures so much?'

He looked at me and smiled. Behind that graceless curtain of hair his eyes were really quite beautiful, with lashes as long and thick as a girl's. 'This isn't an ordinary camera,' he said, this time, I noticed, without stuttering. 'Through this, I can see right into your heart. I can see what you're hiding from me. I can tell if you're good or bad, if you've said your prayers, if you love your mother—'

My own eyes opened wide at this.

'You can see all that?'

'Of course I can.'

And at that he gave an enormous grin.

And that's how I was collected.

Of course, I didn't see it that way. Not until much later. But that was when I decided that Brendan Winter would be my friend: Bren, whom nobody wanted; Bren, who had asked me to lie for him to keep him out of trouble.

It began like that; with a little white lie. Then, with my curiosity about someone so unlike myself. Then came the wary affection that a child may feel for a dangerous dog. Then, a sense of affinity, in spite of our many differences; and lastly a feeling that blossomed at length into something like infatuation.

I never believed he cared much for me. I knew from the start where his interest lay. But Mrs White was protective. Emily was never alone, never allowed to talk to strangers. A glimpse over the garden wall; a photograph; a vicarious touch was all that Bren could hope for. As far as he was concerned, Emily might as well have been on Mars.

The rest of the time, Brendan was mine; and that was quite enough for me. He didn't even *like* her, I thought. In fact, I believed he hated her. I was naïve. I was very young. And I believed in him – in his *gift*. I'd failed to meet my mother's standards; but maybe, with Bren, I could succeed. I was his guardian angel, he said. Watching him. Protecting him. And so, stepping through the looking glass, I entered the world of *blueeyedboy*, where everything exists in reverse and every sense is twisted and turned, and nothing ever really begins, and nothing ever comes to an end . . .

I was three months shy of twelve years old the summer Brendan's brother died. No one told me what happened, although rumours of varying wildness had been circulating around Malbry for weeks. But the Village has always considered itself above events in White City. Brendan was ill, and at first I assumed that Ben had died of the same sickness. After that, the Emily affair swallowed up most of the details. The scandal, the public breakdown – all of that kept the Press in business for more than long enough to eclipse one dirty little domestic.

Meanwhile, the Fireplace House had become the focus of everything. Emily White's brief moment of fame would have fizzled out long ago, but for the blast of oxygen delivered to it that autumn by Brendan Winter. Those allegations of fraud and abuse did more to raise Emily's profile than Catherine White ever did. Not that Catherine cared by then – her family was breaking apart. She hadn't seen her daughter for weeks, not since the Social Services had decided that the child was at risk. Instead, Emily had been sent to live with Mr White, at a B & B in the Village, with twice-weekly visits from a counsellor, until such time as the business could be properly concluded. Left at home, Catherine was self-medicating with a mixture of alcohol and anti-depressants, which Feather – never a stabilizing influence – supplemented with a variety of herbal remedies, both legal and illegal.

Someone should have noticed the signs. Amazingly, nobody did. And when the thing exploded at last, we were all of us caught by the shrapnel.

Although we were next-door neighbours, I didn't know much about Mr White. I knew he was a quiet man who only played music when Mrs White wasn't around; who sometimes smoked a pipe (again, when his wife wasn't there to nag him); who wore little steel-rimmed glasses and a coat that made him look like a spy. I'd heard him play the organ in church and conduct the choir at St Oswald's. I'd often watched him from over the wall, as he sat in the garden with Emily. She liked him to read aloud to her, and, knowing I liked to listen, Mr White would project his voice so that I could hear the story as well – but for some reason Mrs White disapproved, and always used to call them indoors if ever she noticed me listening, so I never really got the chance to get to know either of them.

After he'd moved, I'd seen him once, in the autumn that followed Benjamin's death. A season, not of mists, but of winds, that stripped the trees of their leaves and made gritty work of the pavements. I was walking home from school through the park that separates Malbry from the Village; the weather was half a degree away from snow, and even in my warmest coat I was already shivering.

I'd heard he'd given up his job to care full-time for Emily. This decision had met with a mixed response: some praised his devotion; others (for instance, Eleanor Vine) felt it wasn't appropriate for a man to be left alone with a girl of Emily's age.

'He'll be having to bathe her, and everything,' she said, with clear disapproval. 'The thought of it! No wonder there's talk.'

Well, if there was, you can bet that Mrs Vine was behind it some-how. Even then, she was poisonous: spreading slime wherever she went. My mother had always blamed her for spreading rumours about my dad; and when once or twice I played truant from school, it was Eleanor Vine who informed the school, rather than telling my mother.

Perhaps that was why I felt a link between myself and Mr White; and when I saw him in the park, Mr White in his Russian-spy coat pushing Emily on the swing, I stopped for a moment to watch them both, thinking how very happy they looked, as if there were no one else in the world.

That's what I remember most. Both of them looking so happy.

I stood on the path for a minute or so. Emily was wearing a red coat, with mittens and a knitted cap. Dead leaves crackled under her feet each time the swing reached its lowest arc. Mr White was laughing, his profile slightly averted so that I had time to look at him; to see him with his defences down.

I'd thought him quite an old man. Older by far than Catherine, with her long, loose hair and girlish ways. Now I saw that I'd been wrong. I'd simply never heard him laugh. It was a young and summery sound, and Emily's voice against it was like a seagull crossing a cloud-less sky. I realized that the scandal, far from driving them apart, had strengthened the bond between these two, all alone against the world and glad to be together.

It's snowing outside. Wild, yellow-grey flakes caught in the cone of the corner streetlight. Later, if it settles, then maybe there will be peace over Malbry; all sins past and present reprieved for the day beneath that merciful dusting of white.

It was snowing the night that Emily died. Perhaps if it *hadn't* been snowing then, Emily wouldn't have died at all. Who knows? Nothing ends. Everybody's story starts in the middle of someone else's tale, with messy skeins of narrative just waiting to be unravelled. And whose story is this anyway? Is it mine, or Emily's?

13

They should have seen it coming, of course. Catherine White was unstable. Ready to lash out at the cause of her pain – rather like me, if you think about it. And when Patrick White brought Emily home after her performance –

Well, there was an argument.

I suppose they should have expected it. Tension had been building for months. Emotions ran high in the household. In her husband's absence, Mrs White had been joined by Feather, who, with her alternative therapies, her conspiracy theories, her walk-ins and ghosts and Tomorrow Children, had pushed Catherine White from her volatile state into a full-blown neurosis.

Not that I knew that then, of course. It was late September when Emily left home. Now it was mid-January, with the snowdrops just beginning to push their little green heads through the frozen ground. In all those months of observing the house, I'd barely seen Mrs White. Just once or twice, through the window – a window still hung with Christmas lights, although Twelfth Night was long gone, and the Christmas tree with the tinsel on it was turning brown on the back lawn – I'd seen her standing, looking out, a cigarette trembling at her lips, gazing at nothing but snow and a sky that hissed like white noise.

Feather, on the other hand, was always hanging around the place. I saw her almost every day: fetching the groceries; bringing the mail; dealing with the reporters that still turned up from time to time, hoping for an interview, a word, a picture of Emily –

In actual fact, Emily had barely been seen by anyone. Released by the Social Services when the Peacock case collapsed, she had since moved in with her father, who, every alternate weekend, took her to see her mother in the presence of a social worker, who made careful notes and wrote a report, the gist of which was always that Mrs White was, as yet, unfit to be left alone with Emily.

That night, however, was different. Mr White wasn't thinking clearly. It wasn't the first time that Catherine had threatened to kill herself, but it was her first realistic attempt; averted by Feather's intervention, and by the swift action of the paramedics who had hauled her out of the cooling bath and performed first aid on her slashed wrists.

It could have been worse, the doctor said. It takes a lot of aspirin to actually kill someone outright, and the cuts on her wrists, though fairly deep, had not touched the artery. But it *had* been a serious attempt, grave enough to cause concern – and by the next morning, which happened to be the day of Emily's final performance – the story had reached such giant proportions that it could no longer be contained.

How small are the building-blocks of our fate! How intricate their workings! Remove just one component, and the whole machine ceases to function. If Catherine had not chosen that particular day to make her suicidal gesture – and who knows what sequence of events led to that final decision – bringing Bodies A, B and C into malign conjunction; if Emily's performance that day had not been quite so compelling; if Patrick White had been stronger, and had not given in to his daughter's pleas; if he hadn't defied the court ruling and taken Emily to see her without a social worker being present; if Mrs White had been in a brighter mood; if Feather had not left them alone; if I had worn a warmer coat; if Bethan had not come outside to look at the newly fallen snow –

If. If. If. A sweetly deceptive word, as light as a snowflake on the tongue. A word that seems too small to contain such a universe of regret. In French, *if* is the yew tree, symbol of mourning and the grave. If a yew tree falls in the woods –

I suppose Mr White meant well. He still loved Catherine, you see. He knew what she meant to Emily. And even though they were living apart, he'd always hoped to move back in, that Feather's influence would fade and that Emily, once the scandal had died, could go back to being a real child instead of a phenomenon.

I'd been watching the house since lunchtime from the coffee shop across the road. I caught it all on camera; the shop had closed at five o'clock, and I was hiding in the garden, where an overgrown clump of leylandii right up by the living-room window offered suitable cover. The trees had a sour and vegetable smell, and where the branches touched my skin they left red marks that itched like nettlerash. But I was nicely shielded from view – on one side by trees – whilst at the window the curtains were drawn, leaving just a tiny gap through which I was able to watch the scene.

That was how it happened. I swear. I never meant to hurt anyone. But standing outside, I heard it all: the recriminations; Mr White's attempt to calm Mrs White down; Feather's interjections; Mrs White's hysterical tears; Emily's hesitant protests. Or maybe I just *thought* I did – in retrospect, Mrs White's voice in my memory now sounds a lot like Ma's voice, and the other voices resonate like something heard from inside a fish tank; creating booming bubbles of sound that burst in nonsense syllables against the whitened glass.

Clickclick. That was the camera. A long lens resting on the sill; the fastest exposure the shot can take. Even so, the pictures, I knew, would be blurry, nebulous, unclear; the colours blooming around the scene like phosphorescence around a shoal of tropical fish.

Clickclick. 'I want her *back*! You can't keep her away – not *now!*'

That was Mrs White, pacing the room, cigarette in one hand, hair like a dirty flag down her back. The bandages on her cut wrists stood out a ghostly, unnatural white.

Clickclick. And the sound tastes like Christmas, with the sappy blue scent of the leylandii, and the numbing cold of the falling snow. *Snow Queen weather*, I thought to myself, and remembered Mrs Electric Blue and the cabbagey reek of the market that day, and the sound her heels had made on the path – *click-click-click*, like my mother's.

'Cathy, please,' said Mr White. 'I had to think of Emily. None of this is good for her. Besides, you needed to rest, and—'

'Don't you fucking *dare* patronize me!' Her voice was rising steadily. 'I know what you're trying to do. You want to get some distance from me. You want to ride the scandal. And when you've pinned the blame on me, then you'll cash in, like all the rest—'

'No one's trying to blame you.' He tried to touch her; she flinched away. Underneath the window, I too flinched; and Emily, her hand at her mouth, stood helplessly to one side, flying her distress like a red flag that only I could see.

Clickclick. I felt the touch on my mouth. I could feel her fingers there. They felt like little butterflies. The intimacy of the gesture made me shiver with tenderness.

Emily. Em-il-y. The scent of roses everywhere. Flecks of light shone through the curtains and scattered the fallen snow with stars.

Em-il-y. A million lei.

Clickclick – and now I could almost feel my soul rising out of my body. A million tiny points of light, racing towards oblivion –

And now Feather was joining in, her strident voice drilling through the glass. Somehow, once more, it reminds me of Ma, and the scent that always accompanies her. Cigarette smoke and the lurking scent of L'Heure Bleue and the vitamin drink.

Clickclick, and Feather was in the can.

I imagined her trapped and drowning inside.

'No one asked you to come here,' she said. 'Don't you think you've done enough?'

For a moment I thought she was talking to me. *You little shit*, I expected her to say. *Don't you know it's all your fault?* And maybe this time it is, I thought. Maybe this time she knows it, too.

'Don't you think you've humiliated Cathy enough, with your bastard living right next *door?*'

A pause, as cold as snow on snow.

'What?' said Mr White at last.

'That's *right*,' said Feather triumphantly. 'She knows – *we* know – everything. Did you think you could get away with it?'

'I didn't get away with it,' said Mr White to Catherine. 'I told you all about it. I told you straight away, a mistake I've been paying for these past twelve years—'

'You told me it was *over!*' she cried. 'You told me it was a woman at work, a supply teacher who *moved away—*'

For a moment he looked at her, and I was struck by his air of calm. 'Yes, that was a lie,' he said. 'But all the rest of it was true.'

I took a step back. My heart gave a lurch. My breath bloomed huge and monstrous. I knew that I shouldn't be there, that by now Ma would be wondering where I was. But the scene was too much for Yours Truly. *Your bastard.* What a fool I'd been.

'How many *other* people knew?' That was Mrs White again. 'How many people were laughing at me, while that Irish bitch and her fucking *brat—*'

Once more I approached the glass, feeling Emily's hand on my cheek. It was cold, but I could feel her heart beating like a landed fish.

Mum, please. Daddy, please –

No one but I could hear her. No one but I could know how she felt. I stretched out my hand like a starfish, pressing the fingers against the glass.

'Who told you, Cathy?' said Mr White.

Catherine blew smoke into the air. 'You really want to know, Pat?' Her hands were fluttering like birds. 'You want to know who gave you away?'

Behind the window, I shook my head. I already knew who had told her. I knew why I'd seen Mr White giving money to Ma that day; I understood his pity when I'd asked him if he were my father –

'You hypocrite,' she hissed at him. 'Pretending you cared about Emily. You never really wanted her. You never really understood how *special*, how *gifted* Emily was—'

'Oh yes, I did,' said Mr White. His voice was as calm as ever. 'But because of what happened twelve years ago, I've allowed you far too much control. You've made our daughter into a freak. Well, after today's performance, I'm going to stop all that once and for all. No more interviews. No more TV. It's time she had a normal life, and time you learnt to face the facts. She's just a little blind girl who wants to please her mother—'

'She isn't normal,' said Mrs White, her voice beginning to tremble. 'She's *special*! She's *gifted*! I know she is! I'd rather see her dead than be just another handicapped child—'

And at that, the subject under discussion stood up and began to scream: a desperate, penetrating cry that sharpened into a bright point of sound, a laser that sliced through reality with a taste like copper and rotting fruit –

I dropped the camera.

Миииииии-ииииииии-ииииииииит!

For a moment, she and I are one. Twins, two hearts that beat as one; a single oscillation. For a moment I know her perfectly; just as Emily knows me. And then, as suddenly, silence. The volume falls. I'm suddenly aware of the vicious cold; I've been standing here for an hour or more. My feet are numb; my hands are sore. Tears are running down my face, but I can barely feel them.

I'm having trouble breathing. I try to move, but it's too late. My body has turned to concrete. The illness I suffered after Ben's death has left me wasted and vulnerable. I have lost too much weight over too short a time; my body's resources are used up.

A wave of terror engulfs me. *I could die here*, I tell myself. *No one knows where I am.* I try to call out, but no sound escapes; my mouth is starchy with fear. I can hardly breathe; my vision is blurred –

Should have listened to Ma, Bren. Ma always knows when you're up to no good. Ma knows you deserve to die –

Please, Ma, I whisper through lips that are papery with cold.

> *Snow had fallen, snow on snow*
> *Snow on snow –*

Silence has enveloped me. Snow deadens everything: sound; light; sensation –

All right, then let me die, I think. *Let me die right here, by her door. At least I'd be free then. Free of her –*

The thought is weirdly exhilarating. To be free of Ma – of

everything – seems like the culmination of every desire. Forget Hawaii; all I need is a moment longer in the snow. Just a moment, and then, sleep. Sleep, without hope, without memory –

And then from behind me comes a voice.

'Brendan?'

I open my eyes and turn my head. And it's little Bethan Brannigan, in her red coat and her bobble hat, looking at me from over the wall like something out of a fairy tale. Little Bethan, otherwise known as *Patrick's brat from next door,* and whose parentage – kept secret for years – Ma must have threatened to reveal –

She scrambles over the garden wall. She says: 'Bren, you look *awful.*'

The snow has stolen my voice. Once more I try to move, but my feet are frozen to the ground.

'Wait here. You'll be all right.' Bethan, even at twelve years old, knows how to cope in a crisis. I hear her run to the front door. She rings the bell. Someone comes out. Snow falls from the burdened porch with a dull *ch-thump* on to the step.

Mr White's voice cuts through the night. 'What's happened, Bethan? Is something wrong?'

Bethan's voice: 'It's my friend. He needs help.'

Mrs White, shrill with hysteria: 'Patrick! Don't you *dare* let her in!'

'Cathy. Someone's in trouble—'

'I'm warning you, Patrick!'

'Cathy, please—'

And now, at last, my legs give way. I fall on to my hands and knees. I lift my head and see Emily, at an angle by the door. Syrupy light spills languidly on to the unblemished snow. She is wearing a blue dress, sky-blue, Virgin-blue, and at that moment I love her so much that I would be happy to die in her place –

'Emily,' I manage to say.

And then the world shrinks to a speck; the cold rushes in to engulf me, footsteps come running towards me and –

Nothing.

Nothing at all.

14

You are viewing the webjournal of **Albertine**.
Posted at: 00.23 on Friday, February 22
Status: restricted
Mood: drained

The Press has a poor vocabulary. It works according to certain rules. A house fire is always described as a *blaze*; a blonde is always *bubbly*. Murders are always *brutal*, as if to distinguish from the more compassionate kind. And the death of a child (better still, a *tot*) is invariably a *tragedy*.

In this case it was almost true: a mother's love tested beyond endurance; friends who failed to notice the signs; a husband too willing to rally round; a freak combination of circumstances.

They blamed the media, of course, as they would for the death of Diana. The ultimate tabloid accolade of being known by one's first name alone is reserved for Jesus, royalty, rock stars, supermodels and little girls who have been kidnapped or killed. Headlines love those dismembered names – those Hayleys and Maddies and Jessicas – implying some kind of shared intimacy, inviting the nation's collective grief. Wreaths and angels and teddy bears; flowers piled knee-high on the street. Emily's legend was reinstated, of course, in the wake of that terrible tragedy.

Tragedy? Well, maybe it was. She had so much to live for. Her talent. Her beauty. Her money. Her fame. So many legends had already grown about her little person. Afterwards, those legends grew into something almost approaching a cult. And the surge of grief that surrounded her death was like a group ululation that mourned and repeated: *Why Emily? Why not some other little girl?*

Well, I, for one, never mourned for her. As *blueeyedboy* might say, shit happens. And she was nothing special, you know; nothing out of the ordinary. He told me himself that she was a fake – a rumour that was buried with her under that white headstone – but death made her untouchable, just one step removed from the holy choir. No one doubts an angel. Emily's status was assured.

Everyone knows the official tale. It needed little embellishment. After her TV performance that night, Emily went home with her father. A quarrel – the cause of which remains unknown – flared up between the estranged couple. Then came one of those incidents that no one could have predicted. A young man – a boy, a neighbour of theirs – collapsed outside the Whites' house. It had been a cold night; snow lay thickly on the ground. The boy – who might have died, they said, if his young friend hadn't asked them for help – was suffering from exposure. Patrick White took both children inside and made them cups of hot tea, and while Feather tried to determine why they'd been there in the garden at all, Catherine White was left alone – for the first time in months – with Emily.

At this point, the time-scale becomes unclear. The sequence of events that night may never be fully understood. Feather Dunne always claimed that she last saw Emily at six o'clock, though forensic evidence suggests that the child was still alive up to an hour later. And Brendan Winter, who saw it all, claims not to remember anything –

In any case, the facts are these. At six or maybe six thirty, while the others were dealing with Brendan, Catherine White ran a bath, in which she drowned nine-year-old Emily before getting in herself and taking a bottle of sleeping pills. And when Patrick went to look for them later, he found them curled up together in the bath, stellated with fragments of glitterbomb –

Oh yes. I was there. I'd refused to leave Brendan alone. And when they discovered Emily, we were peering around the bathroom door; invisible as only children can be in such traumatic circumstances . . .

It took me some time to understand. First, that Emily was dead;

next, that her death was no accident. My memory of things exists in a series of images bound together by hindsight; a scent of strawberry bubble bath; glimpses of naked flesh seen through a bathroom mirror; Feather's useless peacock screams and Patrick repeating, *Breathe, baby, breathe!*

And Brendan, watching silently, his eyes reflecting everything . . .

In the bathroom, Patrick White was trying to revive his daughter. *Breathe, dammit, baby, breathe!* – accenting each word with a hard push aimed at the dead girl's heart, as if, by the force of his own desire, he might somehow restart the mechanism. The pushes, increasingly desperate, degenerated into a series of blows as Patrick White lost control and began to flail at the dead girl, thumping her like a pillow.

Brendan pressed his hands to his chest.

'Breathe, baby. Breathe!'

Brendan began to gasp for air.

'Patrick!' said Feather. 'Stop it. She's gone.'

'No! I can do it! Emily! *Breathe!*'

Brendan leaned against the door. His face was pale and shiny with sweat; his breathing, rapid and shallow. I knew all about his condition, of course – the mirror-response that made him flinch at the sight of a graze on my knee, and which had caused him such distress the time his brother collapsed in St Oswald's Chapel – but I'd never seen him like this before. It was like a kind of voodoo, I thought; as if, even though she was already dead, Emily was killing him –

Now I knew what I had to do. It was like in the fairy story, I thought, where the boy gets the ice mirror in his eye and can only see everything twisted and warped. *The Snow Queen*, that was the story's name. And the little girl had to save him . . .

I took a step in front of him, blocking his view of Emily. Now it was I who was in his eyes, mirrored there in winter-blue. I could see myself: my little red coat; my bobbed hair, so like Emily's.

'Bren, it wasn't your fault,' I said.

He flung out a hand to ward me off. He looked very near to passing out.

'Brendan, look at me,' I said.

He closed his eyes.

'I said *look* at me!' I grabbed him by the shoulders and held on to him as hard as I could. I could hear him struggling to breathe –

'Please! Just look at me, and *breathe*!'

For a moment I thought I'd lost him. His eyelids fluttered; his legs gave way, and we fell together against the door. And then he opened his eyes again, and Emily was gone from them. Instead there was only my face, reflected in miniature in his eyes. My face, and his eyes. The abyss of his eyes.

I held him at arms' length and *breathed*, just breathed, steadily in and out, and gradually his breathing slowed and shifted gently to match my own, and the colour began to return to his face, and tears spilled from my eyes – and his – and I thought once again of the story where the girl's tears melt the fragment of mirror and free the boy from the Snow Queen's curse – I felt a surge of fierce joy.

I'd saved Brendan. I'd saved his life.

I was there now, in his eyes.

For a moment, I saw myself there, like a mote inside a teardrop. And then he pushed me away and said:

'Emily's dead. It should have been you.'

15

I really don't remember much about the rest of that evening. I remember running outside in the snow; falling to my knees by the path; seeing the snow angel that Brendan had left by the front door. I ran to my room; lay down on my bed under the blue-eyed Jesus. I don't know how long I stayed there. I was dead; a thing with no voice. My mind kept going back to the fact that Bren had chosen *her*, not *me*; that in spite of everything I'd done, Emily had beaten me.

And then I heard the music . . .

Perhaps that's why I avoid it now. Music brings too many memories. Some mine, some hers, some belonging to both of us. Maybe it was the music that brought me back to life that day. The first movement of the *Symphonie fantastique*, played so loudly from inside the car – a dark-blue four-door Toyota sedan parked in the drive of the White house – that the windows trembled and bulged with the sound, like a heart that was close to breaking.

By then, the ambulance had gone. Feather must have gone with it. Mother was working late that night – something to do with the church, I think. Bren was nowhere to be seen, and the lights were out in Emily's house. But then came this gust of music, like a black wind set to blow open all the padlocked doors in the world, and I stood up, put on my coat and went outside to the parked car. The engine was running, I noticed, and a rubber pipe fixed on to the exhaust led into the driver's side window, and there was Emily's father, sitting quietly in the driver's seat; not crying, not ranting, just sitting there, listening to music and watching the night.

Through the car window, he looked like a ghost. So did I, against the glass; my pale face reflecting his. All around him, the music swelled. I remember that especially; the Berlioz that haunts me still, and the snow that covered everything.

And I realized that he, too, blamed himself; he thought that if things had been different, then maybe he could have saved Emily. If he hadn't let me in; if he'd left Brendan outside in the snow; if some-one else could have taken her place.

Emily's dead. It should have been you.

And now I thought I understood. I saw how I could save us both. Perhaps I could make this *my* story, I thought, instead of it being Emily's. The story of a girl who died, and somehow made it back from the dead. I had no thought of revenge – not then. I didn't want to take her life. All I wanted was to start again, to turn on to a clean page and never think of that girl any more, the girl who had seen and heard too much.

Patrick White was looking at me. He had taken off his glasses, and without them, I thought he looked lost and confused. His eyes with-out the lenses were a bright – and oddly familiar – blue. Yesterday he had been someone's daddy – someone who read stories, played games, gave kisses at bedtime, someone who was needed and loved – and who was he now? No one; nothing. A reject, an extra – just like me. Left on the pile while the story goes on somewhere else, without us.

I opened the passenger door on his side. The air was warm inside the car. It smelt of roads and motorways. The hose, attached to the car exhaust, fell out as I released the door.

The music stopped. The engine went off. Patrick was still looking at me. He seemed unable to speak, but his eyes told me all I needed to know.

I closed the door.

I said: 'Daddy, let's go.'

We drove away in silence.

16

You are viewing the webjournal of **blueeyedboy**.
Posted at: *01.09 on Friday, February 22*
Status: *restricted*
Mood: *contrite*
Listening to: *Pink Floyd*: 'The Final Cut'

No, it wasn't exactly my finest hour. Don't think I'm proud of what I said. But, in my own defence, let me say that I'd suffered a great deal already that day, and that suffering gets passed around in ever-increasing circles, like the ripples from a flung stone as it strikes the water's surface –

It should have been you. Yes, that's what I said. I even meant it at the time. I mean, who would have missed Bethan Brannigan? Who was she in the scheme of things? Emily White was unique; a gift; Bethan was nothing; nobody. Which is why, when Bethan disappeared, she was caught in the headlines, pipped at the *Post*, eclipsed in the mourning for Emily.

Front-page headlines: *EMILY DROWNED! MYSTERY DEATH OF CHILD PRODIGY.*

In the wake of such momentous news, everything else takes second place. *LOCAL GIRL DISAPPEARS* barely makes it to page six. Even Bethan's mother waited until morning before reporting her daughter's absence to the police –

I have very little memory of what happened after that. I made it home; that much I know. Ma noticed I was feverish. She put me to bed, where I was to stay. Headaches, stomach cramps, fever. The police came round eventually, but in the circumstances I was unable to tell them much. As for Mr White, it took them forty-eight hours to realize that he, too, had vanished –

By then, of course, the fugitives were long gone. The trail was cold. And why, they thought, would Patrick White have kidnapped a child he hardly knew? Feather revealed a motive, confirmed by Mrs Brannigan. The news that Bethan was Patrick's child delivered a much-needed blast of oxygen to the story– and once again, the hunt was on for the missing girl and her father.

Patrick's car was found by the road fifty miles north of Hull. Brown hairs taken from the back seat confirmed that Bethan had been in the car, although of course there was no way of knowing how long ago that had been. Meanwhile, bank receipts showed Patrick White emptying his savings account. Then, after three cash withdrawals of ten thousand pounds each, the credit trail stopped abruptly. Patrick was running on cash now. Cash is nicely untraceable. Sightings of a man and a girl were reported to the police from Bath. Two weeks and a city-wide search later, these reports were dismissed as a hoax. More sightings, this time in London, were also judged unreliable. An appeal from Mrs Brannigan met with a similar lack of result.

Nearly three months later, with no solid evidence to the contrary, folk were beginning to wonder whether Patrick, unhinged by the tragedy, hadn't staged a murder-suicide of his own. Ponds were dredged; cliffs investigated. In the Press, Bethan acquired the first-name status that often precedes a grisly discovery. Candles were lit in Malbry church, *To Angel Beth God Loves You*, et al. Mrs Brannigan led a series of prayer campaigns. Maureen Pike held a jumble sale. Still the Almighty stayed silent. Now they kept the story alive merely on speculation; the life-support of the world's Press, a machine that can be kept running indefinitely (as in the case of Diana – twelve years gone, and still in the headlines) or switched off at the public's whim.

In Bethan's case, the decline was fast. A cut rose swiftly loses its scent. *BETH – STILL MISSING* wasn't a story. Months passed. Then a year. A candlelit vigil in Malbry church marked the anniversary. Mrs Brannigan was diagnosed with Hodgkin's lymphoma, as if her God hadn't tortured her enough. That made the papers for a while – *TRAGIC BETH'S MUM IN CANCER SHOCK* – but everyone knew the story was dead, covered in bedsores and waiting for someone brave enough to turn off the machine at last –

And then they found them. By accident; living in the back of beyond. A man had been rushed to hospital after suffering a sudden stroke. The man had refused to give his name, but the young girl accompanying him had identified him as Patrick White, and herself as his daughter, Emily.

A STROKE OF LUCK! blazoned the Press, never at a loss for a suitable cliché. But the story itself was less easy. Eighteen months had passed since Bethan Brannigan had disappeared. During most of that time she and Patrick had been living in a remote Scottish village, where Patrick had home-schooled the child, and where no one had even suspected that this bookish man and his little girl might be anything other than what they had appeared to be.

And this child – this shy and reticent fourteen-year-old who insisted her name was Emily – was so unlike Bethan Brannigan that even her mother – now bedridden, in the terminal stages of her disease – was hesitant to identify her.

Yes, there were similarities. The colouring was similar. But she played the piano beautifully, although she never had at home; referred to Patrick as *Daddy* and professed to remember nothing at all of the life she had led eighteen months ago –

The papers had a field day. Rumours of sexual abuse were the most common, of course, although there was no reason for any such assumption. Next came the conspiracy theories, digested versions of which were disseminated in all the best journals. After that, the deluge – dumbed-down diagnoses from possession to psychic transference; from schizophrenia to Stockholm syndrome.

Our tabloid culture favours simple solutions. Quick fics. Open-and-shut cases. This case was unsatisfactory; messy and unfathomable. Six weeks into the investigation, Bethan had still not opened up; Patrick White was in hospital, unable – or unwilling – to speak.

Meanwhile Mrs Brannigan – still known to the tabloids as *Bethan's Mum* – had sadly since given up the ghost, giving the papers one more excuse to misappropriate the word *tragedy*, which left poor Bethan alone in the world, except for the man she called *Daddy* –

It must have come as a shock to learn that Patrick really was her father. Certainly, they mishandled it; and then Dr Peacock compounded the harm, changing his will in her favour, as if that could somehow erase the past and banish the ghost of Emily –

It can't have been easy for her, poor thing. It took years to recover even the semblance of normality. Taken into care at first, then into a foster home, she learnt to fake what she did not feel. Her foster parents, Jeff and Tracey Jones, lived on the White City estate. They'd always wanted a daughter. But Jeff's good humour turned sour when he'd had too many drinks, and Tracey, who'd dreamed of a little girl to dress up in her own image, saw nothing of herself in the silent, sullen teenager. All emotion suppressed and concealed, Bethan found her own ways of coping. You can still see the scars of those early years, their silvery traces down her arms, beneath the ink and filigree.

Talking to her, looking at her, there's always the sense that she's playing a part; that Bethan, just like *Albertine*, is only one of her avatars, a shield thrown up against a world in which nothing is ever certain.

She never told them anything. They assumed she had blocked the memory. I know better, of course; her recent posts confirm it. But her silence ensured Mr White's release; the charges against him were quietly dropped. And although the Malbry gossips never stopped believing the worst, father and daughter were finally left to get on with their lives as best they could.

It was years before I saw her again. By then, like myself, she was someone else. We met almost as strangers; made no reference to the past; talked every week at our creative-writing group; then she wheedled her way into my life until she found the right place to strike –

You thought *she* was in danger from *me*? Quite the opposite, I fear. I told you, I'm incapable of harming as much as a hair on her head. In fiction, I can do as I please; in real life, I'm condemned to grovel before those people I most hate and despise.

Not for very much longer, though. My death list gets shorter day by day. Tricia Goldblum; Eleanor Vine; Graham Peacock; Feather Dunne. Rivals, enemies, parasites – all struck down by the friendly hand of Fate. Well, Fate, or Destiny, or whatever you want to call it. The point is it's never my fault. All I do is write the words.

The moving finger writes, and, having writ –

But that's not strictly true, is it? To wish for the death of an enemy, however well-crafted the fantasy, is not the same as taking a life. Perhaps this is my *real* gift – not the synaesthesia that has caused me so much misery, but this – the power to unleash disaster on those who have offended me –

Have you guessed what I want of you yet, *Albertine*? It really is very simple, you know. As I said, you've done it before. The line between the word and the deed is all about execution.

Execute. Interesting word, with its spiky wintergreen syllables. But the *cute* makes it strangely appealing; sentence to be carried out, not by a man in a black hood, but by an army of puppies . . .

You mean you really haven't guessed what you're going to do for me? Oh, *Albertine*. Shall I tell you? After everything you've done so far, after all we've been through together – *Pick a card, any card –*

You're going to kill my mother.

PART SIX

green

1

You are viewing the webjournal of **blueeyedboy** *posting on:*

badguysrock@webjournal.com

Posted at: *01.39 on Friday, February 22*

Status: *public*

Mood: *nasty*

Listening to: *Gloria Gaynor*: 'I Will Survive'

She has changed her name a number of times, but folk still call her Gloria Green. Names are like tags on a suitcase, she thinks, or maps to show people where you've been, and where you think you're going. She has never been anywhere. Just round and round this neighbourhood, like a dog chasing its tail, running blindly back to herself to start the whole charade again.

But names are such portentous things. Words have so much power. The way they roll like sweets in the mouth; the hidden meanings inside each one. She has always been good at crosswords, at acronyms and wordplay. It's a talent she has passed on to her sons, though only one of them knows it. And she has an immense respect for books; although she never reads fiction, preferring to leave that kind of thing to her middle son, who, despite his stammer, is brighter than she'll ever be – too bright, perhaps, for his own good.

His own name, in Anglo-Saxon, means *The Flaming One* – and though she is terribly proud of him, she also knows he's dangerous. There's something inside him that doesn't respond; that refuses to see the world as it is. Mrs Brannigan, the schoolteacher at Abbey Road, says he will grow out of it, and tacitly implies that if Gloria attended church on Sundays, then maybe her son would be less troublesome. But as far as *blueeyedboy*'s Ma is concerned, Mrs Brannigan is full of shit. The last thing *blueeyedboy* needs, she thinks, is another helping of fantasy.

She suddenly wonders what things would have been like if Peter Winter hadn't died. Would it have made a difference for *blueeyedboy* and his brothers to have had some fatherly influence in their unruly lives? All those football matches they missed, the games of cricket in the park, the Airfix models, the toy trains, the fry-ups in the mornings?

But there's no use crying over spilt milk. Peter was a parasite, a fat and lazy freeloader good for nothing but spending Gloria's money. The best he could do was die on her, and even then, he'd needed some help. But no one walks out on Gloria Green; and surprisingly, the insurance paid up; and it turned out so easy, after all – just a pinch on a tube between finger and thumb as Peter lay in hospital –

She wonders now if that was a mistake. *Blueeyedboy* needed a father. Someone to sort him out. To teach him a sense of discipline. But Peter couldn't have coped with three boys, let alone such a gifted one. His successor, Mr Blue Eyes, was never even an option. And Patrick White – who, in all ways but one, would have made the perfect father – was, sadly, already spoken for; a gentle, artistic soul whose offence was a lapse of judgement.

Guilt made Patrick vulnerable. Blackmail made him generous. Through a judicious combination of both, he proved a good source of income for years. He found Ma a job; he helped them out; and Gloria never blamed him when, in the end, he let her go. No, she blamed his wife for that, with her candles and her china dolls, and when at last she saw her chance to serve Mrs White a backhanded turn, she told her the secret she'd kept for so long; setting in motion a chain of events that resulted in murder and suicide.

But in spite of his parentage, *blueeyedboy* is different. Perhaps because he feels things more. Perhaps that's why he daydreams so much. God knows, she has tried to protect him. To convince the world he is too dull to hurt. But *blueeyedboy* seeks out suffering like a pig rooting for truffles, and it's all she can do to keep up with him, to correct his mistakes and clean up his mess.

She remembers a day at the seaside once, when all her boys were very young. Nigel is off somewhere on his own. Benjamin is four years old and *blueeyedboy* nearly seven. Both are eating ice cream, and *blueeyedboy* says that his doesn't taste right, as if just watching his brother eat is enough to diminish the flavour.

Blueeyedboy is sensitive. She knows this only too well by now. A slap on another boy's wrist makes him flinch; a crab in a bucket makes him cry. It's like some kind of voodoo; and it brings out at the same time both her cruel and her compassionate side. *How is he going to manage*, she thinks, *if he can't cope with reality?*

You have to remember it's only pretend, she snaps, more harshly than she means to. He stares at her from round blue eyes as she holds his brother in her arms. At her feet the blue bucket is already beginning to stink.

'Don't play with that. It's nasty,' she says.

But *blueeyedboy* simply looks at her, wiping ice cream from his mouth. He knows dead things are nasty, but he still can't seem to look away. She feels a stab of annoyance. He collected the damn things. What does he want her to do with them now?

'You shouldn't have caught those animals if you didn't want them to die. Now you've upset your brother.'

In fact, little Ben is completely absorbed in finishing his ice cream, which makes her even more annoyed (although she knows it's irrational), because *he* should have been the susceptible one – after all, he is the youngest. *Blueeyedboy* ought to be looking out for *him* instead of making a fuss, she thinks.

But *blueeyedboy* is a special case, pathologically sensitive; and in spite of her efforts to toughen him up, to teach him to look after himself, it never seems to work, somehow, and she always ends up looking after him.

Maureen thinks he is playing games. *Typical middle child*, she says in her supercilious tone. *Jealous, sullen, attention-seeking.* Even Eleanor thinks so; though Catherine White believes there's more to him. Catherine likes to encourage him; which is why Gloria has stopped bringing *blueeyedboy* to work, substituting Benjamin, who plays so nicely with his toys and never seems to get in the way –

'It wasn't my fault,' *blueeyedboy* says. 'I didn't know they were going to die.'

'Everything dies, ' Gloria snaps, and now his eyes are swollen with tears and he looks as if he is going to faint.

A part of her wants to comfort him, but knows that this is a dangerous indulgence. To give him attention at this stage is to encourage him in his weakness. Her sons all need to be strong, she thinks. How else will they take care of her?

'Now get rid of that mess,' she tells him, with a nod in the direction of the blue bucket. 'Go put it back in the sea, or something.'

He shakes his head. 'I d-don't want to. It smells.'

'You'd better. Or God help me, you'll pay.'

Blueeyedboy looks at the bucket. Five hours in the sun have brought about a rapid fermentation in the contents. The fishy, salt-water vegetable smell has turned to a suffocating reek. It makes him gag. He begins to whimper helplessly.

'Please, Ma—'

'Don't give me that!'

At last, now, his brother is crying. A high, fretful, icy wail. Gloria turns on her hapless son. '*Now* look what you've done,' she says. 'As if I didn't have enough to deal with already.'

She shoots out a hand to slap his face. She's wearing cork-soled sandals. As she snakes forward to hit him again, she kicks over the blue bucket, spilling the contents over her foot.

To Gloria, this is the final straw. She dumps Benjamin on to the ground and grabs hold of *blueeyedboy* with both hands, the better to take care of business. He tries to escape, but Ma is too strong; Ma is all wire and cables, and she digs her fingers into his hair and forces him down inch by inch, pushing his face into the sand and into that terrible, yeasty mess of dead fish and fake coconut, and there's ice cream melting over his wrist and dripping on to the brown sand, but he dare not let go of his ice cream, because if he does, she'll kill him for sure, just as he killed those things on the beach, the crabs, the shrimp, the snail, and the baby flatfish with its mouth pulled down in a crescent, and he tries very hard not to breathe, but there's sand in his mouth, and sand in his eyes, and he's crying and puking and Ma screams: 'Swallow it, you little shit, just like you swallowed your brother!'

Then, suddenly, it's over. She stops. She wonders what has happened to her. Kids can drive you crazy, she knows, but what on earth was she thinking of?

'Get up,' she says to *blueeyedboy*.

He pushes himself up from the ground, still holding his melted ice-cream cone. His face is smeared with sand and muck. His nose is bleeding a little. He wipes it with his free hand; stares up at Ma with brimming eyes. She says: 'Don't be a baby. No one got killed. Now finish your fucking ice cream.'

Post comment:
Albertine: (*post deleted*).
blueeyedboy: *I know. Most of the time, words fail me, too . . .*

2

You are viewing the webjournal of **Albertine**.
Posted at: 01.45 on Friday, February 22
Status: restricted
Mood: uncertain

At last, a version of the truth. Why bother, at this stage in the game? He must know it's too late to go back. Both of us have shown our hand. Is he trying to provoke me again? Or is this a plea for compassion?

For the last two days both of us have stayed indoors, suffering from the same imaginary bout of flu. Clair tells me by e-mail that Brendan hasn't been to work. The Zebra, too, has been closed for two days. I didn't want him coming here. Not before I was ready.

Tonight I came back for the last time. I couldn't sleep in my own bed. My house is too exposed. So easy to start a fire there; to set up a gas leak; an accident. He wouldn't even have to watch. The Zebra is more difficult, built as it is on the main road. Security cameras on the roof. Not that it matters any more. My car is loaded. My things are packed. I could set off immediately.

You thought I'd stay and fight him? I'm afraid I'm not a fighter. I've spent all my life running away, and it's far too late to change that now. But it's strange, to be leaving the Zebra. Strange and sad, after all this time. I'll miss it; more than that, I'll miss the person I was when I worked there. Even Nigel only half-understood the purpose of that persona; he thought the *real* Bethan was someone else.

The *real* Bethan? Don't make me laugh. Inside the nest of Russian dolls, there's nothing but painted faces. Still, it was a good place. A safe place, while it lasted. I park the car by the side of the church and walk along the deserted street. Most of the houses are dark now, like flowers closing for the night. But the neon sign of the Zebra shines out, spilling its petals of light on the snow; and it feels so good to be coming home, even for a little while –

There was a present waiting for me. An orchid in a pot, with a card that reads: *To Albertine*. He grows them himself; he told me so. Somehow that seems very like him.

I go inside. I log on at once. Sure enough, he's still online.

I hope you like the orchid, he writes.

I wasn't going to answer him. I'd promised myself I wouldn't do that. But what harm could it do now, after all?

It's beautiful, I type. It's true. The flower is green and purple-throated, like a toxic species of bird. And the scent is like that of a hyacinth, but sweeter and more powdery.

Now he knows I'm here, of course. I expect that's why he sent the orchid. But I know he can't leave until his usual time of a quarter to five, not without alerting his Ma. Leave now, and she would ask questions, and *blueeyedboy* would do anything to avoid making Ma suspicious. That keeps me safe till four thirty at least. I can indulge myself awhile.

It's a Zygopetalum 'Brilliant Blue'. One of the fragrant varieties. Try not to kill it, won't you? Oh, and what did you think of my fic, by the way?

I think you're twisted, I type back.

He answers with an emoticon, a little yellow smiley face.

Why do you tell these stories? I ask.

Because I want you to understand. His voice is very clear in my mind, as clear as if he were in the room. *There's no going back from murder, Beth.*

You should know, I rattle back.

That emoticon again. *I suppose I ought to feel flattered*, he says. *But you know that's only fiction. I could never have done those things, any more than I could have thrown that rock – my wrist still hurts, by the way. I guess I'm lucky it wasn't my head –*

What is he trying to make me believe? That it's all coincidence? Eleanor, Dr Peacock, Nigel – all his enemies wiped from the board by nothing but a lucky chance?

Well, no, not quite, he answers. *Someone was working on my behalf.*

Who?

For a long time he does not reply. There's nothing there but the little blue square of the cursor blinking patiently in the message box. I wonder if his connection has failed. I wonder if I should log on again. Then, just as I am preparing to sign out, a message arrives in my inbox.

You really don't know who I mean?

I have no idea what you're talking about.

Another of those silences. Then comes an automated message from the server – *Someone has posted on badguysrock!* – and a note which simply says:

Read this.

3

You are viewing the webjournal of **blueeyedboy** posting on:
badguysrock@webjournal.com
Posted at: 01.53 on Friday, February 22
Status: public
Mood: hungry
Listening to: The Zombies: 'She's Not There'

He calls her Miss Chameleon Blue. You can call her *Albertine*. Or Bethan. Or even Emily. Whatever you choose to name her, she has no colour of her own. Like the chameleon, she adapts to suit the situation. And she wants to be all things to all men – saviour, lover, nemesis. She gives them what she thinks they want. She gives them what she thinks they *need*. She likes to cook, and in this way she feeds her need to nurture. She can recognize all of their favourites: knows when to add or hold the cream; senses their cravings almost before they themselves are aware of them.

It is of course for this very reason that *blueeyedboy* avoids her. *Blueeyedboy* used to be fat, and though that was twenty years ago, he knows how easily he could go back to the boy he used to be. Chameleon knows him too well. His fears, his dreams, his appetites. And he knows that certain cravings were never meant to be satisfied. To look at them directly would be to risk the most terrible consequences. So he uses a series of mirrors, like Perseus with the Gorgon. And, safe behind the darkened glass, he watches, waits, and bides his time.

Some people are born to watch, he knows.

Some people are mirrors, born to reflect.

Some people are weapons, trained to kill.

Does the mirror choose what to reflect? Does the weapon select the victim? Chameleon doesn't know about that. She never had any ideas of her own, not even when she was a child. Let's face it, she barely has memories. She has no idea of who she is, and she changes her role from day to day. But she's trying to make an impression, he knows. She wants to leave her mark on him.

Impress. Impression. Impressionist. What interesting words. To provoke admiration; to make a statement; to leave an indentation. One who pretends to be someone else. One who paints a picture using only little dabs of light. One who creates an illusion – with smoke and mirrors, with portents and dreams.

Yes, dreams. That's where it all begins. In dreams, in fic, in fantasy. And *blueeyedboy*'s business is fantasy; his territory, cyberspace. A place for all seasons, all seasonings; a place for all flavours of desire. Desire creates its own universe; or at least it does here, on *badguysrock*. The name is nicely equivocal – is it an island on to which penitents are cast away, or is it a haven for villains worldwide, in which to indulge our perversions?

Everyone here has something to hide. For one, it is his helplessness, his cowardice, his fear of the world. For another, an upright citizen with a responsible job, a lovely home and a husband as bland as low-fat spread, it's a secret craving for dark meat: for the troubled, the wicked, the dangerous. For a third, who yearns to be thin, it's the fact that her weight is just a kind of excuse; a blubbery blanket against a world she knows will eat her otherwise. For a fourth, it's the girl he killed the day he crashed his motorbike: eight years old, on her way to school, crossing on a blind bend. And along he comes at fifty an hour, still tanked up from last night, and when he skids and hits the wall he thinks: *That's it, game over, dude.* Except that the game keeps on going, and just at the moment he feels his spine give way like a piece of string, he notices a single shoe lying on its side in the road and wonders vaguely who the hell would leave a perfectly good shoe in the gutter like that, and then he sees the rest of her, and twenty years later, that's *all* he can see; and the dreams still come with such clarity, and he hates himself, and he hates the world, but most of all what he really hates is their terrible, fucking sympathy –

And what about *blueeyedboy*? Well, like the rest of the tribe, of course, he's not exactly what he seems. He tells them as much; but the more he does, the more they're prepared to believe the lie.

I never murdered anyone. Of course, he'd never admit the truth. That's why he parades himself online; strutting and strumming his base desires like a peacock's courtship ritual. The others admire his purity. They love him for his candour. *Blueeyedboy* acts out what others barely dare to dream; an avatar, an icon for a lost tribe that even God has turned away –

And what of Chameleon, you ask? She is not one of *blueeyedboy*'s closest friends, but he sees her, if sporadically. They do have a kind of history, but there's nothing much here to move him now; nothing to hold his attention. And yet, as he comes to know her again, he finds her more and more interesting. He used to think she was colourless. In fact, she is merely adaptable. She has been a follower all her life, collecting ideologies; although so far she has never had a single idea of her own. But give her a cause, give her a flag, and she'll give you her devotion.

First she followed Jesus, and prayed to die before she woke. After that, she followed a boy who taught her a different gospel. Then, when she was twelve years old she followed a madman into the snow just for the sake of his blue eyes, and now she follows *blueeyedboy*, like the rest of his little army of mice, and wants nothing more than to dance to his tune all the way to oblivion.

They meet again at her writing class when she is just fifteen years old. Not so much a writing class as a kind of soft-therapy group, which her counsellor recommended to her as a means of better expressing herself. *Blueeyedboy* attends this group primarily to improve his style, of which he has always been ashamed, but also because he has learnt to exploit the appeal of the fictional murder.

There's a woman he knows in the Village. He calls her Mrs Electric Blue. And she's old enough to be his Ma, which makes it quite disgusting. Not that *he* knows what's in her mind. But Mrs Electric is known to have a predilection for nice young men, and *blueeyedboy* is an innocent – at least, he is in matters of love. A nice young man of twenty or so; working in an electrical shop to pay his way through college. Slim in his denim overalls, no pin-up, but still, a far cry from the fat boy he was only a couple of years ago.

Our heroine, in spite of her youth, is far more adept in the ways of the world. After all, she has had to endure a great many things over the years. The death of her mother; her father's stroke; that hellish blaze of publicity. She has been taken into care; she is staying with a family in the White City estate. The man is a plumber; his ugly wife has tried and failed many times to conceive. They are both fervent royalists: the house is filled with images of the Princess of Wales, some of them texturized photographs, others paint-by-numbers kits in acrylic on cheap canvas. Chameleon dislikes them, but says very little, as always. She's found that it pays to keep silent now; to let other people do the talking. This suits the family just fine. Our heroine is a good little girl. Of course, they ought to know by now: it's the good little girls you need to watch.

The man, whom we shall call Diesel Blue and who will die with his wife in a house fire some five or six years later, likes to be seen as a family man; calls Chameleon *Princess* and at weekends takes her to work with him, where she carries his big box of tools and waits while he chats with a series of jaded housewives and their vaguely aggressive husbands, who all think that plumbers are rip-off merchants and that they themselves, if they so desired, could easily fix that gasket, that tap, or put in that new storage heater.

It's only Health and Safety gone mad that does not permit them to do so; and so they are sour and resentful, while the women make tea and bring biscuits and talk to the silent little girl, who rarely answers back, or smiles, but sits with her oversized sweatshirt hiding most of her body, and her little hands poking out of the sleeves like wilted pale-pink rosebuds, and her face as blank as a china doll's under the curtain of dark hair.

It is on one of these visits – to a house in the Village – that our heroine first experiences the furtive joy of homicide. Of course, it wasn't *her* idea; she lifted it from *blueeyedboy* at their creative-writing class. Chameleon has no style of her own. Her claim to creativity is based on imitation. She only attends class because he is there, in the hope that one day he will see her again, that his eyes will meet hers and stay there, transfixed, with no reflection of anyone else to mar his concentration.

He calls her Mrs Electric Blue . . .

Nice move, *blueeyedboy*. All names and identities have been changed in the hope of protecting the innocent. But Chameleon recognizes her; knows the house from her visits. And she knows her reputation, too: her taste for young men; her erstwhile disgusting liaison with our subject's elder brother. She finds her pathetic, pitiable; and when Mrs Electric Blue is found burnt to death in her house a few days later, she cannot find it in herself to grieve, or to even care about it much.

Some people like to play with fire. Other people deserve to die. And how could a tragic accident have anything at all to do with that good little girl who sits so still, and who waits so patiently by the fire while her father fixes the plumbing?

At first, even *blueeyedboy* doesn't guess. At first he thinks it's karma. But, with time, as his enemies falter and fall at every stroke of the typewriter key, he begins to see the pattern emerge, clear as the flowered wallpaper in his mother's parlour.

Electric Blue. Diesel Blue. Even poor Mrs Chemical Blue, who set the seal on her own demise by wanting things so nice and clean, beginning with that nice, clean boy in her fat niece's therapy group.

And Dr Peacock, whose only true crime was to find himself in our hero's care; whose mind was half-gone anyway, and whose chair it was so easy to push off the little home-made ramp, so that next morning they found him there, his eyes jacked open, his mouth awry. And if *blueeyedboy* feels anything, it's a dawning sense of hope –

Perhaps it's my guardian angel, he thinks. *Or maybe it's just coincidence.*

Why does she do it, he asks himself? Is it to safeguard his innocence? To take his guilt and make it her own? Or just to attract his attention? Is it because she sees herself as executioner to the world? Is it because of that little girl, whose life she collected so eagerly? Is it because to be someone else is her only means of existing? Or is it because, like *blueeyedboy*, she has no choice but to mirror those around her?

Still, in the end, it's not his fault. He's giving her what she wants, that's all. And if what she wants is guilt, what then? If what she wants is villainy?

Surely, he's not responsible. He never told her what to do. And yet, he feels she wants something more. He senses her impatience. It's always the same: *these women*, he thinks. *These women and their expectations.* He knows that it will end in tears, as it always has before –

But *blueeyedboy* can't blame her now for what she is considering. He was the one who made her, who shaped her from this murderous clay. For years she has been his golem; and now the slave just wants to be free.

How will she do it? he asks himself. Accidents happen so easily. A poison slipped into his drink? A humdrum gas leak? A car crash? A fire? Or will it be something more esoteric: a needle tipped with the venom of a rare South American orchid; a scorpion slipped into a basket of fruit? Whatever it is, *blueeyedboy* expects it to be something special.

And will he see it coming, he thinks? Will he have time to see her eyes? And as she stares into the abyss, what will she see staring back?

Post comment:
JennyTricks: *THINK YOURE SO CLEVER, DONT YOU?*
blueeyedboy: *You didn't like my ficlet? Now why am I not surprised?*
JennyTricks: *BOYS WHO PLAY WITH FIRE GET BURNT.*
blueeyedboy: *Thank you, Jenny. I'll bear it in mind . . .*

4

He calls me a golem. How hatefully apt. The golem, according to legend, is a creature made from word and clay; a voiceless slave with no purpose but to do its master's bidding. But in one of the stories the slave rebels – did you know that, *blueeyedboy*? It turns against its creator. What then? I don't remember. But I know it ended badly.

Is that what he really thinks of me? He always was conceited. Even when he was a boy, despised by almost everyone, there was always that arrogant side to him; the enduring belief that he was unique, destined some day to be someone. Perhaps his Ma did that to him. Gloria Green and her colours. No, I'm not defending him. But there's something twisted about the idea that boys can be sorted like laundry; that a colour can make you good or bad; that every crime can be washed away and hung out on the line to dry.

It's ironic, isn't it? He hates her, and yet he's incapable of simply walking away. Instead, he has his own means of escape. He's been living inside his head for years. And he has a golem to do his work, moulded to specifications.

He's lying, of course. It's only fic. He's trying to breach my defences. He knows my reluctant memory is like a broken projector, incapable of processing more than a single frame at a time. *Blueeyedboy*'s account

383

of events is always so much better than mine, high-resolution imaging to my grainy black and white. Yes, I was full of confusion and hate. But I was never a murderer.

Of course, he knew that all along. This is his way of taunting me. But he can be very convincing. And he has lied to the police before, incriminating others to hide his guilt. I wonder, will he accuse me now? Has he found anything in Nigel's flat, or at the Fireplace House, that he could present as evidence? Is he trying to play for time by drawing me into a dialogue? Or is he playing the picador, taunting me into making a move?

Boys who play with fire get burnt.

I couldn't have put it better. If this is his plan to disorient me, then he is treading dangerous ground. I know I ought to ignore him now, just get in the car and drive away, but a feeling of outrage consumes me. I have played his mind games for far too long. We all of us have; we indulge him. He can't bear the sight of physical pain, but he thrives on mental suffering. Why do we allow it? I ask. Why has no one rebelled before now?

An e-mail arrived a moment ago. I picked it up on my mobile phone.

Re: Everyday care of orchids.

   In my absence, I would be grateful if you might agree to care for my orchid collection. Most orchids do better in a warm, humid environment away from direct sunlight. Water sparingly. Do not allow the roots to soak. Thank you. Aloha,
blueeyedboy

I don't know what he means by this. Does he expect me to cut and run? All in all, I don't think so. More likely he is toying with me, trying to put me off my guard. His orchid is on the back seat of my car, anchored between two boxes. Somehow I don't want to leave it behind. It looks so inoffensive, with its clump of little flowers.

And then a thought occurs to me. It comes with the scent of the orchid. And it seems to clear, so beautiful, like a beacon in the smoke.

It has to end somewhere, don't you see? I've followed him down this road too long, like the crippled child after the Pied Piper. He made me like this. I danced to his tune. My skin is a map covered with scars and the marks of what he has done to me. But now I can see him as he is, the boy who cried murder so many times that, finally, someone believed him . . .

I know his routine as well as my own. He'll set off from home at four forty-five, pretending, as always, to go to work. I'm sure that's when he'll make his move. He won't be able to resist the lure of the Pink Zebra, with its warm and welcoming light, and myself, alone and vulnerable, like a moth inside a lantern . . .

He'll be driving his car, a blue Peugeot. He'll drive down Mill Road and park at the corner of All Saints' Church, where the snow has been cleared away. He'll check the street – deserted now – and then he'll walk up to the Zebra, keeping to the shadows around the side of the building. Inside, the radio is playing loudly enough to mask the sound of his entry. *Not* the classical station today, though I have no fear of music. That fear belonged to Emily. Now even the *Symphonie fantastique* has no power over me.

The kitchen door will be on the latch. Easy enough to open it – glancing up at the neon sign as he does – the strobing words; PINK ZEBRA, with their phantom smell of gas.

You see? I know his weaknesses. I'm using his gift against him now, that gift he acquired from his brother, and when the *real* scent assails him, he will simply dismiss the illusion as he has so many times before – at least until he walks inside, and lets the door close after him.

I have made an adjustment to the door. The handle no longer turns from the inside. And the gas will have been on for hours. By five any spark could ignite it: a light switch, a lighter, a mobile phone.

I won't be there to see it, of course. By then I will be long gone. But my mobile can access the Internet, and I have his number. Of course, he has to *choose* to go in. The victim selects his own fate. No one forces him inside; no one else is responsible.

Perhaps, when he's gone, I'll be free again. Free of these desires of his that mirror desires of mine. Where does the reflection go after the mirror is broken? What happens to the lightning after the storm is over? Real life makes so little sense; only fic has meaning. And I have been fictional for so long; a character in one of his stories. I wonder, do fictional characters ever rebel, and turn on their creators?

I only hope it's not over too soon. I hope he has time to understand. Walking blind into the trap, I hope he has a moment or two to cry out, to struggle, to try to escape, to beat his fists against the door, and finally to think of me, the golem who turned on its master . . .

5

You are viewing the webjournal of **blueeyedboy**.
Posted at: 04.16 on Friday, February 22
Status: restricted
Mood: optimistic
Listening to: Supertramp: 'Breakfast In America'

No sleep tonight. Too many dreams. Some people dream in Technicolor. Some only dream in film noir. But I dream in total-immersion: sound, scent, sensation. Some nights I awake half-drowned in sweat; others, I don't sleep at all. Then, too, the Net is my solace; there's always someone awake online. Chat rooms, fan sites, fic sites, porn. But tonight I'm lonesome for my f-list, my little squeaking chorus of mice. Tonight, what I need is to hear someone say: *You're the best, blueeyedboy.*

And so here I am, back on *badguysrock*, watching perfidious *Albertine*. She has come so far – I'm proud of her – and yet she still feels the need to confess, like the good little Catholic girl of old. I've known her password for some time. It's really quite easy to find out, you know. All it takes is a careless gesture: an account left signed in on a desktop while someone pours a cup of tea, and suddenly her private posts are open for that someone to read –

Are you checking your mail, *Albertine?* My inbox is crammed with messages: plaintive whimperings from Cap; tentative noises from Chryssie. From Toxic, some porn, snagged from a site called *Bigjugs.com*. From Clair, one of her *memes*; along with a dull and cretinous post about Angel Blue and his bitchy wife, about my mother's mental health, and about the wonderful progress she thinks I made in my last public confession.

Then, there's the usual junk mail, hate mail, spam: badly spelt letters from Nigeria promising to send me millions of pounds in return for my bank details; offers of Viagra; of sex; of intimate videos of teenage celebs. In short, all the flotsam the Net brings in, and this time I welcome even the spam, because this is my lifeline, this is my world, and to cut me off is to leave me to drown in air like a fish out of water.

At four o'clock, I hear Ma get up. She doesn't sleep well either, these days. Sometimes she sits in the parlour watching satellite TV; sometimes she does housework, or goes for a walk around the block. She likes to be up when I leave for work. She wants to make me breakfast.

I select a clean shirt from my wardrobe – today it's white, with a blue stripe – and dress myself with some care. I take pride in my appearance. It's safer that way, I tell myself; especially when Ma's watching. Of course, I don't *need* to wear a shirt – my uniform at the hospital consists of a grubby navy-blue jumpsuit, engineer boots with steel-capped toes and a pair of heavy-duty gloves – but Ma doesn't need to know that. Ma's so proud of her *blueeyedboy*. And if Ma ever found out the truth –

'B.B.! Is that you?' she calls.

Who else would it be, Ma?

'Hurry up! I made breakfast!'

I must be in her good books today. Bacon, eggs, cinnamon toast. I'm not really hungry, but this time I need to humour her. This time tomorrow I'll be having breakfast in America.

She watches me as I fuel up. 'There's my boy. You'll need your strength.'

There's something vaguely disquieting about her mood this morning. To start with, she is fully dressed: discarding her usual dressing gown for a tweed skirt-suit and her crocodile shoes. She's wearing her favourite perfume – L'Heure Bleue, all powdery orange blossom and clove, with that trembling silvery top note that overpowers everything. Most curious of all, she is – what can I say? I can't quite call it *happy*. In Ma's case, you could count those fleeting moments on the fingers of a one-armed man. But there's a cheeriness in her manner today; something I haven't seen since Ben died. Quite ironic, really. Still, it'll soon be over.

'Don't forget your drink,' she says.

This time it's almost a pleasure. The taste is a little better today, perhaps because the fruit is fresh; and there's a different ingredient – blueberries, blackcurrant, perhaps – that gives it a tannic quality.

'I changed the recipe,' she says.

'Mmmm. Nice,' I tell her.

'Feeling better this morning?'

'Fine, Ma.'

Better than fine. I don't even have a headache.

'Good of them to give you time off.'

'Well, Ma, it's a hospital. Can't be bringing germs to work.'

Ma conceded I had a point. For the past few days I've been sick with flu. Well, that's the official story. In fact, I've been otherwise engaged, as I'm sure you can appreciate.

'Sure you're all right? You look a bit pale.'

'Everyone's pale in winter, Ma.'

6

You are viewing the webjournal of **blueeyedboy**.
Posted at: 04.33 on Friday, February 22
Status: restricted
Mood: excited
Listening to: The Beatles: 'Here Comes The Sun'

I bought the tickets on the Net. You get a discount for booking online. You can choose where to sit; order a meal; you can even print out your own boarding card. I chose a seat by the window, where I can watch the ground fall away. I've never been in an aeroplane. I've never even caught a train. The tickets were rather expensive, I thought; but *Albertine*'s credit can stand it. I snagged her details a year ago, when she bought some books from Amazon. Of course, at that time she had fewer funds; but now, with Dr Peacock's legacy, she should be good for a few months, at least. By the time she finds out – if ever she does – I'll be nicely untraceable.

I haven't packed much. Just a satchel with my papers, some cash, my iPod, a change of clothes, a shirt. No, not a blue one this time, Ma. It's orange and pink, with palm trees. Not much in the way of camouflage; but wait till I get there. I'll blend right in.

I log on for the last time, just for luck, before I set off. Simply to read my messages; to see who hasn't slept tonight; to check for any surprises; to find out who loves me and who wants me dead.

No surprises there, then.

'What are you doing up there?' she calls.

'Hang on, Ma. I'll be down in a sec.'

390

And now there's time for one more mail – to *albertine@yahoo.com* – before I'm ready to go at last; by noon today I'll be on that flight, watching TV and drinking champagne –

Champagne. Sham pain. As if sensation of any kind could ever be anything other than real. My guts are afizz with excitement. It almost hurts for me to breathe. I take a moment to relax and concentrate on the colour blue. Moon-blue, lagoon-blue, ocean, island, Hawaiian blue. Blue, the colour of innocence; blue, the colour of my dreams –

7

You are viewing the webjournal of **blueeyedboy** *posting on:*
badguysrock@webjournal.com
Posted at: *04.45 on Friday, February 22*
Status: *public*
Mood: *anxious*
Listening to: *Queen:* 'Don't Stop Me Now'

She must have taken off her shoes. He never even heard her. The first he heard was the door as it shut, and the sound of the key as she locked it.

Click.

'Ma?'

No answer. He goes to the door. The keys were in his coat pocket. She must have taken them, thinks *blueeyedboy*, when he went back upstairs. The door is pitch pine; the lock, a Yale. He has always valued his privacy.

'Ma? Please. Talk to me.'

Just that heavy silence, like something buried under snow. Then, the sound of her footsteps receding softly down the carpeted stairs.

Has she guessed? What does she know? A finger of ice slips down his back. A tremor creeps into his voice; the ghost of the stutter he thought was lost.

'Please, Ma!'

In fiction, our hero would break down the door; or failing that, crash through the window to land unharmed on the ground below. In real life, the door is unbreakable – though, sadly, *blueeyedboy* is not, as a leap from the window would surely confirm, sprawling him in agony on to the icy concrete below.

No, he's trapped. He knows that now. Whatever his Ma is planning, he thinks, he's helpless to prevent it. He hears her downstairs; her steps in the hall; her shoes on the polished parquet floor. The rattle of keys. She's going out.

'Ma!' There's a desperate edge to his voice. 'Ma! Don't take the car! *Please!*'

She hardly ever takes the car. Still, today, he knows she will. The café's only a few streets away, down at the corner of Mill Road and All Saints'; but Ma can be so impatient sometimes – and she knows that girl is expecting him, that Irish girl with all the tattoos, the one who has broken her little boy's heart –

How did she know what he was planning? Perhaps it was his mobile phone, left on the hall table. How stupid of him to have left it there so invitingly. So easy to open his inbox; so easy to find the recent dialogue between her son and *Albertine*.

Albertine, she thinks with a sneer. A rose by any other name. And she *knows* that it's that Irish girl, already to blame for the death of one son, now daring to threaten the other. A wasp in a jar may have killed him, but Gloria knows that Nigel's death would never have happened but for *Albertine*. Stupid, jealous Nigel, who first fell for that Irish girl and then, when he found out his brother had been following her, taking photographs, had first threatened, and then used his fists on poor, helpless *blueeyedboy*, so that Ma had had to take action at last, putting Nigel down like a rabid dog lest history repeat itself –

Dear Bethan (if I may),

I suppose you must have heard the news by now. Dr Peacock passed away the other night at the Mansion. Fell out of his wheelchair down the steps, leaving the bulk of his estate – last valued at three million pounds – to you. Congratulations. I suppose the old man felt he owed you something for the Emily White affair.

I have to say I'm surprised, though. Brendan never told me a thing. All that time he was working for Dr Peacock, and never thought to tell me

about this. But maybe he mentioned something to you? After all, you're
such good friends.

I know our respective families have had our differences over the years.
But now that you're seeing both my sons, perhaps we can bury the hatchet.
This business comes as a shock to us all. Especially if what I've heard is
true; that they're treating the death as suspicious.

Still, I wouldn't lose any sleep over that. These things blow over in time,
as you know.

Yours sincerely,
Gloria.

Yes, *Ma* wrote the letter, of course. She has never flinched from her
duty. Knowing that Nigel would open it; knowing that he would take
the bait. And when Nigel came round that day, demanding to talk to
blueeyedboy, she was the one who deflected him, who sent him away
with a flea in his ear – or at least, with a wasp in a jar –

But now her only surviving son owes her a debt that cannot be
repaid. He can never leave her now. He can never belong to anyone
else. And if he *ever* tries to run –

Post comment:
blueeyedboy: *Comments, anyone? Anyone here?*

8

You are viewing the webjournal of **blueeyedboy** *posting on:*
                              badguysrock@webjournal.com
Posted at: *04.47 on Friday, February 22*
Status: *public*
Mood: *devious*
Listening to: *My Chemical Romance: 'Mama'*

She ought to have seen it coming, of course. She ought to have known he would end up this way. But Gloria is no expert on child development. To her, *developing* is something he does in his darkroom, alone. She doesn't like to think of it much. It's like the nasty old Blue Book, she thinks, or the games he likes to play online with those invisible friends of his. She has looked into it once or twice, with the same faint dutiful distaste as when she used to wash his sheets, but only for his protection; because other people don't understand that *blueeyedboy* is sensitive; that he is simply incapable of ever standing up for himself –

The thought makes her eyes mist over a little. For all her steely hard-headedness, Gloria can be strangely sentimental at times, and even in her anger, the thought of his helplessness touches her. It's always been at these moments, she thinks, that she loves him best of all: when he's sick, or in tears, or in pain; when everyone else is against him; when there's no one to love him but her; when all the world thinks he's guilty.

Of course, *she* knows he's innocent. Well, of murder, anyway. What *else* he may be guilty of – what crimes of the imagination – is between *blueeyedboy* and his Ma, who has spent her whole life protecting him, even at her own cost. But that's her son all over, she thinks: sitting in the nest she has built, like a fat and flightless cuckoo chick with his beak perpetually open.

No, he wasn't her favourite. But he was always the luckiest of her three unlucky boys: a natural survivor in spite of his gift; a chip, she thinks, off the old block.

And a mother owes it to her son to protect him, no matter what. Sometimes he needs to be punished, she knows; but that's between *blueeyedboy* and his Ma. No stranger raises a hand to him. No one – not his school, not the law – has the right to interfere. Hasn't she always defended him? From bullies and thugs and predators?

Take Tricia Goldblum, the bitch who seduced her elder son – and caused the death of her youngest. It was a pleasure to take care of her. Easy, too: electrical fires are always so reliable.

Then Mrs White's hippie friend, who thought she was better than they were. And Catherine White herself, of course, so easy to destabilize. And Jeff Jones from the estate, the man who fostered that Irish girl, and who some years later, in the pub, dared to raise a hand to her son. Then there was Eleanor Vine, the sneak, spying on Bren at the Mansion, and Graham Peacock, who cheated them, and for whom the boy had *feelings* –

He was the most rewarding of all. Tipped over in his wheelchair and left to die alone on the path, like a tortoise half-out of its shell. Afterwards, she went upstairs and relieved him of his T'ang figurine, the one with which he taunted her all those years ago, and which she carefully placed in her cabinet along with the rest of her china dogs. It isn't stealing, she tells herself. The old man owed her *something*, after all, for all the trouble he has caused her son.

But in spite of everything she has done for him, what gratitude has *blueeyedboy* shown? Instead of supporting his mother, he has dared to transfer his affections to that Irish girl from the village, and worse, has tried to make her believe that *she* could have been his protector –

She'll make him pay for that, she thinks. But first, to take care of business.

Now, from upstairs, she hears his voice, accompanied by a banging and slapping at the bedroom door. 'Ma! Please! Open the *door!*'

'Don't be such a baby,' she says. 'When I get back, *then* we can talk.'

'Ma, *please!*'

'Don't make me come in—'

The sounds from the bedroom cease abruptly.

'That's better,' says Gloria. 'We've got a lot to talk about. Like your job at the hospital. And the way you've been lying to me. And what you've been up to with that girl. That Irish girl with all the tattoos.'

Behind the door, he stiffens. He can feel every hair stiffening. He knows what's in the balance here, and in spite of himself he is afraid. Of course he is. Who wouldn't be? He is caught inside the bottle trap, and the worst of it is, he *needs* to be caught; he needs this feeling of helplessness. But she's there on the other side of the door like a trapdoor spider poised to bite, and if any part of his plan goes wrong, if he has failed to compensate for any one of those minute variables, then –

If. If.

An ominous sound, tinged with the grey-green scent of trees and the dust that accumulates under his bed. It's safe under the bed, he thinks; safe and dark and scentless. He listens as she puts on her boots, fumbles with the front-door key; locks the door behind her. The *crump* of her footsteps in the snow. The sound of the car door opening.

She takes the car, as he knew she would. His begging her not to do so now ensures her cooperation. He closes his eyes. She starts the car. The engine ratchets into life. It would be so ironic, he thinks, if she had an accident. It wouldn't be his fault if she did. And then, at last, he would be *free* –

Post comment:

blueeyedboy: *Still no one here? Right, then. I guess that leaves me all on my own for Stage 4 . . .*

9

You are viewing the webjournal of **blueeyedboy** *posting on*:
>   **badguysrock@webjournal.com**

Posted at: *04.56 on Friday, February 22*

Status: *public*

Mood: *cautious*

Listening to: *The Rubettes*: 'Sugar Baby Love'

I think you must have guessed by now that this is not an ordinary fic. My other fics are all accounts of things that have already happened – though whether they happened quite as I said is up to you to determine. But this little story is more in the way of being a work-in-progress. An ongoing project, if you like. *A breakthrough in concept*, as Clair might say. And like all conceptual work, it isn't entirely without risk. In fact, I'm more or less convinced that it's all about to end in tears.

Five minutes to drive to the Zebra. Five more to see to business. And after that – *Whoops! All gone!* – here comes the explosive finale.

I hope they'll look after my orchids. They're the only things in this house that I'll miss. The rest can rot, for all I care, except for the china dogs, of course, for which I have special plans of my own.

But first of all, to get out of this room. The door is pinewood, and well-made. In a movie, perhaps, I could break it down. Real life demands a more reasoned approach. A multi-tool with a screwdriver, a file and a short-bladed penknife should help me deal with the hinges, after which I can make my exit unimpeded.

I take a last look at my orchids. I notice that the *Phalaenopsis* –

otherwise known as the moth orchid – is in need of re-potting. I know exactly how she feels; I, who have lived for all these years in the same little, airless, toxic space. Time to explore new worlds, I think. Time now to leave the cocoon and to fly . . .

It occurs to me as I work on the door that I ought to be feeling better than this. My stomach is filled with butterflies. I'm even feeling a little sick. My iPod is packed in my travel bag; instead I turn on the radio. From the tinny speakers comes the bubblegum sound of the Rubettes singing 'Sugar Baby Love'.

When I was a little boy, mistaking *baby* for B.B., I always assumed that those songs were for me; that even the folk on the radio *knew* that I was special, somehow. Today the music sounds ominous, a troubling falsetto sweeping across a fat layer of descending chords to a mystic accompaniment of *doop-shoowaddies* and *bop-shoowaddies*; and it tastes sour-sweet like acid drops, the ones that, when you were a child, you poked into the side of your mouth to make your tastebuds shudder and cramp, and if you weren't careful, the tip of your tongue would slide over the boiled-sugar shell and snag on the sharp-edged bubbles there, and your mouth would fill with sweetness and blood, and *that* was the taste of childhood . . .

Nyaaa-haaaa-haaaa-ooooooooooooooooh

Today there's something sinister in those soaring, sustained vocals; something that tears at the insides like gravel in a silk purse. The word *sugar* is not sweet: it has a pink and gassy smell, like dentist's anaesthetic, dizzy and intrusive, like something boring its way into my head. And I can almost see her there – right at this moment, *here* and *there* – and the Rubettes are playing at migraine volume in the Zebra's tiny kitchen, and there's a smell, a sickly-sweet, gassy smell that cuts through the scent of fresh coffee, but Ma doesn't really notice that, because fifty years of Marlboros have long since shot her olfactory organs to hell, and only the scent of L'Heure Bleue cuts through, and she opens the door to the kitchen.

Of course I can't *quite* be sure of this. I could be wrong about the radio station. I could be wrong about the time – she might still be in the car park, or by now it might even be over – and yet it feels completely right.

Sugar baby love
Sugar baby love
I didn't mean to make you blue –

Perhaps there was something, after all, in Feather's tales of walk-ins and ghosts and spirits and astral projection; because that's how I feel now, lighter than air, watching the scene from a place somewhere on the ceiling, and the Rubettes are singing – *aaaah-oop shoowaddy-waddy, doop-showaddy-waddy.* And now I can see the top of Ma's head, the parting in her thinning hair; the packet of Marlboros in her hand, the lighter poised above the tip; and I see the superheated air ripple and swell like a balloon inflated beyond its capacity, and she calls out – *Hello? Is anyone there?* – and lights a final cigarette –

She has no time to understand. I never really intended her to. Gloria Green is no wasp in a jar, to be caught and disposed of at leisure. Nor is she a seaside crab, left to die in the simmering sun. Her passing is instantaneous, and the hot draught sweeps her away like a moth – *Pfff!* – into oblivion, so that nothing, not even a finger, remains for *blueeyedboy* to identify, not even a measure of dust large enough to rattle inside a china dog.

From my room I can almost hear the dull *cr-crumpf* of the explosion, and it's like crunching a stick of Blackpool rock, all sharp edges and toothache, and although there's no way I can know for sure, I am suddenly certain, in a surge of wonder and indescribable relief, that I've done it at last. I'm free of her. *I'm finally rid of my mother –*

Don't tell me you're surprised, *Albertine.* Didn't I tell you I knew how to wait? Did you believe, after all this time, that this could have been an *accident*? And did you really believe, Ma, that I didn't know you were watching me, that I hadn't clocked you from the first time you logged on to *badguysrock*?

She appeared on the scene some months ago in response to one of my public posts. Ma isn't what you'd call computer-literate; but she accessed the Net through her mobile phone. After that, it can't have been long before someone, somewhere, steered her towards *badguysrock*. My guess is Maureen, via Clair; or maybe even Eleanor.

In any case, I'd expected it; and I'd expected to pay for it, too, though I knew she would never make any direct reference to my online activities. Ma can be strangely prudish at times, and some things are never mentioned. *All your nasty stuff upstairs* is about the closest we ever got to discussing the porn, or the photographs, or the fics that were posted on my site.

I have to admit I enjoyed the game: playing with fire; taking risks; taunting her to reveal herself. Sometimes I went a little too far. Sometimes I got my fingers burnt. But I had to know the boundaries; to see how hard I could push them both; to calculate the precise amount of pressure I could exert over the mechanism before it began to break down. An artist needs to understand the medium in which he works. After that, it was easy.

Don't feel guilty, *Albertine*. You had no way of knowing. Besides, in the end she'd have gone after you, just as she did with those others. Call it self-defence, if you like. Or maybe an act of redemption. Anyway, it's over now. You're free. Goodbye, and thank you. If you're ever in Hawaii, call. And please, look after my orchid.

Post comment:

10

You are viewing the webjournal of **blueeyedboy**.
Posted at: *05.17 on Friday, February 22*
Status: *restricted*
Mood: *sick*
Listening to: *Voltaire*: 'Snakes'

At last. The door pulls away from the hinge. I'm free to leave. I pick up my bag. But the ache in my guts has worsened; it feels like a piece of bramble scoring my stomach lining. I go to the bathroom; I wash my face; I drink a glass of water.

God, it hurts. What's happening? I'm sweating. I look terrible. In the mirror I look like a corpse: deep shadows around my eyes; mouth bracketed with nausea. What the hell is wrong with me? I felt so good at breakfast.

Breakfast. Ah. I should have known. Too late, I remember the look on her face; that look of almost-happiness. She wanted to make me breakfast today. Cooked me all my favourites. Stood over me while I ate it. The vitamin drink tasted different – and she *said* she'd changed the recipe.

For God's sake, it was obvious. How could I have missed what was happening? Ma up to her old tricks again – how could I have been so *careless?*

And now it feels like shards of glass are grinding away at my insides. I try to stand up, but the pain is too bad; it doubles me up like a penknife. I check the status of my f-list. There has to be someone awake by now. Someone who can help me.

A message through WeJay should bring help. Ma has taken my mobile phone. I type out my SOS and wait. Is there nobody online?

Captainbunnykiller is feeling OK.

Yeah, right. The fucktard. Too scared to leave his house now in case he runs into the boys from the estate. In passing, I notice that *kidcobalt* has been removed from Cap's f-list. Oh, well. Colour me surprised.

ClairDeLune is feeling rejected. Well, yes, probably. Angel has finally had enough, and has written to her personally. His tone, which is cool and professional, leaves Clair with no illusions. Rejection hurts at any age; but to Clair the humiliation is even more of a blow. *sapphiregirl* is gone from her f-list. So, I see, is *blueeyedboy*.

And Chryssie? Once more, she is feeling sick. This time, I almost sympathize. Looking at her f-list this morning, I notice, with diminishing surprise, that *azurechild* has been deleted. I immediately check for *blueeyedboy*. There, too, I am absent.

Three strikes? It's more than coincidence. I scroll quickly through the rest of my f-list, checking accounts and avatars. *BombNumber20. Purepwnage9. Toxic69. All* my friends. As if they had all decided as one to leave me marooned on *badguysrock* –

Of course, there's nothing from *Albertine*. Her Webmail account is marked as *dormant*; her WeJay as *deleted*. I can still look up her old posts – nothing online is ever lost, and every word is hidden away in caches and encrypted files, the ghosts in the machine. But *Albertine* is gone now. For the first time in over twenty years – perhaps for the first time in his *life* – *blueeyedboy* is quite alone.

Alone. A bitter, brown word, like dead leaves caught in a wind trap. It tastes like coffee grounds and dirt, and smells like cigarette ash. Suddenly I feel scared. Not so much of being alone as for the absence of those little voices, the ones that tell me that I'm real, the ones that say they see me –

You understand it was fiction, right? You know I never killed any-one? Yes, some of my fic may have been in bad taste, even a little sick, perhaps, but surely you don't believe I could ever have acted out those things?

Do you, Chryssie?

Do you, Clair?

Seriously. It wasn't real. Artistic licence, anyone? If it sounded genuine, if you were nearly *convinced*, then – surely that's a compliment, proof that *blueeyedboy* kicks ass –

Right, guys? Toxic? Cap?

I try to get down the stairs again. I need to call a taxi. I have to get out. I have to escape. I have to be on that plane at midday. But I feel like I've been cut in half; my legs can barely hold me. I make it to the bathroom again, where I throw up until there's nothing left.

But I know from experience that this doesn't help. Whatever she used is in me now, working its way through my bloodstream, shutting down all systems. Sometimes it lasts for days, sometimes weeks, depending on the dosage. What did she use? I don't know. I have to call that taxi. If I crawl, I can reach the phone. It's in the parlour, with the dogs. But the thought of lying there, helpless, with those china dogs looking down at me, is more than my brutalized nerves can take. The snakes are loose in my belly, and now there is no stopping them –

Damn, I feel sick. I feel dizzy. The room is spinning choppily. Black flowers open behind my eyes. If I just lie here, quietly, then maybe things will be OK. Maybe in time I can regain some strength, enough to get to the airport, at least –

Bip! It's the sound of the mailbox. That bittersweet electronic sound. One of my friends has messaged me. I knew they wouldn't leave me here. I knew they'd come round eventually.

I crawl back to the keyboard. I click on the symbol for *message*.

Someone has commented on your post!

I flick back to my most recent entry. A single line has been added there. No avatar. Just the default pic; a blue silhouette inside a square.

Post comment:

JennyTricks: *NOT BAD AT ALL FOR AN AMATEUR. NOT TOO REALISTIC, THOUGH.*

She ends it with an emoticon: a little winking smiley.

No way. No *way!* A finger of sweat runs down my spine. My

stomach's filled with broken glass. It has to be a joke, right? Nothing but a bad joke. Right from the moment she first logged on, thinking she was so clever.

Oh, please. As if I could have missed her, with that ridiculous username –

JennyTricks.

Genitrix.

And its colour is sometimes Virgin-blue, and sometimes it's green, like market-stall baize, and it smells of L'Heure Bleue and Marlboros, and cabbage leaves and salt water –

Post comment:
blueeyedboy: *Ma?*

No. No. Of course not. I heard the explosion, for God's sake. Ma isn't coming back, not today, not ever. And even if she had escaped somehow, then why would she choose this medium, instead of simply driving home and dealing with me face to face?

No, someone's trying to mess with my mind. My guess is *Albertine.* Nice try, *Albertine.* But I've been playing these games for much too long to be freaked out by an amateur.

Bip! Someone has commented on your post!

I consider deleting the message unread. But –

Post comment:
JennyTricks: *SO HOW ARE YOU FEELING,* **blueeyedboy?**
blueeyedboy: *Never felt better, Jenny, thanks.*
JennyTricks: *YOU NEVER COULD LIE TO SAVE YOUR LIFE.*

Well, that's a debatable point, *JennyTricks.* In fact I've survived for as long as I have by doing precisely that. Like the princess Scheherazade, I've consistently lied to save my life for rather more than a thousand and one nights. So, Jenny, whoever you are –

> Post comment:
> **blueeyedboy:** *Tell me, do I know you?*
> **JennyTricks:** *NOT AS WELL AS I KNOW YOU.*

Seriously, I doubt that. But now I'm beginning to be intrigued, in spite of the pain that comes and goes like the waves under Blackpool pier. *In pain.* What a phrase. Like a mouse inside a bottle. In any case I'm trapped here, and rather than think about my circumstances – which, let's face it, don't look good – it's easier to stay here, to grab the line that's being offered, to keep up the dialogue, which at least is preferable to silence.

> Post comment:
> **blueeyedboy:** *So, you think you know me?*
> **JennyTricks:** *OH YES. I KNOW YOU.*
> **blueeyedboy:** *Is that you,* **Albertine***?*

She responds with another smiley. The pixellated yellow face looks like a grinning goblin. It hurts to type, but the silence is worse.

> Post comment:
> **blueeyedboy:** **Albertine***? Is that you?*
> **JennyTricks:** *NO, THAT BITCH IS GONE FOR GOOD.*

Now I'm convinced it's Bethan in there. How did she get Ma's password? Where is she logging on from? It's good she doesn't know I'm sick. She may not even know I'm here. For all she knows I'm at the airport, logging on from the business lounge.

> Post comment:
> **blueeyedboy:** *Well, it's been fun, but I have to go.*
> **JennyTricks:** *YOU'RE NOT GOING ANYWHERE.*
> **blueeyedboy:** *Oh, but I am. I'm flying south.*
> **JennyTricks:** *NOT IN THIS LIFETIME, YOU LITTLE SHIT. WE*
> *HAVE THINGS TO TALK ABOUT.*

Bitch, I'm not afraid of you. In fact, I'm feeling better. I'm going to get up in a minute, pick up my bag, call a taxi and then I'll be off to the airport. Who knows, I may even find the time to deal with those dogs before I go. Still, for the moment I think I'll stay here, crunched up like a contortionist, keeping the pain at bay with words as it opens its jaws to swallow me –

> **Post comment:**
> **JennyTricks:** *YOU WAIT HERE. I'M COMING HOME. I'M COMING TO TAKE CARE OF YOU.*

She's bluffing, of course. She has no idea. But if I didn't know better right now, I might even feel a little afraid. She has Ma's voice down so accurately that I can feel my hackles trying to rise, and the back of my shirt is clammy with sweat. But all the same, it's just a bluff, based on what she knows of me. She knows it's a weakness of mine, that's all. She's shooting in the dark. I've won, and there's nothing she can do about it –

> **Post comment:**
> **JennyTricks:** *THINK YOU'RE SO SMART, DON'T YOU? YOU SHOULDN'T HAVE TRIED TO CHEAT ON ME. AND IF I FIND THAT YOU'VE LAID AS MUCH AS A FINGER ON ANY OF MY CERAMICS I'LL BREAK YOUR FUCKING NECK, OK?*

OK, game over, *JennyTricks*. I think I've exhausted my tolerance. Places to go, people to see, crimes to commit, and all that jazz. There are plenty of opportunities for a man of my skills in Hawaii. Plenty of places to explore. Perhaps I'll message you from there. Till then, Jenny, whoever you are –

11

You are viewing the webjournal of **blueeyedboy**
Posted at: 05.32 on Friday, February 22
Status: restricted
Mood: scared
Listening to: Abba: 'The Winner Takes It All'

OK. *Joke over*, thinks *blueeyedboy*. This isn't funny any more. She knows too much about him, of course; it's almost beginning to get to him. He stands up, though it hurts terribly. The room does one of those choppy swoops. He holds on to his desktop to keep from falling over.

Bip! That mailbox sound again. This time he ignores it. He slings his bag across his shoulder, still leaning on to the desk for support.

Bip! Another message. *Someone has posted on badguysrock!*

But he's halfway across the landing now, leaning on the banister. *Badguysrock* is an island from which he is suddenly desperate to escape. Each step he takes is an effort, but he'll walk out if it kills him. No crawling for *blueeyedboy*. He's going to make that fucking plane –

He's concentrating so hard that the sound of the car hardly registers, and when it stops on the driveway it takes him some seconds to react.

Police, here already? thinks *blueeyedboy*.

A car door slams. He hears the crunch of footsteps approaching in the snow. A door key ratchets and turns in the lock. The front door opens quietly. He hears the sound of boots on the mat. A double thud.

Then the sound of bare feet across the parquet hall floor.

They found the keys. That's all, he thinks. They let themselves in. Two detectives. He can see them in his mind's eye: a man and a woman (there's always one). He will be plain and businesslike; she will be kinder, more sensitive. But – why did they take their boots off, he thinks? And why on earth didn't they ring the bell?

'Hey!' His voice is rusty. 'Up here!'

No one replies. Instead, a scent of cigarette smoke winds its way up the stairwell. Then comes a small and slithery sound, like a snake – or a long piece of electrical cord sliding across a polished floor.

Panic wrenches at him now. He falls against the banister. He tries to get up, but his legs are on strike. Cursing, he crawls back into his room. Not that *that* will protect him now; the door is off its hinges. But there's always his computer, he thinks; his refuge; his island; his sanctuary.

He logs back on to *badguysrock*. Two messages await him.

He reads them as the room spins dizzily around him. His eyes are streaming; his head sore; his stomach filled with razor blades.

From the stairs, relentlessly, comes the sound of footsteps.

'Who's there?' His voice is raw.

'Ma, please? Is that you?'

No reply but those feet on the stairs, coming up so steadily. With shaking hands, he begins to type. The footsteps reach the landing. A slithery sound on the carpet. *Blueeyedboy* types faster. He cannot, *dare* not, stop typing. Because if he stops, he'll have to turn round, and then he'll have to *look at her* –

But of course, this is only fic. *Blueeyedboy* doesn't believe in ghosts. Even as he types the words he knows that this is *Albertine*. She couldn't leave him after all; she stopped to read her mail, then turned back, knowing that he needed her help. And the phantom reek of Marlboros is only in his mind, he thinks, and the scent of L'Heure Bleue is so powerful that it cannot possibly be real. No, it's only *Albertine*, who has come to save him –

'I knew you wouldn't leave me, Beth.' His voice is weak and grateful.

Albertine makes no reply.

'You gave me a hell of a scare, though. I thought you were my mother.' He tries a laugh, which sounds more like a scream. That slithering sound comes closer.

'I guess that makes us even now. I'll even admit I deserved it.'

Still no reaction from *Albertine*. Behind him the footsteps come to a stop. He can smell her now, a rose in the smoke.

She says: 'I brought your medicine.'

'Ma?' he whispers.

'Ma? *Ma?*'

Joanne Harris is the author of the Whitbread-shortlisted *Chocolat* (made into an Oscar-nominated film starring Juliette Binoche and Johnny Depp) and seven other best-selling novels: the latest is *The Lollipop Shoes*. Her hobbies are listed in *Who's Who* as 'mooching, lounging, strutting, strumming, priest-baiting and quiet subversion'. She plays bass guitar in a band first formed when she was sixteen, is currently studying Old Norse, and lives with her husband and daughter in Yorkshire, about fifteen miles from the place where she was born.

www.joanne-harris.co.uk